PRAISE FOR

"Cannibalism. Murder. Rape. Absolute brutality. When civilizations ends...when the human race begins to revert to ancient, predatory savagery...when the world descends into a bloodthirsty hell...there is only survival. But for one man and one woman, survival means becoming something less than human. Something from the primeval dawn of the race. "Shocking and brutal, The Devil Next Door will hit you like a baseball bat to the face. Curran seems to have it in for the world ... and he's ending it as horrifyingly as he can."

—Tim Lebbon, author of *Bar None*

"Tim Curran is one of those guys that people talk about when you speak of ultra-violent and gory horror. Books like Biohazard, or The Devil Next Door are a couple that I've read that made my stomach turn. I was wondering where Blackout might lead me when I got this from the publisher to review...Tim Curran builds on this with every turn of the page. Each of the characters have their own unique perspective and voice of the events, and the group survival mentality is in full effect. He does a great job of getting across just how dire of a situation this is through their actions and dialogue. Every bit of it had a purpose and moved this story forward."

—Reviewed by Joe Hempel, *Horror Novel Reviews*

"Tim Curran's, The Devil Next Door is dynamite! Visceral, violent, and disturbing!"

—Brian Keene, author of *Castaways and Dark Hollow*

"Nightcrawlers is a monster story and an ode to H. P. Lovecraft. I would say that this story has two of Lovecraft's in it: The Colour Outer Space and Facts Concerning the Late Arthur Jermyn and His Family. It is also completely Tim Curran. Curran manages to own the story and the monsters within it. But one cannot deny the spirit of Lovecraft...So, having read the rest of the story, I can say that I had a great time reading it. You do get to know the characters more and more the deeper you go in, and one thing that surprised me is how much we got to know one character when she wasn't even in it for very long. Throughout the story, including the ending, Curran shows his talent for creating actual frightening scenes that can linger long after reading them. If you let them. And you should. It is why we read horror after all, isn't it?"

—*Darkness Dwells*

"Dead Sea is an epic horror novel, and delightfully claustrophobic and reminiscent of Lovecraftian lore, a lengthy voyage into a genuinely chilly, fog-drenched horror novel that all fans should experience."

—*The Paperback Stash*

"Horror is a lot of fun, and Worm is proof of that. If you're looking for very complex plots with descriptive passages that belong in classic Russian novels and characters with full back stories, look elsewhere. However, if you're looking for a taut, fun, grisly read, ignore the stench and sink your teeth into this one."

—Gabino Iglesias, *HORROR DNA*

"Tim Curran has a way of slinging words to create grotesque imagery that makes you cringe and yet you find yourself absorbed, frantically turning the pages to see what kind of gruesome avenues he takes you down. SOW is a quick and thoroughly enjoyable read. This is eye-popping madness, paranoia realized, body horror most foul. Curran takes what should be the one of the happiest times in someone's life and turns it on its head. Really this is a story for anyone who craves a good, creepy yarn. If you're a Curran fan and you haven't read this one, you'd better rectify that. If you haven't read Curran yet (what?), this is just as good a place as any to start as any. Think Rosemary's Baby dunked in a bathtub full of acid and you begin to touch on the madness that is SOW"

—Robert Essig, *Splatterpunkzine*

"Okay so I rocked on with this collection, Tasmaniac have kicked a major here kids, and I've found a new must read Writer whose name is now chiselled into my tree of counted sorrows. One of the best collections of the year in terms of quality and content, full recommendation this book is one that you simply cannot miss assuming you can get a copy before the print run is depleted. Take down the name Tim Curran, you are going to be hearing a lot about him in the coming years."

—*Scaryminds*

THE BRAIN LEECHES

AND OTHER ELDRITCH PHENOMENA

THE BRAIN LEECHES

AND OTHER ELDRITCH PHENOMENA

TIM CURRAN

ISBN: 978-1-957121-29-1

Text © 2002 - 2022 by Tim Curran

Cover Artwork © 2022 by K. L. Turner

Interior and cover design by Cyrusfiction Productions

Editor and Publisher, Joe Morey

Weird House Press
Central Point, OR 97502
www.weirdhousepress.com

CONTENTS

WHEN THE SEA RUNS HOT AND COLD

1

They were on the return leg from the Grand Banks, dragging their mid-water trawl for cod and flounder, just north of Sable Island. Twice they'd hauled in their nets and twice the catch was pathetic. Some cod, mostly scrod, very few market fish. Lots of by-catch or garbage fish. A sad state of affairs.

Staring out into the gray morning void of the North Atlantic, Bricker told Eddie Braun, "Keeps up like this and it's gonna be a bust. Bank'll take the fucking boat."

"We just need a pinch of luck, Skip. Just the one pinch."

Diminishing returns.

Everyone was getting less these days. Even the autoliners and stern trawlers were taking a real beating. Bricker could remember very well fishing these very waters in the old days with his old man and when they returned to port, it was because the pens were full to the gunwales.

Ancient history.

Commercial fishing had started declining in the seventies and it had been a greasy slope ever since. Bricker and the crew of the *F/V Jezebel* had been out a month fishing the Grand Banks and they didn't have shit to show for it. The fish-hold could handle an easy fifty thousand pounds, but the pens probably had less than ten in them now. Cod, haddock, and redfish packed down in melting ice. Mostly wee little things. Legal, but barely.

If the bank hadn't owned the majority of the *Jezebel,* Bricker would've sold her off for cash, crewed on another vessel. But he couldn't do that. He had people depending on him. Like creditors, for example.

And that was the way it was going.

The men—Garrick, Hanley, Pete Searles, and old Johnny Muller—were quiet, subdued. The bawdy jokes and good-humored yelling and rivalry of the old days was gone. Bricker knew he was witnessing the death of an entire way of life, a traditional way of life, as he looked out across the working deck and watched the gray angry sea spouting foam over the bow.

"HAULING TIME!" he called out from the doorway of the wheelhouse. "DEAD STOP!"

2

The *Jezebel* was a fresher, an ice-filled side trawler. She had to stop dead in the water to recover her nets. As the thrum of the diesels died out and the crew readied themselves, Bricker lit a cigarette lee side of the wheelhouse. The trawl winch started, bringing the nets in.

Haulback.

Everyone was tense. What was in the nets was their bacon, their livelihood. If it was a good haul they'd be jumping for joy; bad and they'd be quiet as stones in a churchyard, beaten men whose backs were nearly broken.

When the nets came over the side, everyone saw it: a tangled black mass nearly covered in a mound of fish.

Eddie Braun spit the cigar butt out of his mouth. "What the Jesus is that?" he said.

Searles wiped his hands off on his sea bibs. "Shark...some kinda shark?"

"Ain't no shark," Braun said.

Just about everyone was gathered around now, standing there in yellow oilskins, swearing in low voices as water and sea slime poured from the nets and washed over their rubber boots and out the scuppers.

Nobody knew what the hell it was they had hooked onto forty fathoms below, but, to a man, they didn't like it. And these were guys who couldn't wait to dump the catch onto the deck for sorting, got giddy about it like kids anxious to tear into presents under the tree.

But not this time.

They knew it wasn't right. So, they got no closer. They stood there staring at the thing, their nostrils full of its pungent, cloying odor.

"What the hell, Eddie?" Bricker asked, coming down the ladder from the wheelhouse.

But Braun, who usually couldn't keep his mouth shut, just shook his head.

Bricker came over. His trawl was torn up; he could see that much. Great sections of net were frayed, even completely ripped open. Something had been at her. "Jesus fucking Christ in a handcart," he said, already tabulating in his head the price of a new pelagic trawl. He grabbed a boat hook and pulled lines and netting aside. "Sonofa...*bitch.*"

Heaped in cod, tangled in trawl lines, the thing was just lying there, not moving, not even seeming to breathe. Bricker saw what looked like a human shape in the nets...or near human. It had two arms and two legs, that much was certain, its flesh a lustrous, oily greenish-gray spotted with brown.

"Like a...a mermaid or some such shit," Hanley said.

Johnny Muller stroked his long white beard, running fingers over his seamed face. "That's no mermaid, son. That's something that walks below."

Bricker just stared; his mouth dry as sawdust. *No, not a mermaid. More like the Creature from the Black Lagoon's ugly sister.*

It had the head of a fish with gasping blubbery lips, bulging unblinking eyes, and pulsating fins running down the sides of its neck. Its four-fingered hands were like those of a toad—long, blunt, and rubbery-looking, webbed with a pale membranous flesh you could nearly see through. Same for the feet. It had two sets of rising ridges at its back that feathered out into spiny fins and looked much like the pectorals of a flying fish only much more skeletal.

It was, all in all, perfectly horrible.

The crew of the *Jezebel* kept their distance and these were men used to all the crawling, slimy, multi-finned, and tentacled horrors of the deep.

It gazed up at them, huge black eyes swimming in yellowed irises. They were not the vapid eyes of a fish or the cold, predacious eyes of a reptile, but somehow bright and alive and intelligent. Almost human in curiosity and depth.

There was a spiny crest atop its head that was pink-tinged like the other fins…but now it was paling as if the blood was being sucked away or starved of oxygen.

Bricker found himself staring at its belly which was huge and white, painfully distended. *That a belly filled with spawn?* he wondered. *This goddamn evil looking mother of a fish is pregger?* The very idea made his blood run cold. Something like this breeding pretty as you please. Christ, it was almost more than he could take.

Eddie Braun whistled low under his breath. "What do you make of it, Skip? Not human, not fish, but one Jesus mean-looking guppy. How the hell we gonna put this in the catch log?"

"Sea monster," Garrick said breathlessly. "A good goddamned sea monster, Skipper. Wicked ugly, too."

"Aye," Johnny Muller said in a low, wounded voice. "Sea monster. That's for sure. Put her back over the side, Skip. Put her back down in the black lower fathoms where she belongs."

Hanley shook his head. "That would be a bullshit mistake. She's probably worth more than we'd see in ten good seasons."

Bricker was speechless. Whatever it was, it began to move in the net, trapped and fighting, gills fluttering like Chinese fans, mouth opening and closing and revealing a spread of needle-like teeth that were meant to grasp and hold on. As he watched, its struggles slowed.

It was dying.

3

Long before they'd hauled the thing aboard and he saw it looking at him like some childhood nightmare with those flat black, lidless eyes, Bricker had known *something* was going to happen. He'd felt it as a chill along the bridge of his spine. It was something fishermen got from time to time and it had nothing to do with the wind or weather.

4

A premonition, maybe.

A silent, intimate death knell.

He feared the feeling as did all who worked the sea.

It always foretold of shit luck, a bad run, a poor catch. And as he stared down that morning at what was struggling in the net, breathing with a moist hiss of trapped sub-sea gases, he could feel that anxiety filling his soul with dark matter, with scuttling terror-bright things he could not hope to put a name to—*maybe you won't be coming back from this trip, Brick, maybe this is the last one, the final voyage. Sea's always hungry and it's eaten better men than you. A rogue wave…a roll the boat can't right herself from…shit happens. Men aren't supposed to catch what you caught and you know it. The Devils of the sea are meant to spawn in darkness, not be exposed to the light.* He couldn't shake the unease. It seeped his veins with ice and threaded his belly with weakness. His brain felt like a buzzing swarm of fear-glutting flies, all of them growing fat on his dread.

Superstition. That's all.

Thirty years fishing the grounds, thirty years of hardship, struggle, and heartbreak, barely making enough to cover expenses and keep the boat going, always looking for that one perfect haul, the golden egg that would put him in the black and never quite finding it. Close maybe a time or two, but never quite there.

And then, by fate or luck or sheer coincidence, the golden egg fell right into his lap. Who was he to question it?

That thing's a goldmine and you know it. Woods Hole or Scripps will pay millions for it. You can quit fishing, go down to Florida. Do any goddamned thing you want. You get this thing to port, you and your boys are going to be rich men. You'll be pissing in golden toilets and wiping your asses with twenty dollar bills. And that ain't something to sneeze at, Brick. Creditors off your back. You could buy a couple boats, rig 'em out, and crew 'em how you please.

If you get to port, that is.

4

Bricker looked at the creature.

It looked at him.

It stared at him with dark, translucent eyes that were tunnels leading to an anti-human blackness that was indescribable. There was no warmth in those eyes, yet they were not the eyes of a senseless beast, something that lived to eat or be eaten. This was beyond that. Far beyond that. The difference between a pebble and a black pearl. There was a cold intelligence in them.

And a hatred that was literally beyond comprehension.

"Ye want my opinion, Skip? Do ye?"

All the crew looked over at Johnny Muller. He worked a plug of chew in his cheek, turned his head, spit over the rail into the misting fume. "Throw that bastid back into the depths. It's a devil and ye can see that just looking in its eyes. It comes from a world ye don't want no truck with, understand?" He studied the fear-bleached faces of the men watching him. "She's preg, Skip. Full of roe. Best toss her back or ye'll have the death of her spawn upon ye."

"Don't do it, Brick," Hanley said, always on the hunt for things green and spending. "Don't goddamn well do it. This is your ticket. You piss this away and twenty, thirty years from now you'll still be kicking yourself. You'll be telling tall tales of this day while you're shitting your pants."

"Don't listen to that whore," Muller said. "He'd cornhole a codfish for a shiny nickel."

Bricker looked over at Eddie Braun, his mate. "Well?" he said.

Braun whistled out of the space between his teeth. "Shit, Brick, don't ask me. I bet that god-awful mermaid would bring real cash…but it might bring real Jesus trouble, too."

Bricker studied the faces of his crew. Eddie Braun and Garrick couldn't make up their minds. Hanley was greedy for a slice of the pie. Pete Searles stood with old Johnny Muller.

"I ain't throwing her back," Bricker finally said. "You know what this thing is worth? *Millions.* You'll all get a cut, same as the catch. We can write our own ticket with this bitch. She goes into one of the pens and then we sell her off to the highest bidder once we make port."

Muller sighed and shook his head. "I'll want no cut of her. She might be worth a fortune to them scientical types, but ye better think about how much yer life is worth. Ye all better think on that." He looked at them all in turn. "Because if ye think, any of ye, that ye'll make port with this...this *horror* aboard, yer fucking wrecked, everyone of ye. Ye'll be sucking black mud at the bottom by this time tomorrow. Mark them fucking words."

While the others looked spooked or suspicious like Eddie Braun, Hanley stepped forward. "Weather's clear, Johnny. Not shit between us and the Cape. We'll make it just fine."

Muller shook his head, grumbling about young fools and idiots married into one, how they and their lives are soon parted. "No, ye won't. Not a one of us'll see land again. What's out there...*it* won't allow it."

"Shitting superstition," Hanley grumbled. "Old wives' tales."

"It's struggling," Garrick said.

It was. Thrashing about in the net, it looked pitiful even for a sea monster. Its body trembled and it made a weird croaking sort of noise that almost sounded like the dry, pained rasp of a woman. And then...the creature contorted with muscular spasms and there was a gushing, liquescent sound. It seemed to burst like a swollen seedpod, a flood of slimy discharge bubbling from between its legs and oozing over the decks.

It stank like sun-washed dead fish.

"Spawn," Eddie Braun said, trying to keep his stomach down. "She was preg, all right."

It flooded past their boots in a yolky, eggy mass—dozens of pink round ova caught in a sticky, juicy ocean of birth jelly. The creature was female, all right, gravid with eggs, and she continued to shudder as she aborted her roe, her blank ichthyic face emoting something quite near despair and melancholy.

"Oh Christ," Searles said, turning away.

Bricker stepped back, trembling. His throat was dry, his tongue pasted to the roof of his mouth. A weird sort of screeching blackness broke open in his brain and for one insane, hysterical moment, he could *hear* the death-cry of her young echoing through his head in a squalling/squealing/shrieking resonance of agony.

Oh, we sure as Christ did it now. We murdered a generation of them pollywogs and there's going to be hell to pay.

The others stepped away from the discharge and *out* of it, shaking it off their boots. But not Johnny Muller. He stood right in it, his leathery face set in stern lines, his green eyes shining and beady. "That cuts it then," he said. "We ain't none of us making it home now."

5

"What do you think, Skipper?"

Bricker was sitting in his swivel chair in the wheelhouse, the other men lounging around, waiting to hear what he had to say. All of them, that was, save for Johnny Muller who had spoken his piece and would say no more on the subject. He was below. It was in Bricker's hands now and he knew it.

He stared out the Plexiglass windows that circled the house, studying the flat seas off the bow. The former owner of the *Jezebel* had decided that his bridge needed some sprucing, so he decorated it in what could only be deemed as Cape Cod classic: the lower walls adorned with nets, clam rakes, trap floats, and diving helmets, all of them bolted in place.

Bricker had never removed them.

"What's there to think?" he said. "Do you boys want to be rich or do you want to scrounge out a living until you die or the sea takes you?"

Eddie Braun toyed nervously with the brim of his Red Sox cap. The others waited for him to speak. As the mate, he was their chosen mouthpiece. "It's like this, Skip. I've known Johnny for twenty-six years. He's got a lot of wind and bullshit in him, but he's got a good sense of things. He thinks that thing will bring us bad luck. Maybe these boys don't believe in the jinx and maybe they do, but they want to know your gut feeling on it."

Bricker wondered if he should tell them the truth, that just the sight of the thing or the stink it put up his nose made him feel bad inside. And scared. Scared like he'd never been before and hoped he never would be again. No, he wasn't going to hoist any of that on them. It was only natural that a freakish beast like that would get the superstition and primitive fears stirred up in a man.

"What I think is that if we throw that thing back overboard, we're going to regret it the rest of our lives," he said, his voice calm and authoritative. "Throwing it over like by-catch is like throwing away a winning lottery ticket."

They did not look convinced.

8

He cast an eye to Hanley. "How about you? You've had your greasy paws in my wallet ever since you crewed up. You want to put this in practical terms for everyone?"

Hanley couldn't decide whether he'd been insulted or praised or both. "Skip's right," he said to the others. "The labs or museums will want this thing. If they don't, a carnival will pay big to put something like that on display. And you better damn well know I ain't talking thousands but *millions.* Far as we know, this thing is one of a kind. It's priceless."

There was some grumbling, but like any good fishermen, the dollar always won them over.

"Sure," Braun said. "Why not?"

Searles and Garrick just looked at each other. They were caught, trapped in-between what their hearts whispered and what the greed in their souls was shouting in their ears.

Hanley beamed.

The VHF and single sideband radio were bolted to the ceiling. Now and again you could hear boats hailing each other through the static. A call was coming in.

"F/V *Devilfish* calling *Jezebel.* You boys alive over there?"

Bricker stood up and grabbed the mic. The *Devilfish* was another trawler out of Cape Cod, part of the fishing fleet. Her captain was an old friend of Bricker's, Danny Sprenger. They were steaming about 40 miles northeast of the *Jezebel's* position.

Bricker was about to speak into the mic…then hesitated. On the radar screen, he saw a huge green blip heading in their direction. Panic welled inside him. Then it was gone. There was nothing on the screen. Not so much as a boat within spitting distance. He blinked his eyes, feeling that unreal sense of doom once again.

What in the Christ?

"*Devilfish*, this is *Jezebel.* Go ahead, Danny," he breathed into the mic.

"You getting any joy over there, Brick?"

"Some. We're heading in."

"Us, too. We got forty in the hold and I'm calling that good," Sprenger said. "You full up?"

9

"Hell no, not even close," Bricker told him. "But we got something else, something special."

"Caught yerself a mermaid, did you?"

There was dead silence in the wheelhouse. Cigarettes were not lit and pipes not packed, itches not scratched and bodies did not shift wetly in oilskins.

Bricker pulled off his coffee. "Not quite. You'll see it on the dock. First round's on me at the Tap."

"Roger that, *Jezebel*."

Bricker sat back down. It was Sprenger's standard joke, *Did you catch a mermaid?*, but today it left a funny, hollow feeling in his belly. He sighed. Swallowed. "Not only are we gonna be rich, boys," he said, "but we're going to be famous. Every nature documentary and monster-hunter show on the tube will want to interview us. Might be movie deals, book deals…shit, you don't know what something like this might turn into. Now, you all got bills. You can pay 'em off. You can buy anything you want. You can buy your own goddamn boats if it tickles you. That's what it comes down to: you want to keep struggling or do you want to dance down Easy Street for once in your fucking lives?"

"Johnny said the thing smells like death," Searles said.

"Wicked stinks, that's for sure," Garrick put in.

Yes, the beast certainly had a fishy, gray water smell about it—one that was concentrated, rank, and pervasive. But a lot of things from the deeps had nasty odors about them, Bricker knew. Some deep-water squid, for example, had a real foul, dead smell about them, even fresh ones.

He lit a cigarette and offered his pack around. "Things from the sea smell bad…I got to sit here and remind you about that? Trust me, when we make port, you don't smell much better."

The men laughed. Bricker had an easy way about him. He knew how to ease their minds and they had absolute confidence in him. They would have followed him straight into hell and he knew it.

The wheelhouse door opened and Johnny Muller was standing there. He did not look happy. He looked, if anything, haunted and maybe even devastated. "She's dead," he said. "The creature's dead."

With that, he left, grumbling under his voice and everyone in the room was filled with an anxiety they could not truly fathom.

"That settles it," Bricker said, blowing out smoke. "The bitch is ours. Wrap her up in the net, stow her in an empty pen. Ice her. Lots and lots of ice. Cover her. Keep her fresh."

It was time to go home.

6

At first, it was a milk run.

Bricker steamed full ahead, cutting a path between Sable Island and the northward flow of the Gulf Stream's headwaters. He figured they'd make Cape Cod in seven days, eight at the outside. The weather was fair, the seas were low, nothing but the constant throb of the diesel engines. Johnny Muller was still grumbling away like an old gypsy woman prophesying death, but the others were coming around just fine and the usual talk of sports and women was replaced by talk of money and how to spend it.

As he kept an eye on the radar, autopilot, and the GPS video plotter, Bricker kept seeing the creature's eyes looking at him and despite the fishy, unblinking glare, there had been something accusing in them.

Like twin, dark, deep-sea mirrors of unrelenting hatred.

He'd seen that look only once before in an animal. When he was twelve, a giant squid had stranded itself in a tidal pool off Provincetown. The sea had gone back out, trapping it. The squid was thirty-odd feet long, not the largest giant ever stranded, but to his fevered twelve-year-old imagination that September day, it was the demon of the deep. The ship wrecker, the man-eater, the ultimate horror of the depths. The fucking kraken of lore. As it lay there, slowing dying, surrounded by a crowd of onlookers, the water only covering half its immense girth, it looked at Bricker. Its eyes sought him out and held him. In them was a wrath that was smoldering black. It knew its life was nearly played out. It also knew that had it lived, had it survived, it would have become the gargantuan monster of every sailors' nightmare. And as it looked at Bricker, sluggish and weak, it assured him that had they met in the open ocean, it would have shown him no mercy.

Its hatred had been complete.

Maybe he'd been reading too much into it, but since the creature had spilled her spawn on the decks and he'd heard that shrill bawling in his head, there had been a guilt that he could not understand.

Just quit it, he told himself. *You're letting it all lay on you the wrong way. This is the golden egg you been waiting for, stop questioning it, and stop looking for wolves behind every tree.*

But he could not get past that constant feeling of dread worming at his belly.

7

Doing ten knots, near on eleven, the *Jezebel* steamed forward by the sheer might of her 350 horsepower turbo-charged diesels, her sharp bow slicing through the choppy seas and her stern leaving a spreading white wake aft. The boys were down in the galley, playing cards and watching movies, a few snoring in their bunks which were stacked one atop the other in the starboard hull. All except for Johnny Muller, that was, who was standing out on the whaleback, gripping the gunwale and studying the sea through narrowed eyes.

Bricker had seen him do that for hours, as if he was seeing something out there nobody else could. And today he was more intense than ever.

By seven that night, the seas had risen to sixteen feet and the wind was gusting at 25 miles per hour, the barometer continuing to fall which meant something was building out there, somewhere.

Christ, they were calling for clear skies and calm seas not three hours ago, Bricker thought.

He checked the weather fax and an emergency bulletin came in right away:

Maritime warning. Dangerous storm front developing. Cycling E-NE at 45 KTS. Forecast accelerating winds 50 to 80 KTS, gusting to 90 near center. Seas to 50 ft and building.

Shit.

Bricker felt an icy chill take hold of him, wondering deep down if this was it, if this was the source of the bad feeling he'd had since the beginning of the voyage. He told himself that he did not for a moment believe in things like prophecy…yet, as a sailor, he'd seen and sensed things that made belief sometimes come far too easy.

First thing he did was radio his position to the rest of the fleet, cod boats and swordfish boats, out of the Cape and Gloucester. The lot of them were in roughly a hundred-mile semi-circle steaming south-southwest. He hailed the *Devilfish,* chatted nervously with Danny Sprenger. He hailed the *Peggy Lee,* the *Sarah T,* the *Greenback* and the *Charlee Donovan.* He knew their skippers and they knew him. They all agreed on one thing: they were heading into the mouth of hell.

And the entire time all he could think of was what was iced down in the fish-hold.

On the intercom, he said to the crew, "Boys, we're heading into some weather. I want everything battened down. I think…I think we're going to take a real beating."

His crew was a good crew and Eddie Braun led the charge, barking orders to everyone out on the whaleback as the winds began to pick up and rain started to fall, the *Jezebel* heaving in the rolling seas as if it was going through birth contractions.

The biggest fear in a storm, of course, was that breaking waves would flood the decks and holds, so every porthole and watertight hatch was secured. Equipment and tackle were stowed. Bilge pumps were checked, filters cleaned, bilge drained. Scuppers opened. Barrels of fuel and water were lashed down. Anything that could conceivably break loose and cause damage or injury was stowed or anchored down. Braun went through the engines, generators, EPIRB beacons, survival suits and rafts. He checked the batteries and handed out seasickness pills while up in the wheelhouse, Bricker manually plotted a course on the chart in case his electronics went FUBAR.

They were ready.

8

By nine that night, the *Jezebel* was at roughly 42° north latitude, 57° west longitude and she was getting battered by big seas. Rain was lashing the decks and high winds were making the wire stays and outrigger cables scream with a high, hollow moaning that was so loud you had to shout over it.

"What in the Jesus is going on up there?" Eddie Braun called over the intercom. "I got boys puking their livers out down here, Skip."

"Don't know, Eddie," Bricker told him. "But she's coming at us now and she's plenty bad."

Bricker could hear the other captains in the fleet squawking over the sideband about this building mother of a freak storm. How could the NOAA not have seen it coming? What pissing use were weather ships and weather buoys and fucking Doppler radar if they couldn't see a black-hearted hell like this one brewing for days?

Bricker stayed at the helm.

He dropped both port and starboard stabilizers into the water, to see if the birds, as they were called, could give the *Jezebel* some stability.

He drank black coffee.

He chain-smoked.

But he did not close his eyes even for a second.

In conditions like that, no captain left the wheel. Autopilot was disabled. This was the kind of sea only a man could fight through using experience, gut instinct, and perseverance. Capabilities far beyond those of a machine.

Once, several years before, off Nantucket Shoals, the *Jezebel* had gotten into some real weather and he had stayed at the wheel for thirty-six hours straight. He pissed in a bucket. He chewed amphetamines. He mainlined the blackest, strongest, gut-tearing coffee Eddie Braun could brew. When he got home, he couldn't sleep for two days…partly because he was wired like a junction box and partly because after nearly three days of pounding rollers, he couldn't close his eyes in a bed. It wasn't *moving*. Every time he did, he thought he was back on the *Jezebel* and she was taking a final foundering descent to the bottom.

Standing there, glaring through the windows at the foaming white seas and black water breaking over the bow, he knew he was in the shit again. A pea tossed in a wind tunnel.

The crew was down below and they were scared.

There was weather and then there was *weather*. It took a lot to turn these boys, but this storm was the one. They watched videos. They sipped from flasks of whiskey. They thought about their wives and children, mothers and fathers, maybe remembering a few prayers from childhood as dry tears squeezed from their eyes because they knew, they knew down in their marrow, that this was the one. The widow-maker. This sea was black and pissed-off, opening before them like a bottomless grave.

And it was just getting its wind up, nowhere near on to full bite just yet.

"F/V *Jezebel*," a crackling voice said over the radio. "F/V *Devilfish* here. Brick, we're up at forty-six and all hell's breaking loose. Seas are rising and the wind is unholy. What you got down there?"

"No joy here, Danny," Bricker said into the mic. "It's coming on like I never seen it before."

"I was thinking of making port but I don't dare turn abeam in this sea," came the reply.

"Roger that, Danny. We're riding into hell down here. I'm reading forty-foot waves cresting to fifty. Anemometer registering winds on up to sixty an hour. Don't know if I can hold her."

"Keep me posted, Brick."

"I'm hoping to."

Bricker gripped the wheel in white-knuckled hands, the violent sea churning and crashing around the boat, yanking at the rudder. It took all his strength to hold it steady as wild conflicting currents swept the surface of the water and hit the *Jezebel* from below like rams.

He thought about his ex-wife.

He thought about the blue of his daughter's eyes, how her eight-year-old laughter could fill him with sunshine for days.

And he thought about his father who had gone out in 1964 on a swordfish boat and was lost in a storm, body never recovered.

Keep a warm berth for me, Dad, 'cause I think I'm coming home to you soon.

Now and again, a wave cresting at forty-five feet would strike the *Jezebel* to port and she'd flounder helplessly before stabilizing. Then the boys down below would start calling on the intercom, asking if they should get into their survival suits. Their voices were frantic and Bricker did everything to calm them.

But he was far from calm and was making no long-range plans.

It was one hell of a ride and no roller coaster in the world could compare with climbing those big waves and sliding down their backsides into the troughs between. Sometimes it was a smooth descent, but often the sea just disappeared beneath the *Jezebel* and she came crashing down.

Night was coming on and the deck lights were burning bright, but in that steady torrent of gray, driving rain there was hardly any visibility. Even with the big spotlight atop the wheelhouse cutting an opening into the murk, all Bricker could see was the whipping rain, a thundering maelstrom of breaking waves flooding over the bow, and the sea beyond which was a raging, angry chaos of forty and fifty-foot breakers smashing into one another with gouts of white foam, sliding right over the top of one another, creating gushing dark mountains of rolling water and the *Jezebel* was heading downsea right into it.

More than once, he caught sight of a wall of water big as a two-story house moving past them, sliding beam-to of the boat. He knew any of them could have rolled the *Jezebel* effortlessly. As it was, he was threading the needle and every moment in the tempest seemed like an eternity.

Around 9:30, as the storm became less of a weather pattern and more of a primal monster filled with wrath, Johnny Muller came into the wheelhouse in a barrage of rain and wind. It took some time to get the door closed again.

"Say it," Bricker told him. "You been nursing it ever since we brought that ugly bitch of a fish aboard, so say what's on your mind. I ain't got time to stroke it out of you."

Muller managed a half-smile that was near to a frown. Water dripping from his oilskins and sou'wester, he held onto the rail and tested his sea legs against the pitch and give of the *Jezebel*.

Nobody knew how old Johnny Muller was, but by all accounts, he'd been working the Grounds for fifty years if not sixty. His face was fissured like pine bark, his long beard and trailing hair white as November's first snow. But that he was an equal to any man that crewed the *Jezebel*, nobody doubted. His chest was huge like an oak stump, arms thick and corded, shoulders broad and squared-off, hands powerful and sure. The young guys kidded him, calling him "the old man of the sea" and "Methuselah" to which he replied that he had moles older than they, that the lot of them were nothing but weak-kneed, sallow-bellied, drool-nosed tommycots still pissing yellow in their ditties, a fine dew of mother's milk still warm upon their lips.

"Okay, Skip. Yer straight with me and I'll be straight with you. Fair enough. Here's what I got to say. Ye think I'm acting like some crazy old coot saying we ain't gonna make port? Piss on ye. Ye sealed it for the lot of us when you wouldn't throw that thing down into the deeps where it belongs," he said, nearly shouting above the wailing of the wind. "Ye ain't been at this game long as I. Half the ships I crewed on are on the bottom now or scrapped in dry dock, along with the men who sailed 'em. Ye don't know what I seen in them years and I sure as hell don't have time to learn ye. That thing…that sea-bitch ye brought aboard…aye, not the first to get tangled in a net. They live down below, they say. Got cities and what not on the bottom beneath the deepest reefs. To bring 'em aboard is a curse and to look 'em in the eye is death. They got a god same as we do and what yer seeing out there is the rage of that god, and sure as the sea out there is running hot and cold and black at its core, that rage is coming for us. Straight on. And when ye see it, call it Dagon, for it answers to no other."

With that, Muller left.

Bricker didn't have time to argue sea lore with him. He'd been around the docks and crewed the fleets for a good many years by then and he had heard things. But despite that and despite the fear turning in his stomach like a drill bit, he could only face what was out there as a storm. A freak storm. One that came up out of nowhere and would eat lives by the handful, but a storm nonetheless.

To think otherwise would be to give into weakness.

He would not allow that.

The radio was popping with static, but the voices of other ships could be heard, swordfish boats and trawlers, longliners and tuna boats, freighters and factory ships. Sometimes the crazy weather would carry their signals so close it sounded like they were standing in the wheelhouse with Bricker, others times they were nothing but ghost voices drowning in some voracious sea of noise.

Shortly after Muller went on his way, one of them came through on

Channel 16. Not particularly clear, but clear enough that Bricker could hear the terror on the voice of its captain. *"Mayday! Mayday! Mayday! This is F/V Sarah T. out of Gloucester! My position is 41 North and 65 West! We have jeopardy! This is an SOS! Repeat: this is an SOS!"* came the voice. *"We're going down! We're going down! We been hit by something! God help us...IT'S COMING BACK, OH DEAR CHRIST IT'S COMING OUT OF THE SEA AGAIN—"*

Within seconds, every captain on the band was trying to raise the *Sarah T.*, Bricker included, but she was gone. Another captain from the tuna boat *Sea Hound* came over the band saying that he saw the *Sarah T.* get swallowed by a wave...but he sounded nervous and disoriented, admitting finally that he couldn't be sure it *was* a wave, just something dark and swift rising with the cresting sea and when it passed, the *Sarah T.* was no more. They were looking for survivors, but there was nothing.

Not so much as a floating seat cushion.

9

Just after he signed off with Bricker on the sideband, Danny Sprenger, captain of the *Devilfish,* saw his own ship thrown into jeopardy. She had been taking a horrific beating and had lost most of the tackle off her decks, but that was minor in comparison to what came next.

Sprenger was at the wheel in the pilothouse, his mate—Jacobee—working the throttle. The seas were crashing over the bow, green and frothing, churning white water. When the latest barrage cleared and the *Devilfish* started its climb up the face of a cresting sixty-footer, Sprenger gripping the wheel for dear life and Jacobee giving the engines full throttle, they both saw an immense wall of water coming at them.

A black and godless wave towering right above them a hundred feet or more.

Sprenger reached absently for the radio mic, but by then, of course, it was useless: there was nothing coming over the band but the crackling electrical noise of the storm itself, the dead and droning sound emitted by its chaotic heart.

Jacobee shouted and then the wave came down and for one impossible second, both men saw that it was more than a wave but a towering titanic shape of reaching limbs that seemed to be emerging *from* the wave.

Then the water hit them, blowing out all the windows in the pilothouse, flooding the bridge and sweeping the decks clear of barrels of fuel and fresh water, what tackle remained and life rafts, peeling away the masts.

There was a crackling of electronics burning out, the stink of fused wiring and smoke.

Sprenger was tossed, rolled, then found himself thrashing in black, boiling water.

The *Devilfish*, bow to the sea, was flipped over, then rolled onto her side, and then, somehow, she seemed to recover. Sprenger swam up through the water and out the pilothouse door. He emerged gasping for air to see that his boat was being held by something immense, forced down into the water. The sea was wild and churning, right up to the gunwales and flooding over onto the decks.

The rocking motion threw him across the whaleback and then back into the pilothouse.

He saw a gigantic mass of writhing tentacles, stout and stubby, as some huge marine beast boarded his ship, driving her under with its weight. A shapeless, contorting mass of flesh above the tentacles, a body mottled green and pink and brown against pale pulsating tissue.

And eyes, eight or ten eyes, perfectly round orbs that were a lurid purple-red and the size of beach balls.

Through the rain and thrashing water, he saw a jutting head, a slobbering mouth like a train tunnel opening wider and wider, scuttling forelegs at its lips, spike-like teeth and licking tongues coming at him.

But that was all he saw as water filled the cabin and the pilothouse was smashed flat.

He was dead long before the *Devilfish* rolled to the bottom in a shattered, mangled heap.

10

The *Jezebel* had her own jeopardy.

The pounding seas were beating the hell out of her. She was rising to meet each wave, barely making it again and again. Bricker knew damn well that it was only a matter of time before they would be pushed back down into the sea to the point that they could not recover and the *Jezebel* would either pitchpole, get driven into black water, or take a final, devastating roll into the depths below.

As it was, she was creaking and groaning, the wind tearing her apart as the rain and waves tried to drown her.

Fuel barrels were breaking loose out on the whaleback.

Eddie Braun and Johnny Muller were up from below to secure them, trying to stay on their feet in the pounding rain and screaming wind as the sea broke over the gunwales, drenching them and tossing them about deck. Muller got his hands on Braun and got him down as the barrels rolled past them up to the wheelhouse ladder, then came rolling back as the bow rose to meet a wave, all of them firing off the stern like depth charges.

But they were still at the mercy of the storm.

The wind kept knocking Muller down as he tried to reach the hatch to go below, dragging Braun with him. Then the wind punched into him, a crashing spray of water knocking Braun to the stern and nearly washing him overboard.

Bricker threw the boat in autopilot and went out into the blow. Braun was getting pummeled by foaming green water, the stern dipping into the sea and disappearing, only to reappear a few seconds later with him barely hanging on.

Bricker slid across the whaleback as an ocean of water flooded the deck and sprayed out the scuppers. The pitch of the ship tossed him to his knees again and again. He called out to Braun that he'd get a line to him and Braun called back, "GET THE HELL ON THAT WHEEL, SKIP! STEER THIS CRATE! WE'RE STARTING TO ROLL!"

Bricker knew he was right, but Eddie Braun was his best and oldest friend in the world and he knew he could not abandon him to the elements even at the cost of the boat. He just couldn't do it.

As he tried to uncoil a spool of nylon rope, the seas kept breaking against the sides of the ship with a sound like an artillery barrage. She pitched forward, bounced, heaved, rode up the crests of crashing seas and slid back down into their troughs. Boarding seas inundated the decks with yellow foam and spindrift. There was nothing to do but hold onto the gunwales and pray. The wind was howling at sixty-five knots by that point which was enough to lift up a man and throw him two-hundred feet if not a quarter mile. Waves were conflicting now, coming from every direction and crashing into one another.

As he wiped salt from his eyes, Bricker caught sight of a wall of water bearing down on them that had to be cresting to seventy feet. By luck or providence, it split open and died out before it hit the bow.

He edged his way along the gunwale towards Eddie Braun, swallowing water and blinking salt from his eyes. He heard something at that moment rising up in the storm: a roaring noise that sounded more like some primordial beast than any wind.

"ROGUE!" Johnny Muller called out.

Bricker saw it.

He looked right at it.

It was descending on the stern, its black shadow falling right over Eddie Braun. Steep and cresting, more than sixty feet in height, it came down like an avalanche and engulfed the decks, stripping away gear and barrels and ripping a life raft from its mount and sending it careening off into the storm.

When it passed, Eddie Braun was gone.

Bricker started screaming when he saw the wave coming down because it was not merely a barrier of rushing water, but a shadowy mass that concealed a horror beyond imagining: a reaching, pale and segmented limb ending in something like a mottled albino spider with wriggling legs…a *hand,* it was some kind of hand with claw-like fingers that had to be the size of telephone poles…and beyond—barely hidden by the cresting water, shadows, and pelting sheets of rain—a yawning mouth like the jaws of a skeletal fish, opening and opening, appendages writhing at its perimeter, gigantic teeth sliding from pink gums.

It was this that took Eddie Braun.

Then Johnny Muller was pulling Bricker up the wheelhouse ladder as spray, foam, and wind tore at them.

"Dagon," he said, spitting out water. *"Dagon has come…"*

11

Below decks, it was a tempest.

Water was flooding down through hatch covers ripped free in the storm. Anywhere there was an opening, a crack, a minute crevice, in came the water until it was waist deep in the galley as the *Jezebel* lifted and canted, rose up and crashed back down, swaying and jerking and pitching wildly.

The lights were flickering overhead.

The water was rising, the pumps failing. Soon the engine compartment would flood and the batteries would go. As Hanley tried in vain desperation to slip into his survival suit, getting dunked and thrown against the bunks and submerged face-first, Garrick and Searles fought in vain to open the companionway hatch that had slammed shut with the violent motion of the ship, swelling with the water, and refusing to budge.

Searles and Garrick were screaming, fighting to stay on their feet as the ship lurched and the water rose and the galley became a splashing pool of floating dishes and books and DVD covers, boxes of rice and plastic bags of frozen vegetables and sacks of potatoes and onions and beer cans and pretty much anything else that wasn't tied down.

Then the lights went out.

Garrick fought forward and banged on the intercom which was dead, fearing that above decks all had been swept overboard and the cabin was about to become a tomb.

The lights flickered back to life weakly.

The boat veered straight up and the men were thrown into the drink along with just about everything else. As the *Jezebel* righted herself, their faces emerged from the dirty water. Just in time to hear a curious groaning from the bulkheads beyond the bunkroom. It became a low groaning, a shifting, and then as the boat climbed yet another wave, a sudden and deafening *boom* like an explosion as the bulkhead separating the cabin from the fish hold let go and a mountain of ice and fish came flooding down over them, washing Searles and Garrick under.

Hanley fought up from beneath the ocean of ice and bobbing fish and saw the creature they had netted floating a few feet away.

Then he saw two forms rise up to either side of it…things like *her:* hunched-over shapes, green, gray, and scaled, gills at their necks opening and closing with moist sucking sounds. They stood almost like men, but were monstrous, abyssal horrors, spined and sharp-finned, tiny marine parasites wriggling at their pale white bellies. Their faces were the faces of fish—blubbery lipped, noseless, eyes huge and bulging grotesquely, shining like smoky, yellowed glass.

There was hate in those eyes: primal, enraged, merciless…yet something else, too, and was it not pity and remorse but maybe something akin to anguish.

They made croaking sounds like toads.

Hanley heard…*music.* Maybe it was in his own head, but as he looked at them he heard a whispering, ancestral music of pelagic depths and sunken reefs, abyssal planes and subsurface currents. The music of the tides, of waves crashing on silent beaches and sluicing over foggy headlands.

It was *their* music.

As it filled his head, layering and feathering, drowning him in silken fathoms, he saw towering coral cities squatting on murky seabeds or rising up amongst the wrecks of rotting green-masted schooners, split-hulled fishing boats, and rusting freighters turned turtle. Everything—city and wreck— was encrusted with marine growths, heaped barnacles, and multi-colored shells amongst waving kelp forests. Cities so old they were sinking into the mud and slime and accumulated detritus of silt, bones, and mollusk shells, the gutted husks of missing ships.

When the lights finally went out, something rose from the icy water behind Hanley and a fish-stinking hand with webbed fingers wrapped around his face, compressing, crushing.

He moaned and fought at first, tearing his hands on sharp spines.

Then he accepted, cocooned and enshrouded in secret green depths.

Then the lights went out for good. Things still moved amongst the ice and bobbing fish and debris, but they were not the forms of men.

12

Johnny Muller almost had Bricker through the doorway to the wheelhouse when another wave crashed down on them…only this one was not just water, but a heaving tonnage of slime and dead fish that buried the decks, flattening Bricker and washing Muller over the side in a fetid wave of rotten cod, flounder, redfish, and shark. He emerged in a sea of carcasses, fighting to stay afloat, fingers clawing through a bubbling muck of putrescence, but finally going under, weighted down, sinking away and borne under by the waves.

Bricker saw none of this. He climbed into the wheelhouse as waves drenched him and wind-driven rain hit him like grapeshot. The radio was gone now: the steel masts holding the antennas had been stripped away and he was alone on the dying *Jezebel*, as alone as any man can possibly be.

And in his mind there was but a single voice: *I'll see her through, yes sir, I'll see her through.*

The engines were still running and the rudder was answering, so he threw every last ounce of himself and the boat into the fight as the wind howled with freight train intensity and the *Jezebel* shook and rocked and waves broke over the bow and rain pelted the slimed decks.

A thundering wave was coming and Bricker clenched his teeth. It was a sixty-footer and he drove right at it, climbing its face until it seemed the engines would dog out and then the boat broke the crest and as it came sliding down the other side, picking up speed as it went, he saw the next wave coming right on top of the other: this one an easy two-hundred feet in height—roaring and booming and crashing.

And then the sea seemed to open up like a great hole had been carved through it and he could see the devil coming at him through the funneling hollow, the primal and spectral fish-god known as Dagon driving right at him in a burning, boiling expulsion of hissing sea-fog—something colossal that rose as high as a three-story building on a coiling, swimming raft of tentacles…a nebulous, pulsating, multi-limbed mass that was equal parts tentacular cephalopod, segmented marine worm, bony crustacean, and undulant bathypelagic mutation…primeval and noxious and seething.

"HERE COMES THE JEZEBEL, *YOU SONOFABITCH!"* Bricker shouted. *"RIGHT DOWN YOUR FUCKING THROAT!"*

24

Gaining speed as the boat raced down the backside of the sixty-footer, Bricker let out one last agonized and defiant scream and drove the *Jezebel* right at its tormentor, the sharp-chinned bow slicing into the gelid mass of Dagon at maximum velocity in a rancid gushing of gelatinous tissues, yellow burning steam, acrid rotting fish stench, and a gargantuan outpouring of toxic slime that engulfed the boat from stem to screw in a web of ooze.

Then the wave above mercifully crested, crashed, and all was lost in a convulsive vortex of rushing gray water and writhing blackness that shattered the wheelhouse windows and gouged open the hull, the decks buckling as the ship pitchpoled, driven down into the churning dark seas.

Bricker was knocked off his feet, banged and bounced from ceiling to deck to bulkhead as water rushed into the wheelhouse with devastating hydrostatic pressure and the electrical system shorted out with a crackling explosion of blue sparks.

As the *Jezebel* went under, the emergency lights lasted long enough so that he could see, as his mind fell into a field of steel gray, the huge and malevolent jellied eyes of Dagon peering in at him just before squirming, squamous tendrils filled the wheelhouse like tree roots, taking hold of him as his lungs were filled with water.

13

Six hours later, the storm was downgraded from a Force 12 tempest to a mild blow and even that diminished and faded. Then the seas of the North Atlantic were curiously flat, silent, and glassy as if the storm had sucked away every last bit of building potential energy of the vast sea itself, bleeding it out in one massive kinetic thrust.

Twelve ships were lost with all hands.

Six others floundered but their crews were rescued, save a few.

The *Jezebel* did not sink. It was found floating derelict off the southern tip of Nova Scotia by a fishing party. The Coast Guard boarded her within the hour. She was a devastated wreck, holds flooded, bulkheads collapsed, decks stripped clean, whaleback severed by a huge jagged crack.

It was a mystery how she stayed afloat with a split hull.

The Coasties discovered that her decks were badly stained and pitted by some corrosive marine secretion, origin unknown. They found no exotic unknown animal below decks, but what they did find were the bodies of Captain Bricker, Hanley, Searles, and Garrick all neatly packed away in ice in the one remaining fish pen that had not been breached.

How that had come to be, they did not speculate.

CULT OF THE BLACK SWINE

Riggs blew into town with a bad attitude and a .44 Smith in a speed rig under his left arm. He carried a picture of the Winslett girl inside his coat and another of Red Olney, the guy who had supposedly abducted her. One would lead to the other and that's why he had come to Boomugga, a skid mark in the Pennsylvania Highlands. The sort of hick town where you could take your best girl square dancing on Friday night or buy corn liquor from inbred moonshiners that would make you shit fire.

The Feds had been bird-dogging Olney for six months without catching so much as a whiff of his cologne or snagging a single print or an eyewitness to his existence. The case was still open, of course, but there were only so many agents in the Bureau and priorities were always changing.

That's where Riggs came in.

He had his private cop's license and had spent five years as a prohibition agent during the bootlegging days and another twelve in the Sixteenth Precinct in South Philly. He had all that to recommend him and nothing but time on his hands. For the right price, he'd chase down anyone—cheating husbands, playful wives, embezzlers on the run, and cheap hoods on the lam—and with a near 100% success rate, he came highly recommended. There wasn't much he wouldn't take on for a price. Case in point, Old Man Winslett. He owned four Steel Town factories, two refineries, and three rust belt foundries. He definitely had the scratch. He wanted to bring the tragedy of his granddaughter's kidnapping to an end one way or another—if she was alive, he wanted her back; and if she wasn't, he wanted a body to bury.

So, Riggs came to Boomugga.

The first thing a private dick was supposed to do when he stepped onto foreign turf was to appraise the local bulls of his intentions: why he was there and what he was after. But Riggs didn't have the time for that. There was no law in Boomugga and the county sheriff was down in Allentown. Riggs had no intention of tracking him down and greasing his backside. He knew how things worked with these local john laws, how connected and intermarried they could be to their constituents. Last thing he needed when he was this close was word getting out and fouling his investigation.

He'd handle it his own way.

The best way to deal with these country shitheels was to blindside them, throw the goods at 'em and watch 'em squirm. You started by laying on the honey like you were old pals and if that didn't bring the bees, you started breaking bones. That's how Riggs had handled these hillbillies as a prohibition agent and that's how he'd handle them now.

Maybe the feds had drawn a blank on Red Olney, but he had resources they didn't. Word had it Olney was hiding amongst his people in Boomugga. Riggs would run him to ground because it was the one thing he was good at. He was going to find out what happened to the Winslett girl one way or another. How that played out was entirely up to Red Olney. If he cooperated, Riggs would get what he wanted, slap the bracelets on him and bring him in warm and breathing. If he didn't, he'd drag him in full of holes and cold as a dead carp.

That's the way it had to happen.

Riggs had 15,000 reasons to see that it did and all of them were green and folding.

First thing he did was to canvas the town. There were less than 500 souls in Boomugga, so it didn't take very long. The second thing he did was to roll his heap up to the local café, Pauline's. He'd grab a stool and mingle with the locals, get a feel for things from them.

Pauline's was a dive with torn red leather booths, chipped Formica tables, and the requisite stools polished smooth and shiny by generations of asses.

"What'll it be?" a hard-looking redhead with highly inflated assets asked him.

"How's the hamburgers?"

"Thick and rare with plenty of fried onions and pickles," she told him.

"Make mine twins. No garbage, lots of mustard, and throw some cheese on 'em. And a chocolate milkshake to wash 'em down with."

"You got it, mister."

She dropped him a wink and made sure he got a shot of her abundant cleavage for future reference. She was his type, all right. Cute and stacked, a smirk to her mouth and shake to her bosom. He just bet she was plenty good with both. A girl like that a guy would follow anywhere.

As she called out his order to a slab of pork with bushy eyebrows and a grease-stained paper hat, Riggs looked around. The locals leaning over their sandwiches and soup were muttering in low voices to one another, but they paid him no mind. He had the feeling that whatever they were jawing about, it had nothing to do with a stranger in town. His gut feeling was that something was in their collective craw, something that was worrying and preoccupying them.

His milkshake came in a steel cup, his hamburgers on a blue-flecked plate. The former was cold and good, the latter juicy and mouth-watering. He polished them off and ordered a coffee.

The redhead announced that her name was Sally, so Riggs swapped tags with her.

"Just Sally?" he asked, getting a sudden feeling.

She smiled. "Sally Olney," she admitted.

Bingo. Sometimes as a private detective you played a hunch and things worked out.

"What brings you to this hellhole, Steve?"

He shrugged. "I peddle insurance—life, home, fire, you name it. That's my racket. It pays the bills. Got an appointment in Bethlehem day after tomorrow, so I'm just laying over. Recommend a room for a few days?"

"Two blocks down, past the blinking light. Ma Steuben. She'll take care of you." Sally studied him very closely, looking troubled. "Ma'll be glad to have you."

"I'll look her up."

"You want my advice?" she asked. "Don't bother. Get the hell out of here. Drive over to Bethlehem. There's some good hotels there, lot better than Ma's."

Riggs had the funniest feeling that she was warning him off. "Something wrong with staying here?"

"No, of course not. But you can do better. A lot better."

"I'll take Ma Steuben's," he said.

She shrugged. "Well, nobody can say I didn't try."

It looked like she was on the verge of telling him something and from the look on her face, it was something bad. But at the last moment, she shook her head and went off to tend to her other customers.

Well, ain't that just something? Riggs mused.

He sipped his coffee and pulled off a Lark, thinking about mixed signals. He was getting them not just from Sally, but from the whole damn town. Nobody had been unfriendly to him exactly, yet he had the nagging feeling there was another level at play here. Things unsaid.

Sally came back and he noticed, with a bit of disappointment, that her flirtatious air had vanished now. She looked serious, deathly serious.

"Olney," Riggs said. "Olney, Olney...now why does that name sound familiar? You have any celebrities in the family?"

She rolled her eyes. "It's probably familiar because of my cousin Red—third cousin, that is. They wanted him for kidnapping some girl. There was a statewide manhunt for him, but they never got him."

"Yeah, that must be it."

She looked around. "Some people said he went into hiding around here somewhere. Who knows? Only one that would know is his old man, Dash. Both of them were damn weird and everyone in the family kept their distance."

Riggs was going to ask her more, but the slab of pork working the grill shouted: "SALLY! CUSTOMERS!"

It was time to leave.

Riggs stepped outside into the chill air, cupping another Lark in his hands and giving it some flame. He puffed away, thinking. Autumn leaves blew up the walks, making sounds like scraping claws. People passed. None of them were unfriendly, but, again, preoccupied. Something was eating away at this whole damn burg and he just wondered what it might be. The only way to figure it out was to maybe hang around, see what transpired.

He didn't waste time because it wasn't his way. A phone book told him exactly where Dash Olney lived. It was a short distance, so he legged it. He took a left off the main drag, followed a peeling whitewashed fence plastered with tatters of ancient circus posters and political flyers until he reached a decrepit neighborhood of sagging houses with dirty kids chasing balls up the street. Yards were overgrown, trees gnarled, bushes untrimmed. About what he figured. Shit-nothing towns like this, they were always the same. Only the names changed.

303 Hickory was easy enough to find. It was a sagging two-story that hadn't seen a lick of paint since Taft was in office. The upstairs windows were boarded, plank siding coming loose, pigeon shit staining the roof white.

Riggs walked by it twice like he was lost, seeing if he attracted any attention. He didn't. In Boomugga, nobody noticed anything. They were all blank-eyed, empty-skulled wind-up dolls, bovine, senseless things like cattle being led by a Judas Goat into the stockyards. The image of that resonated with him, but he shrugged it off. He had real work to do.

Feeling eyes crawling on him like flies, he went up the steps to the front door and knocked. He could feel somebody on the other side deciding whether to open it or not. Reaching their decision, the door creaked open on its hinges. Dash Olney was a skinny little guy that could have slipped through cracks if he turned sideways. He wore green workpants and suspenders, a dirty gray t-shirt. His eyes were the color of mud puddles.

"Yeah?"

"Mr. Olney? Name's Steve Riggs. I need to ask you a few questions and I'd appreciate you answering them."

"And if I don't wanna?"

"You can either talk to me or the feds. Your choice."

"Another cop, eh?" He shook his head. "Or maybe you're something else?"

"That's about it."

Riggs eeled his way through the door and followed Dash into a living room crowded with tatty furniture, beer bottles, and yellowed newspapers. Dash fell into a rocking chair and appraised Riggs with dead eyes.

"Well?" he said.

"I want to ask you about your son."

"Figured." He lit a cigarette, his face vanishing in a cloud of smoke. He made a sound in his throat that was somewhere between a chuckle and a cry. "I knew you'd come. It was only a matter of time. You're looking for the girl and you think I can point you towards her. That it?"

Riggs nodded. "Yes."

Dash blew out another cloud of smoke, licked his lips. "FBI tried to find her and couldn't. What makes you think you can? What's so special about a guy like you?"

"I find people. It's what I do. People seem to think I'm good at it."

"Well, ain't that something? But I'll save you some trouble, bloodhound. I don't know where Red is. If he's about, then you best put your nose to the ground and sniff him out."

"Oh, I will. You can count on that."

"And while you're at it," Dash said in a low, threatening voice, "maybe you ought to consider the fact that she's gone because she needs to be. Then maybe you'll have enough common sense to leave well enough alone."

"Meaning?"

"Meaning, you're the detective, you figure it out."

Maybe Dash thought he was going to get excited and smash his teeth out, but there was no need for that. As Dash had been jawing, Riggs had seen something through the sheer curtain over the window that looked into the back yard—a shape that peered out from behind a sap house out there. And that was all he needed to see.

But he played the game because Dash expected it. "I don't like a guy who speaks in riddles. Sooner or later, I'll find your son. Then I'm coming for you."

Dash blinked a couple times. "If he's here, then you gotta find him because that's how it works. I don't know anything."

"Fair enough. Be seeing you."

Riggs left the way he came in. He played it the way it had to be played. He did not try to get a look at the backyard. That would be for later. Right now, he was a man in a hurry with a hundred things that needed attending to.

Funny how things are, he got to thinking. Just a few hours before nobody paid any attention to him. They were neutral. Now, out of the blue, they were wiggling around him like hungry cats. Eyes were no longer averted, no longer disinterested. People either went out of their way to say hello and pump his hand, welcome to Boomugga, or they parted at his approach like the Red Sea as if he was some kind of wheel that ran things.

Funny.

He was planning on a late supper at Pauline's, grab some grub, rub noses with Sally, see what came of that. Then he had business over at 303 Hickory.

But before that, he tracked down Ma Steubens so he'd have somewhere to hang his hat for the night. Two blocks down past the blinking light, Sally said. By that point, the road had turned to a dirt run and the sidewalks were wooden and root-buckled.

He parked the heap outside a ratty, used up Victorian and hopped out, following a flagstone path through a jungle of weeds to a slouching porch. A sign nailed to a newel post read, ROOMS 25¢ a night. This was the place all right.

Riggs didn't bother knocking; he sashayed right in. There was a narrow staircase right in front of him, a sitting room off to the right. That's where he found Ma Steuben. She was sitting there with a couple other antique dames, reading in a muttering voice from an old hide-bound book on her lap. He couldn't make out what they were saying, some kind of foreign tongue, guttural and strange.

As he came in, he heard one word: "Nyarlathotep."

One of the old bats had said it. Hell kind of word was that? It made no sense, yet it seemed to gain traction in his mind—*Nyarlathotep, Nyarlathotep, Nyarlathotep*. It had a sing-song quality to it. He couldn't shake it. As he stood there, it kept hitting him in the brain like a fist.

"Can I help you?" a voice asked.

"You Ma?" he said.

She closed the book on her lap with a snap. "Who wants to know?"

"A guy who needs a room."

"Then I'm Ma."

The two other old ladies whispered things under their breath and vacated the room, their shadows crawling after them like pet snakes. One of them used a black, knotty cane that looked like the dead branch of a tree. *Tip-tap, tip-tap,* it went. Ma studied him earnestly with dreary eyes set in red, pouchy sockets. Her thinning hair was white and weedy, a permanent scowl etched onto her mouth.

She pressed a hand against the cover of the book, the title of which looked like Latin. "What business you say you were in?"

Riggs gave her his own smirk. "Let's just say I'm a man on a mission and leave it at that."

Ma nodded, uttering something which could have been a cough or a cackle. "Well, I'll not be the one to stand in the way of a man obeying higher powers. No, sir. Twenty-five cents like it says out front. You want breakfast, it's another ten cents."

"Just the room."

"So be it."

"What are the house rules?"

"Ain't none. Not for a man on a mission."

She seemed to get a special joy out of that, but he didn't ask why. He had better things to do than to chat it up with some crazy old broad. She walked him up the stairs to his room. Every third or fourth step, she paused and looked down at him like he was the most entertaining thing she'd ever seen. When she did that, it raised his hackles. It was as if just for a moment, he saw something under her skin, another face grinning at him, maybe a dozen of them and each one brooding over a terrible secret old as time.

The room was small and cramped, typical Victorian, the gaudy floral wallpaper peeling up near the ceiling which was frescoed with water stains.

"Well, Mr. Riggs," she said, "I hope you find that girl you're seeking."

Riggs tensed. He didn't like other people knowing his business, especially not in Boomugga. "Never said I was looking for anyone."

"You didn't have to. I didn't get to be this damn old without being able to read faces, even faces like yours that don't want to be read." She stared him down, her dreary eyes suddenly wide and bright with something like anticipation. "I hope you find the Winslett girl. I surely do. She's close to hand and I know it same as you do. Go out there and find her. It'll be a blessing for one and all, son."

She closed the door and he heard her talking to herself with what almost sounded like glee.

Riggs sat down on the bed. He could hear the wind in the trees outside. A fly buzzed at the window. His own thoughts collided inside his head. He opened his mouth to say things, but no words came out. They were all in his mind, a jumble of conflicting thoughts and ideas, distorted imagery and abstract impressions. His entire body began to tremble and he was powerless to stop it. He clenched his teeth tightly so he did not scream because he could feel it building in him, reaching a rising crescendo of nameless horror.

And then it was gone as if it never was.

He sat there, his face blank, his heart beating, his lungs breathing. Something had him and he knew it. He could feel it crawling under his skin and worming at the base of his brain. *Nyarlathotep.* There would come a time when it would make sense, but that time was not now.

He had things to do.

He was in far too deep to back out now.

35

Pauline's was a bust. Sally wasn't on and seeing her had been the only bright spot in a particularly dismal evening. He sat before the window, listening to leaves scraping up the walks, hunched over a plate of chicken-fried steak and hushpuppies, chewing methodically but tasting nothing. It was dark out and he sensed, rather than saw, shapeless forms moving past the window. In the café, the locals watched him breathlessly, as if waiting for him to do or say something revelatory.

He finished his Coke, smoked a cigarette, and thought about those things he would do now. How he would accomplish them and the reverberations of those very actions.

When he stood up to leave, everyone watched. They studied him as he pulled on his trench coat and fedora. He paid his bill and went out to his heap. He did not look behind him, because he knew they would be watching, all lined up at the window with awful things in their eyes. Mentally goading him on like a gladiator going into the arena.

There were things going on all around him and maybe there had been from the very first but he had been too thick-headed to notice, too mired in his own pursuits. He had the most awful feeling that nothing he did and nothing he had come to do were secret any longer. Everyone knew. They were all with him in spirit—anxious, longing, and eager.

He parked the heap a half a block from 303 Hickory. He sat there behind the wheel, smoking, thinking, looking around. Sending his mind out to see if it made contact with anything or anyone. He didn't want an audience now. He didn't want anything but the girl. In the light of his cigarette, he studied her picture. Her name was Rita. She was fourteen years old.

After about twenty minutes, nothing riling his instincts, he stepped out of the car. The night was windy and dark. There was a light mist in the air. He left his hat on the backseat and started out for 303. He felt tense, which was understandable, and afraid, which was not. By nature, he was icy, cold, and emotionless. His nerves did not jump; they were dead snakes. They barely crawled. But tonight, everything was alive inside him, everything seemed to be in conflicting motion. Nothing would settle in place.

"Do what you came to do," he said under his breath.

Yes, that's all there was to it. Like he told Ma Steuben, he was a man on a mission. There was no more to it. The locals in Boomugga might've been out of their heads, but that wasn't his business. Only the girl. Old Man Winslett wanted her and he was going to get her or the guy that snatched her. This was Riggs' meat and potatoes.

The wind blew leaves in his face as he stepped into Dash Olney's yard. Latticed moonlight shone through the trees in yellow blades. There was a single light on in the house. Riggs edged along the hedges, feeling the weight of the .44 at his side. Now it was strictly about money. Anyone got in the way of that, he'd burn 'em.

There was the shack out back.

Probably a sap house like he'd thought. Maybe a smokehouse. Too big for a privy. He slipped in closer, moving a few feet, listening, feeling for trouble, then moving a few more. When he reached the shack, he knew someone was in there. Maybe they were waiting for him, maybe not. He would need to do this aggressively. Experience taught him that he needed to stay on the offensive. Always be the crusader, never the defender.

He stood before the door.

He pulled out his heater, flashlight in his other hand. All he had to do was lift the latch and charge in. Yet, he hesitated. An old fear had consumed him, one that he had not felt since he was a child and his mother had forgotten to shut the closet door completely. It was a fear of unknown things, primeval things, shadows that slithered around the edge of reason.

He would not be owned by it.

Using the flashlight, he quietly lifted the latch free. Then he yanked the door open and went right in, going down low in case the lead started flying or fists sought his face. But there was nothing. He was vaguely disappointed because this was not at all how it had played out in his mind. There was too much fear and rage and random energy inside him. He needed to spend it on something.

The shack was empty save for a trapdoor set in the concrete floor. It was an open invitation and he knew he had to go down there. In the flashlight beam, his heart pounding in his throat, he could see a sort of symbol on the trapdoor lid. Odd sort of thing like a squiggly star with a staring eye at its center. He kneeled down, touching it. It seemed to be carved or burned right into the wood. He had no idea what it meant, but it made fear squirm in his belly like worms.

He grabbed hold of the pull ring and lifted it up. A hot smell of decay wafted out at him. There was light down there and a set of iron rungs leading down to it. He was expected and he knew it. He stuffed the flashlight into his coat pocket and started down. He didn't hesitate—he went down fast, looking for trouble. There was sort of a tunnel in front of him, the walls made of sweating brick. The light was at the end. The closer he got to it, the stronger was the stench of oozing grave slime. It made his stomach contract.

There was a heavy wooden door before him now with that same arcane symbol etched into it. Partially open, it beckoned to him like a finger. Breathing in deeply, he jumped forward and kicked it open all the way. He felt a pungent heat, smelled candles and curious spices, and saw a loping shape vaulting toward him. Again, there was no hesitation. He'd been in plenty of tight spots and his instinct prevailed—he fired two rounds from the .44 and somebody cried out, dropping to the dirt floor.

Red Olney.

He was struggling, gut-shot and bleeding out rapidly. He was gasping for breath, freshets of gore bubbling from his lips. He was thin and dirty. It looked like he'd been used to mop the floor of hell.

Riggs stood there with the gun in his hand, looking down at him. "It didn't have to be this way, you know. It didn't have to be this way at all." He looked around the room with its cobwebbed beams overhead, the grimy brick walls. "You tell me where she is, I'll get you a doctor."

Red laughed with a choking sound and expelled a glob of blood. "Don't...want no doctor." He breathed with a liquid rasping sound. "Knew you'd come...I tried...God knows I tried to keep...keep her from them..."

"What are you talking about?"

"That's what it...what it was about, you fool," Red managed, shaking with spasms and from the look on his face, each one was an agony. "Keep her from them. They need her...what lives in her...but they couldn't come get her...not with the elder signs...couldn't cross the barrier..."

It was crazy talk. Delirium. Riggs had seen plenty of men die and sometimes they got like this, talking lunacy as they passed over. You couldn't pay much attention to it. Yet, in the back of his mind, things were fitting together and adding up. The symbols were powerful. He'd felt that himself and he'd known the moment he saw them that they were not there on the doors by accident. There was a logic behind everything in Boomugga.

"Where's the girl?"

"In…there."

Another door, another damn symbol etched into it. Riggs stepped over Red Olney and pushed it in. A fire was burning in a central pit. It painted the walls with Halloween tongues of orange and black. Shadows danced around him like pagan devils.

He stepped in there and right away something shriveled inside him, twisted up and broke apart like chaff before a scythe. He leaned in the doorway, trying to suck air through clenched teeth. His eyes bulged like those of a decompressed fish. It felt like a thousand fingers were scratching around inside his skull. The atmosphere was poison. The smell was hot and diseased, like an open gangrenous wound. A palpable, revolting stench that covered him like an insect swarm, crawling up his spine and nesting in his hair, filling him and seeping from his pores.

But it wasn't the worst thing.

That was the girl—Rita Winslett—who dangled in the air before him like an engorged human fly. Naked, contused, and expanding with each breath like a blowfish, she was suspended spread-eagled in a web of silver wires the thickness of fishing line. Each one pierced her, threaded through her body, and was fixed to the rafters overhead in a grisly network. But none of it seemed random. There was some esoteric, deranged pattern to it, an eldritch configuration. They were strung through her face and back and belly, puncturing her legs and arms. All of them ran just under the skin and her own weight had tented her flesh, pulling it up into spikes and stretched pouches.

She was hairless, her flesh a mottled pink. Her eyes were spirals of color, her black-lipped mouth opening and closing.

Riggs stumbled forward, appalled, sickened, and angry. It was an atrocity. And even as a wizened voice in his head screamed at him not to disturb the network, not to release the girl from the elaborate cat's cradle that nullified her awful potential, he was doing just that—snapping the lines, yanking them from the rafters, freeing her. Then he had the girl on the floor and he was pulling the wires from her one after the other, casting them aside in a spidery tangle.

"There," he panted, sour sweat beading his face. "It'll be all right now."

It was at that moment as she fixed him with the black whirlpools of her eyes that he realized that she had not bled a drop. Then she reached out a palsied hand and he took it, her flesh spongy and oozing with something like fish oil. She was cold. Unbearably, painfully cold despite the rancid heat in the room. Her black maw opened and he saw gnarled teeth like shards of glass, then she bit into his hand, clamping down on it, tearing it open and sucking up the blood that ran free.

Riggs fell back in agony, his mind spinning, the walls closing in. He fought through it and when the girl made to bite him again, he conked her with the butt of the gun and she dropped limp at his feet.

He wrapped his bleeding hand with a handkerchief, his mind going in and out of focus. Then he seized her by the ankles and dragged her through the doorways. He nearly passed out as he pulled her up the ladder, but finally he had her in the shed. He carried her out into the night and they were waiting for him—the residents of Boomugga.

Old Man Winslett was there. He was grinning like a yellow skull. "I told you he was the one," he said. "Now Mr. Riggs, bring the child forth so that the cycle might complete itself."

Riggs sank to his knees, dropping the girl and going out cold.

It could have gone on for weeks or months; there was really no way to know. Thinking was hard because there were layers to his mind—what was, what had been before, what could never be, and what would come next or not at all. Like intermeshing gear wheels, spinning and grinding and throwing off sparks and filling his head with hot smoke so he did not know where he was or even *what* he was.

They kept him in a pen that was less than three feet wide and not even five in length. He could not straighten his legs; he could barely turn from side to side. There were other pens, he knew, dozens of them. Dash Olney was in one of them. Sometimes he heard him screaming at night. Like the others, he was drugged, stunned like a spider stung by a hornet.

The citizens of Boomugga came and went. They chanted strange things in strange tongues. They told Riggs how wonderful he was delivering the avatar to them. That he was special. Prophecy said he would come over the mountains and he had. Praise the night and the hunger, praise Her, praise the sow, praise the Mother of all things that would come to them now, walk amongst them, the earthly spawn of the Crawling Chaos, the blessed Haunter of the Dark, He of many masks.

Riggs kept hearing only one word in his head: *Nyarlathotep, Nyarlathotep, Nyarlathotep*. It was a germ that invaded him, sickened him, sucked the blood from his soul.

They wanted him to eat and they brought great platters of spicy, greasy meat. But he knew that to taste it would bring disaster. He did not know what form it would take, but his intuition told him it would be the end of all he knew. The meat terrified him because he feared it would make him like them, like the cultists of Boomugga, part of some immense, ravening beast whose body was made of the meat-eaters. They were its flesh and blood, bone and marrow, sinew and nerve endings and skin. It breathed with them, *as* them. Their hearts beat, filling the beast with blood. And the beast grew hungry.

And it had a name: Rita Winslett. He had freed her from her prison and now she would become their living god. If he ate the meat, he would become the meat. He would fawn at her feet like the others.

This was what they wanted more than anything because it was part of the ancient cycle. In their houses, in bedrooms and living rooms, attics and cellars and dark closets, they clawed like rats in walls. They chattered their teeth and gnawed their fingers and dreamed of the meat as it dreamed of them. He heard them rasping, hissing, and slavering at night.

They starved him until he gave in, the animal in him stuffing itself with the meat which was sweet and rich, deliciously juicy and succulent. Once he had tasted it, he could eat nothing else. They brought him more and he devoured it. When he did not have it, he howled in pain like an addict until they let him have his fill. And day after day they did. He ate and ate until he was swollen and obese and the meat juices dripped from every pore.

In his fattening pen, he was insatiable.

Then one day, maybe a month later or two or nine for that matter, as he lolled in the filthy straw of his pen, the cage door was opened. In fact, all of them were. Sally stood there. It took Riggs a moment or two to remember who she was.

"I'm getting you out," she told him.

By that point, he couldn't even stand, so he crawled. They all crawled. A herd of swill-fattened hogs, pink and oily and stinking. Covered in flies and their own waste, they followed her up the ramp and out of the hot darkness where they had been kept. They inched along behind her until they reached the altar. They were in a church. That's where they had been kept and now, they were paraded out by Sally, the Judas Goat, to be shown to the residents of Boomugga like stock.

The pews were crowded. Hands were raised, making sign, and mouths chanted. Ma Steuben was there, as was Old Man Winslett who had crafted the entire scenario so that Riggs would bring them what they needed. Like a puppet, he had been manipulated expertly.

Sally put a rope around his neck and led him away. He was special. He had delivered the girl. She was up on the altar, too, and what happened next happened very quickly. The avatar was revealed. There was a crackling, bursting sound, then a loud echoing thunder like a sonic boom as the Crawling Chaos spawned in the semi-human, tortured mass of Rita Winslett.

She expanded like a fleshy balloon and sheared open, a foul soup of bubbling gray plasma flooding out, steaming and hissing. And from that placental ooze, a massive polymorphic, maggoty form rose up on a sea of squirming tendrils and flaying tentacles. It was black as India ink, glistening and palpitating, a pulpous geyser of flesh and worming appendages. Its huge flabby body vibrated and spasmed as it lifted its bulk to be worshipped, its head like that of a boar but horribly distorted and grotesque. Its blood-filled eyes gleamed with cosmic hunger, its snout ending in a sucking black maw filled with rasping teeth.

It snorted.

It squealed.

It shrilled.

This was the Black Swine, this was what was worshipped as a god in Boomugga, this was the shadow that darkened the town and poisoned its marrow.

As it squealed out its dominance and birth, its followers in the pews began to revert to their true forms, popping like chestnuts, splitting open like blood-swollen ticks. Riggs saw them as he saw his entire world now—through marred glass. The cultists were lolling, flaccid swine, pink and porcine monstrosities that squirmed and writhed with repulsive gyrations. They looked upon their god with blazing tiny red eyes set in sloughing pig faces, snouts opening to reveal jutting fangs and gouts of black foam. They grunted their delight and acquiescence.

And the Black Swine, voracious from the long ages, accepted its sacrifices. Clouds of whirring insects rose from its filthy mass with a sound of buzzsaws. To its ravenous appetite, the world was a succulent meat pie dripping with hot juices, mankind but tender morsels to be chewed slowly and savored. It towered over the naked, wriggling offerings, pulsing tentacles flensing them open, crushing them with its tumescent girth, opening their skulls like lids and scooping out their brains like soft-boiled eggs spooned from shells. It was an immense tsunami of flesh and appetite, rendering its sacrifices to polished white bone.

Riggs, broken, insane, spinning on a steel-gray axis of atavistic loathing and stark terror, watched every moment of it.

"Now," Sally told him, "we become part of her and never know death."

He shook his head to say no, that he would not be part of such an obscenity, but the throbbing corpulent mass of the Black Swine pulled him in with the others. They were planets and moons held in a dark, eccentric orbit around *her*. They gathered like puppies begging treats and she exposed rows of quivering, distended teats to them. This was the end game, he knew and she was the source. Once resurrected, this spawn of Nyarlathotep had to be satiated with human sacrifice in this terrible ceremony and once fed, she would feed her disciples, giving them the milk that would prolong their lives another century.

The dark secret of Boomugga was secret no longer.

When his turn came, he did not hesitate—he took the phallic teat into his mouth, sucking on it until the rancid milk of the Black Swine filled him, engorged him. And in his head, new vistas and webs of stars opened in some dead-end space. He was remade in her image, reborn, spawned anew. Blessed be the holy meat and the sacred pap, and blessed be the name of the Black Swine, the Earth Mother, the Daughter of the Dark Demon, the great interdimensional hog whose appetites were boundless.

THE ELDRITCH EYE

Long before the bandages came off, there was an itching and a pulling, a sense not of healing but of growth and change and strangeness. Art felt it and knew something was not exactly right, but he had trouble putting it into words that would make any kind of sense.

He had never been a hypochondriac.

He wasn't the sort of guy who got a pain in his chest and associated it with an oncoming heart attack or thought that indigestion was bleeding ulcers. The body was a complex thing, he knew, and it only stood to reason that some days there would be aches and pains. Same way that some days your car ran like a thoroughbred and others days, it took its time starting and didn't have any get up and go.

But this…this thing with his eyes, it was different.

Something was going on.

Something was not right and for the life of him, he just couldn't put a finger on it what it was exactly. He only knew that it was not normal and it did not belong. He tried to tell Lynn about it, but all she did was nod like she understood, but obviously she did not understand at all.

"You've just had surgery, Art," she said in that condescending tone of hers, the one she reserved for small animals, children, and silly men who thought something abnormal was happening to their eyes. "You had both your eyes operated on for god sake and you've been bandaged and blind for two weeks…is it any wonder you're out of sorts?"

"But it's not that…not exactly."

"Then what?"

But, again, the words failed him. "Something's just not right. I know it's not right. They feel weird. They itch all the time."

"That's called healing."

"But—"

"No buts about it, Art. You've never had surgery before. I have. I had my appendix out when I was seventeen and I had a pin put in my hip when I was twenty-five and broke my leg skiing," she told him. "It's no fun. I know that. When the healing starts, it drives you crazy. It feels like you could scratch your skin off. Been there, done that. But if you're worried, I'll give Dr. Moran a call."

The way she phrased things made him feel like some crazy old woman beset with imaginary illnesses. She was right, of course, for the most part. He *had* just undergone surgery and been blindfolded with bandages for two weeks. His vision had been failing in both eyes for years and when he finally got it checked out he was diagnosed with advanced retinitis pigmentosa, ARP, a hereditary disease which causes the retina to degenerate. No surprise, really. His mother had been functionally blind by the time she was fifty. But things were different now. There were technologies and procedures that weren't available back then. Dr. Moran had grafted fetal tissue to replace that which was damaged due to the disease. The surgery was pretty commonplace and had a 90% success rate.

Nothing to worry about.

Yet, something was happening and he just could not explain it.

But he gave in. "No, don't call him. The bandages are coming off in three days anyway."

"Now you're being sensible."

Art just wondered how sensible she'd think he was if he told her that sometimes at night he'd wake and sense a nameless sort of movement behind the bandages. Not his eyes blinking or rolling of their own accord, but a crawling, wriggling motion in there like something was trying to get out.

The bandages came off.

Dr. Moran removed them in a room that was nearly dark so the brightness wouldn't cause Art any discomfort. He unwound them carefully and slowly. Art gradually adjusted to the sudden intrusion of light. After two weeks of darkness, it caused him pain, but right away he knew there had been results. Things that had been fading and growing obscure, like the details of faces, were much sharper. He could actually see the stunning blue of his wife's eyes.

"And it'll get better, Mr. Reed," Moran told him. "Given time, you'll see things you never thought you would in ways that will astound you."

"See?" Lynn said. "I told you everything was fine."

"Hmm? What's this?" Moran said.

He was a thin, nervous little man with an assortment of odd twitches and trembles, but his hands—long-fingered and delicate—were steady as a rock. When he spoke, and he had an inclination to ramble nearly incessantly, the corners of his lips were beset with little tremors.

Art honestly wished that Lynn hadn't brought it up. "I don't know. My eyes just felt…funny."

"Funny strange, eh? Well, that's no surprise, is it? Of course, your eyes felt funny. Surgery does that to them. A change, a difference, a transformation even. Trauma is to be expected." As he spoke, he examined Art's eyes with a head-mounted ophthalmoscope that looked like some crazy virtual reality device with its jutting binocular lenses. "Good, good, good. I like what I see. Things are progressing just fine. You may never have the twenty-twenty vision you had as a boy, Mr. Reed, but then again, you just may! You just may! You stick with me and we'll work wonders, absolute wonders!"

Lynn left the room to fill out some paperwork for the insurance and Art set his chin on the biomicroscope so Moran could make a close examination of the frontal structures of the eye, the cornea and iris and lens. Next came the visual field tester and the keratometer which, Moran told him, was a very handy device for measuring the curvature of the cornea and the smoothness of the ocular surface.

Then it was all over, just a regimen of eye drops that Moran explained to him in detail. One was an antibiotic, another a topical anti-rejection ointment, and still another a steroid to speed healing.

Finally, Moran sat back, studying Art from behind his own huge dark-rimmed glasses. They made his protuberant eyes look even larger. Art always wondered why he didn't have some corrective surgery done, Lasik or something. But he supposed it was the old story. Same reason the cobbler's kids never had any shoes or the mechanic drove around in a beater.

"Questions? Questions? Do we have any questions today?" Moran asked, mouth twitching.

"No," Art told him. "I guess you covered it all."

"What about this funny feeling you mentioned?"

Art tried to explain it the best he could, which was much easier without Lynn in the room humoring him. He told Moran about the itching and the sense of movement.

"Well, well, well, that's interesting, isn't it? Hmm. I grafted complete sections of tissue to your eyes, Mr. Reed. Why? Because the implantation maintains those oh-so vital connections between the transplanted retinal cells. What you're feeling is nothing more than your eyes reacting to the transplant and putting the tissue to good use. Growing and healing and making you well."

"But should it feel like that? Like something in my eyes is moving?"

"Of course it should, of course it should. Development, progression."

Art wanted to believe him. This guy was a retinal specialist. Maybe he was a little odd, but he came well recommended and was supposed to be one of the best. He did many of these procedures every week. Yet, that sense of something abnormal remained. Even as Moran talked in great depth about tissue grafting and the miracles it could bring about, he could feel something in his eyes. Maybe just behind them, a pulling and a sliding, a swelling motion like something was coming to term in there that did not belong.

"You just give it time. Mr. Reed," Moran said. "And you'll get used to it."

But he did not get used to it.

Two weeks later it was still going on, only worse. Oh, his vision was excellent and he had no complaints about that. He was seeing perfectly, but still his eyes itched and watered and sometimes they drove him crazy with that wriggling, pulsating motion that reminded him of the beat of tiny hearts. Very often he'd come awake in the dead of night and they'd be wide open and staring. He told Lynn about it, but she asked him how he could possibly know if they were wide open when he was sleeping. He'd probably just opened them as he woke and *thought* they'd been wide open.

But, again, she did not understand and Art could not find the words to explain it.

His eyes were acting…*independently* of him. Like they were doing things of their own volition. That was absolutely insane and he did not dare mention it to her, but it was as if they had a mind of their own. They seemed to *want* to look at things. Things he himself had no interest in seeing. At least, that's how it seemed. He would find himself staring for an interminably long time at a housefly brushing its forelegs together or maybe gazing intently at the texture of tree bark or the moon hanging in the sky. Things like that, natural things, had never interested him. He liked sports. He was an ESPN junkie. Basketball and football, baseball and soccer. Anything. But whenever he sat down in front of the TV to watch those things or even a movie, his eyes began to get sore, to feel dry and aching and all he could do was close them.

His eyes did not want to look at sports or current events or action movies, they were interested in other things. They had no use for TV, but they did like books. Art was not much of a reader, but suddenly he found himself going to the library and pouring over books on zoology and anatomy, physics and mathematics. Boring textbooks that he could not pull his eyes away from. He tried to read them but they were so dull, none of it made sense. Yet, his eyes kept looking, scanning the pages and photographs and diagrams. They seemed particularly interested in pictures of other worlds and distant stars and clusters.

He was losing his mind.

He knew he was losing his mind. They were *his* eyes. They did not have any will of their own or any independent intelligence. They were essentially tools that had evolved to help animals orientate and survive in a three-dimensional world. But if that was true…then why couldn't he look away from those boring texts? Why did his eyes throb and ache whenever he tried? And why couldn't he watch TV or do any of the things he liked? Why was it that it seemed like they were taking charge, that they owned his vision and would use it to suit their own ends and only their own ends?

One night, lying awake in bed as his eyes studied the full moon drifting outside the window, he thought: *Don't you see what's happening? That tissue Moran put in is not normal tissue. It's something else, something that does not belong. It's not becoming part of your eyes, it's making your eyes part of itself.*

But that was crazy thinking.

It had to be crazy thinking.

A few nights later, he woke up and his eyes were again wide and staring, this time at the stars out the window. His head was even inclined on the pillow to give them a better view of the constellations. He got out of bed, his heart hammering and his breath coming in short, sharp gasps. He tried to blink his eyes shut, but he couldn't.

They refused.

He went into the bathroom, splashing water in his face and then putting some eyedrops in. It did no good. His eyelids would not close. It was as if the muscles controlling them were paralyzed. Panicking, he wondered if he should wake Lynn or not. He stared at himself in the mirror, knowing something was wrong, terribly wrong.

His eyes were unnatural.

And as he watched, they began to change.

The lids shriveled back even further, looking pale and vestigial, the eyes themselves becoming grotesque, glassy, golf ball-sized alien orbs. The sclera were no longer white, but sort of a pale bubble gum pink and the irises that had always been such a deep chestnut brown were a brilliant, crystalline red suffused with metallic threads of yellow. There were no pupils. The irises had consumed them and as he watched, they seemed to be ever expanding, pressing out into the whites themselves…or where the whites should have been.

He panicked.

Trying to breathe, trying to think, trying to make sense out of something essentially senseless, he pressed a finger to his left eye. There should have been some pain, but there was nothing. No sensation whatsoever as if his nerves were no longer connected to those bulging ruby orbs. But what made him jerk his finger away was the *feel* of the eye. Not like ordinary tissue, but soft and pulpy to the touch like the flesh of rotting fruit that you could sink your finger into.

It was revolting.

The thing that made him want to scream was the sudden, almost hysterical realization that he was not only looking at those eyes, but they were looking at *him*. Studying him, appraising him, somehow appalled by what they were seeing as if he were some slithering monstrosity, something they despised and would have liked to crush. He could not stop looking at them...or they at he. They seemed to be growing larger and larger, utterly dominating his face, red and leering and positively obscene. A gelid membrane covered the entire ocular surface of both eyes, magnifying what was beneath.

"What are you?" he heard his voice say. *"What in the fuck are you?"*

As if in answer, they began to move in their sockets, rolling and squirming, tears of clear fluid running from them. And the most disturbing thing was that not only were they growing brighter, but they were actually moving independently of one another...the left keeping an eye on him in the mirror while the right looked around, up and down and to either side.

He let out a little cry and pulled himself away from the mirror.

What he saw was not earthly possible. It just wasn't. He was hallucinating. The fetal tissue had caused some sort of bizarre infection and he was feverish. Yes, the sweat was rolling down his face and he felt dizzy, nauseated. He would simply wake Lynn and she'd get him into Moran at the hospital and things would be put right.

That's it. That's all there was to it.

As he moved towards the bathroom door, he was amazed at how very clear his vision was. How he could see the inlaid woodgrain of the door and the smudges of overlapping fingerprints on the knob. A fleck of dust in the air was so distinct he could make out its spherical shape and spiky texture. He left the light on and walked out into the corridor.

Or he would have.

Except as he tried to, he slammed right into the door itself. It was closed. He had closed it, yet *he could see right through it* as if it were transparent. He reached out a trembling hand and, yes, he could feel its surface, but it was like it was made of the clearest glass.

Practically hyperventilating, he looked around.

Yes, the walls were fading and he could see into the spare bedroom, the linen closet, even his own bedroom at the end of the hall, Lynn curled up and sleeping. Not only could he see her, but he could see her *perfectly.* In the darkness he could see her skin, the pores set into it. The fine hairs on her forearm. A mole on her left hip. Even the small thatch of dark hair between her legs.

Jesus, he was seeing right through the blankets and right through her pajamas and, yes, right through *her* and the mattress beneath and the carpet beneath that.

He pressed a fist to his mouth so he would not scream.

Everything was transparent, physically solid, but visually intangible. He could see the downstairs rooms under his feet as though he were standing on a sheet of glass. He could see the kitchen table as if it were in bright daylight, not pitch darkness, the individual flecks of mica in the countertop, a crumb of toast that looked like a boulder.

It was enough.

He made his way down the hallway…and then he went blind. His vision was shut off like a switch was thrown. When he tried to go towards his bedroom, there was absolute blindness; when he turned towards the stairs, his sight returned.

But he knew why.

The eyes did not want him alerting his wife. They had other plans. They wanted him to go downstairs. They demanded that he go downstairs and then he did, step by step, wishing to God he could close them so he would quit seeing the world as *they* saw it.

Downstairs, he fell into his recliner, not knowing what else to do. He thought of calling out for Lynn, but he was nearly afraid to. Because if he did, they would know it and he was not so much afraid of what they might do to him, but what they might do to her. There was nothing to do but wait and hope it passed. He sat there in the darkness, terrified of the world around him, seeing it as they saw it: a monstrous and threatening place, a confining place that was like a cage to them.

"Please," he said. "Please just stop it, please just make it go away…"

But it would not go away.

Maybe what was growing in his eyes was only incubating before, but now it had been born and was fully cognizant of the world around it. He was staring upward, looking right through the ceiling and the second story and even through the attic, peering through the roofing tiles far above and the latticed, ghostly tree branches beyond.

He was seeing the stars in the sky.

There was a thick cloudbank over the city and there was no way he could see them, but he was. They were growing brighter and larger as his telescoping sight pushed away from the Earth at a dazzling speed and looked into the very marrow of the cosmos itself.

That's when he finally screamed.

Because the human brain was not conditioned to take in what the eyes were showing him. It was not designed to look beyond the pathless wastes of deepest space and into the primal furnaces of those far flung suns themselves.

But what the eyes showed him next was even more awful.

Not only was he looking through the walls, the trees, and everything, but he was seeing stars in some far distant cosmos…except they were not stars, but eyes, thousands of eyes that looked down on the world of men with a cold, merciless intellect.

No, no, no…God, not this, not…this…

But his eyes felt no pity for him and his tiny mammalian brain.

They showed him another world out there, one that pressed in so very close that he could almost touch it, even though it must have been such a vast distance away that it was probably incalculable. They were showing him a linkage of fourth-dimensional space, a nightmare anti-world of impossible curvatures and perverse geometry, a prismatic asymmetrical abyss of blazing colors that was actually the seething, godless darkness beyond the rim of the known universe. Steaming crystalline worms left slime trails of polychromatic bubbles and hunching, loathsome shadows devoured time and space and even themselves.

That's when he really started screaming.

Because he was certain that those things, those *entities*, were seeing him as well.

And the idea that he might be trapped in that macabre multi-dimensional pit with them was enough to drive him stark, raving mad.

There could be no doubt any longer: the transplanted tissue was of no ordinary nature. It was a parasitic life form given birth in his sockets and he was now nothing but a host to it.

The knowledge of this was what finally made him go out cold.

Lynn found him in the chair in the morning.

She shook him awake and he looked at her, expecting her to scream at the very sight of his eyes, but she didn't. She just wanted to know what the hell he was doing down here sleeping in a chair.

His eyesight was perfectly normal. He could not see through her or the walls or anything. He rushed into the bathroom and examined his eyes. They were certainly larger than normal, but not discolored or in any other way mutated. Whatever had happened last night had now retreated.

But it's still there, he told himself. *You know it's still there. Whatever's generating from that tissue in your eyes, it's still there.*

When he got back, Lynn was waiting for him. "Would you like to tell me what this is all about?" she demanded.

"I think I'm insane," he said.

"Is that all? I've put up with that for years."

"I'm serious, Lynn. I've never been more serious in my life."

There was no way around it, so he told her everything that had been happening and particularly what had happened last night. He spoke calmly even though he wanted badly to rant and climb walls and maybe even laugh his ass off at the sheer absurdity of what he was saying or the even greater absurdity of what fate had dumped in his lap. But he did none of those things. His delivery was cool and formal.

When he was done, Lynn looked at him for a moment or two, perhaps sizing him up for a straightjacket or a psychiatrist's couch. Finally, she smiled, and then chuckled. "Oh, you almost had me, Art. You almost had me."

"It's the truth," he said. "I'm telling you the truth."

She saw that he was or at least that he seemed to think so. "C'mon, Art. Would you please knock this shit off already? My God, you dreamed it all. It was a nightmare. That's all that happened. You have to see that."

"I want that damn tissue taken out of my eyes."

"Stop it, Art."

"I want it taken out."

"You *are* crazy," she said. "Moran saved your eyesight and you want him to take that gift back? Sorry, Art, but that's not only absolutely crazy, it's ludicrous. Do you honestly expect me to sit here and believe this crap about things living in your eyes? Monsters or aliens or whatever the hell you're talking about?"

He felt like she was not only pushing him into a corner, but holding him there with her foot against his throat. "Please, baby, you have to believe me."

"Believe what? That you want Moran to reverse the procedure? To set you back on the course of blindness? Well, I don't believe that and I sure as heck do not believe you can see through walls or into hell itself."

"I didn't say it was hell."

"Okay, *Wonderland*. What Alice saw when she looked through the looking glass. Another dimension."

"Lynn…"

She held up a hand. "Whatever. Art, I love you. I've always supported you in every way, but I can't support this. It's…it's just crazy. Why don't you tell me what this is *really* about?"

"I already have."

"Bullshit."

She was really getting angry now. Lynn was a good kid, he knew, and you could trust her and count on her and she'd never let you down. But there were limits and Art had just crossed the line. More than crossed it, he had danced drunkenly over it, clicking his heels. Had he come strolling down the stairs wearing some of her lingerie and talking like Bette fucking Davis, she could not have been more distressed.

"Please, Lynn, *please…*"

"I don't believe any of that shit and neither will anyone else, Art. Tell me what it is. Did you suddenly get some half-assed, misguided conscience in the eleventh hour because they used fetal tissue from an aborted baby? Is that it? Well, you and your conscience have fun, Art. Have a good old time with your dark glasses and your white cane selling fucking pencils outside city hall."

He had an overwhelming desire to slap that mouth right off her face. "Listen to me, Lynn. Just shut up and listen. I'm not going to fight with you. I'm not going sit here and tell you what an insensitive bitch you're being, because I think you probably already realize that. I'm in trouble. I'm in bad fucking trouble. Something has happened. Something impossible. Something that is scaring the living shit right out of me. All I'm asking for you is to discuss it with me. Is that too much?"

She pursed her lips and wiped some moisture from her eyes. "I'm sorry, Art. I'm just…I'm worried about you."

"I'm worried about me, too. So worried, in fact, I'd rather be blind as a bat than be able to see the things I've been seeing."

"I guess there's no point in me saying again that you maybe had a nightmare?"

"None. I wish it were true, baby, I really wish it were. But it's not that simple. None of this is."

She thought it over for a time. "Okay, Art, I'll play Devil's Advocate. How about that? You said your eyes changed, right? Well, they look normal now. They're not bulging and red and weird like you said."

"They were." He got up close to her. "Look closely. Look at them very… closely."

She sighed. "They look okay."

"Are you sure?"

She shrugged. "Well, I mean, they seem bigger than they used to be, I guess. But not huge or anything. There's some little bumps on them." She shook her head and sighed. "They're just eyes, Art."

"They weren't last night."

"Art, just listen to yourself. You're telling me there's things living in your eyes. Things that have grown from that transplanted tissue. Things that are letting you see as *they* see. Do you know how that sounds?"

"Paranoid? Crazy? Like I think there's a tissue conspiracy going on? That I've gone full Joe fucking Rogan? Yes, dammit, I know how it sounds. Maybe they look fine now, but they were not fine last night. That's when the weirdest stuff always happens, Lynn. At night. That's when I feel things moving in them, growing, changing. They're active at night, whatever these things are, they're nocturnal. Maybe that's why they're hiding now."

Oh, it sounded rich, all right, just completely loony. Like something a little kid might say. *The boogeyman only comes out when you turn off the light, mommy. He won't come out if you're in the room.*

"I think they're taking over somehow, Lynn. I think they're beginning to assert themselves. They're testing the waters, stretching their legs, whatever you want to call it. They make me look at things I have no interest in."

"Art…"

"They make me look at the stars. They're fascinated by the stars."

"Art, please…"

"You think I'm nuts? Okay. How about the textbooks, Lynn? How about that? You know me. You've been married to me for fifteen years. Have I ever had any interest in science or higher math?"

This was evidence she could not refute. "No. No, you haven't. You always hated that stuff."

"I still hate it. Do you think I understand any of that shit? I have a high school education, Lynn. I don't know shit about biology and chemistry and astrophysics and differential equations."

"But you read it."

He shook his head. "No, Lynn. *I* don't read it. *They* read it."

"So they're controlling your mind, too?"

"Yes, maybe, I don't know. I'm just a host for them. That's all I am. They compel me to do things and I'm not even aware of it. Sometimes, like when I go and get those books or read highbrow shit off the internet that I can't even pronounce, it's like something in me has shut down. Like I'm just a machine and they're at the controls. They're curious, Lynn. They're curious about us, about this place. It's not like where they're from."

"Which is?"

"I have no idea."

"What do they want?"

Again, he shook his head. "No idea. I only know that they're getting stronger, Lynn."

She considered it for a time even though it was plain that she did not buy any part of it. "This is beyond me, Art. If it's happening or if it's not, it's still way beyond me. I'm going to make you an appointment with another ophthalmologist. If something's really going on with your eyes, something fantastic, then there'll be signs, changes. The anatomy will be different. Right?"

"Yeah, I guess it would."

"Okay, I'll find you a specialist and get you a complete exam."

"It takes months to get in to see those people."

Lynn offered him a sharp smile. "I can be very convincing."

There was hope now. A shred, but it was something. And a starving man will eat just about anything. At least the wheels were turning. Things would happen. If it was all in his head then they'd discover that, too. If that was the case, there was always therapy…or confinement and drugs.

Oh, Christ. How could it be happening? How could any of it possibly be happening?

Art sat there in the chair, almost willing the mutation to happen. Wanting those alien red orbs to reassert themselves so that Lynn would believe him absolutely. He really needed that. But…what if he was going insane? *No,* he knew unequivocally that he was not. He'd noticed something odd happening the day after the operation and that feeling had not lessened, it had grown geometrically. He was not a hypochondriac and he was not paranoid or wildly imaginative. His fantasies never went any farther than having sex with leggy cover girls or maybe the Detroit Tigers winning the pennant again like they had in 1984. That was the extent of it. What was happening here was certainly not his imagination. It was something much larger, something infinitely malefic and horrible.

Sitting there, he began to feel activity in his eyes.

Not like last night, but something much subtler and insidious. What was happening was inside his eyes or just behind them, maybe at the roots of his optic nerves. He could feel things moving and undulating in there, tiny cords and tentacular growths spreading out from the back of his eyes and enveloping the nerves like threads of dry rot moving through wood, following them back to his brain and implanting themselves there in fertile soil, ingesting and assimilating gray matter, neurons and dendrites and synapses, making his mind into what they were—

He sat bolt upright, listening to Lynn in the other room talking to someone on the phone.

It was too late.

It was all too late.

She could make him all the appointments with all the best eye specialists in the world, but it would do absolutely no good. He would never see those doctors. He would never be *allowed* to see them.

For *they* would never let it happen.

Lynn got him an appointment with a Dr. Galen Friday morning.

But it was only Wednesday night and Friday was an eternity away when something was sprouting in your eyes, spreading out its vile rootlets and webbing your entire nervous system.

That night, he lay in bed next to Lynn. She was sleeping and the only reason for that was because he had feigned sleep himself so she had given up the watch for the night. So now he was alone. Alone with what was growing in him. It began to happen right away, he could feel his eyes enlarging and soon enough he could not close his eyelids. There was a fierce burning as his ocular physiology and chemistry was altered, as what hid behind his eyes in the daylight now emerged to consider its new world. He could feel them not only physically now, but mentally and even psychically.

They were sentient.

They were aware.

He decided that they must have thought the human race was sloppy and primitive and inefficient in comparison to themselves. Something to be used as hosts, draft animals, but nothing more. Wherever they came from— whatever multi-dimensional gutter of reality or *anti*-reality for that matter— things were not as they were here. There was no cumbersome hardware, just a perfectly seamless and functional organic technology. They did not invade in rockets or subjugate other races with anything as impossibly crude as weapons or brute force. They invaded at the subatomic, nuclear level, manipulating mankind's very biology and exploiting it to their own ends, using the very cellular matrix as raw materials to replicate themselves in a world where they were fantastic aberrations at best.

It was simple really.

And in its simplicity, there was a stark malevolence.

Maybe it was completely natural wherever they came from and Art was pretty certain he would never know where that was any more than he could know the origin of a particular virus that gave him the flu. But maybe that's how these things evolved. On Earth, it was said that life sprang from the sea. Simple one-celled creatures evolved into multicellular organisms and colonials and ultimately into advanced forms such as plants and animals. Maybe the evolution of these things was far different. A sort of parasitic evolution. Using existing cellular matter from other life forms, they modified and converted it, laying the groundwork for themselves, altering genetic codes to bring themselves into being.

And maybe the cow jumped over the moon, too, and the little fucking boy ran away with the spoon.

He would never know.

But the fact that he was even able to contemplate such things showed him that their forced reading program had not been a complete waste. He'd learned a few things, not that any of it did him one bit of good.

He found himself sitting up on one elbow, a cold sweat drenching him, his heart pounding and his head aching, his eyes burning like hot blades had been stabbed into them.

He tried to think at *them*, to make them know he was there, that he was alive and aware and that they had no right to use him like this, to parasitize all that he was for their own purposes. But if they could hear him, they gave no sign. He was a dumb beast of burden and they would converse with him no more than a man would converse with a donkey that carried his packs.

He was staring at Lynn.

Or rather, *they* were staring at Lynn. They were looking through the blankets and through her flesh, marveling at the biological profusion and the intricacies of the physiological machinery therein. Art was seeing these things, too. Repelled not so much by what was inside Lynn, but the *way* in which those eyes showed it to him, the way they must have seen not only the human machine, but all things of flesh and blood—as something to be dissected and rendered to their base anatomies and basal chemistry. Not the engines which fired brains which allowed men and women to make music and write poetry and to love one another, but as mechanistic things that could be altered, re-engineered, taken apart and put together as they pleased.

A knife.

The thought emerged in his head unbidden, a cold and alien thought. Had he thought it or had they?

Use a knife.

Yes and no. He had thought it, but so had they. What he heard in his head was not their voices or even reflections of the same, but just some primitive translation of their thoughts and objectives, the best his mind could do at transcribing what it was they wanted.

She can be opened with a knife. The membrane can be severed with a knife.

Something in him cringed and something else cried out. If he had had a voice, he would have screamed loud and clear. But even that was gone. They had infested not only his eyes, but his brain, and he was powerless over the cold immensity of their will.

A knife. A simple vertical incision, lengthwise through the thoraco-abdominal cavity, severing the epidermis and dermis and musculature, and we can begin our investigation.

Art pulled himself away. He pulled himself right off the bed and stumbled out into the corridor. What they wanted, what they intended on doing, was monstrous and awful beyond words.

Imagine holding her still-beating heart in the palm of your hand.

He choked back a cry and fought his way downstairs even though they had shut his vision off. But if they thought that was a punishment, they were sadly mistaken. There was serenity and peace to being blind. Better that than looking on those things they could show him or doing those things they demanded of him.

But they fought.

They fought hard, not only with blindness and searing agony in his eyes, but with a thrumming mindless pain in his head that made him dizzy, squeezed tears from his eyes.

"You want a knife…" he managed. "I'll get you a knife…oh yes, I'll get you a knife…"

Laughing under his breath, he found a carving knife in the kitchen drawer. He was tired and run-down and beyond caring. He brought the knife up, seeking his left eye with the tip. He would start with that one, carve it out at the roots and then proceed to the other.

And he almost got away with it, too.

But in the end, they numbed his arm until it was dead and rubbery and absolutely limp.

On his knees on the kitchen floor, he tried to formulate a plan, a way out, something, anything. But there was nothing. Only a mad acceptance of it all. He could not only feel them in his eyes now, but in his brain, wrapping themselves around his thoughts and free will. All he could think about was Dr. Moran, the man who had placed that alien tissue in his eyes. And the more he thought of him, the angrier he became.

Given time, you'll see things you never thought you would in ways that will astound you.

Yes.

That's what Moran had said. It had struck him strange at the time, but then Moran was nothing if not strange. But it had been more than a simple odd, offhand comment from doctor to patient; it was a confession and possibly even a warning.

Moran had done this on purpose.

And as the realization of this filled him, Art felt activity in his eyes. A new activity, a degenerate hothouse profusion, a nameless fleshy cultivation and germination. Whatever was in them was growing, expanding, blossoming, replicating its own genetics with his chemistry and his biology, feeding off him and leeching him dry. It would live and thrive and reproduce…and he would die.

As he sat there, knowing it all to be true, there was a searing pain in his left eye as something viscid and moist like a slimy spider leg emerged, the tip of it tapping against his cheek. Then another and another like the tentacles of an octopus reaching from its lair and examining the surrounding terrain.

There was only one thing left to do: he had to go see Dr. Moran.

Moran had given him his home number in case of an emergency and Art used it without further delay.

"Dr. Moran? This is Art Reed. You performed a transplant of tissue into my eyes."

"Yes, yes. Is there something wrong?"

"Yes, there is. I'm going over to your office now. I'll meet you there."

"Mr. Reed, I—"

"I'll meet you there."

Then the sound of Moran swallowing. "Yes."

Art scrawled Lynn a note, something about going for a walk, and left.

Maybe they didn't want Art going to see Moran and maybe they did, regardless the pain in his eyes multiplied beyond anything he had known before. As he drove, trying to stay on the road, it felt like his eyes had doubled in size if not tripled. They swelled in their sockets, threatening to explode the very orbits they were set in. The pain was red-hot and ice-cold, wet and tearing and unspeakable. Things stretched and wriggled and bunched like muscles. By the time he reached Moran's deserted office building, there was a wet ripping in his right eye that made him cry out.

Moran had opened the doors and he was waiting for him.

"What in the fuck have you done to me?" Art said.

Moran was still nervous and twitching, but there was something empty and beaten about him now. "I did what was expected of me, Mr. Reed. I did what *they* demanded."

"I should kill you," Art said, his vision blurring momentarily, fresh tears splashing down his cheeks. But not tears of sorrow or even pain, but just fluid releasing like a woman whose water had burst as what grew inside her prepared to be born.

"Go ahead. You'd be doing me a favor, I suppose." Moran seemed completely noncommittal to the idea of violence. It did not look as if he would even fight back or raise a hand in his own defense. "But understand, it won't change anything. I didn't do any of this because I wanted to. I did what they made me do."

"How many of these transplants have you performed?'

"Hundreds."

"Jesus Christ."

Moran shook his head. "No, no, not all of them were like…yours. I never know. There's no way I can know. It's only after the operation that I discover that they have migrated into the tissue I used in order to propagate themselves. They invade the fetal tissue, Mr. Reed. Somehow, some way. They use it to regenerate themselves at the molecular level. A few atoms, then a molecule, then an entire cell body. What dark genius, eh? What other organ would give them such mastery and what other sense would so surely hand them the keys to the city?"

Art was dizzy, feeling like he was going to pass clean out. They were sucking the blood out of him. "Who…*what* are they?"

"I don't know. They've never shared that with me."

"But you go on infecting people with them?"

"I don't have a choice, Mr. Reed." Moran rubbed his own eyes, buried his face in his hands. "I lost my sight in a car accident. My optic nerves were damaged beyond repair and then months later, my vision began to return.

They chose me because I was an eye surgeon. I was the one who could give them a foothold in this world…and a window."

"But you could have fought!"

"There's no fighting. There's no violence. They abhor such things. Primitive, animalistic reactions and they'll have no part of them. They have infested me as they've infested you. I can no more stop them than a car can stop me from driving it or an oven can stop me from cooking with it. We're machines to them, Art. Can't you see that?"

Moran pulled his hands from his face and then there was no doubt.

His eyes were red and crystalline, set with knobs and bumps and protrusions. They were immense and oozing like raw egg yolks, a clear slime running from them, a series of gelatinous feelers sprouting forth like the wavering, transparent tentacles of a deep-sea anemone.

Art's vision darkened and went completely. He was a host, a nursery, a Petri dish and nothing more. But he could still feel and what he felt was a blazing, white-hot agony as the spawn in his eyes was birthed. He could feel them unwinding and worming, spreading out their feelers like the fingers of an unclenching hand. The sounds were hideous…slithering and sliding and slopping. He felt those feelers erupt from his/their eyes. Felt them reaching upward towards the ceiling and the stars far above, the empty black wastes of space beyond. That was what they understood. The yawning, soundless gulf of mad darkness. Art stumbled forward because it was what they demanded. His dripping and jellied feelers reached out to touch those of Moran. There was a joining and a communion.

And as they were born, Art dropped away into fathomless blackness.

When Lynn woke the next morning, she found Art's note and saw it as a good thing. Evidence that maybe he was coming around, finally leaving the house and rejoining the world at large. Maybe, maybe. Hopefully.

Well, if he was doing his part, then she would do hers.

It had come to her when she woke up. A simple plan, really, but maybe exactly the sort of thing that would bring her husband out of his dementia and back to her. They always said that the way to a man's heart was through his stomach and she supposed that was true. There was also another school of thought which said that the way to a man's heart wasn't through his stomach, but via what was in his pants. Both viable theories, in Lynn's way of thinking. But her friend Laura Klyman, who was more than a little rough around the edges, put it best: "Lynn, there's no man on Earth that can't be won over with a good blowjob and a T-bone steak."

It was funny. It was crude. But it was also *true.*

So, Lynn walked down to the market and picked up a nice bottle of wine, some baking potatoes, salad fixings, and a couple huge T-bones two inches thick. She would, this day, make Art forget all about monsters living in his eyes. It would begin with the wine and end with the steaks, and in-between, there lie the magic like the meat between two slices of bread.

When she got home, she called out for him. "Art? Are you here, honey?"

Well, she knew that he was.

She could sense it.

She climbed the stairs and by the time she reached the top, her good mood began to melt away, replaced by a growing fear. He was not in their bedroom. She found him in the spare room. She looked at him in the chair by the window and everything she was ran cold inside her, puddled at her feet, and evaporated.

It was not the sight of her husband's corpse that made her scream—slumped there in the chair, head thrown back, mouth contorted in death-agony. Or even his bloody, empty eye sockets or the way they looked, like something immense had pushed out of them, expanding them like birth canals until the skeletal orbits around them shattered.

No, it wasn't that.

It was the two things that had left clear slime trails like those of slugs down her husband and up the wall to their present position. Huge, cantaloupe-sized balls of pulsating jelly with a feathering web of tissue dangling from each like optic nerves that had been ripped out at the roots. They were threaded with an intricate system of bright blue vein tracery and set, at the very centers, with brilliant red crystalline orbs like monstrous, swollen pupils...or perhaps nuclei.

From them reached long, transparent tendrils, dozens of them, that waved and vibrated in the air as they reached for what they needed most.

Her eyes.

THE HORROR OF MANY MOUTHS

Sister Agnes Elizabeth

Sisters of the Sacred Blood
14 Old Elm Road
Loxley, West Virginia

Your Most Esteemed Excellency,

How wonderful it was to receive your missive this past week. But let me bring you up to date.

Concerning Wenna DeShambry, she was delivered unto us by a local farmer name of Woodgate, who discovered the child curled up in a drainage ditch at the edge of his property. The Sisters of the Sacred Blood are, of course, a contemplative order, a community of lay sisters devoted to the Holy Rosary. Our charity and mercy to the unfortunate and poor is well-known, so it was not unusual for the child to be brought to us for sanctuary until it was deemed by the Superior of the convent what actions would be taken on behalf of the child's welfare. As I had recently received my nursing certificate, I was present at the examination of the girl.

The child was filthy, hungry, and exhausted. After bathing and feeding and a brief rest, we examined her in some detail. We found her to be emaciated, bruised, and swollen from insect bites. We applied balms and cleaned her wounds. I myself stitched-up several of the deeper contusions. She was cooperative, though paranoid and frightened. She refused to speak or to give any indication as to where she had come from.

She was undoubtedly the victim of grave physical and mental abuse. Her back was set with ragged scratches as were her limbs. Whether this was from abuse or from crawling through brambles and briars, we could not say. Her breasts and abdomen were riddled with infected sores. The most striking of her injuries were punctures in both wrists and ankles, all slightly smaller in girth than an average pencil. We, of course, noted these wounds as they were consistent with the phenomena of stigmata as understood by the Holy Church. At times, when under duress or emotional excitement, the child bled freely from them.

For the next month or so, the sisters were extremely patient and careful around Wenna. Gradually, she began to speak, telling us her name, but refusing to speak of the ordeal that had brought her to us. Her family name was not unknown to the convent in particular and the diocese in general. Long had there been rumors of the most unpleasant nature whispered about that clan and their depravity.

After Wenna was stronger and her numerous wounds had healed, she was given work with the other sisters and was found to be quite diligent and resourceful, possessed of a strong back and non-complaining disposition. Like most sons and daughters of the hill-clans, she was no stranger to hard work and a simple lifestyle, which was all we could offer her. She was especially talented in gardening and brought our flowerbeds and meager crops to luscious bloom with attentive care. Many of us, myself included, were hopeful that the Superior would admit her into the Order, as she would have been a boon for us.

Interestingly enough, the wounds at her wrists and ankles continued to bleed at odd times and particularly during masses and rosary in the chapel. A priest from Wheeling named Father Freed came to us and examined the apparent stigmata, but we—the sisters and I—never learned of his findings or report to the bishop.

I was charged with Wenna's medical care and found her to be of an extremely resilient constitution. She responded quickly to good food and rest, the ointments and medicinals I treated her with. Other than her apparent stigmata and the state of her mind, I was concerned with her menstrual cycles. She seemed to bleed on a daily basis. Dr. Bartol, a physician long associated with the convent, had been called in originally to make a more thorough examination of Wenna. With the Superior's permission, I called him in again on the matter of the child's menstruation.

Dr. Bartol gave Wenna a complete cervical exam, concerned as I was about the possibility of uterine cysts or fibroid tumors of the uterus itself. He found none of these, but deduced that Wenna was possibly with child. A fact that I had been speculating upon for some time. A blood test proved our assumptions correct…though even this did not explain the child's excessive bleeding. Dr. Bartol suspected a possible hormonal imbalance.

Within days of Wenna's positive pregnancy test, her vaginal bleeding ceased and this almost overnight. It's important that I mention here that the sisters and I questioned Wenna as to who the father of her child might have been. But each time the subject was broached, she fell into a fit of hysterics and bled voluminously from her apparent stigmatizations.

She began to give us trouble. No more could she be counted on to help in the gardens or kitchen. When duties were allotted to her, they generally went undone. We did not attribute this to laziness or sloth on her part, but to a gradual disintegration of her mental health which was marked by bouts of hysteria and anger that were generally followed by spells of lethargy and depression. During this time, it was not unusual for her to sleep twelve and fourteen hours a day. Often, when a task had been handed her—and gradually, you understand, only the simplest of tasks could be entrusted to her—she wandered off and was found in the forest later with no explanation as to how she had come to be there. Though more than once, she mentioned something concerning the "Dark Man in the Woods" and the "Holy Covenant of the Ravening Mother."

On several occasions, she was discovered in the chapel in a state which greatly disturbed many of the sisters. Naked and bleeding from the wounds in her wrists and ankles, she would be found on the altar mocking Christ's agony on the cross—standing stiffly with arms stretched out straight to either side. Several times, she also bled from her scalp in imitation of the crown of thorns, something not unknown among stigmatics. Upon the altar, seemingly in a trance and completely unreceptive, it would take several of us to bring her back to her room on account we could not force her limbs out of the "crucified" position and would have to carry her in this manner. She would be extremely stiff and cold to the touch as of a corpse.

Things reached the point where Wenna had to be confined to her room and watched over. She was not allowed to be alone. And even with these precautions, she managed to slip away and we would find her wandering naked in the woods, gibbering mindlessly and often pointing at the sky. When questioned, she would tell us—with an odd childlike innocence— that she had answered the "Call of the Mother of Many Shapes," but when questioned further, would become fearful and agitated, saying she dare not speak Her Name.

The attending sisters could never adequately explain how it was they had fallen asleep when on duty and for days afterward, they would be plagued by terrible nightmares and night-chills. I should make note of the former here. The sisters seemed to be tormented by the same nightmare, interestingly enough. They claimed to dream of a space beyond the one we know, that a dark man beckoned them to join him in some terrible multi-dimensional hell where they would sign a book in blood, vowing their obedience to a certain monstrosity at the very center of cosmic chaos.

It was at this time that again Father Freed came to make an examination of Wenna. Her state of mind had nearly disintegrated and was accompanied by the most alarming phenomena. The Superior was quick to ascribe what we saw as evidence of mystical rapture or ecstasy, divine trances not unknown among stigmatics. But the sisters were not so sure. There were still occurrences of catalepsy and somnambulism, but these were becoming rare. Wenna's rooms became practically unlivable for us slated to watch and pray over her. They were either unaccountably hot or freezing cold. Prayer candles inexplicably melted into pools of wax within minutes and, at other times, sheaths of ice formed upon the walls.

Sister Patrice claimed she fell into sort of a fugue, and upon waking, that there were muddy tracks upon the floor in the form of cloven-hoofed prints. I did not witness this personally, nor can I substantiate Sister Teresa's assertion—one that left her in a perpetual state of fear for many days—that Wenna's left hand had become the hairy claw of a beast.

I should also mention the mental collapse of Sister Angelica. She claimed that she witnessed Wenna being summoned by a primeval horror in the shape of a huge, winged black goat who taught her how to walk through walls via application of some debased mathematical equations that could intersect the space we know with that we do not. That if Sister Angelica would sign the book, the goat would show her the wonders and blasphemies of the "corpse-city of R'lyeh".

Finally, no less than two sisters were put "on guard" as we began to call it, feeling more like soldiers and less like Sisters of the Order.

Wenna's physical condition was not improving. She could not keep down any food, whether grains or vegetables, broths or meat. Within minutes of ingesting them, she commonly vomited them back up. She was able, however, to drink water sparingly. Increasingly, she grew emaciated, though her belly continued to swell and the first movements of her child were evident. Often, she cried and whimpered and at other times, assailed the sisters with the most vulgar profanities, insisting that she needed raw meat and blood, that nothing else would sustain her. She told me that she would die if not fed the flesh of young children.

It was Dr. Bartol's opinion that she needed to be placed in a hospital, but Father Freed said she was not to be moved. The Superior submitted to Father Freed in all such matters, no doubt on orders of Your Worship. The sisters were told they were not allowed to speak with Wenna outside of the most general queries concerning her comfort and illnesses. And by that point, many of the sisters were only too happy to consent.

The Superior herself, a most harsh and pragmatic woman, confessed to me that she believed the entire convent to be under spiritual attack by the Devil or assorted demons. The diocese exorcist was called in to cast out devils that grew fat on unknown sins, but it was a failure for our plight did not lessen. Medically, it seemed that the convent was plagued by an endless series of infirmities. The sisters displayed rashes and lesions, uncontrollable diarrhea and painful vomiting. Fevers ran rampant. They came down with bouts of influenza and pneumonia and whooping cough. More than one had to be hospitalized. The convent buildings began to smell of bodily discharge and soiled bandages, infected sores and puss-saturated wrappings. The overall spirit of the sisters, which had always been one of resilience and resolve, began to deteriorate at an alarming rate. The Superior was distressed and even that staunch, unflinching woman was showing signs of weakness and oncoming mental collapse.

A disease, a pathogen, had invaded the Order and blackened its roots, turning indomitable spirits to something low and coarse. The very blood of the convent was infected. Within that grim run of weeks, Dr. Bartol quarantined the entire convent and fought epidemics with antibiotics, but to no avail. Three sisters expired. Save one, they were advanced in years.

Many of the sisters were of the mind that the epicenter for these insufferable maladies was Wenna DeShambry. A few went so far as to say her breath, which was markedly hot and offensive-smelling, was filling the convent with germs. That the girl exhaled contagion. Regardless, the ailments were lengthy and generally unexplainable. And as bodies were weakened, so were minds.

But let me add here that not only were the sisters devastated by sickness, but so were our gardens and produce. Flowers wilted and died, crops were set by blight and rotted in the fields. The convent was a graveyard, a place of illness and despair and dying. And by that point, very few were rejecting the idea that some evil had been visited upon the Order and that the origin of this was Wenna herself.

These maladies, I will say, were not only physical, but psychological as well. And, yes, possibly spiritual. I saw mental degradation occurring on a daily basis. Many of the sisters screamed and ranted and had to be sedated and confined to their rooms. Much like Wenna herself, they began to demand meat and blood. We quarantined a group of sisters in the north wing under orders of Reverend Father Freed, who was of the opinion that their particular maladies were perhaps spiritual, rather than merely physical or mental. Again, as the nursing sister, I attended to their medical needs. The Superior ordered all those physically able to pray the rosary in the chapel for hours at end, seeking His deliverance from our ills.

Meanwhile, the afflicted and quarantined group of sisters worsened to the extreme. They wailed nearly nonstop, hysterical and overwrought, tearing their own clothes and those of the others, scratching themselves and biting one another, reveling in the blood and pain and anguish. Sharp objects had to be removed, for the sisters sought physical penitence by cutting and puncturing themselves, beating themselves bloody with anything at hand. I myself witnessed much of this and it was a terrible sight. Cut and lacerated, they writhed about naked and bleeding on the floor, crying out that they were possessed by what they referred to in their mania as the "Mother of Many Mouths". That they were her vessels, her womb, her dark cup of fecundity that would soon overflow.

Wenna grew no better during this time. Those of us able, saw to her care, praying vociferously and ignoring the blasphemous things she screamed. Reverend Father Freed continued to interview her. To my knowledge, neither he nor the diocese exorcist actually began the rite of exorcism over her (though many wished they would). They had their reasons, I assume, and those reasons were not for me to know. Wenna had become particularly vile in every way—physically, mentally, and of spirit. She had been altered to some fat and lolling slug, hairless and gray-toothed, a greasy creature smelling of rotten meat. She continually secreted foul-smelling slime and something like a gray bile. We cleaned and bandaged her constantly while she screeched and spit in a dozen different voices and dialects, very often whispering profanities to us in Latin, German, and French, dead languages that none but Reverend Father Freed seemed to recognize. He told me that she was speaking Aramaic regularly, as well as several Semitic tongues known only from ancient fragmentary sources.

She claimed to be a prostitute from Galilee that seduced Jesus and gave birth to his offspring, a "hairy goat-child" that chewed its way out of her womb, killing her "with a beautiful agony" in the process. She also told me that she was a brothel-keeper from Carthage that had been burned for devouring her own children and serving their tainted meat and bones to Roman conquerors during the Third Punic War.

I asked her what was happening to the quarantined sisters and she laughed at me, saying—in some bastard form of French that was near-nonsensical—

that "as the stars are made ready and the black spheres roll in the spaces beyond our perception, so shall them from Outside that have been called up lay with the daughters of men".

And then, a few days later, something incredible happened. I went into the quarantined rooms with a few sisters to administer treatments and we discovered an abundance of meat. Salted joints of pork and smoked hams, raw yellow chickens and slit rabbits and bloody shanks of beef. They dangled from beams overhead and were secreted beneath blankets and red-stained sheets. And bones…many nibbled bones scattered about the floor so that they crunched under foot wherever we walked. The sisters themselves lay amongst this ravaged flesh, smeared with blood and grease and fat, completely naked and speechless, their eyes glassy and fixed. They had gorged themselves again and again and from what we saw, I had no doubt they had purged themselves in the finest Roman tradition so that they could yet again fill themselves.

The room had become a slaughterhouse, scraps and bones scattered about. The sisters were splattered with blood, lard smeared over their faces and chests, their fingers cold and red-stained. I believe that they had attacked their larder like animals, tearing and rending and glutting themselves. One of the sisters had a wedge of bloody meat between her thighs and another was chewing on it, licking it.

We had no idea how they got the meat. None whatsoever. Our own pantry was stocked only sparingly, you understand, and none of what was in that room was from the convent's stores. The sisters in question were locked in that room. Being that there were no windows, no method of egress, then how did they come by any of it? It was pointless questioning them for they were completely dazed and near-catatonic. The entire episode disturbed the sisters, as you can imagine, but here is something that brought them to near-frenzy: all of the quarantined sisters bore the identical stigmatizations of Wenna DeShambry. Neither Father Freed nor the Reverend Mother could account for it.

Now, I would be remiss if I did not mention Sister Joline. She was quite advanced in age, having been of the Order for well over fifty years. She was what you might call semi-retired given that she was severely affected by senility and dementia precox. We cared for her and, generally, she was no trouble. But, like everything else at the convent, she was touched by the degeneration. She began slipping outside and wandering off into the fields and forest in the dead of night. She would be found on the stoop in the morning, gibbering and cackling, pointing up at the sky (like Wenna). It was a bad omen, we thought, given that we had become quite astute in spotting terrible portents by that point. We had hoped it would pass with Sister Joline, but when she was discovered in her bed, a gassy stench of spoiled meat in the air, we expected the worst. We were not disappointed. On one of her nocturnal jaunts, she had found a wormy woodchuck and slept with it, cooing over it, kissing it as if it were a favored child.

"I do Her bidding," she told us. "Her of many shapes and many faces."

After we cleaned her up, the Superior and I attempted to find out what was behind Sister Joline's sudden bout of derangement. Before this, her mental difficulties were never anything more extreme than forgetfulness or speaking to those long dead, sometimes reliving her childhood. Nothing more dangerous than that.

We tape-recorded what she said, as Father Freed insisted. Here is what Sister Joline told us:

"Oh, have I not celebrated the holy eucharist? Have I not spent my life in His service, praying, Reverend Mother, praying only for a simple life of spiritual purity and a death of blessed union with our savior, Jesus Christ? Have not my ways been His? Have I not shown great mercy to the poor and unfortunate and have I not lived a life free of sin so that I would be welcomed into His house as His consecrated bride of spirit? Can any deny my willing sacrifice? Can any find ill in my ways which were always in accordance with divine law and scripture?

"Can you answer me that, Reverend Mother, or why He has forsaken us? Abandoned us to that Other what would toy our souls into stark oblivion? The Father, and the Son, and the Holy Ghost...how they abandon us in dire times, do they not? Now the other...has he a name! He is the Mighty Messenger from the black chasms, the Crawling Chaos! He remembers eternal all that I have forgotten, he knows of my sins and sets a table so that he may sup upon them! He chews and fills and remembers, does he not? Certainly! He knows how I prayed for death and the comfort of the grave, the embrace of the all-knowing blind

worm that gnaws! He knows how I have touched myself and how I have lusted for the firm young flesh of our sisters, the hot darkness between their legs that I can smell…the honey and sugar and woman-meat my tongue can taste!"

At his point, Sister Joline became hysterical. Some hours later, we recorded the following:

"Tell us, Reverend Mother, of the Dark Man of the Black Coven in the high woods! You must speak the Three Words from the Roman crypt! I know! I know! For have I not signed the Black Book in my own blood? Have I not consorted with the Dawn Mother whom is worshipped by the headless lambs as the Magna Mater? Shall we not bring her offerings and fill our fertile wombs with her Dark Young? The vessels were filled at May-Eve, were they not? Did we not all gather with Wenna, the Sister of the Shriveled Worm? Were we not made holy and sanctified by the touch of the Mother? Yes! Like the child, we were nailed to the altar in the sacred wood where our screams called out the hallowed words as our wombs were consecrated by the Dark Man, our vessels filled with the seed of the Split Mother of Vermin! She who was the consort of the Nameless One! Cybele and Cerunnos and Artemis! The Black Madonna and the Old Hag of Midsummer: Gather in Her Name and make fertile! Iä! Iä! Iä! Shub-Niggurath! The Black Goat of the Woods with a Thousand Young!"

Basically, most of the transcript (which covers some five pages) ran on like this. Sister Joline spoke in some detail that the convent could only be sanctified through the blood of the sisters, through their suffering and sin and madness. That we would all make the Sign of the Dark Mother, that the sisters' own blasphemy and rending of vows was "its fruit and wine and straw."

So, you can certainly see, your Excellency, the dire straits which the Sisters of the Sacred Heart found themselves in. A malign, unspeakable influence had taken hold of the convent. And it is now, that I should tell you yet another horrendous and shocking thing. Dr. Bartol and I, whilst making detailed examinations of the quarantined sisters (whose ranks were swelling by the week) deduced that all of them within childbearing years were, in fact, pregnant. Cervical exams and blood tests confirmed this. It was impossible, of course, but the fact remained. Now, no men are allowed in the convent and although the Holy Church accepts the miracle of virgin birth, the idea of mass virgin birth was immediately rejected by the Reverend Mother. She, as many, suspected diabolical influences and became quite concerned with what Sister Joline (and others of the quarantined) had alluded to: this mysterious altar in the dark woods and the terrible ritual which the sisters claimed to have undergone on the night of May-Eve. Essentially, like Wenna DeShambry, that they had been "crucified" by having nails pounded through their wrists and ankles so that some malevolent entity might fill them with its seed.

Regardless, all twelve of the quarantined were expecting and as the weeks rolled by, their pregnancies moved at an accelerated rate until it seemed that within six weeks they appeared like women in their final trimester. It was, of course, quite disturbing. As per your decree, the above information never left the walls of the convent. What those of us who tended to the sisters experienced, was never spoken of nor alluded to in any form. And it was not until your letter and your request for a full accounting of the events leading up to the mass birthing that I dared so much as mention it. We sisters of the Order of Sacred Blood know how to keep our secrets, as the Superior has pointed out to me on many occasions.

I must admit here that I was not untouched by what was going on around me. Though I try to be cool, clinical, and detached in all matters, my dreams were mad and feverish and in the light of day, perfectly insane. I dreamed that I strode out amongst the cold, black wastes between the stars, following a terrible, reedy piping to the center of ultimate chaos where a terrible old woman with the face of a toad compelled me to sign the dreaded *Book of Azathoth* in my own blood. She promised that I might hold court with the Black Goat with a Thousand Young in the secret woods on the sacred night of breeding when the stars tremble in the sky and primal blasphemies become known to the adept.

I often woke trembling and feverish from these dreams, certain I could hear the beating of a thousand tiny hearts.

I suppose I could go on for countless pages concerning the degradation and desecration of the Order, the myriad phenomena witnessed, the evidences of dark nature worship and trafficking with those from beyond the known spheres, but let us get to the night in question, the culmination of these horrors as it were. As you have no doubt heard, your Excellency, the conclusion of the events I write of occurred toward the end of June, on Midsummer night.

It began when my most trusted confidant, Sister Marie Anna, came to me and admitted that the Reverend Mother had been missing all day. I was ignorant of this matter, being that all my time was spent watching over the quarantined sisters and their coming events. Together, we searched the convent, but could find her nowhere. This became more disconcerting when Sister Marie Anna admitted that for many days, the Superior had been spending time out in the dark woods beyond our walls.

But that was only the first revelation of that night. The second I discovered several hours later—the quarantined sisters were gone. Like the Reverend Mother, they had completely disappeared. And those who watched over them could not recall them leaving. Well, as you can imagine, this was of great concern considering the physical state of the quarantined. We had no time to lose. We had already made a thorough search of the convent and grounds, so, procuring several flashlights, we went out into the woods to search for the missing.

It was a dark night, the moon but a sliver in the sky. For several hours, we walked the known trails deep into the forest and then, just as we were about to abandon our search, Sister Marie Anna told me that she saw light in the distance. My hand trembles as I write this. Let me compose myself and continue without emotion or duress.

There was indeed the flickering of firelight. It came from a deep, forgotten hollow in the darkest part of the woods. I could describe to you the mist that played around us like phantoms as we descended the narrow trail into the crowded, black thickets. How the stars seemed to pulsate above with a freakish luminosity or how, try as I might, I could not identify a single constellation. The trees were gigantic, gnarled things, entirely denuded, reaching towards the stars like withered hands breaking the mold of a grave. The whippoorwills were piping madly, what seemed hundreds of them, in a shrill, rhythmic chant that raised the hairs on my neck. Sister Marie Anna was genuinely terrified, clutching her rosary beads with one hand, praying for divine protection.

The firelight grew brighter, painting the trees with licking tongues of orange and yellow light that guttered eerily, creating leaping long-limbed wraiths and grotesque witch-shapes that seemed to fly through the trees.

Sister Marie Anna gasped as we finally stepped into the secret glade. Gigantic, lightning-blasted trees surrounded us, their skeletal limbs scraping together though there was no wind to prod their swollen, moss-dripping boughs.

What we saw in that shadow-riven clearing I can scarcely believe. Sister Marie Anna fainted dead away at my feet.

This was the secret place in the woods, the lonely dark glade that had drawn the sisters by moonlight. This was the hellish hop-ground of the thing which had eaten Sister Joline's mind. In this hollow, the sisters had been summoned to participate in the darkest rituals of the witches' sabbat.

I must proceed carefully now.

In the clearing, I saw the terrible scaffolds Sister Joline had ranted about where the sisters had been fixed in place with nails through their wrists and ankles, so that their wombs could be filled with the vile seed of the Black Goat of the Sabbath.

Yes, they had been here on the night of the seeding…and they were here now.

Before me, I saw five distinct bonfires that burned brightly, each marking the point of a pentagram that had been burned into the earth. And by their jumping, hissing flames, at the very center of the magic circle there stood a titanic, slime-covered idol of incalculable age. Quarried from some ancient gray-black stone, it depicted a wholly fetid monstrosity like a horned goat with spreading wings and glittering crystalline eyes. I heard voices shouting and singing profane chants and I saw not only members of the local degenerate hill-clans, but the Reverend Mother and Sister Joline. They performed a sinuous, counter-clockwise dance around the idol, shrieking madly. All were naked and greased with fat. Some wore hideous waxen fetish masks representative of the idol towering above them.

Terrified, yet somehow exhilarated and moonstruck, I stepped forward knowing I could not go back. It was too late for that. Behind me, the awful thick-boled, decay-encrusted trees with their rippling, serpentine limbs had closed any avenue of escape. I nearly lost my footing as tangles of phosphorescent bones burst from the blackened, spongy earth. This had long been a site of human sacrifice to the inbred locals.

I said the sisters were all there and they were—beyond the bonfires, their heads, all twelve of them, were impaled upon spikes with a thirteenth added: Wenna's (she being the original vector of infection to the convent). Yet...*yet,* I heard them screaming obscenities into the night.

Nearly out of my mind, I stepped ever forward, my limbs quaking, the muscles jumping spasmodically beneath my skin. My mind whirled with hallucinatory imagery. I was witnessing a primeval ritual far older than the world I knew, a debased and iniquitous pre-human ceremony remembered only in eldritch witch tales, but whose origins were beyond the rim of known space.

Hysterical with it all, my mind melting like tallow in my skull, I saw something grisly and insane that even now I cannot accept—the headless bodies of Wenna and the sisters were ringed around the idol. The dancers had hidden them from view, but no more. They parted so that I might witness what a shrieking, alien voice in my brain told me was the Sacred Spawning of the Black Goat on this, the sacred Night of the Thousand-Faced Moon.

And the moon above, your Excellency...it was no longer a sliver, but full and bloated and the color of blood. It was many times the size of the full moon we know.

Laughing madly as devil shapes careened around me and the heads cackled behind me, I sank to my knees in delirium. The headless bodies were moving, you see. They were gyrating, contorting, corpse-white limbs flailing in the call of that unearthly moonlight. With a horrible convulsive rhythm, the headless lambs thrust their pelvises towards the idol. It was the time of the birthing and I saw the abdomen of each body inflate and then quite literally explode in a rain of tissue and blood.

And then...oh yes, and then, as the dancers made the sign of the goat, the spawn of Shub-Niggurath were brought into this world. I suppose I went a little mad at the sight of the Dark Young hatching from those writhing corpses—wriggling, gelatinous things like squirming oyster-gray pupae, coiling embryonic horrors that seemed to be composed of wormy feelers, reaching flaccid tentacles, and countless mewling mouths, larval horrors that would one day ride the star winds and bring horror into the world of men.

A great burning hot cyclone of wind pushed the trees apart as their mother stepped forward to claim her children. My mind filled with the hell-fire of imploding nebulae, I looked upon Shub-Niggurath, the great dark mother, that quivering garden of fertility whose horror was so great that the puny, insignificant minds of men had re-channeled it into the Black Goat of the Sabbath because her physical reality was so repulsive, so horrifying, that the mere sight of her drove her worshippers insane. My memory is distorted and disjointed, but I saw...I believe I saw... an immense noxious cloud of undulating black protoplasm, a fungoid horror of stomping hooves and pulsating vermiform flesh crawling with wriggling white grubs, a great seething cauldron of boiling gas and pulsing tissue and tentacles and screeching mouths and huge milk-swollen teats—something which simultaneously existed in this world yet was part of another.

I am thankful that the curvature of the third dimension only allowed me that brief glimpse of She from outside of time and space, the horror of many mouths.

After that, I remember very little. That monstrous creature had seeded its young in the sisters, then, on that holiest of nights, her monstrous wailing progeny were born. The sisters' heads had been removed so that they would not be able to witness this blessed event. They had been sacrificed to the Dark Mother and the cycle of the goat was complete.

So, as you can see from this missive, your Excellency, all proceeded as per our plans, just as promised in the holy book, *De Vermis Mysteriis*. Soon, the spawning will be a worldwide event and for this we are thankful.

I believe I have served my master well.

All praise the Dark Mother and her Divine Young,
I remain your servant of the Yellow Sign,

Sister Agnes Elizabeth
Yogg-Sothoth Neblod Zin

THE SLITHERING

E ven now, so many dread years later, I can scarcely speak of what I saw at that rotting house on the moors. And, worse, what saw *me*. That obscenity that haunts me still, sucking my mind dry like a leech year by year.

I was lost. That's how it started. Lost in that grim desolation of moorland. I was out hiking, something of an amateur naturalist, and that is how I came to horror and horror came to me.

As night came on, the sky went from a dismal leaden gray to a boiling black like the contents of a witch's cauldron. Shadows, long-limbed and grotesque, began to creep up from hollows and steaming mires. The wind called out in a mournful dirge amongst those pathless wastes, skirting hummock and drainage pits. It sounded like the shrill voices of entombed souls.

And it reminded me, with a chill up my spine, just how late it was and how terribly alone out there I was.

I had strayed from the main path and then strayed from it again, gotten myself turned around amongst the bogs, climbing over rotting trees, and scaling steep crags. All in search of marsh orchids—twayblade, northern, and heath spotted.

And that's where dusk found me.

Amongst the damp mounds of sphagnum moss and heather, steadfastly examining some common lichens, meadowsweet, and an especially large butterwort. I should've been on my way an hour, two hours before, but there I still sat, lost in the dreamland of nature.

Soon enough, the rain started coming down.

I got to my feet, lost in that maze of heather and sedge, no shelter for miles, steadily saturating like a sponge as water ran in rivers off the brim of my hat and flowed down the back of my neck. I was cold and wet and there wasn't so much as a dead tree to hide under. I grabbed my stick and made my way across the moorland, but it was hopeless by night. I couldn't find the path. All around me was lowland bog waiting to swallow me alive. The rain poured down and the mist grew thick, mud sluicing over by boots.

About an hour into it, the rain still coming down, I spotted the house atop a sloping and grassy ridge.

A high, leaning structure wrought from crumbling stone, tangled in vines and creepers, scrub oak growing in dark profusion around it. The grounds were weedy and wild, the vegetation clotted and unpleasant. I'd come across other deserted farmhouses that morning amongst the uplands, shacks really, windows boarded-over and walls bowed.

They'd been abandoned for decades.

But this place?

Even before I saw that dim, yellow light in the windows, I had known instinctively that it was occupied. I had the most unsettling sensation of being watched. From the house or the moors, I did not know. But it gripped me and I climbed up the hill and threw myself at the door of that sprawling house, the stink of rank vegetation making me almost nauseous.

I pounded on the locked door for a full five minutes before it was opened.

And then only a crack. A crack through which by sputtering lamplight I saw a sliver of face…aged, yellow, and worn like the leaves of an ancient book. That single red-rimmed eye appraised me with something like fear.

Then a voice, dry and scraping: "Who…who knocks?"

"Bassett," I said, feeling the damp of the night like fingers at the back of my neck. "David Bassett…I'm a tourist lost on the moor."

The door opened another crack and I could feel the warmth of the old place beckoning and something beyond—a weird, eldritch stink of unwholesome age that I did not care for at all. I suppose a house like that which had stood some three hundred years or more had a right to such an odor, yet I found it inexorably loathsome. For here was not just the smell of time, but the smell of unhallowed memory, of advanced decomposition, of embalmed things resting uneasily in nitrous oblong boxes.

It made my blood run cold, made me want to run from that awful place and never look back.

"Bassett, Bassett," the old man said, opening the door wide. "So you would be a traveler, eh? A babe lost in the woods and I would be the one to give you shelter within these here walls? Aye, is that what you ask?"

"Yes," I said, the water dripping from me.

He was carrying an antique lantern and now he held it up, studying me apparently in some detail. Satisfied, he peered into the storm behind me to what I might be hiding out there. Suspicious? No, he was paranoid to the extreme.

"All right then, Mr. Bassett, then shelter I would give you. You say you're a tourist…but others have come, aye, many of them claiming to be things which they were not. Come off the moor, they did…them knocking in the dead of night which no man would allow across his threshold." Then he shook his head, those sparse white locks trembling down his neck like white ribbons. "But I would not turn you away, not on such a night."

Then we were inside, that huge oaken door shut behind us. The old man said his name was McKerr, just McKerr, and that his family had occupied that very house since just after the Puritan Revolution. With his lamp held high, he led me down a narrow corridor and into something like a sitting room with a flagstone floor and a huge hearth crackling with fire, exposed smoke-blackened beams high overhead.

I sat before that wonderful fire, the wetness steaming off my back.

"I'll get you a cup and a dram," McKerr said. "That much I'll do."

There are old people and then there are old people. And McKerr was a relic. He was long and narrow, rawboned like a framework of sticks stuffed with dead leaves, the thinnest veneer of cellophane used for flesh. His skin was loose, nearly transparent like that of a brine shrimp. You could see all the cords and arteries that kept him animate and alive. His shaggy hair and bushy beard were the color of hoarfrost and what teeth he had were crooked and discolored. And those eyes…wide, bright, *hunted* like those of a rabbit hiding from a swooping owl.

The walls of that cavernous room were set with moldering tapestries, archaic realist paintings, and crowded shelves of ancient books, rotting and wormy-smelling. As we passed them on our way in, I tried to read the titles, but my Latin is weak and my Arabic nonexistent. Something about those heaped, hidebound books with their curious bindings and rusty iron hasps disturbed me as did the arcane symbols that were carved into them.

The whiskey was good and the coffee even better. Playing the good host with varying degrees of success, McKerr wrapped me in a musty-smelling blanket and asked how it was I came to be on the moor. So I told him in some detail, but he was either rude or utterly disinterested and probably both.

"Did…did you see anything out there?" he asked me, those eyes of his hooded and conspiratorial. "Out on that moor? A shape? A hulking figure perhaps?"

"No, nothing." Something about his tone made my skin positively crawl. "What…what do you mean exactly?"

But he just shook his head, held a finger to his lips, demanding quiet. With a cocked head and darting eyes, he listened, perhaps hearing something I could not. All I could make out was the rain on the roof, that wind making the old timbers creak and groan.

"You heard nothing, then?" he put to me. "When…when the night came down and the rain started? You heard no sounds? Nothing…*unusual?* A noise…a slopping noise? A slithering in the distance?"

I shook my head.

"Did you not feel watched by unseen eyes?"

I admitted that I had and McKerr began to shake. He made an odd sort of whimpering sound in his throat and gasped.

"Ah, then," he said, nodding, "so it is tonight, is it? Aye, so I was told."

"What do you mean?" I said, barely able to keep the fear from my voice. "What's tonight?"

He grinned at me and the overall effect of that sallow, wrinkled face and crooked teeth was appalling. He looked like some morbid human rodent, something malevolent that had sharpened its teeth on bones. And his eyes… dear God, they were filled with an eerie, malefic light that stripped my mind to the bare bones. Yes, he was disturbed. Certainly, he was mad. But can insanity be communicable? For as he looked upon me, and yes, *through* me, I could feel that gnawing madness in me, too. Maybe I was exhausted and worn thin from my adventure on the moor, but I didn't think so. That seed of lunacy was inside me…growing, germinating, sprouting in black, slimy coils. Maybe it was the way he seemed to stare right through me, seeing unknown things I could not see and hearing things I could not hear. And though I could not physically sense them, I could *feel* them. Lurking shadows and crawling shapes, things primal and nameless and degenerate.

He poured me another whiskey. "Tonight is the night of my inheritance, you see. Aye, it is the legacy of a depraved bloodline, a godless and terrible heritage that all the McKerr men succumb to in their final hours when their minds grow weak and their bodies grow slow and no more can they fight that awful malignance which reaches out to them from out of space and out of time." He laughed bitterly at the idea of it. "But I am rambling and you are growing concerned, eh? Well, perhaps I should explain, explain why you must leave this house."

I wasn't sure if I wanted him to.

"What I tell you now happened during the Puritan Revolution, the so-called English Civil War, some three centuries past, Mr. Bassett. You see my grandfather, some six generations removed, was an officer with the Royalist cavalry under the Marquess of Newcastle and Prince Rupert. Not so far from here, as the crow flies, was the staging ground for the bloody and decisive Battle of Marston Moor where the Royalists engaged the Roundheads of Oliver Cromwell beneath a yellow harvest moon…"

McKerr spoke in some depth of the battle as if he had been there, but such memories are thick as blood in some of the older families of Yorkshire. I was glad for the diversion from those other things he had hinted at, things I did not want to know about. Apparently, the Civil War was going poorly for the Royalist forces in the north of England. The Marquess of Newcastle was forced to retreat to the fortified city of York where he was harassed bitterly by the Parlimentary forces of Sir Thomas Fairfax. Prince Rupert broke the siege with some 14,000 soldiers loyal to the crown, cavalrymen and infantry. McKerr's ancestor was one of them. Fairfax broke off the siege and later that day, both Royalist and Parlimentary armies engaged in the area of Marston Moor at dusk. The Roundheads numbered themselves at some 27,000, a numerically superior force to Rupert's beaten and bedraggled 14,000 that had been fighting for days without rest. The Royalist cavalry was soundly defeated during several hours of bloody fighting that cost them some 3,000 men. In the coming days, York would surrender to Parliament and, in doing so, the north of England would be effectively lost for the king and gained by Cromwell.

"Aye, you can imagine it, can't you, Mr. Bassett? The senseless and diabolical slaughter beneath that glowering harvest moon. And now…let me tell that which is not in any history book, but true nonetheless." McKerr poured himself a whiskey, gulped it down in one swallow. "Yes, now my ancestor—Douglass McKerr—found his regiment to be cut off from Lord Newcastle's main force, pushed back into the oaks and willows and mires of Wilstrop Wood. They were surrounded and it was war to the knife, a vicious struggle for survival.

"Imagine it under the baleful eye of that bright yellow moon: a slaughter. No quarter asked for and none given. Bodies strewn in every direction, in whole and part, the air thick with the stench of blood and powder, the screams of the dying. The Roundheads could smell victory that night and they pressed ever forward, decked out in steel armor corselets and iron helmets decorated with sashes of orange, the Royalists falling back, their red sashes splattered with mud and blood. It was a grim turn of events. The Roundhead cavalry rode in for the kill, bolstered by infantry and pikemen in their steel cuirasses and waves of musketeers with their matchlock muskets. It was a massacre for that cut-off band of Royalists…or would have been."

"Something happened?" I said.

McKerr flashed me that perfectly awful grin again. "Oh yes, by Christ, something certainly happened. Something that sent Fairfax's Roundheads running…hundreds and hundreds of them, climbing right over the tops of their comrades."

"What?" I asked. "A counterattack?"

"Of a sort," McKerr told me, that malign witch-light in his eyes again. "Of a sort, Mr. Bassett."

What he told me next made me certain he was raving.

"I would tell you of Douglass McKerr," the old man said to me, the firelight painting up his narrow face with shadows. "For every clan has its black sheep or black hand and this family is no different. Aye, Douglass McKerr was what might be called a wizard or a witch. It was said he escaped more than one noose during the witch hunts of those dire days. It was no secret that he studied damnable hell-books that should have been burned to ash. Books of ancient wisdom and godless blasphemy that I scarce have the courage to tell you of. But know, Mr. Bassett, that what I say to you is no twice-told tale, no colorful sprite of family history embellished upon and re-embellished through the centuries. Understand that. Understand that Douglass McKerr was a sorcerer of the worst ilk and that is a dire and horrendous secret that generations of McKerrs have protected, even though, in the end, it cost them their lives. So, I will tell you all there is to tell, things no stranger has ever heard."

"Why?" I said. "Why tell me?"

"Because I am the last of my line," McKerr admitted. "There are no others after me. I am the last of the McKerr's and tonight…yes, tonight I will die." He paused, studying me intently. "Do you believe in such things, Mr. Bassett? Witchcraft and the like?"

I wanted to lie, but I didn't dare. "No, no I don't."

"All the better, all the better. Oh, what sweet wine is your skepticism. Once I was young and arrogant and sure like you…but now? Yes, now I know better and am that much the worse for it." He sucked down another whiskey and he was shaking so badly that even with both hands, he could scarcely get that steel cup to his lips. "So you do not believe in witchcraft and necromancy and the summoning of noxious elementals? Aye, Douglass McKerr's enemies did not believe either. They thought it was folktale and legend, the stuff of children's tales and old wife's banter.

"But is it folktale, Mr. Bassett, that my ancestor once raised his hands to the sky amongst the old Druidic ruins on the moor and the sun did not shine for three days? And is it legend that Douglass McKerr barely escaped the gallows in Newton for the witching of several prominent families and not one month later, something flickering and burning like a forest of quivering

ropes slid down from the heavens and when it left, aye, when it left there was
no more Newton? And is it the stuff of children and old wives that Douglass
McKerr's own wife was given to some demon out of space and time on an
altar of children's bones and that some nine months later, she gave birth to a
boneless thing that ate its way out of her womb? You would say that's fantasy
and folklore and chimney-corner whisper, would you not? But I put it to
you, my fine and naïve friend, *that I saw that abominable and centuried thing
that devoured its mother! Aye, I was the one that destroyed it so that no more
would it scream and howl in the family vault beneath our feet…*"

Madness. Dear God, I was trapped in that decaying, odious house with
a raving lunatic. Yes, certainly the gloomy atmosphere of the place and my
morose host had gripped my imagination and my nerves had cannibalized
one another for a time, making me feel things that were not there. But that
was at an end now. What he was talking about was sheer fantasy. I couldn't
let myself see it in any other way. McKerr was insane and I had to keep that
in mind.

"When the rain stops," I said. "I'll be on my way."

That made him laugh. Laugh? No, he cackled horribly, wheezing and
coughing like I was the biggest buffoon he'd ever met. And maybe I was.
Maybe this was all some game he was playing on me, some grand joke, and
I was the punchline.

"Ah, my boy, now you can't wait to leave, eh? Can't wait to be free of
this old fool and his dementia." He laughed again and it was a raw, bitter
sound. "Well, I will not see another day, Mr. Bassett, so do me the courtesy
of hearing an old man's final confession."

What could I say to that? I wasn't trying to be rude. It was the last thing
on my mind. But…well, I had to get a grip on my nerves. None of what he
claimed could possibly have been true.

I swallowed. "Douglass McKerr was an officer, you say," I put to him,
trying to get our conversation on a sane path again.

"Aye, an officer he was and how does such a man gain a commission? A
man who was at best a recluse and at worst a conjuror of the vilest nature?
Well, some say it was by sorcery, but you may draw your own conclusions."
McKerr stared into his empty cup for a time. "Now, as I told you, the

Roundheads were pressing ever forward, the Royalists hiding in Winstrop Wood, beaten, bloodied, low on ammunition and spirit. What a pretty fix that was. All seemed to be lost until my ancestor interceded."

"What did he do?"

McKerr refused to look at me. "He called something up…something that has tormented my family ever since."

"What do you mean?" But I knew. I figured I knew.

"He invoked an entity…something ancient and hideous, something that slithered down from the sterile plains and cosmic graveyards beyond the withered edge of the universe…a thing, a monstrosity, a livid and hungering nightmare," the old man said to me, drool hanging from his lower lip, his eyes filled with a bottomless darkness. "Yes, Mr. Bassett, using old words culled from those profane books of his, he summoned a living contagion, a slithering horror from the putrescent subcellar beyond time and space as we know it! What sort of thing? Something primal and pestilent, an evil and sinister malignance that crawls in the black slime of what is and what can never be! A viscid haunter of the dark…"

Of course, it was madness, but how could I not be unmoved by any of it? How could I not let those words settle into me and destroy me? In that awful house of creeping shadows and ominous portent with the rain lashing and the wind moaning…I was just beside myself with fear, with apprehension, with I did not know what.

As I tried to pull back from McKerr, he leaned closer until I could smell the sour fetor of his breath. A smell that told me he was putrefying inside, going black and foul to his core. And it was no wonder…living in that shadow-riven house on the desolate moor, his mind gone to ruin.

"Yes, Mr. Bassett, my ancestor called down that thing, but nothing comes without a price. It was a verminous and repellent thing he called down and it demanded sacrifice. So, sacrifice was given…the Roundheads." McKerr paused, breathing hard now. "The thing…it did not want their flesh and bones, you see, it wanted their *minds*. It wanted to fill its belly on the raw intellects of those advancing soldiers and it did. It sucked the minds of a hundred dry, the rest turned into gibbering mad things as that quivering and serpentine nightmare slithered about them."

McKerr did not describe this imaginary beast in any detail. Only that it coiled and slithered and devoured. But that was enough, my mind could supply the rest. Supposedly, this thing came with a reeking, shivering mist, turning the Roundheads around and slithering about them, vacuuming their minds dry. By the time they realized there was something among them, something hunting them in that seeping fog, they were terribly disorganized and terrified, shooting and stabbing each other, fleeing in all directions, many of them swallowed alive in the bottomless fens.

"And since that night, this thing has plagued my family, Mr. Bassett. That terrible sacrifice given it was not enough…it returns each generation to devour the mind of a McKerr man in his final days. We feel it out there, of course, circling us, gradually draining our mental energies one sip at a time, but it is not until our final days that it comes to drink its fill."

McKerr was no good after that.

He told me I had to leave at once, but we were dead in the teeth of the storm, so he gave me a room upstairs that was dirty and cobwebbed, stinking of age and mold. I did not sleep. I could not sleep after what I had been through. And it was just after midnight that I heard him scream. It was a scream beyond mere terror, but something agonized and bestial like an animal being slaughtered.

I ran down the stairs, screams echoing through those vaulted rooms. I knew the thing had come. Despite my urbanity and reason and logic, I knew it had come for him. Such things cannot be, you say, and I told myself the same. But as I came down those creaking stairs I could *feel* it…feel that invidious and bleak alien presence filling that rotting old house like the plague.

And McKerr?

Yes, I found him. He was still in that shadowy sitting room, but he was not alone. I smelled something like corpse gas and black river mud, odors I could not even put a name to. The thing itself…that unnamable inheritance of the McKerr's…was an abomination, like some huge slug formed of quivering gray jelly, a wormlike and undulant thing with dozens of wavering stalks tipped by black nodes which I knew were eyes. Eyes that looked upon me with a cold and glaring appetite. McKerr was being absorbed by it,

92

assimilated, head-first he was being drawn into a steaming orifice dripping with a black and acidic slime.

I only saw part of the thing, that which the flickering firelight described to me, but it was enough. I had a feeling that the beast had no true dimensions as we understood them, that it's fungous and serpentine body might well have reached beyond the stars themselves.

I ran.

I did not try to help McKerr. I ran out into the storm and the mist and the night, nearly out of my mind. Seeing such a thing was bad enough, but I had more than seen it…I was seen *by* it. Marked. I felt its morbid intelligence sliding through my mind, nibbling and chewing and tasting. I knew it then as I know it now as I will know it intimately at the very hour of my death.

For in my final days, it will come for me.

It will come to eat my mind and those of my children and my children's children for a thousand generations for only then will it be satisfied.

THE PENUMBRA OF
EXQUISITE FOULNESS

Camilla: Oh please, please don't unwrap it! I can't bear it!

Cassilda: (Setting the wriggling bundle before them.) We must. He wants us to see.

Camilla: I won't look. I refuse.

Cassilda: It squirms like an infant, but how soft it is like a worm.

Camilla: Its lips move…but it makes no sound. Why doesn't it make a sound?

Cassilda: (Giggling now.) It cannot. Its mouth is filled with flies.

The King in Yellow, Act I, Scene 4.

*I*n chaos, I found purpose. In bedlam, purity of vision. That is the skin of my story. And the blood and meat of my little tale is that you can only hide from insanity *within* the cloak of insanity. This will make precious little sense to those of you who've never opened the book—blessed are the meek and ignorant—but to those of you who have (and you are many, aren't you?) it will make all the sense in this world…and out of it.

Now let me confess, let me expose the yellowed bones of my tale. Once the idea occurred to me, I had no choice but to see it through and do those things that were demanded of me. Let's call it a blind compulsion. That will sit easier with most. A mental derangement, an insanity, a stark mania.

With that in mind, listen: on a perfectly ordinary Tuesday morning, I gave baby Marcus a bath. I sudsed him up and rinsed him thoroughly because a clean baby, so soft and pink and fine-smelling, was a happy baby. As he gooed and gurgled, the madness pierced me like hot needles. I tried to shake it from my head, but I couldn't get rid of it anymore than I could shed my own skin. So, I leaned there against the tub, a sweat that was foul-smelling and cool running from my pores.

It was communion. Something—I dare not say what—had made me part of it. I had been named, chosen. And in my head, a voice, a very soft and smooth voice, said to me, *The King comes now. He comes for what is his and you are made ready.*

A fathomless darkness sucked my mind into nether regions and I saw black stars hanging over a gutted landscape. My hands were no longer my own but instruments of something malevolent that crowded the thoughts from my brain. They—the hands, looking jaundiced and almost *scaly* in the weak bathroom fluorescents—seized Marcus by the throat and held him beneath the sudsy water until he stopped moving, until his cherubic face was erased and replaced with that of a bluing corpse-child, lips blackening and pink skin mottled, eyes like staring black holes looking straight into the vortex of my soul.

Once the act was complete, I sat there, tears running down my face.

Sobbing and whimpering, I studied the hands that had just murdered my darling little boy. I studied them in detail, knowing they were not my hands but those of another, one that did not belong but crept in silent, silken moonlight.

Baby Marcus sank like a rock. That is crude, but perfectly descriptive. He would resurface, I knew, when the time was right. And in my horror, I could envision that moment: his puckered face breaking the tepid, bubbly water like lips parting, his voice cutting deep into my brain like a scalpel.

The hot needles burning deeper, fed by the kindling of unspeakable guilt, I opened my wrists with a razor, staring at the corpse of my baby drifting like a swollen dead cod at the bottom of the tub. As blood bubbled from my gashed arteries in scarlet rivulets and freshets, I dipped a skeletal white digit into the ragged, spurting inkwell of my left wrist until it was dyed a brilliant red. The vibrancy of my glistening fingertip fascinated me. Without further ado, while the ink of life was still wet and running, I sketched out the form of a simple stick man on the white tile wall of the bathroom in slashes of crimson. It wasn't until I had drawn in the ruby blobs of its eyes and the tattered mantle blowing out from it that I began to scream. It was then that my stick figure became something much more and I saw it move as it has moved in my nightmares ever since.

As I slowly came out of it, there was panic. It filled my mind until it seemed I had no mind. Grimly, with great burning intensity, I held onto my sanity as reality flew apart inside my head and out of it. I screamed again. I must have screamed for I heard a voice echoing amongst the black and uneasy stars that pressed in from all sides. The walls of the room were gone. And when I looked up, there was no ceiling, there was no roof above, only the inverted sickle of a scarlet moon dripping its black blood onto my face.

Later, after my neighbor called 911, I was stitched-up—much against my feeble will. My neurotic soul sought death and death was denied it. So be it. I was held in the psych ward where I was heavily sedated and restrained because I saw the haunted onyx eyes of the cold dead thing in the tub and they created a grim alchemy in my brain.

I told the staff feverishly about *The King in Yellow*, how Act II had thrown open the doors of nightmare perception and plunged me screaming into a phobic void. But they would not listen. And the more they would not hear my words, the more certain I was that they already knew them.

I was incarcerated, of course. While the courts decided what to do with me, I underwent some two months of recuperation and intensive therapy. At the close of which, I was brought before the police psychiatrist for yet another interview.

"Why?" he asked me. "Why did you do it?"

"If you have to ask that, then it's beyond your understanding."

He smiled gently as if I was something to be pitied. "Enlighten me."

"Enlightenment is dangerous."

He had no idea how close he was to the abyss, but I refused to give him the final push.

I studied the scars on my wrists. They had healed into pink whorls, spiraling pink whorls like distant galaxies that captured the eye and drew it deeper into Archimedean complexity. It was there that I saw what no man or woman should ever see: the Sign. It was sketched on each wrist in an intricate weal of healed flesh. Once my eyes had discovered it, I could not look away. It owned me and I knew that my service to the King had only just begun.

The police psychiatrist pegged me with questions, of course. He was intrigued that Marcus's father—dear, lost David—had committed suicide and that I had no family and no friends. He was only doing his job and I tried to be helpful. I did not want to involve him in the greater cosmic horror of the things I knew to be true, the things that had forced David to put a noose around his throat. Keeping with that, I kept my wrists out of view and when he asked questions whose answers might be dangerous to him, I remained mum. But he was insistent. As he jabbed, I parried. It was exhausting subterfuge, but in the end, I would not confess the secret of the Hyades.

My next stop, of course, was prison. I was sentenced to ten to fifteen years. I was not alone there; many of the women had killed their own children and some had killed the children of others. At night, they would rage and cry and beg God for deliverance but there was never any deliverance. There was only the cool concrete silence winding out interminably.

One night, as I lay there beaded in the sweat of fear that the darkness always brought, a drug trafficker called Mother McGibb started calling out to God for forgiveness. Not just for herself, but for all the animals in all the cages squatting in the dirty straw of their lives. And maybe He heard her because a violent storm gripped the prison in its teeth. The more Mother cried out for divine intervention, the more the torrential fury outside built. The wind screamed and sheets of lightning flashed in the sky as rain lashed those high gray walls.

"SISTERS!" shouted Mother above the cacophony of the storm. "SISTERS! HEAR WHAT I SAY: THE LORD IS VENTING HIS WRATH FOR WHAT WE HAVE DONE AND THE SIN IN OUR HEARTS! BOW YOUR HEADS AND MAKE PEACE WITH HIM SO THAT HE MAY COME UNTO YOU IN THE FINAL HOUR!"

Some of the women yelled for her to shut up and others rattled tin cups and hair brushes against the bars of their cells. It was quite melodramatic. Soon, it seemed, everyone was awake and frantic, crying out in anger and remorse as the thunder boomed and the prison shook like a wet dog. The wind was howling and I was certain it was calling out the names of the incarcerated. The scars on my wrists burned interminably.

"HE HAS A PLAN FOR THIS WORLD!" said Mother. "AND HE WATCHES ALL FROM HIS LOFTY THRONE IN THE HYADES! HE WILL ALIGN THIS WORLD WITH ALDEBARAN, FOLLOWER OF THE SEVEN SISTERS! MAKE HIM WELCOME! TREMBLE BEFORE HIM! ACCEPT THE LIVING GOD SO THAT HE MAY LAY HIS HANDS UPON YOU!"

The lightning was flashing continuously by this point, thunder echoing down the sullen corridors of the prison, punctuating the fearful voices of the incarcerated. I was shaking, mouthing the words of Mother McGibb even though they tasted like poison on my tongue. It was then that my cellmate, Gretta Leese—doing twenty-to-life for multiple homicide—took hold of me, wrapping her arms around me as if I were a child frightened of the dark and what lurked in it (which was very true).

"Don't listen!" Gretta said into my ear. "She's a false prophet and her words are iniquity! The god she calls out to is not the god of anyone sane or righteous! Don't listen! Do you hear me? *Don't listen!*"

But even though Gretta clamped her hands over my ears, I could hear the words of Mother McGibb just fine as if they were spoken in the hollows of my skull.

"WE SHALL LOOK FOR THE SIGN, SISTERS! HIS SIGN! THEN WE SHALL KNOW THAT WE ARE AT ONE WITH HIM! THAT THE SON OF HASTUR WALKS THESE LANDS AND THE BROTHERS AND SISTERS OF MAN SHALL BOW THEIR HEADS AS HE KNOCKS AT THE DOOR! WE SHALL BE BROUGHT FORTH INTO THE BODY OF THE PALLID MASK AND WE SHALL MAKE OFFERINGS ONTO HIM AND GIVE PRAISE TO THE KING IN HIS TATTERED MANTLE!"

By that point, the guards had had more than enough of it. Mother

McGill was told to quiet down and when she didn't, they hauled her down to solitary where, I heard, she continued to rant and rave. But I didn't need to be told that—the stigmata of my wrists burned throughout the night.

Month after month, the prison psychiatrist picked and pecked at me in search of some tasty red meat, trying in vain to understand my inner workings, the motivation for my crime and (what she called) a deep-set delusional disorder. She was convinced the wellspring of it all was David's suicide. Although I advised against it again and again, she insisted on hypnotherapy.

Our first few sessions were a complete bust. Then, on the third or fourth try, I came out of it and she began asking questions that I dared not answer. She had jotted down things I said while under—"the Pallid Mask" and "darkest Carcosa" and "Cor Tauri, the Festival of the Bloody Heart"—but I refused to comment on any of it. In fact, to my credit, I acted as if I had never heard of such rot and practically accused *her* of multiple delusions.

But I was not completely stubborn. I tried to be cooperative when and where possible. The psych badly wanted to understand me and my psychosis. The way she spoke of the latter, you would have thought it was a living, breathing thing like some immense, fear-swollen parasite or an evil conjoined twin. She found it perplexing that I, an apparently loving and kind single mother, well-educated, well-bred, and quite successful, could commit such a crime as if status precludes one from darkest folly. I parried with her a bit, telling her that when things were so right, they had a way of going so wrong.

But she was no fool. She wanted answers and she planned on having them, even if that meant slicing my brain wafer-thin and putting it under a microscope. She had a great deal of passion for my dilemma and I was pretty certain that she had some scientific paper in mind that would win her accolades amongst her peers. I understood ambition. She wanted to know the root cause and I explained it to her (in the most general and antiseptic way). It was the book, *The King in Yellow*. I had discovered it in the historical collection of St. Aubin's College. As a full professor of Medieval History, I had access to those things which were denied others. I read the book, knowing quite well its fearsome reputation, and suffered the consequences. She claimed that the book did not exist and its namesake, the King himself, was a fantasy. I explained that for those who were chosen (*cursed*, might be a better word), he was occasionally visible in the distorted glass of certain antique mirrors or in pools of October rain. I had once glimpsed his numinous shadow at sundown, an immense and ragged form hovering over the city. I could tell her no more. Already, I knew, the ether of this world was beginning to fracture.

That the King was close, I did not doubt. That he was reaching out for me was a given. That became very apparent to me one summer day as we trimmed weeds amongst the graves at the prison's potter's field. Here were acres of withered crosses and crumbling sandstone markers invaded and sometimes engulfed by infestations of devil's gut, hairweed, and woodbine.

We spent the better part of a week cleaning it all up. Creepers had even grown up the wall of the little stone mausoleum. I was one of those who peeled the knotty growths free and when I did, revelation of the worst sort awaited me. For there, etched by a knife, was the very image I had drawn on the bathroom wall in my own blood that terrible night: *the King.* He was a stick figure and nothing more, but as I stared upon him, he became three-dimensional—fleshing out like a flower blooming until I could see the juicy running orbs of his eyes that bled like crushed berries and the vibrant colors of his tattered mantle. They drew me in closer and closer until I heard my own voice say, *"Oh, please, King, not again, not so soon."*

I have no idea how long I stood there, transfixed, but soon enough a guard came. "What do you think you're doing? Get back to work."

I pointed one trembling hand at the wall. "But…but he won't allow it."

"There's nothing there, can't you see that? Get back to work."

Oh, the rapture of ignorance. The guard did not see what I saw and how I envied the sheer simplicity of his mental processes. Simplicity, I began to believe, was close to divinity. I dreamed of it and wished for it, but once you have opened the book and seen the dark star and the hollow moon, there is no going back. No one can ever close that staring third eye that shows you hidden things in this world and beyond.

I could go into great, prolix detail about other such occurrences, but I present only the latter to illustrate my point. The penumbra of the king was creeping closer and it would compel me to do the most awful things.

All of which brings us to my last night in prison. After some six years, I was paroled. And the only reason I was paroled was because I was clever. I kept my nose clean, yes, but there was more to it than that. After a time, but not too soon as to appear suspicious, I accepted what the prison psychiatrist told me and volunteered for therapy sessions. That made her happy. I accepted all that she told me, sometimes repeating verbatim what she said, and that made her even happier. There was no book and no King. It was all delusion and fantasy. And that was how I won my early release from the cesspool of the prison.

But let us consider my last night there for a moment.

Long after midnight, I opened my eyes. There was something in the cell with me and it was not Gretta. This was something born from the womb of secret darkness. I could hear it breathing like wind in a chimney flue. It was standing near to me. Its body was a grotesque, heaving sack, its face white and soft, glistening like a mushroom damp with dew. I could see little of it and I was grateful for that. When it spoke, its voice was wet, nearly gelatinous: "You have found the Yellow Sign?"

"No," I muttered. *"No."*

Then a single pulpous hand like a flaccid starfish touched my wrist and the scars there burned like phosphorus. "It has been sent and you have found it."

I was released with very little fanfare. My parole officer was a man named Meecham who I instinctively did not trust. He was a smallish man, thin as a swamp reed, with a chin so sharp you could've sliced cheese with it. His right eye was blue, blinking all the time, but the left just stared. It was oddly large and green, but not a good sort of green, but the green of stagnant ponds and mildew. Frogspawn. It was gummy and jellied-looking.

"What I want you to keep in mind," he told me, "is that what happened is over with and you have a new life now. A new purpose. I will help you fulfill that purpose. Do you understand?"

I told him that I did. At which point, he pulled out a large envelope and out of it he took the book.

"Do you know what I have here?" he said.

I was trembling. "I don't want to see it."

"But you must, you must. You see? It's no book at all."

What I was looking at was not *The King in Yellow*, but only a sheaf of papers that I recognized instantly. These were the doodlings I had done after finishing Act II. The work of a madwoman, certainly. Drawings of stars and distorted planetary bodies, surreal landscapes and cities with misty towers that rose against the face of a rising moon. All of it was dominated by mindless scribbling that looked like the work of a child and numerous spiraling forms that seemed to connect it all together.

"There is no book. There never was a book. Do you believe that?"

"Yes," I managed, turning away from those awful spirals that made my wrists burn. "Yes."

He slid the papers back in the envelope. "Excellent. Then we can begin to craft the new you. And you do want that, don't you?"

I told him I did. I was afraid not to. He was playing a merry obscene game and I knew it. For even as he spoke, I noticed that the edges of his mask were beginning to fray.

Over the next few weeks as I settled into my role as ex-convict and former child murderess, there were things that did not sit right with me. I had the most disquieting sense that the world was no longer spinning safely and smoothly on its axis. Something had changed. I told myself it was only my perception of the same, but I was not convinced. Whomever or whatever had been in control of the universe before was in control no longer. Guardianship had changed hands. Maybe others were unaware of it, but I saw the signs immediately. They were subtle, but apparent—the arcing of sunlight at the horizon near dusk, the misaligned curvature of certain angles, the gathering of immense pale moths outside my window, and (the most telling) the frightening progress of a certain shadow that was getting closer by the day.

Meecham settled me into a halfway house with the other ex-cons. It was a unisex place, the men's quarters up the staircase to the left and the women's up the right. Regardless of gender, they shared one thing in common: the stare, that awful cataleptic sort of stare as if they were looking at something far in the distance no one else could ever see. The majority of them stayed in their rooms, pacing back and forth as if they were still in their cells, uncomfortable with the outside world. I suppose the higher physics of unlimited space was beyond their comprehension after being caged so long.

One of the women, an old lady everyone called Marge, hanged herself my first week there. She left a suicide note that said simply, ONLY THE LEFT EYE MAY SEE. But before she slipped the noose around her throat, she took an apple corer and took out the offending orb. She set the bloody glob in a teacup and then killed herself. And so very quietly that the woman in the next room didn't even hear her.

The woman next to me cried a lot at night. She had dead eyes that reminded me of pools of gray rainwater. It was said that she had murdered her own child. I understood her pain. Sometimes in the middle of the night, I would wake up thinking Marcus was crying and I had to feed him. My breasts would ache incessantly, but then I'd remember that Marcus was dead and that I was alone. *Oh, David, you do understand, don't you?* Often, I'd stare out the window, certain I could hear a baby crying somewhere in the night, lost and alone. But it was all in my head. More than once, I was certain I had spied Marcus in a baby carriage. But that was impossible…unless the time had come.

Next door, night after night, I could hear the crazy woman rocking back and forth in her chair, *squeak, squeak, squeak.* Sometimes it went on until dawn. She often sang lullabies in a shrill, scratching voice that made my skin crawl. I wasn't truly terrified until I heard a baby crying over there. It wasn't possible. I knew it wasn't possible. Yet I heard it and there was no mistaking it or the moist sucking sound of an infant feeding.

Finally, after too many haunted and sleepless nights, I inquired about my neighbor. "She can't have a baby in there," I said to Kim, one of the other girls. "She killed her baby."

"Hell are you talking about? You're the one that murdered your baby. Only you."

That was only one of many items that convinced me the world was lopsided and stretching itself inside out. Let me tell you of another. I woke one night certain that I was not alone in my room. A search proved otherwise. I went to the window, staring at my reflection in the glass. And it was then that I saw not my room reflected behind me but some deranged seesaw landscape with an immense lake over which dangled black, guttering stars. On the shore of the lake I caught sight of a tall, crooked figure in scalloped tatters that blew about it like a shroud. I knew who it was. It could only be the King in Yellow and he was striding in my direction.

That was enough in of itself, but it was not all. You see, the spiraling scars on my wrists that revealed the Yellow Sign were spreading. It was not possible and I knew it, but the evidence was all-too apparent: the intricate pink whorls had spread up my arms and down onto my chest. I traced them with my fingers and they were upraised like burns and unbelievably intricate. Their geometry was not only Archimedean in nature, but hyperbolic or inverse. If the eye followed their vortexual progression, the Yellow Sign was always revealed. And when it was seen, you could look beyond it and see the skeletal towers of Carcosa rising into a red-hazed sky through which Aldebaran and the Hyades peered through sickly yellow cloud banks like swollen eyelids.

After that, I must admit my memories are not as lucid as I would like. It seemed that everything started to get obscured. My world was leaning a little too far this way or that and where the angles met, I was afraid of what I might see. It was like looking through cellophane, everything became oblique, obscured, inverted. The King was turning my world upside down as he crept closer, ever closer to claim me as his own.

Now to the next few items on my list.

I awoke another night and I could hear whispering voices next door that disturbed me greatly. After a time, I pressed my ear against the thin wall and listened. This is what I heard: *"You won't be the one, you know. It is I who'll wear the crown…not you! I have been made ready by His hand and the crown was promised to me in a dream of withered roses! I alone have plumbed the black depths of Lake Hali and I alone have climbed the towers and cried out the sacred names above the Hill of Dreams! All will soon bow down before me, the child of Hastur!"*

Whether it was the crazy woman speaking or the child itself, there was no way of knowing. I wanted to go over there and make them stop, but I did not dare. I knew if I opened that door, I would see a fleshy spiraling that would suck my mind from my skull.

One afternoon after stepping off the bus, I stood on the sidewalk before the halfway house, trembling with fear. It was changing like everything else. It was no longer some simple, shabby three-story house but a cyclopean, rising black monolith that wavered and shuddered as if it could no longer hold its shape. It filled the sky, its icy shadow enveloping me in the frozen cerements of the King himself.

But it did not end there, oh no. When the house became nothing but a house again, I went to my room. After lying on my bed for an hour or so, I went to the window and I saw not my world but the scarlet-litten city of Carcosa with its forest of twisted, rising towers overlooking a warped anti-world of clustering black ruins. I could see the Lake of Halli, its dark flat waters reflecting an immense moon of blood. On the shore stood the King in Yellow beckoning to me amongst the crushed shells of a thousand disciples.

I pulled the shades so I did not have to see the twisted nightmare vistas of that anti-world and particularly its king. For three interminable days and three torturous nights, I hid there in my boxlike room, waiting for a tread on the stair or, worse, for the gossamer material of this world to wear thin from its constant friction against that intrusive other which threatened to intersect all that we know. The penumbra of the King's shadow grew closer and closer by the hour.

My second day of self-imposed isolation, I dared peek around the drawn shade and what I saw was the shadow edging closer to the house. Of course, others would say it was only the shadow thrown by the looming building across the street, but I know better. For each evening at dusk as I watched its grim approach, I clearly saw that diabolic penumbra creeping ever forward on a thousand tiny legs.

By the night of the third day, I knew I was trapped. I should have escaped while there was time and maneuvering room. The reality I had known my entire life was fragmenting, giving way to the tidal thrust of a limitless blackness without form. Each time it began to come apart, I heard something like a crackling or sizzling and awful pains swept over me...following, yes, following the exact patterns of the spiraling cicatrisation that covered my entire body now much as electricity will follow the path of a copper wire. When the pain ceased, I would see—if only momentarily—my room turned topsy-turvy and inside out, remade by the hand of another into some poor, crude replica whose walls oozed a mephitic pink slime and whose ceiling was loose and spongy. Dear God, even the floor was like some nasty jelly as if I were not squatting on tiles but on the accumulated soft putrescence of dozens of over-ripened corpses.

Then it would pass.

But I knew, given time, it would engulf my world and there would be no going back. For three nights I watched the moon hanging above the city like an immense peeled eyeball studying the nocturnal scrambling of those creatures who would soon tremble before a new and malefic god. It throbbed like a heart, pulsing with each abnormal beat, filling itself with blood, getting stronger and larger, fleshing itself out for the final act.

There were things that needed doing and only I could do them. I plotted carefully and waited. When I heard that poor demented woman slip downstairs, I went to her room and found the door ajar. It smelled strange in there, hot and briny like tidal flats on a scorching summer day.

Passing by the bed, I went to the bassinet under the window, pushing aside the flowing lace. The baby stared at me with curiosity and innocence.

"Again, oh King, must I do it yet again?"

The moon was peering through the window and looking at its face, I saw voids, glistening depths, and some demented stygian dead-end space where black stars shiver in a nightmare cosmos. Soon, I would travel there.

As I hesitated in my sacred task, the penumbra of the King in Yellow crept ever closer. I heard the crackling-sizzling sound and the stigmata of my elaborately scarred body went electric with pain. Right away, the room began to alter. It mutated, morphed, going liquid like hot corpse fat and cooling into something perverse and insane. It was a room as envisioned by a lunatic: a surreal, *anti*-real, expressionistic tangle, a black and red framework of jagged shards of glass, warped doorways that led into black pathless wastes, and windows that looked onto the pulsating face of the grinning, sardonic moon.

But I completed my task and when they charged into the room, I held up the blood-dripping, mangled offering to the King. I saw then that there were no secrets between us. They knew that I had tied the noose that David hanged himself with—dear God, he had *begged* me to after glimpsing the book—and they knew I brought Marcus to term only to offer him to the mighty King at summer solstice.

"I have won and now I ascend to the throne! It is my right as concubine of Hastur! It is I who shall wear the crown and I who shall rule over darkest Carcosa!"

As they approached me, I tossed the offering at them so the King would know that I was righteous and pure. Then carefully, calmly, and with exacting precision I showed them the knife I carried. How the face of the moon glimmered along its blade. Then, with the finesse of a surgeon, I slit along the outer edges of my mask and began to peel it free so they could see what I hid beneath, the face the world would soon worship and tremble before.

THE BLOWFLY MANIFESTO

They found the bodies in a slum tenement that stank of yellowed bones, human excrement, and rusting lives.

Close, so very close. Five minutes earlier, Trask knew, and they would have caught old Crawling Face with his hands deep in the pie, licking cherry filling from his skeleton fingers. They traced him here at the edge of town where the immense sewage lagoons were black, gummy lakes lit by flames of burning methane. Here the houses were crowded together, rising tall and dirty from the heaped garbage and gutters blown with rubbish and human remains.

Trask followed the other bulls down streets paved with broken bottles and rusting tin, where shabby hotels boasted clear blue neon and rats clustered in warped slum doorways, pimps hawking cybered-up whores with pre-installed virtual reality/virtual memory chips, externalizing the girl of your dreams.

Up narrow stairways perfumed with cat piss they went, finding a door at the top. On the other side, arcing flashlight beams white swords slashing open the darkness and making it bleed like an opened vein…there was death. Death that was amused and happy with itself, lewd and leering. It stank of violence and worms, the dander of buzzard's wings. The accumulated stink of it was a foulness Trask could taste on his tongue like pennies plucked from a dead man's eyes.

The air was so silent—save for the sound of meat fly wings cutting it—that he could hear the dissolution of the corpses themselves: a dry and husking sound like plums or peaches in a dehydrator.

The bulls said nothing.

Not even to themselves.

One of them lit a cigarette and the smoke he exhaled became a ghost of the dead that haunted them all as it drifted man to man to woman. Yes, another slaughterhouse and this one so drenched with blood and seeped with remains that it would need to be hosed out. Stepping through the congealed pudding of blood and flesh debris, the bulls found a second room. Like the first, it was exceptionally dark—no windows, no working lights, as if illumination of any sort was an infection to be kept at bay. Trask noticed that not only were the windows carefully boarded over, but every crack and crevice was stuffed with rags. Darkness was celebrated here. They found more bodies, but these were much older. Like onions decaying in dark cupboards, they had rotted to black peelings.

Trask went back into the other room where the stink of putrescence was fresh and vomitous, clouds of flies rising from human fruit fermented down to a vile wine that seeped into the floorboards.

He knew there was nothing to say.

Once again, the victims here died willingly, crowding themselves into these rooms. Did they sit and wait while Crawling Face danced merrily from one to the next, disemboweling them?

Was such a thing possible?

Slit, slit, slit. Good evening to one and all. How are you and how's the mizzes and the chattery young-squirts? Crawling Face must have chatted with them as his hands became postmortem knives and his mouth whispered sad stories of lust crimes and blood-spattered rooming houses. Hooks and blades and embalming needles for fingers, he did his bit, *slit, slit, slit,* slashing like pendulum blades. When he was done, he must have stood there, admiring his work.

Sickened, Trask studied the words on the wall written in blood.

As always, gibberish that was not Latin nor Runic script exactly, but old, very old, pre-human perhaps if such a thing could be. The only identifiable word was the signature: *CRAWLING FACE.*

"He's at it again," one of the bulls said, as if there could be any doubt.

But Trask was not interested.

He found something wrapped in red velvet cloth. A black crystal threaded with glaring red striations like a fine networking of blood-engorged veins. It fit neatly in his hand, pulsing warm in his palm like the heart of a newborn. Growing hot, it scalded his flesh, biting into the meat of his palm like barbwire. As his eyes bulged from his head and his brain became a boiling chemical cauldron, his mouth filled with a vile sweetness of sugar, rusty iron, and human fat that was gagging. The world distorted, inverted, was turned inside out and made to bleed. He felt burning heat and icy cold, a weird fission energizing the air around him in a smoldering plutonium steam as iridescent particles wormholed through him, his mind laced with a spiderweb of black glass. A third eye opened and he saw beyond the pale, into unwinding spiral galaxies and nebulas collapsing under their own atomic weight, then beyond into the black void of some dimensional closet.

The boards were torn off the windows and sunlight filled the room, sunlight whose beams swam with motes of dust and motes of skin. Right away, the light closed Trask's third eye, praise Mother.

He blinked and saw the real world, but his tongue was still in the anti-world. "Cthulhu fhtagn," he said.

"You say something?" another bull asked.

"No," Trask told him, "I said nothing at all."

Beneath the pink gasoline sky, Trask moved deeper into the suffocating heat of the city, just another sleek-bodied shark finning its way through the black waters of oily despair. The wind was warm, shivering around him like gelatin. It smelled of human grease and bubbling black mud. The gutters were aswarm with hawkers and sellers like a corpse with its attendant flies. Drifting past Chinese brain laundries and detox halls, he passed sallow-faced whores selling pale meat and Fixers pushing contraband VR chips that would turn your mind to crackling white ice and let you see the face of your god before your brain spilled from your ears in a soupy mush of warm-sweet memory pain.

Trask knew the taste of it, all right. For ten years, he'd drifted through the gutters with the rest of the human garbage, hiding in his cage of addiction, interfacing the virus of need, haunting toxic graveyards and bone shops, ever hungry. But it was eating lunch with the damned: you eat it and it eats you.

Mother saved him.

Praise Mother in the highest.

"Anything?"

"I'm flatlining out here," Trask said, looking around the square with its teeming crowds like spider monkeys clustering on rotting vines. A bagged-out whore offered him a kiss of teeth and a hot breath smile. He could smell the cool, dead Victorian sex blowing off her. She was swollen with lust like a barrel. He edged past her, white leprosy flesh brushing his own. A café. He wriggled his way through the crowd like an eel moving upstream. "Gotta be fifty people in here sucking latte. Not getting a single spike on the screen."

"He has to be there," the voice said over the net. "The drone marked him not ten minutes ago."

"Is the drone still on-line?"

"Yes."

"Link me, Control. I want a positive signature."

The interface took less than a second and right away, Trask found what he was looking for: the rogue was an old man with a face torn by scars into a Braille that wanted to be read. He wore a dirty overcoat like a sheath of atrophied flesh. How he could go on day after day without being chipped was just beyond Trask. What did guys like him do with themselves? Wandering around in a fog, soft-stepping through dead-end alleys and the gray lost spaces of the human arcade. No guidance, probably thinking things that would get them in trouble.

He gave Trask the creeps. All the offline types did.

The old man was worse, of course. Bodies all across the city, dozens of them. Crime scenes like blood-dipped human stockyards. The only connective tissue from one victim to the next was the old man...but was he the one? Did he carve them up like Sunday hams, fingerpaint that word on the walls: Crawling Face?

Whenever Trask tried to think about it, to play connect the dots, lost in the deep fugue, wiring conscious to sub-conscious, Mother got nervous and threatened to shut him down. She didn't like her chippies doing too much thinking. And Crawling Face, he knew, made her nervous, very nervous.

Who is Crawling Face, old man? What does that name mean?

The old man's eyes passed over Trask but did not *see* him. Trask's well-scrubbed, almost sterile appearance made him chameleonic, gave him the ability to blend in like a smudge on a wall. Five minutes after someone talked to him, they forgot what he looked like. He was nothing if not bland and unremarkable.

The old man managed to palm a few credits for a cup of tar from a brassy, high-end woman whose pink shiny skin gleamed in the dirty light. A cloud of perfume rose from her and burned his eyes like wafting mustard gas. Her own eyes were turquoise, somehow depraved and filled with bitterness as if she'd seen things she could not get her mouth to speak of.

Trask watched her, becoming more and more curious. He rawdogged her, tapped illegally into her neural net and ran her through Mother, parsing her life. Mother said her name was Marjorie Bates. Matrix engineer, CyberPath Global. *Shit.* Trask broke the link. The lady was well-chipped, have no doubt, definitely not a rogue. Mother was never wrong. Mother was the neuroplex of CyberPath Global, she was wired into the heads of billions of users. The Pathway was created so all could share a bright, comfortable, and carefully orchestrated vision of today, tomorrow, and yesterday. Blessed be the name of Mother.

Outside the window, Trask scoped a couple of Mother's Little Helpers: Cryoborgs all. Hard to miss them: black sharkskin-fleshed, blood-drained complexions, eyes like dark shell holes filled with shattered white glass and black cinders. They smelled of chemical sterility and fused circuitry, reptilian brains hot-wired with bio-peripherals, minds amping on vectors, fusion binaries, and Boolean X-Ys. They patrolled the terminal landscape like carrion crabs on a polluted beach. They moved on and Trask let out a breath of stale air. He walked up to the old man, let his hand drop on the old party's shoulder like Miss Muffet's spider.

"I need to talk to you. This is official," he said.

The old man whirled around, made Trask as one of Mother's bulls instantly. His face went gray into a hysterical mosaic of terror, his eyes like hazy smoke rings.

Before Trask could properly collar him, he was gone, jumping away like a compacted spring, moving with a fluid dance through the sea of bodies out there. He got caught up in a pack of feral-toothed junkies dusted yellow from the compulsory anti-viral mistings that were used to keep weaponized bio-particles on the down low. The junkies circled him, slavering and hungry, drug-bellies growling for Laotian Redline and Sicilian Blue Spider, bas-relief tracks tattooed on their arms. They wanted to cook-up, to dissolve into memory-hazes of pre-protoplasmic bliss, meet their makers, star-headed and fish-eyed.

Mother's Little Helpers moved in for the kill, mindless Mother-hive drones, cheapjack old school TV Daleks that must exterminate. The old man wiggled free. The junkies scattered, all except two which were absorbed into the communal flux of Mother. The Cryoborgs, eyes like black glass and bald heads gleaming with plexi-composite temporal hardware, nabbed them, made them ready for the mind dance: brainwashing and identity modification. *We scrub your brain and re-boot you in five minutes or your next visit is free,* as the rogues liked to say.

"Shit," Trask said over the net. "He's a runner."

"He's tagged, Three. Don't make a scene. Play it smooth."

Trask helped himself to the old man's cup and pulled a scan on it, picking up a latent from the old man's thumb. He ran it through Mother. Interesting. Charles Tollan. So that was their boy. He'd run a biocybernetic team back in the old days. In fact, he'd worked for CyberPath for twenty-two years, had been one of the original designers of the Pathway. How did a guy like that end up panhandling for credits and sleeping in alleys? And how did he fit into the butchery of Crawling Face?

"That's our boy, Three. Get him before the Cryoborgs do."

"Can't you put a net on them?"

"No can do. Autonomic control, Mother-generated."

Trask understood. Like antediluvian anti-virus software launched from the motherboard…except they had legs, blank minds, twisted Mother-love, and were relentless in their pursuit of undesirables in need of chipping.

Back out into the excrement of the Big Ugly, Trask took in the wreckage and massing bodies, filled his head with the dead ammonia stink of a metropolis trying to sanitize its own germy surfaces. He watched faceless hags selling skin, narco-monkeys pushing psycho-synthetics and level 4 nirvana chips that could open up your third bleary eye and shut the other two permanently. Hawkers with voices like off-key barrel organs groaned, moaned, and coveted second-hand ID chips, psionic dust, and lost children. Fixers with minds like slag pits and deadheads with polished teeth of crystal sugar rubbed shoulder-to-shoulder with cyberjacks and ecto-phrenologists carting hollow-socketed wares. Here were tapeworm medicaments and writhing pestilence, freakshows and melting waxworks of the inhuman condition. Filth and squalor, entropy and state-sponsored sterility.

An embalmed-looking woman with a slack mouth and slattern mind stopped him. "How about a light?" Trask gave her one, lighting her coffin nail that was half synth-tobacco and mostly free-form Ganja called Man in the Moon, bioengineered hemp that would toast you for hours. "Why don't you come back to my hovel? I got some rock to burn. I'll shoot you with some pink and wreck your mind."

"Another time."

The old man tried to pull the fade again, but Trask logged his signature on infra-scan. He tightened his fields and ran his qualifiers. Everything he needed to know was displayed on the synth-lens of his left eye. The implant was painful, like mainlining rock salt into his cornea, but without it being a cop was like being a painter without a brush. And Mother insisted.

Trask moved on through the masses. *Hello. How are you? A pleasant evening to you.* The crowd flowed around him, liquid and sluicing. Too many voices, too many neurals overloading his interface. He shut it down, let himself breathe for a moment. He still had the old man—Tollan—and followed him at a discreet distance, tracking him carefully on infra-scan. Hunter and prey, but sometimes role-reversal was the norm. Sometimes rogues baited cops, drew them in and yanked their chips like gold teeth. You had to be careful. Cop identity chips brought heavy credit from the Asian syndicates.

"You on him, Three?" the voice said over the net.

"Like a mole."

"No heavy stuff. Mother doesn't want that. He gets out of hand, bring him back. A night in the Gutters ought to soften him," Control told him, referring to the MCC, the Metropolitan Correctional Center, a Medieval lice-hopping, rat-infested gaol by all accounts.

"Will do, Control."

But Crawling Face…

Trask kept imagining him, seeing some skull-smiling, doll-eyed, lamprey-mouthed night-haunter sucking in oxygen and breathing out pure methane vapor, a crawling infectious rot steaming from the shadows in a deadly chlorine mist, fingers sharpened in gutters and teeth like needles, multi-deranged and uttering a grim hysterical laughter. Not padded room, Thorazine-juicing-crazy in the conventional sense, but maybe believing that he…or *it*…and the city were clinging together in some maggoty graveyard symbiosis.

The old man cut into an alley and Trask followed, so close he could almost swim in his shadow. But right away he started getting the heebie-jeebies like crickets crawling up his bellyskin and down his spine. He could feel things moving around him, grotesque oblong shapes swimming in the ponds of mulling darkness. He moved forward, leather boots creaking on the concrete. He shut down his camo-screen. One moment he was a blur moving against the filthy bricks, the next, a man.

Tollan was there waiting for him.

A wasted stick figure whose breathing was the gurgle of ancient pipes in slum tenements. Trask just stared at him, trying to lubricate his tongue with words but the well was dry. The old man…Trask couldn't remember his name suddenly. It was there, then gone like a bat winging through his head and the more he tried to remember, the more that name was hot metal smoke on the wind searing the inside of his skull. The old man's eyes did not blink. They were feral-red baboon eyes…*Mother have mercy*…like blood-hot peepers peering from a dank bone-strewn cave. As if the old man had the bread and Trask was the meat that filled the space in-between.

Something momentarily softened around the old man's greasy mouth. He said: "Please…please just go away…I'm trying to disconnect."

By then Trask, veteran of so many blood wars and Mexican stand-offs, had filled his hand with an automatic. His voice was easy. It slid forth like oil on polished glass. "I'm not here to hurt you," he told the old party. "Just relax. I only have questions. There's been murders out in the Big Ugly. Bad shit, friend. CyberPath has traced you to each scene. I want to know your connection. We can do that here or we can do it in the Gutters."

"You want to know if I'm Crawling Face."

"Are you?"

"Yes, I'm Crawling Face. In fact, we're *all* Crawling Face."

"Make sense."

"I made a mistake. A bad mistake."

"Tell me."

The old man tried to, but none of it made sense. Not really. Something about hyperdimensional physics, vortexual displacements, and gravity sinks, the acceleration of angles and spatial derangements. That Mother was the key. Mother had worked out the variables and opened the door to what lay beyond.

"You're talking in riddles," Trask said, because even though it was intriguing, he could feel Mother getting restless at such talk.

But the old man did not hear him.

He was going on in some drug-addled, mind-fuck of a delirium about "the latticed doorway of the 5th Linkage" and "the festering polychromatic slum of frozen shadows" and "the labyrinthine tangle of intersecting mirror worlds." Stuff that was somehow disturbing, yet clearly the vomit of a mind wholly self-entrenched in a boozy tar pit. Trask kept trying to interrupt him, but his voice was not heard. The old man wanted him to know things and spoke to him through red lips speckled with white foam: *"You don't know and you don't listen. Mother teaches and Mother guides, but Mother is the enemy and the architect of Crawling Face…she has seeded it in billions of heads as it was seeded in her…she knows…she knows there are holes in the world and cracks in the continuum…and when you look through them…"*

"You're making no sense," Trask told him.

"I make sense of the senseless. Crawling Face! The keeper of the keys of the dark spaces between the stars, the shadow boxes, the mother-womb primal chaos of the anti-world."

"What does this have to do with anything?"

"Everything! Crawling Face has another name but I dare not speak it! The Cult of the Writhing Men, the Temple of the Boneless Woman…it was known that He, the Haunter of the Dark and the Bloody Tongue, would come, for His voice echoes in the void and only He is the Face-that-Crawls! Mother is not who she once was…"

"You're out of your fucking head," Trask told him.

"The crystals," the old man gasped. "They're falling through the rift! You've seen them! They're everywhere! There's one in your pocket. You're part of the matrix!"

Lunatic stuff, but Trask pulled out the crystal if for no other reason than to show the crazy old man that it was harmless. He found himself staring into it…and like before, things happened—he was seeing through darkest, unhallowed space to where a glaring three-lobed eye stared back.

No, no, no…

He saw many things, his thoughts brushing against the black satin facades of nightmare worlds. Mother should have stopped it, but she did not. His vision blurred; his head spun with strobing spokes of white light. But as he blinked it away, he saw that the old man had moved closer and something serpentine and bloated was filling his mouth like a fleshy eel, that his face was the bulb of a morbid crypt flower that wished to bloom, that his nose had gushed with a black-red expistaxis of blood…then the old man touched him with a hand that felt like the beslimed tendrils of an abyssal jellyfish and… *sweet Mother*…it was like a thousand hornets drilling their stingers into him at the same time.

He gasped. He shuddered. Pinpoint explosions erupted in his head and he twitched with clonic spasms, smelling the acid of burned-out batteries and dirty ozone, his brain filled with yellow vapors and quicksilver pulsations.

His eyes opening like flapping window shades…he saw the world unzip and expose its meaty gross anatomy, worming blue-green spheres gnawed at its pink, juicy tissues, revealing a churning black mist of lambent glow and shining multi-lobed diamond eyes—

Then he was back, panting, down on his knees, flesh gray as stove ash, a squealing sound coming from his throat like that of a peeled cat. He breathed in and out as phantoms swept through his vision, trying to feel for the here and the now, not sure where he was or *what* he was. There was a sucking feeling of dark velocities and vast spaces closing up behind him like lips, his body aching like he'd passed through a violent enemy flak of powdered glass. His brain seemed to vibrate in his skull, half-blurred memories and distortions flying through the field of his mind. Deranged geometrical shapes like trapezoids and octahedrons that crawled like worms. Moon-ladders rising into gulfs of seamless buzzing blackness. Tiers of protoplasmic slime and cuboids that inched slug-like in vacuums of suspended metallic dust. The universe itself shaking, pulsating, splitting open like an egg to disgorge a shivering fetal-headed excrescence with a body like a quivering sack of ropes.

Trask blinked his eyes for maybe the tenth time and it was gone.

The old man was still standing there stiffly as if in a trance, then his rheumy eyes fluttered open in a shadow-latticed face. They were like sink holes plunging into suffocating depths, windows looking into a room of blight and decay.

Over the net: "Three? Three? Are you there?"

Trask heard his own voice: "Ph'nglui mglw'nafh Cthulhu R'lyeh wgah'nagl fhtagn…"

Maybe the old man laughed with a sound like glass shards crunching under boots or maybe the noise was that of things stirring in backward, upside down spheres of time-space, but Trask saw his eyes, felt their heat. They were bright purple neon burning in the night, globular suns setting over poisoned dead worlds. The old man's flesh went to a jelly of bubbles, tendrils and tongues bursting forth from each until he was something like a wiggling mass of phosphorescent fingers, crawling and slithering things infesting him as his face and form liquefied into a plastic peristalsis of noxious organic profusion—

"Three, please respond immediately!"

Trask's gloved fist remembered the lethal contours of the automatic it gripped. It squeezed the trigger. Slugs punched the old man right between the eyes…or where they might have been if they hadn't slid from their housing in gelatinous globs. There was a metallic, echoing *clang!* as the rounds chewed into the green grimy dumpster behind him, going right through the metal, taking fragments of skull and brain with them. The old man dropped to the cool concrete and something like a glistening white worm fattened on soft tissues slid from his mouth. It sucked away blood and screams and the sugary marrow of burst bones.

And as Trask watched, it divided, then divided again, becoming a writhing plexus of worm-meat that netted the old man's remains and gorged itself on them before dissolving away into a fleshy pool of stringy mucus and steaming bile.

"Three? Your connectivity is coming and going…hell's going on?"

Trask, the inside of his throat swabbed with vomit, blinked his eyes. All he could see was the bullet-perforated corpse of an old man.

What the hell was that?

Glitch or something. For a moment there, everything rippled and Trask thought he was cashing out. Was it Mother? He wasn't so concerned for himself as with the possibility that Mother might crash. If the Pathway went, only chaos could ensue. This was what he knew to be true; he was conditioned to accept this as the ultimate inevitability.

Not Mother, asshole, but the death throes of Mother. The crystal, the crystal, the shining trapezohedron—

It was still in his hand, burning into his palm. He tried to toss it, but it didn't seem to want to leave his hand. *Get rid of it, you must get rid of it.*

"Three…goddammit! Your signals are erratic…"

His brain was disjointed now, the different spheres raging against one another as a spontaneous discharge of electrical energy shot through his nervous system. He heard a static crackling in his ears, felt a prickling up and down his spine. Mother was going to shut him down and he knew it.

"Three! Talk to me! Mother's getting aggravated!"

Trask heard the voice, but it was meaningless to him. Jibber-jabber, words as indecipherable as the buzz of mosquitoes. Abstract, entirely abstract. He heard a sharp beeping in his ears, a whine in his skull. And displayed on his synth-lens:

CYBERPATH GLOBAL, INC.
THIS PROGRAM IS UNRESPONSIVE
IT HAS PERFORMED AN ILLEGAL OPERATION
IT WILL BE SHUT DOWN IN TWELVE SECONDS

"Jesus Christ, Three…talk to me…you're being hibernated," said the voice of Control. *"Talk to me…"*

Trask tried to throw away the crystal again and Mother shot more electricity into his head. She wanted him to keep it. He was seeing too much and knowing too much. He was afraid to use his eyes. The world, the Big Ugly around him…it was synthetic, it was a skin, it was growing threadbare and he could see through it, see—

A blasphemous fairyland netherworld, which was neither here nor there. The howling discordant stellar noise of pulsing silence. Ghetto wasteland of screaming moonlight, cackling mortuary corridors, warped stairwells leading into black chasms of dripping nothingness. Corroded metal afterbirth—

IT WILL BE SHUT DOWN IN EIGHT SECONDS

Fuck. The countdown was underway and Trask felt things scuttling in his belly like land crabs, hot wires arcing in his chest, the reticulations of a python squeezing the breath from his throat. He wanted to speak, knew he must speak…but oh sweet quantum Mother…the words were leaping around in his head, but they couldn't find his tongue to make themselves known—

IT WILL BE SHUT DOWN IN SIX SECONDS

Control…control…I can't speak because my mouth doesn't work…my throat is paralyzed…help me oh sweet Mother help me I don't want to be shut down…I don't want my brain scrubbed…I don't want to be re-chipped and re-booted…I

IT WILL BE SHUT DOWN IN FOUR SECONDS

Then his voice coming out of his throat in a fluting scream: *"Control... control...I glitched...I glitched...but I'm back..."*

"Shit, that was close, Three."

SYSTEM SHUTDOWN STANDBY

"It was like a sheet on a line," Trask said. "Blowing around...it lifted and I saw through this world into the next."

"Come again, Three?"

Trask shook his head. "I think I was uplinked with Crawling Face."

"He rawdogged you?"

"No...I think it was psionic."

SYSTEM SHUTDOWN ABORTED

"You better watch it, Three. Play it real cool."

Trask said he was ice now, nothing but ice. But he knew better because something was happening and he could not put a name to it.

In the blue silence of his brain, there were voices. Although he refused to listen, he could not help hearing what they said. They told him that he was no longer hyperthreading in the liquid optical matrix of Mother, but scraping at the altar of something else entirely, something that had infected Mother. But Trask didn't want to hear that; it was too much like what the old man said. But the voices persisted. Mother was corrupting from the inside out.

Mother?

Mother?

But Mother would not answer or respond to such heretical ideas. Something had happened, something infinitely bad, and Mother was taking the Big Sleep and the results were in the streets. *Chaos.* Mother had tried to shut him down and it wasn't because he was unresponsive, but because he had tried to get rid of the crystal. For all her omnipotence, Mother knew and knew damn well that there was something much bigger than herself, something immense and dark that had invaded her like a cancer. She had communed with it now and as the old man had said, Mother was not who she once was.

As he eased his way through the streets, Trask reached out not just for Mother but for Control…but they were both gone, swallowed alive by the vapid evil pestilence that had invaded the Pathway neuroplex. He was off-network and the primary interface had broken down, mnemonics gone, quantum drive auto-cannibalizing itself.

All those chips in billions of heads, Trask got to thinking, all connected to Mother and now all connected to something else that was parsing every chipped brain out there, a malignant parasite mega-wired to every mind, glutting itself on parities and metadata, output and input, boot sectors and vectors, draining the power of those minds and sucking the blood from the cybersphere—

Trask's head hurt.

The thinking, the thinking, all the directionless random thoughts in his head with no overseer to direct them. *Oh, Mother, sweet Mother, help me, help me.* The electric lights were flickering above the streets, retro-neon sparking out, three-dimensional halo images moving against the faces of buildings like wriggling corpse-worms. Steam rose from sewer gratings and clouds of acrid-smelling ground mist tangled his legs.

He saw the crowds like mindless, scuttling insects, worming and writhing, leggy things clustering over the corpse of the Big Ugly, feeding off it. They quivered and danced, chanting and screeching, crying out in words that made no sense, yet…at the root core of the neuroplex interface in his brain… made all the sense in the world. Such chaos. What were they doing? An effigy was raised up on crude crossbars and set aflame…except it wasn't an effigy because effigies did not scream out for the protection of Mother. More such dummies were burning on every street corner, the crowds hysterical with delight. White-sheeted figures circled around them, but Trask saw that they were not sheets at all.

The noise.

The confusion.

The crackling fire and smoke and insanity.

The city was a crawling, festering cesspool of black malignancy and suffering mindless evil. Maybe this was what it had always been, Trask thought, but Mother's VR mask concealed it. Each night the city's flaxen legs were spread and each morning it picked parasites from its knotted bloody pelt and dropped them screaming into black sewers.

Trying to catch his breath, he looked around and everything was gray and sooty, leaning and tall and rotting. The air stank of industrial waste and baby hides, corpses left to boil in gutter pools. The shadow-dappled streets were Crawling Face's playground and his cobra eyes counted the dead children impaled on hooks in dusty butcher shop windows. The Big Ugly was made uglier as another reality crowded in, usurping the real and magnifying the anti-real.

Screaming, they never seemed to stop screaming.

A rush of bodies, eyes looking up at the misty stars above, a merry-go-round of dancing, lurking shapes and clutching shadows, a circumnavigation of people driven mad by every base desire Mother had forbidden. Uncaged, shrieking with lunacy and moon-fever—

Trask fell to the sidewalk, beating his fists as the cosmos about him whirled and gyrated, shaking the nits from its hide. It was like going cold again, getting off the hard stuff.

Sweet Mother…he could remember it now.

It was not an abstract concept, but a reality. Death-smell. That was the gritty pith of the thing…*death-smell.* That's what his nose was picking up. The death-smell that filled your head and popped in your brain like black blood blisters when you were suffering withdrawals. It wasn't a smell really, but a *lack* of the same. An absence of the perfume of the organic machinery that filled the spaces. It was gone.

And it was gone now.

Mother had been infected by what Tolan had let through and that infection crawled into every chip and on-line consciousness and now it was being fed back to her: refined, lethal, unspeakable.

These were things Trask had known for a long time only Mother, eaten away by a metastasizing multi-dimensional cancer, would not let him (or anyone else) think them. But he was offline now and he could see and he could think. *Remember.* Like a dog digging old bones from a ditch and gnawing them, he was remembering. *Yes, all of us in our dreams...we were supposed to be off-network, but we were cybered-in, we interfaced in our dreams, viruses digging deeper into the neuroplex, parasites laying our eggs in the neural cells of Mother, bringing forth a generation of noxious vermin. But Mother did not recognize it. She was parasitized like a fish that believes that the worm hanging from its gut is part of its body and protects it.*

Screaming as it all came apart around him, sensing something dark and malignant sitting bloated at the center of the neuroplex web, Trask ran.

The crystal in his pocket began to burn and he picked it up and threw it, but too late. Too late. It was glowing, pulsating with energy. He looked across the shattered landscape of techno-ruin and saw dozens and dozens of others holding up their shining trapezohedrons into the night. The Big Ugly was a city named Hunger and meat was its currency.

Trask stumbled along, rabid hairless dogs with blistered skins running in foam-mouthed packs. Eat and be eaten, that was the law of screaming genocide under the watchful gaze of Crawling face. He was coming even now...tri-lobed blood-eye of silver and sapphire watching, watching.

Yes, the stars were right and Trask could feel them burning holes through him. The world of Mother was an orb of rotten, juice-dripping fruit tunneled by worms. It was opening like spread legs, a cleft gushing with slick webby streamers of egg clusters hissing with pink radioactive steam, meaty pearls, pulsing alien honeycombs, clotted cocoons bursting with unformed raw yolk eyes, throbbing soft machinery, an immense deformed jelly fetus slithering from a crystalline placental sheath and the world, the Big Ugly responded in kind becoming becoming—

The Nameless City of rising jagged spires washed by corpse-clotted sewers wherein tumbled rivers of shrieking, undulant fetuses. A ramshackle cellar of morbid creation haunted by worms of polychromatic slime, chains of living bubbles that crawled across the sky. Beneath the hungry shadows of leaning, sharp-peaked roofs and grinning trapezohedron moons, Crawling Face waited.

Glitch.

Glitch.
Glitch.
What was this?
Mother?
Mother?

Trask could feel the chip in his brain interfacing with the neuroplex, being made part of it, connecting, spooling, hot-wiring and uploading. And on the synth-lens of his left eye he saw words:

CYBERPATH GLOBAL, INC.
!!!WARNING!!!
THIS PROGRAM IS INFECTED
BLOWFLY INTIATED
CLEANSING INFECTIVE ORGANISM
SECTOR ERADICATION COMMENCING
BLOWFLY INITIATED
BLOWFLY
BLOWFLY
BLOWFLY
BLOWFLY
BLOWFLY

What the hell?

Trask saw thousands, then millions, and possibly billions of iridescent spheres filling the sky like soap bubbles filling a sink. They expanded and then each popped like rippling ovum, releasing an oblong gelatinous worming shape of pink-gray tumescent flesh with an oval puckering mouth. They swam like blood-leeches filling a pond, raining down on the city and leaving a weird strobing radiant slime-trail of afterbirth in their wake. They swarmed the city like locust-hordes, their mouths chewing through the masses that had held their crystals up to the coming of the Haunter of the Dark, the physical embodiment of Crawling Face who was called in ancient tongues, Nyarlathotep.

This was Blowfly.

This was Mother cutting off the finger to save the hand, Trask knew.

Blowflies fed on carrion, on diseased and infected tissues, and that's exactly what these Blowflies were doing. Anti-viral, anti-infective, suckering, flesh-eating maggots that had been unleashed by Mother to eradicate and cleanse infected sectors…and those sectors were the chipped human brains that had first received the virtual entity of Crawling Face, the psychic emanation of Nyarlathotep, then externalized it to prepare the way by slaughtering the faithful as it must have been in ancient times.

The vermiform carrion-eaters swept through the crowds, cutting through them like buzzsaws, seeking out the psionic and radionic emissions of the chips themselves and neutralizing the brains that housed them. The streets were slaughter yards of human pulp and bone as the Blowfly larva tunneled through them, Cryoborgs and humans falling in great blood-greased headless heaps.

Trask heard them coming for him with their tell-tale droning.

As hell gathered and reaped, he stumbled through the wreckage of black pitted phosphorescent bones drying in cinder-slime corridors of the urban graveyard as the neon Blowfly eels skimmed human rivers in wakes of midnight crystal slime. Mother saw to her own in the end: no more tears, no more cold fears of post-modern angst or techno-despair, the human family dissolving, civilization sucked and leeched by sterile neuro-vampires.

Shattered glass carpeted streets…

…the Haunter sealed back in its bottle of atomic slime…

…the plastic forlorn eyes of Mother's Little Helpers glistening…

…the human garbage stew running wetly in the gutters as VR vectors closed back in to show a synthetic world that was brightly polished and filled with hope and peopled by scavenging graveyard rats. And as the Blowfly program ceased and the larva dissipated into the cyber-nothingness they were formed of, it was the Cyberpath's own voice that cried out in the silence of broken skulls:

Mother, I'm alone. Alone.
Mother
Oh, please, Mother help me

NEMESIS THEORY

1

His first day at Grissenberg, Johnny Coogan heard all about the three guys who'd gone over the wall. Dead of night, lockdown, and still they had gotten out. The hacks were watching everyone closely in case there would be more, some kind of mass escape like on TV, but the cons knew better. The warden could talk trash all he wanted to, but there was no way he was going to put a spin on it. Because there was one thing for sure: people were disappearing from his prison.

2

Over in C-Block, Coogan's cellmate, Luis Cardone, had been a dirt-crazy Latin terror on the streets, an enforcer for the Latin Lords street gang who'd been called the Junk Monkeys in Spanish Harlem because they pushed skag and rock to the poor and underprivileged. But inside the walls—doing life for multiple murder—he had become fascinated by the stars above. He talked at length about nebulas and pulsars and spiral galaxies. It got that way with cons, Coogan knew. When they went behind the walls and their old vices were denied them, they looked inside themselves and found something purely personal to obsess over. And if they didn't, they went insane.

"You ever hear of the Oort Cloud, home?" Luis asked him.

"Can't say that I have."

"It's something I keep dreaming about. The Oort Cloud."

Luis said the Oort Cloud was, theoretically, a misty spherical cloud of water, ammonia, and methane ices that existed just beyond Pluto. He said it was thought to be the remnant of the original solar nebula that collapsed into itself to form the sun and planets. It was also thought to be the home of comets, that gravitational forces of passing stars and the Milky Way itself occasionally dislodged comets that came shooting towards Earth and inner space.

"A passing star every thirty million years—a red dwarf maybe—sets loose a chain reaction of comets that bombard the Earth and cause mass extinctions," Luis explained, totally mesmerized by the subject. "That's called the Nemesis Theory. See, they think this star is a companion star to our sun, a dark star, they call it."

"You say it like you don't believe it."

Luis shrugged. "Oh, I believe it all right. I just wonder sometimes if it's more than that. Maybe not comets that come visiting us but something else…something not dislodged by a star but something that comes here because it *wants* to."

"Like something alive you mean?"

Luis shrugged again.

"Why do you dream about the Cloud?" Coogan asked him.

Luis shook his head. "I don't know. But the dreams are bad, man. Same dream all the time…that there's something out in the Oort Cloud, something watching us, something…terrible. It makes me wonder about the next extinction event."

Luis was a nut, but there was something sincere in his insanity as if he were trying to caution you, warning to the curious, be careful, my brother, for here there be monsters.

At Leavenworth, Coogan had celled with an old-school bank robber named Bobby LeForest who'd been raised right, meaning he'd been around the prison block a few times. Bobby was great, but now and then he'd go crazy and start foaming at the mouth, start shouting at the ghosts of men long dead.

So, all things considered, Coogan understood crazy and figured he could live with it. Besides, when you were in a cage, you had to learn tolerance. And part of that was taking an interest in your cellmate's obsession.

"Hear you didn't like the accommodations at the Hot House, home," Luis said to him, meaning the Leavenworth federal pen.

"Nah. I decided to leave in the back of a bakery truck. Problem was, they caught me."

Luis laughed.

Coogan was sitting on a federal stretch for armed robbery, extortion, and grand larceny, ten years, which ran consecutively with the three years' state time he'd already pulled at Auburn in New York for burglary. And that—the ten years—was only because his lawyer, some greasy Jew that talked out of the side of mouth, plea bargained it down. Otherwise, it would have been twenty, easy. Except…now it was fifteen years because of that escape attempt at Leavenworth that had landed him here at Grissenberg. *Fifteen years.* Some of the cons, especially those doing all day, said you could do fifteen years standing on your head. Wasn't shit. But as Coogan sat there, looking at the walls of his cage, fifteen years was a long time. Fifteen years could squeeze the juice from a man. He'd already been squatting in the darkness of Leavenworth for two years and Auburn Correctional for three, be another seven before he was even eligible for parole.

"Well, I hope you like it here in Griss City," Luis told him. "Even though I know you won't."

Coogan figured he wouldn't either. He could see all those years stretching out before him, an endless black corridor with no light at the end.

Luis was standing over by the window, face pressed up against the iron bars, staring out past them and through the steel mesh beyond. He motioned Coogan over. "Look," he said. "Do you see it?"

Coogan squinted, seeing the towers of Grissenville, a patch of starlit sky above…except that part of it was gone. There was a spiraling arm of blackness cut through it.

"A cloud?"

Luis nodded. "Something like a cloud. Started about a month ago and every night it gets bigger, eats up more sky. It's getting closer to us. You can only see it at night."

Coogan made the connection, of course. "You think it's coming, don't you? What's in the Oort Cloud?"

Luis climbed up into his bunk and stretched out. "Not a matter of what I think, but a matter of what I *know*. Every night, a little bigger, a little closer. Sounds whacked, I know. But you wait…you'll see how things are here… you'll see it getting closer night by night. You'll feel it under your skin. Then I won't be the only crazy one."

3

Chi Chi said they pinched him on a bullshit possession rap, claimed he was mothering two keys of Mexican Brown with intent to distribute interstate and how right they were. He figured his ex had fingered him because he'd beaten her ass when he caught her in bed sharing the goods with her brother-in-law. Beat her, tossed her out into the streets. Thing was, he had two keys of junk sliced into nickel bags fresh from his cutting house over in Bed-Sty—ten naked Panamanian broads, speakee no English, sitting around in a sealed room, cutting skag with quinine and milk sugar, bagging it up—just waiting for his mules to show, but who shows instead are a squad of DEA narcs that kick down the door, the pigs that blow his house down.

"But that shows you how fucking stupid they are," Chi Chi was saying to Coogan, watching the cons holding court, roosters strutting around with no hens to impress. "Because I had three keys of pure Sicilian in the trunk of my car and they never even looked."

Rosalie flipped when Chi Chi turned his back on her. Went screaming to the feds, fingering his operation. He went to prison, but she—who just had a real hunger for the needle—spiked enough pure cocaine to kill ten men, courtesy of Chi Chi. It was called a "hot-shot" and it was the execution of choice for junkies. Just try and prove it.

The war stories and fish tales were swapped back and forth. It was good to hook up with Chi Chi again, Coogan figured. The two of them had been a real terror at the Hot House. Chi Chi was this tall, wiry street eater who wore his hair in long dreadlocks and had a single gold tooth that winked in the sun. Easy, cool as ice, but don't get him riled.

"What about these escapes?" Coogan asked. "Like a dozen in the last month? Am I hearing this shit right?"

"You are."

"Hell's going on?"

Chi Chi said it was anyone's guess. There didn't seem to be any connection between them, only that somehow, someway, they dropped out of sight... permanently. Grissenberg had a funny way of losing people.

"Some kind of pipeline out of here?" Coogan said, intrigued by the idea.

Chi Chi laughed with a cold, bitter sort of sound. "You got to consider the boys we talking about here. These last three—Tony Babbott, Charley Le Roy, and a big ugly walking slab they called Sludge. LeRoy was a TV star, sure as shit. They featured his ass on one of those America's Dumbest Criminals shows. He was the one who robbed three convenience stores in the tri-state area wearing his uniform from Quik-Lube. You know, the one with his name tag on it."

Chi Chi elaborated. He said Babbott wasn't much smarter. He was a car-jacker. He stole five cars in one night, moved 'em across state lines. By the time he jacked the last one—a late-model Lexus—he was tired, so he decided to unload it first thing in the morning. He parked it in his mother's driveway and went to bed. Somehow, a Lexus sedan stood out in the ghetto and the cops made him right away.

"Yeah, okay, they were both idiots," Coogan said. "What about Sludge?"

Chi Chi laughed. "He weren't no smarter, Coog. Thought his girlfriend was screwing some dude she worked for, so he tracked him down and shot him in full view of like ten witnesses. Only problem was Sludge, with his fifth-grade education and all, couldn't read the name on the mailbox so he tracked down the wrong dude and killed him. Guy he wasted was a U.S. Treasury agent." Chi Chi blew smoke out his nose, laughing. "So that's our three masterminds. You think either of them had the smarts to escape from a Level Five maximum security federal pen? I'm thinking not."

"Then where are they?"

Chi Chi shrugged. "I don't know. They dropped into a big black hole."

Chi Chi said LeRoy and Babbott were cellies, but Sludge was celling with some big oily Albanian drug lord they called Mick the Dick around the block, a.k.a. "The Three-Legged Man," a crude reference to his personal equipment.

"So, okay, Coog, LeRoy and Babbot slip away. But how did Sludge slip away without even waking Mick the Dick up? They were locked in together."

Coogan said he didn't have a clue.

"Nobody does. The other nine missing cons all disappeared at night, after lockdown. Warden's going apeshit."

"Gotta be a connection."

"Maybe there is," Chi Chi said, "and maybe it's not one you or me want to find out about."

When Coogan asked him what the hell he meant by that, Chi Chi just shook his head. "See that fish over there? Standing by the fence?" he said. "That's Eddie Sloat. Recognize the name? You heard about Nithonville? That cult in the mountains of Vermont about three years back? All them bodies? Shit. Another Jonestown. Sloat was the leader. He walked away."

Sloat. Eddie Sloat. Sure, Coogan remembered. Lot of weird shit was being talked about that Nithonville business. Hundreds of bodies. The feds were saying they swallowed poison, but lots of stories had leaked out about the condition of the corpses, how poison could not make bodies liquefy into slime. Some people were even saying that Sloat was some kind of Antichrist, if you could dig that.

Coogan eyed him up. Nothing special. Tall, greasy-looking, black shoe-button eyes scanning the yard.

But there was something about the guy.

He was getting a very strange vibe from him. It wasn't the usual prison thing—antagonism or disrespect or slow-simmering violence—it was something else, something that he could not put a finger on. It made him feel like there was a hole in his belly and everything was waiting to drop right out. Though it was August and warm, a sudden cold gust blew through the yard bringing gooseflesh to his arms. It made a moaning sound as it skirted the blockhouses and chapel, like a wailing dirge blown through a skull.

Coogan kept staring.

His image of Eddie Sloat began to blur, to shimmer like a heatwave… and he *changed.*

Coogan almost fell off the bench. A feeling of stark, unreal terror rose up inside him and he forced it back down. That wasn't Eddie Sloat, it was someone else.

That's Franky McGrath, that's goddamn Franky McGrath.

Coogan figured he'd know him anywhere because he'd watched him die at Auburn Correctional in New York.

Even now he could see McGrath's cold grin as he jointed a body, first the arms, then the legs. That grin…like a dead carp smiling up at you…had haunted Coogan's dreams for years.

Hallucination.

But Eddie Sloat looked just like Frank McGrath all of a sudden.

Coogan could feel reality warping, shattering, and finally unraveling all around him.

An oven-hot dry wind began to blow from Sloat/McGrath and Coogan could smell nitrous age like a brown death-fog blown from a coffin. It was the commingled stench of gangrenous wounds and flesh burnt to ash, of cesspools bubbling with vomit and dripping corpse slime. A vile stink that was unlike anything he had ever smelled before. His febrile human imagination could not define it nor encapsulate it.

And Sloat…McGrath…whoever he was, Jesus, he seemed to crack open like a yellow eggshell and something came pouring and slithering out…a bulbous undulant mass that was webby and bloated, strands and fibers of gelatinous tissue growing through him and out of him, glistening tendrils waving in the air like the tentacles of a squid. The right side of his body was all snotty lacework and living mesh. The left was blown up like balloons, a heaving profusion of pale sacs like the floats of a jellyfish set with purple vein tracery. As he breathed, those sacs expanded with a rubbery sound.

Coogan saw the thing bulge and burst open with a profusion of juicy red tentacles, each one reaching out towards him—

Then it was gone.

He sat there, stunned, shocked, mouth hanging open, a glazed and impossible fear in his eyes.

"You okay, Coog?" Chi Chi said. "Look like you're having a fucking stroke or something."

Coogan swallowed, kept it together. "So what's he doing here?" he managed in a scraping dry voice.

"Feds dropped him on three child murders, all day, life without parole," Chi Chi said.

Coogan looked over towards the fence.

Sloat was standing there, not Franky McGrath. Not some B-movie slime monster.

Fuck is going on here?

Am I losing it?

"Coog?" Chi Chi said, but Coogan did not answer him because it was Eddie McGrath again and he was staring right at him and it was at that moment that something took hold of him, grasping him like hands and squeezing his throat shut. He shook. His eyes rolled white. His vision blurred, ran like hot taffy, and he looked beyond this world and into a ...graveyard. He saw Griss City...but with corpses sprawled out in the yard and through the blocks, mess hall, chapel, and industry buildings. The remains of cons mutilated, stabbed with holes, piped and shanked and pickaxed, many cut in half and others nothing but pools of limbs and entrails, all of it spread about like red-stained paper dollies, an intricate mesh of decomposition melting into a communal carrion...a conga line of corpses dissolving into a red, bubbling jelly.

And above, high above, but getting closer every moment, something like a chaotic maelstrom of spiraling matter and boiling black mist hanging over the prison and irising open like an eye...

Coogan blinked his eyes and it was gone.

"Coog," Chi Chi said, taking hold of him. "You all right?"

Coogan swallowed, shook his head. He saw Grissenville as it was again. No Franky McGrath with death-polished eyes, just Eddie Sloat standing there. "Had a...a...a..."

"Vision?" Chi Chi said. "Thought you saw that peckerwood become something else?"

"Yeah."

"You're not the first. Lot of people afraid of that white boy, Coog," he said, pulling a cigarette from behind his ear and lighting it with a cupped match. "Mmm-hmm, but you'll hear all about that. He has a funny effect on the cons: they either want to piss their pants or they want to kill the fucker."

Coogan didn't say anything. For one crazy second there he thought he saw formless shadows sweeping around Sloat. But he blinked and then it was gone. Heatstroke, hallucination, dust devil madness or something. He balled his hands into fists and steadied himself.

"You're gonna meet all the same types in here you knew in the Hot House," Chi Chi told him. "Only worse. See that fat black dude over there? Yeah, that's Buster Cray. He's a player. Those boys with him, all local talent. Buster's moving junk and blow inside these walls. Check it out. See how Buster's thugs are trolling around by Sloat. Gonna be trouble. Buster wants Sloat dead."

"What's the beef?"

"Personal. That cult Sloat had? One of the corpses was Buster's niece."

"Shit."

Chi Chi said Buster's muscle were all strictly lifers. They had nothing to lose. They did what they were told because he had the green and they had no fear.

Coogan watched them close in on Sloat.

In the joint, becoming a blood enemy of somebody like Buster Cray meant you were on your way to becoming a corpse. Eddie Sloat should have been keeping a low profile, begging the guards to give him protection, throw him in the Protective Custody Unit with all the other snitches, weaklings, and baby-rapers…but he wasn't begging for PCU. In fact, he didn't look afraid at all.

Just…*crazy.*

Chi Chi pointed out another fearsome-looking black dude. "That's Bug-Eye. He's a fucking whack. He's gonna come up behind Sloat and…nope, here come the hacks."

Two guards scoped it out and went over there. Buster's muscle strolled away. Bug-Eye faded into the crowd. Sloat was staring at Buster now and you could almost smell the hatred. Buster turned away, couldn't meet the stare. He looked like a little kid that had just heard claws scratching under his bed.

Coogan studied the gray concrete towers and blockhouses of Grissenberg

Correctional, the seventy-foot red brick wall that hemmed it all in, wondering what it might be like to go over that wall. Or maybe right through the gate.

His mind went back to Franky McGrath: the devil in the dark, the boogeyman licked with white flesh, an Aztec god of sacrifice with yellow bone-slat teeth and eyes glistening white like plump corpse-fed maggots, bright red clown hair swept up in a duckbill d-8 and worn down in spots so you could see the shining Neanderthal skull beneath. Always grinning, grinning, grinning. *Fucker grins like a corpse,* Sean Bolland had once said at Auburn. *You notice that? Like a corpse that just woke up.* Sure, that was McGrath. Always flashing his death-white pearlies, lips pulled back so you could see gray gums and narrow vampire teeth. That grin always made the cautious wonder which graveyard old Franky McGrath had looted through for his cold supper.

Limbs are hard to get free from their sockets, Coog, so don't dick around none, just take a saw and cut 'em.

Coogan found he was suddenly very short of breath, hands with iron fingers squeezing his windpipe shut.

Sloat was over by the fence again…then it was not Sloat, it was Franky McGrath, grinning like a fetish skull in a bokor hut, eyes huge and sewer-dark like toxic oil spills. Coogan could see himself drowning in them, a mastodon sucking into tarry depths. Another gust of wind kicked up, making something in the distance clatter like a wind chime strung with white-polished infant bones. It carried a sudden memory of black death that he knew in his marrow.

Then Sloat again, just Sloat.

"Who did he show you?" Chi Chi said. "I don't know what it is, Coog. But he can hypnotize you or something like a snake. He's bad news, that one. Makes you see things that ain't there. Sends dreams and shit into your head. He's done it with me. You ask Luis about it. Luis knows things. He'll tell you."

Had Chi Chi said something like that and with that rubbery sort of fear in his voice when they were back in the Hot House, Coogan would have laughed. Chi Chi really feared no one. But Sloat had him worked up like he had a lot of them worked up now. "What's his thing? How'd he do this?"

Chi Chi wiped sweat from his face. "I don't know, man. Depends who you ask. Some of these boys in here think he's a witch or warlock or something." Chi Chi shook his head. "I don't bother about that bullshit. But I do know one thing. Those twelve that we lost in the night? Sloat named them all before they disappeared. Pointed at 'em and said they were going on a trip."

Coogan just sat there, pulling off a cigarette, curdled white inside, knowing that this cage he found himself in was like no other he had ever known.

4

FCI Grissenberg was a maximum-security federal penitentiary that housed the very worst of the worst: drug traffickers and contract killers, psychopaths and gangbangers, Mafia soldiers and mass murders, terrorists, racists, mental cases and hardcase predators of every conceivable stripe. It was a pit. Bare-bones Darwinism at its most degenerate: survival of not only the fittest, but the dirtiest and meanest and craziest. A dumping ground haunted by tattooed, dead-eyed monsters that were constantly patrolling the yard looking for weaklings to exploit and victims to torment.

It sat atop a low hill, a mausoleum-gothic, gray-painted madhouse enclosed by high tombstone walls. Beyond those walls, there was nothing but carefully-shorn fields for half a mile in any direction (a con escaped, there was nowhere to hide) and nothing but miles of tangle-dark forest after that. Not even a town within five miles. Within the walls, there were Prison Industry buildings, an infirmary (known as the "Corpse Farm"), an administrative wing, a chapel, and a rectangle formed by concrete cellblocks that looked like drab gray monoliths from the outside and stacked tiers of monkey cages from the inside. Within this rectangle was a hard-packed dirt yard that turned to mud every spring. Year-around, it was patrolled by nervous-eyed hacks who suspiciously—and often *fearfully*—watched the old bulls and hardtimers, but particularly the gangs: the Aryan Brotherhood—the ABs—Jamaican Posses, the Mexican Mafia, the D.C. Blacks, various cliques of outlaw biker gangs like the Hell's Angels, Mongols, and Outlaws.

This was Grissenberg.

This was the cage.

5

Three more escapes. Warden Sheens couldn't believe it. He'd worked for the federal Bureau of Prisons for twenty-seven goddamn years and had seen a total of three successful escapes in all that time and now, in the span of a week, he had five. Which brought the grand total to a dozen in the past month.

And it all started the day Eddie Sloat showed up, Sheens thought, clenching his hands into fists. *The day that puke was processed in from FCI Terra Haute.*

No, no, he wasn't going there. Leave that crazy thinking to the shitheads in the cages; he was above all that. He had to be above all that.

The BOP was jumping up and down on his hairy ass and he was repaying in kind by jumping ass all the way from Captain Getzel to his lieutenants to every goddamn guard on the line. And he told them all the same thing: *this* was unacceptable, *this* was fucking unheard of, and *this* had better goddamn well get sorted out or there was going to be a lot of correctional officers flipping burgers at Mickie fucking Dees.

Getzel tried talking sense to him. "Warden…this is weird…but Eddie Sloat keeps predicting who it's going to be. He names them before they go. He—"

"I don't give a high happy shit what Sloat says, you moron," Sheens told him in no uncertain terms. "Eddie Sloat is a fucking mental case. He belongs in psych, but like every other dysfunctional, disillusioned, demented piece of shit in the system, he gets dumped in my fucking lap. I don't want to hear another word about that drooling, delusional brain-dead squirt of piss. You hear me?"

"Yes, sir," Getzel said, having the feeling that his balls were in the process of being squeezed in a vise.

"Sloat is crazy. End of story. You think I'm going to buy that fucked-up shit the cons are saying? That Eddie Sloat is some kind of fucking prophet or warlock or whatever in the Christ? Jeeee-suuuus, Captain! Enough already!

You get on those monkeyfucks you call correctional officers! I want this goddamn place locked-down! I want every cell turned! I want every man searched! Offer your goddamn rats some cheese and get 'em talking because somebody has to know something! And if they won't talk, take every prisoner to medical and give them a personal finger wave! There's an underground railroad out of this place and I want it closed for business!"

"Yes, sir. It's already being done."

"So get going, man," Sheens told him. "Because right now I have to call a certain congressman with the BOP oversight committee who takes extreme pleasure in using my rectum for a hatbox! Go! *Go!*"

Over the next twenty-four hours every prisoner was duly searched, every cell shaken down…but nothing came to light. Grissenberg was locked down for seventy-two hours, but no one was saying squat.

At least, nothing that made any sense.

6

In the dream, Coogan fell into a darkness that was smooth like smoked glass. Night rushed out with a blackness that was sullen and consuming, all black funeral crepe and graying shroud and spreading ebon mist. It came out as gaunt shadows that pooled and settled, fattening and bloating on their own excess, overflowing their banks and sinking the universe into a pit of crawling darkness.

It made no sense, but this was what he saw and came to know:

He was drawn down a black corridor that echoed with crystalline laughter that shattered around him. The shards were very sharp, he could feel them cut his skin. He was not alone, within and without, there were others pressing in, whispering and humming profane melodies.

He saw eyes like green gemstones, burning a hot indigo-emerald like steaming reactor cores. He was propelled forward into a yawning abyss of mirrored grayness. More eyes watched him, huge slit cat's eyes and tiny bubbling toad's eyes and eyes like yellow diamonds. They followed him in pods and clusters. He found himself in a field of bloated corpse-white growths that came up above his waist. They felt moist and fleshy and vital as they brushed against him, whipping and arcing, coiling over his wrists and crawling up his arms like fleshy vines. They were sticky and damp and he was held fast.

He began to thrash.

He began to scream.

He tore them free in rank, slithering handfuls…then he was stumbling through the viscid garden of threading fungi until he fell panting at the threshold of a city that was like no city he had ever seen before: immense windowless towers of black stone that looked not so much as if they had been built, but like they had *grown* like mineral crystals, polished and shining, reaching up to a sunless and moonless sky of luminescent elliptical green clouds.

Behind him, the fungus rustled with secret undercurrents and tides, whispering and hissing. He looked back but once and thought he saw a dozen distorted faces float from the verdant growths like rising bubbles.

Before him was a single murky oval mouth leading into one of the towers. Inside, it was a shadow-riven cavity that refused moonlight and starlight and anything bright or revealing. A high standing tomb of mystery and dank secret and no light dared reveal its dark glory.

But he could *see,* it seemed, with another sense that was relative to sight yet nothing so crude or rudimentary.

His field of vision was a pulsating pellucid blue phosphorescence. It showed him the room which was spatially deranged, an endless, dizzying space of limitless blackness which reached up into the very heart of the cosmos itself. He was aware of great heights above and plummeting depths below. He moved through the emptiness until he saw twelve cylinders of blue-black metal that gleamed like polished glass.

It was here he stopped.

With that activated, unknown sixth sense, he knew there were living things in the cylinders, conscious and sentient, and that each was aware he was looking at them because they were looking at *him.*

He pulled himself away with horror and then he was leaving the building, being expelled like a pea from a pod, out into the city itself, lost in the mazelike tangle of its streets. And above those towering buildings, rising like a full moon over a stark, dead necropolis…a face.

Immense.

Impossible.

A grotesque, distorted face that was like white graveyard fungi set with huge black doll's eyes and a yawning oval mouth popping open like a blood blister. It drifted closer to him, ethereal and disembodied, coming to swallow the city. He could feel a damp chill of night-black tomb hollows coming off it, smell its breath which was rotting fish and subterranean sewer stagnation.

It whispered something to him that was devastating: *You will be saved.*

7

Coogan came awake gasping for breath. He could still feel that choking, airless void scratching at his lungs. Pawing sweat from his face with both hands, studying his dampened fingers and the dew glistening upon them, he fell to the floor, shaking, his guts coming up the back of his throat like knotted slime-snakes.

"You were dreaming, home," Luis told him, his voice not crusty with sleep, but clear and soft as if he had been watching the whole thing.

Coogan picked himself up off the floor. "I never dreamed liked that before."

"Maybe it was a vision. Maybe you were plugged into something out there. Maybe you should tell me about it."

Coogan lit a cigarette and did just that. He told him about the fields of fungi, the city, the building, the canisters, and about that noxious face rising above it all.

"I could feel it right away...something watching me in the city. Staring down from the green sky."

"And...?"

Coogan sighed and laid it all out. "Today, Chi Chi pointed out Eddie Sloat...but I didn't see Sloat. I saw a guy that's been dead for years. But he was there. He was looking right at me...then it was..."

"What?"

Coogan shook his head, decided to leave the monstrous thing he'd seen out of it.

Luis thought about it for some time. "Funny how all roads lead back to Eddie Sloat in this place." He listened to the night, cocking his head as he did from time to time. "You ain't the only one dreaming of that place, home. Lots of us are. Lot more can't handle the dreams and they get dragged off to Psych. The rest of us…we just live with it. Those canisters. Tell me about 'em."

"Just a dream," Coogan said, blowing smoke at the ceiling. "That's all. Just dreams—"

"Tell me."

"There was something in 'em, something alive. Something that could see me or feel me or know I was there. I can't explain it. Don't ask me to."

Luis just sat there silently. Finally, he said, "I've seen those canisters. Lots of us have. There's something definitely in 'em…only a lot of us don't wanna know what."

Coogan thought it was all fucking crazy and told him so. Sloat sending out dreams to people, making cons disappear in the night. Everyone dreaming the same shit. Fantasy. It was all warped fantasy. Just as bad as Luis and his dreams of something malignant waiting out in the Oort Cloud, creeping a little closer to Earth each night.

"You saw that hole in the sky, Coog. You denying what your eyes show you?"

"Shit."

"Then listen."

"What?"

"Close your eyes, my friend," he said, "and…just…listen. You can hear it out there. *Listen.*"

The cigarette smoldering between his lips, Coogan did just that. And was it hyper-charged imagination or was he really hearing something? A sort of droning, a distant breathing of colossal gulfs…the steady hissing static of dead-end space inching closer and closer.

He crushed out his cigarette and pulled the thin federal-issue pillow over his head to shut it out. *No, I won't listen, I won't hear…THAT. I won't let myself…*

8

Coogan knew what everyone else knew about Eddie Sloat: a gamey mix of fact and bullshit twined so tight it was hard to say where one began and the other ended. Mostly tabloid stuff. Some kind of cult activity in Vermont. A tent city called Nithonville. A brainwashed sect and a mass suicide on a mountain hilltop in the shadow of some weird Druidic-looking stone circle. Sloat walked away. But the majority—nearly 500 men, women, and children—minds ripped open on hallucinogens, did not. Depending on who you asked and what you were willing to listen to, they either slit their throats, tore out their own eyes, or were poisoned…sometimes all three. Rumor had it their bodies were discovered in a morbid, gelid state, and more than one story was floating around that, upon postmortem examination, their brains were missing—and this without a single suture mark, scar, puncture, or pinprick.

One fact was immutable: Eddie Sloat walked away.

Nobody seemed to have a clue who he was before he formed the cult, recruiting members from every imaginable economic, social, and racial grouping, but afterwards, every newsmagazine, network, and police agency followed his every move.

Hunted by the FBI, Sloat moved west. Then the child murders. One in Nevada, another in California, and then a third. The State Police arrested him outside Antimony, Utah. He had the body of his last victim in the trunk. Examination showed no signs of abuse or molestation. In fact, the medical examiner and his people could never adequately determine the cause of death.

At least publicly.

Privately, they knew all too well: the child's brain had been removed. Just like the others. But as to where it was or how it could have been removed from the skull without incision or puncturing of any sort was a mystery.

And one not shared with the public.

But as far as law enforcement were concerned, Sloat had strangled the children and Sloat—defending himself—did not argue the point. He had crossed state lines, so it became a federal matter and that bought him a cage at Grissenberg.

9

Out in the field, it was con vs. con, and everyone—even the guards—were booking action, even though gambling of any sort was strictly forbidden by the BOP.

The two teams were lined up: blacks on one side, whites on the other. The former were gangbangers, traffickers, maniacs sitting on federal time; the latter, bikers, Aryan Brothers, intolerant rednecks that just liked to hurt anything with skin darker than their own. They wore no pads, no helmets. They liked it better that way, venting their aggressions.

Coogan watched as the white quarterback got hit on a screen pass, fumbled, some dreadlocked beast from one of the Jamaican Posses picked the ball up, zig-zagging five yards real sweet and easy, then a massive biker took hold of him, beat him down, and smashed his knee into his midsection about four times in rapid succession. The Jamaican went down, laying there, trembling. The game started getting ugly. Lots of pushing and shoving, racial slurs flying around. The hacks charged over there with their sticks, breaking it up.

Tony Bob, one of the yard hacks, came by, looked Coogan up and down, winked, motioned with his stick at the men in the field. "Hell kind of game is that supposed be?" he said, a vein in his thick neck pulsing. "What the fuck do they call that?"

"Football, boss," Coogan told him.

"Football? I played football two years for Ohio State before my knee locked and you know what? That ain't football."

When he went on his merry way and the cons in the field had been dispersed, Coogan looked over by the chapel.

Sloat was back.

And that baby-raping motherfucker was staring right at him.

He paced back-and-forth in a loose-limbed shuffle. His hair was dark, greasy like an oil spill. It matched the color of his eyes which were black as burnt cork. His face was sunless and pale, nearly bloodless, and it made those simmering ebon eyes look as dark and bottomless as abyssal depths.

"Wait here," he told Chi Chi and Luis. "I want to get a closer look."

"Don't do it," Luis warned him. "Please, man, don't stir things up."

But he was going. Something in him demanded it.

"Watch yourself," Chi Chi told him. "Hacks be eyeballing us."

Coogan crossed the yard, made small talk with a couple old cons over by the bleachers that hadn't seen the light of day in forty years, all the time keeping his eye on Sloat. He left the cons, walked right past Sloat who was standing all alone in the center of the yard, a knife-slash grin cut into his pallid face, his eyes like dead roads through miasmic swamps.

Coogan stopped, lit a cigarette, his back to Sloat.

You really want to do this?

He could feel Sloat watching him and something about that brought a chill like a cold breath at his neck. He turned, wrinkling his nose against a sudden foul odor in the air. It was musky and hot like a reptile house and it seemed to be coming from Sloat.

"Fuck you staring at, asshole?" he heard himself ask.

He stepped closer even though, with that smell boiling hotter by the moment, the idea was repugnant. Sloat just kept grinning and Coogan knew he was going to have to hurt him. It would get him a week in the hole, but it would have to be done because Sloat was staring, grinning like a sawtoothed pumpkin, disrespecting him.

It would be a simple matter.

Coogan was a practiced streetfighter, fast and lethal. His upper body strength was awesome from working the iron pile: shoulders broad and sculpted, neck like a tree stump, arms corded thick with muscle. Even then he could feel it coming over him, the need to hurt this fish, to prove his dominance. His legs were already bending into it, thrumming with power like pistons. He'd swing out with his right and if Sloat was any kind of man he'd try to block it and when he did, Coogan would jab him in the side hard enough to snap a rib.

Closer now, that stench rising and making his stomach roll. "I said, fuck are you staring at?"

If Sloat was afraid, he did not show it. He just stood there, his grin widening until it looked like it would eat his face. So pale he looked like a clown, but not a funny one, but maybe one that drove around with dead children in the trunk of his car.

Coogan could hear Chi Chi and Luis coming to intervene, but he knew Sloat would be on the ground long before they did. Because he could not stop it now. He *needed* to throw this smarmy baby-raper a good beating. Sloat needed to be stomped, squashed flat like some leggy thing that had crawled out from a webby cellar corner.

Then two things happened.

The first was that it wasn't Eddie Sloat standing there, it was Franky McGrath: huge, bristling, death-hunger in his eyes. Then the voice came, hollow and windy from distant gulfs: *"Just like Auburn again, eh, Coog? You and me sharing our dirty little secrets."*

The tattoos on McGrath's arms—things like spiraling symbols and letters intertwined by serpents and clustered eyes and twining wormlike feelers—seemed to be moving, wavering, swirling together like steam rising from a pot, becoming a slithering tapestry of hallucinatory vermiform life.

Coogan felt cold sweat wash down his face.

He heard the high, profane laughter of a child at his left ear.

And then it was Sloat standing there again, his grin ever-widening, an obscene smile of shattered glass. In a hollow sexless voice that seemed to echo from subterranean depths, he said, *"You will be saved."*

"Fuck…fuck did you say?" Coogan managed as his mind screeched with black noise and threatened to close like the petals of a flower.

But then Chi Chi and Luis were pulling him away and he was too weak too fight, leeched dry, numb.

Sloat just stood there, grinning.

But now that Coogan was out of the play, a couple scavengers moved in for their piece of the pie. Two black cellies that were known around the block as Rondo and Mondo and were sitting, cumulatively, on thirty years for narcotics trafficking. They came right up to Sloat and that fool could not stop smiling.

"I figure you pay us a couple bills a week, whiteboy," Rondo said, "and we'll keep you a virgin. How's that sound?"

Mondo giggled. He giggled at everything Rondo said.

Coogan was seeing it, hearing it, knowing how the game was played.

Maybe these two wanted Sloat's love and maybe it was pure extortion, hard to say. But another hardcase BLA banger was watching what was going down real closely and that pretty much gave it away. These two would give Sloat a hard time and the other guy would come to his rescue, protect him, and that's how it would work. He probably paid Rondo and Mondo to do what they were doing.

But again, Sloat did not look afraid.

"You hear what the man said, you whitebread motherfucker?" Mondo told him with absolute threat behind his words.

Rondo was going to take it up a notch but he stopped suddenly. His mouth opened, then closed. Beneath his dark skin, he was pale.

Something had switched here. The aggressor was becoming the victim and you could see it happen just as you could see Sloat feeding on it, pumping himself up with it. His eyes were so huge they seemed to be coming right out of his head like two black glossy eggs. "Will you be saved, my brothers?" he asked them. "Or will you seek communion with the Black Mist?"

Rondo tried to speak, but his throat was filled with a seeping dark sludge; he tried to look away, but Sloat's eyes held him spellbound in a cat's cradle of tomb-dark silences. When he did blink it was with tears of pain for he had been drawn into the black wormholes of Sloat's eyes and been shown something distorted and unreal and grotesque.

Rondo stared in shock at Sloat, drool hanging from his mouth, gibberish falling from his lips: *"Cthulu Fhtagn! Iä Iä Cthulhu Fhtagn!"* Then his hand came out with a razor and he slashed Mondo across the eyes.

Mondo sank to his knees, but did not try to protect himself. He held his hands up in supplication, mumbling something, his eyes crying scarlet tears. Rondo laid open his throat again and again until hot pumping blood sprayed over him like an inkblot, bright red and glistening.

Mondo made a gurgling sound and fell face-first to the ground, dead or near to it.

And by then the hacks were everywhere, knocking Sloat aside and beating Rondo to the ground with their sticks while hundreds of cons stood around and watched silently, their eyes wide, their mouths moving but no sounds coming out.

Chi Chi and Luis had gotten Coogan back to the table by then.

"What kind of shit was that?" Chi Chi said. "You see it? Did you fucking see that?"

Coogan saw all right. He sat there, trying to find his center, trying to tell himself that he had not seen those tattoos move on McGrath's arms. Had not seen them slither and crawl, rising up from the flesh in a multitude of writhing maggoty forms then pull aside like curtains to give him a view of that dead city from his dreams: a necropolis going to slime and rot in the pathless wastes of some interdimensional slum where a loathsome horror rose above the clustered tombstone buildings like a harvest moon.

10

Lockdown again.

Warden Sheens really didn't know what else to do, so he locked his shitheads in their cages and he had Sloat brought below and put in solitary. They told Sloat it was for his own protection, but the truth was Sheens wasn't sure who needed protecting more: Sloat or the rest of the population.

For two days there was nothing to do for Luis and Coogan but to sit in their cells, read, smoke, play cards and do push-ups and sit-ups on the floor. By the second day, Coogan had pretty much avoided the subject of Eddie Sloat as much as he possibly could. Then he gave in.

"What's your take on Sloat?" he finally said. "That shit in the yard?"

Luis did not speak for some time. He stared into space. Then he licked his lips and said, "There was this acid making the rounds in the streets. They called it Third Eye. I pop a tab and expect to zone for four hours, but I don't zone. Something else. My perception is heightened, doors opened, I creep in dark corners of space-time and thread the needle in nameless gulfs where geometric shapes scream and bleed. I stare into the ultimate primal chaos at the center of cosmic creation and touch black crystal towers on dead moons where alien hands have scratched the Yellow Sign into living rock. I scale the Purple Mountains and get funneled into the Great White Space. I am formless and bodiless. But I am not alone. You hear me on this, man? *I am not alone.*"

Coogan pulled off a cigarette, sighing. *Here we go again with the crazy talk.* But he listened, for somehow, he knew it was important. "Who was there with you?"

"Other minds from other places and I brushed against them, tunneling through them as they invaded me and we got tangled together, a big ball of yarn in an endless shadow plane," Luis admitted. "How do you separate one from the other? I was a canvas, home, white and drab and not a single brushstroke to call my own and they—these minds, ancient, ancient minds— they start painting on me and teaching me and instructing me and then I knew what it was to *be* them. Can you understand? These minds...they jump everywhere, through time, through space, from one dimension to the next. They inhabit minds in the past, the present, the future, this world, a million other worlds you never heard of. They have a name, but you don't need to know it. They had many enemies but there was only one thing they were afraid of."

"And what's that?"

"Something out in space, something horrible waiting at the edge of our solar system."

Coogan said, "Something in the Oort Cloud?"

"Yes. An entity...a colony of ancient decayed minds that existed long before this solar system was formed, something that lived in the cold formless blackness, an entity which hates all living things. Something primal and bodiless and destructive. Something that has been called the Million Malignant Minds, but to us is simply *Nemesis.*"

"And what's this shit got to do with Eddie Sloat?"

"It's got everything to do with him, home. He's some kind of conduit to them and I have no doubt of it. He's linked with them and he's responsible for the missing men same as he's responsible for what happened in the yard today and the dreams we've all been having. He's part of what waits out there, what's getting closer every night and if you think I'm fucking crazy, home, well that's just fine. But it'll be dark in an hour and then you look out the window over there and that darkness you saw will be larger and closer. Then, then you tell me how crazy I am."

Coogan sighed. It was all so contrary to everything he was, all he knew, everything he had seen and experienced. "He's…what? Like supernatural or something?"

"I don't know, man. I really don't know," Luis admitted. "But he's part of it." He paused, thinking. "You said he wore the face of a guy you saw die at Auburn."

"Yeah. Franky McGrath."

"I heard of him. Some kind of headhunter for the Lucchese family in New York."

"Sure. He had a lot of bodies out there."

"He died…when?"

Coogan told him that it was four years ago this month.

"Which means shortly after he died, Eddie Sloat turns up with his cult in Vermont. That's interesting."

Coogan liked Luis…but this was madness, it was a private delusion. Crazy sort of fucked-up shit you'd hear from cons sometimes, their minds soft from incarceration, rotting inside out over the guilt of what they'd done and who they were. That's what he kept telling himself, but he couldn't get himself to believe it. He had seen *things* now, felt nameless forces and malefic energies circling him…how could he deny it? Sloat was not human. He couldn't be. He wore McGrath's face, he had the power to send you tripping into weird anti-worlds, and he had *compelled* those two black fuckheads in the yard into destroying themselves. That was power. That was not human.

And there was also what he had shown Coogan that first day in the yard: that crawling monstrosity. And, Jesus, was that Sloat's *true* face?

"How can you know these things?" he asked Luis and Luis just shrugged said, "I feel them. I believe them to be true. That Third Eye fucked me up in ways you can't know, home. I've got senses beyond the normal five. But when I saw him that day, that first day they processed Sloat out into the general population, my skin crawled and I was covered in cold sweat. I had seen things like him when I tripped on Third Eye…maybe not *seen* them, but knew they were there. When I traveled through those outer spheres I became aware that *something* was out there, something was watching me, something was following me, taking great interest in who and what I was. A cold, primal hatred. Can you dig that?"

Luis said he stopped using Third Eye because it had opened up something inside him and it was hard to close back down. The walls of perception had thinned. Reality began to fly apart all around him. He was running with the Latin Lords in those days, he said, moving a lot of heroin and guns in East Harlem, 103rd Street. He was a real terror…but after Third Eye, things were never the same again. He began seeing things, feeling things…things unseen moving around him, interacting with him, toying with him. That's when he knew that something from the outer spheres had followed him back and was dogging him like a ghost.

"It was little things at first, home," he admitted, his voice dry and squeaking. "Things in my room would be moved. Doors would swing open in the dead of night. There would be this foul sewer smell in my closets, coming from under my bed. I lay there, trying to sleep, and I'd hear voices whispering in the walls, hear something scratching like fingernails inside my pillow." He shook his head, shivering. "It just kept getting worse. One night every window in the house shattered at three a.m. What the fuck, I thought. What could do something like that…the windows exploded *out* not in. Explain that, if you can.

"I was scared, I mean really fucking scared. But who could I turn to? A priest? My mother? Shit, nobody would understand and particularly not the street-eaters I was banging with." Luis buried his face in his hands. Head bowed, he said, "I was doing pretty good for myself. Drug dealing, selling guns, working some girls on the side. Just a drug-pushing pimp, but I had lots of scratch in my pockets. I could buy anything or *anyone* I wanted. I had respect, home, and that was because people feared me and feared the Lords. But…well, after Third Eye, I started losing it. I was nervous. I couldn't sleep. Got so I was afraid of the dark. You dig that? *Me.* A fucking Latin Lord, the terror of the Barrio. But, yes, I was afraid. I was spiking all the time. Only time I felt calm was when I spiked some skag, it smoothed me out. Truth was, I wasn't nothing but a junkie. A violent, crazy-eyed junkie who was afraid of his own shadow. And I had good reason. Oh yes, my brother, I had good reason to be."

Luis said he became aware that something was in the house at night, walking around. He'd hear it…*click, click, click.* Like the sound of nails on the floor. He would be paralyzed with fear like a little kid waiting for some hollow-eyed boogeyman to come ghosting out of the closet. In the morning he would find prints, the tracks of what had been in the house.

"Things were walking around in my house, home, things that had followed me back from the outer spheres. I didn't know what they were. The prints they left were not the prints of men…just three-pronged tracks like something had been walking around on the tips of muddy claws." Luis kept swallowing, trying to keep his throat wet. His eyes were wide, red-rimmed, glassy with fear. "I had no doubt *they* were watching me. I couldn't see them because they did not wish to be seen. But one night…on around three in the morning…I saw something come into my room and it was no man. A weird shadowy form moving towards my bed. It did not walk, it *hopped.* And when I screamed…*it walked right through the wall."*

Coogan was listening with rapt attention. He felt like he was tripping himself. It was all absolute madness, but there was no doubt of the sincerity in Luis's voice: he believed absolutely what he was saying and the memories of those days were haunting his bones.

Luis said the fear got stronger because people began to disappear. People in the neighborhood. Members of the Lords. They were being taken in the night.

"By what?" Coogan asked, knowing he had to. "Nemesis?"

"No, not Nemesis," Luis said. "But another race that is in league with Nemesis, being used by it. Maybe it's out of choice and maybe it's out of fear. I don't know."

"They were abducting them?" Coogan said. "These things?"

"Yes, in a way. In a way. Taking them into the sky."

People would disappear, then come back a week later with no memory of where they had been. "They were taken away, then brought back as if something wanted me to know exactly how powerful they were and how weak I was. Like a man plucking ants from a sidewalk crack, home, and sticking them in a jar, returning them later when it amused him to do so."

"For what purpose?"

"Again, I don't know. But these things took people and when they brought them back, they were never the same again. I think they did something with their brains. Changed them, restructured them, what have you. I think…I really think it has something to do with those canisters from the dreams. Something about those canisters."

Luis admitted his thinking was muddled. That time had been very traumatic. Those people who came back seemed perfectly ordinary to others, but to Luis himself them were crawling abominations, monsters. They could pretend around the others, but he could see through them, see exactly the sort of horrors they were. He called this "the taint". The ability to see *them*. He thought they were returned, used as spies or something, like undercover agents or fifth columnists whose job was to watch and wait, report everything they saw.

"Yeah, I know how that sounds, Coog. A-1 fucking loco loony bullshit. Kind of fucked-up thinking that gets you a straightjacket…but I swear it's the truth or what I guessed was the truth. Things just kept getting worse and worse. I was strung out, paranoid, afraid, jumping at sounds, too scared to sleep. I was a wreck. And it was all on account of Third Eye…what it had done to me." He smoked a cigarette and his hands would not stop shaking. His face had the constricted, yellow look of someone nearing a stroke. "I was desecrated, violated, my brain was not the same anymore. You don't know what it was like. All the time…the sounds, the smells, the sense that you are watched like a microbe on a slide…seeing those kaleidoscope dimensions opening all around you like a man looking through a million windows. Imagine that, Coog. Just sitting there watching all those doors around you swing open, the pulsating green matter filling your sight, eyeless horrors and pallid worming things slithering through a primeval ooze of antimatter… and knowing, *knowing* that as awful as that is, there's something far worse that you DON'T see because they do not WISH to be SEEN."

Coogan said, "Take it easy, man. You don't have to talk about this."

Luis wiped sweat from his face. "But I do, home. I gotta get this out." He was breathing very fast now. "At night…oh yes, Coog…at night my third eye would open all the way and I would see a haunted city of towers and spheres and rising cones and pipes. That's when THEY would come: the old, old, ancient ones, the gray ones with the starfish heads and the bright, bright red eyes. They'd feed off me, draining me like a psychic battery. Parasites, Coog, mind parasites. They wanted my memories and my experiences because they were stagnant and dead and dry, nothing inside them anymore but time and dust."

"These were the things you saw walk through the wall?" Coogan asked. "The ones that left the tracks?"

"No, no. I don't know what *they* were. But you'd see them in the outer spheres haunting dead cities, drifting around. All they wanted was to tap into your mind and drink your thoughts and energy and memory. Some kind of parasite…old, old, something that died out long ago and were just ghosts, shades. The ones that were following me, taking people away into the night…they were different."

Luis said it was about that time as he saw things from those other dimensions and felt them moving around him that he just up and lost it.

He found his girlfriend in a room with three of the Lords. All of them had been taken away and returned. They were not right. Their faces often moved like there was something beneath that wanted to get out and he saw something behind their eyes, something watching him. When they got together like that, they would start whispering crazy things, math and physics and the curvature of space, treading the fourth dimension. When he found them *swarming* like that after like the third time, he pulled out a chromed-up Glock nine and emptied the clip into them. He went into hiding and when an FBI agent tracked him down, he shot him dead, too, thinking he was a spy of the things following him.

"I was wrong. He was just some bull, some fed out playing G-man. I killed him anyway."

Luis was promptly arrested and housed in the Metropolitan Correctional Center in New York City awaiting trial. There was no bail to be had for capital murder. Stuck away in the depths of the MCC, things were no better.

They kept him in solitary and time was fluid and utterly seamless. The only way to mark the days was by the periods of sleep or the hours when they let him have a light on. His meals came and went. The hacks would bring him magazines. Gradually, he lost count of how long he had been down there. That distorted sense of perception began to fade. He was probably the only guy in the MCC who was actually glad to be there, glad to be away from what his life had become. After a week, listening to nothing but the beat of his heart, the deathwatch ticking of some internal clock, he felt isolated and abandoned. Paranoia seeped in and he began to imagine there were things in the darkness with him at night—faceless, formless, and malefic.

"I began to hear sounds and I knew they had tracked me down. The things that had followed me back. I could *feel* them around me. In the cell next door, I heard these funny noises…like something wet being dragged across the floor, scratching sounds as if claws were drawn over the wall. At night I would hear this dry, cold cackling like somebody was laughing over there."

One night, unable to stop shaking, Luis looked beneath the sink at the grille down there—a ventilation grille that connected the cells. Steeling himself, he crawled near the grille and flicked his lighter, knowing he had to know, he had to see, he had to confirm that he was not stark raving mad.

Because something was over there.

Something that had come to torment him.

Something from the outer spheres.

He could smell a wet, damp stink. The flickering flame lit up the underbelly of the sink, the pipes, the paint-flaking concrete wall, and the grille itself. Through the steel mesh, he clearly saw eyes staring back at him: six glistening green toad eyes that did not blink.

It went on and on.

"I don't know what it was, home. Not those things…but something else, something like Eddie Sloat maybe."

Night after night, Luis would hear slithering sounds over there, like snakes were moving across the floor and up the walls. Sometimes it would sound like someone wading through a pool of their own vomit. It would go on and on. If he called one of the guards—and they didn't like coming because he was a cop killer—the sounds would fade away.

Then one night as he cowered in the darkness, alone in that cage, feeling nameless things crouching in the shadows, a sense of terror settled into him that was palpable and devastating. It slid into his heart like an icy needle.

There was something fumbling at the grille.

He could smell its hot and fevered breath.

Then it spoke to him:

"I've been following you for years, living in pockets of writhing shadow and creeping through sewers of time-space and slinking through the cold radioactive mud of shattered extradimensional ghettos in the black void. Just another mind of the many. But I've been watching and I've been waiting. In the end, you will crawl and you will slither, but you will not walk as a man..."

Luis was silent then, his tale finally told, and Coogan knew he was the first human being to have ever heard it. The very fact that Luis was sitting in a federal prison and not a madhouse was proof that he had never mentioned a word of any of it to his lawyers or prosecutors or the investigating cops.

"That's it, Coog. Now you know what I know. That sense I developed with Third Eye—sixth sense, psychic shit, whatever—it seemed to go dormant after they stuck me here five years ago...or was it six? Don't matter. Things were calm, quiet. I was a con. I was incarcerated. I was doing life behind bars. I deserved what I got and you ain't gonna hear many of these animals behind these walls admit to that." He shrugged and stubbed out his cigarette. "Yeah, it was all dormant. No dreams, no nothing. Then Sloat showed up. Soon as I saw him...well, it started again. Not so bad, but it's building. And the first time I heard him speak, you know what? I recognized the voice because it was the voice of the thing that had spoken to me in the MCC."

Coogan didn't know what to think about it. A huge conspiracy, one that was not neat or ordered but large and ungainly, lacking boundaries. Luis talked some more and he listened. He believed that primal hatred, Nemesis, was out in the Oort Cloud getting closer to Earth every day. Those other things, the ones that followed him back and abducted people, fooled with their brains, were in league with it somehow. They had an interest in the human race, too. But it was not to exterminate it. They wanted something else.

"But what?" Coogan asked him.

"I don't know, home. But hear me on this: Eddie Sloat is part of Nemesis. Some way, some how. He was what was speaking to me in the MCC. He was born about the same time Franky McGrath died and I'm willing to bet he's been hundreds of people before that. He's the conduit. He's the beacon.

This won't get any better. If we want to stop it, then we have to stop Eddie Sloat."

Staring out the window at the expanding blackness in the sky, Coogan decided that was something that had to happen sooner rather than later. Time was drawing to a close and even he knew that right down to his marrow.

11

Once upon a time, back in the Medieval days of rehabilitation, the hole was basically an iron cell without furniture of any sort. You slept naked in the dirt and darkness and pissed in a crack in the floor. These days, you got a bunk and a toilet and a sink. In the punishment cells, you got twenty-three hours of darkness; in the segregation cells you could burn your light from morning till night. Eddie Sloat was put in the former.

When Captain Getzel and two of his guards led Sloat down below in chains, he could smell the dankness and foul milk of suffering oozing from the concrete walls, feel the darkness and claustrophobia.

He thought it was a good place for someone like Sloat.

Two days later, he stopped by to see how things were going. The guard said Sloat was quiet thus far and they were keeping him in twenty-fours of darkness.

"Let's see if that breaks his ass," Getzel said.

While Sloat was led away in chains to the shower, Getzel inspected his cell.

He looked at the artwork on the walls. Some of it was scratched names, various parts of the female anatomy. But above the bunk there were elaborate scribblings and diagrams of some sort. Just looking at them made him feel cold inside. He looked closer and there seemed to be symbols and numbers mixed in with it, all in cramped handwriting. It looked like some kind of weird math, maybe algebra or geometry…but not the sort Getzel had ever actually seen before.

"What's all that shit?" he finally asked.

The guard shrugged. "Don't ask me."

"He's writing this in the dark?"

"Suspect so, sir."

Getzel liked it all even less now. "Look like calculations of a sort."

"Yes sir, they do."

"How the fuck does he do it in the dark? You sure he ain't got no flashlight hidden up his ass?"

"No sir. We give him a cavity search every day. No lights."

Getzel kept staring at the graffiti.

It *was* math…he could see all the numbers and calculations, lots of interlinking geometrical shapes, but the symbols—like crescent moons and inverted triangles, crossed staffs and clustered orbs—and words he saw were totally foreign to him. There were elaborate formulae here: curves, jarring angles, exotic geometrical shapes similar to complex polyhedrons and antiprisms merging and canceling one another out or transforming into abstract collections of intersecting surfaces and lines. It looked like a freakish combination of math, astrology, and alchemy.

There was something very wrong about it and Getzel began to sweat hot and cold. Maybe it was his imagination, but it seemed that as he traced the figures with his eyes—arriving at the sum of a particular expression that took up half the wall—that the wall itself seemed to shimmer, grow hazy. It looked like it was moving, attempting to fold back on itself.

Struck with an alarming vertigo, Getzel turned away.

"You make sure nobody talks to him," he said, quickly striding towards the door. "He has…has a way with him."

By the time he reached the stairs, all Getzel could think was, *thank God, thank God it's not me down here at night with that freak.*

12

Three days later, when the lockdown was lifted, Tony Bob stepped out of the Prison Industries building and promptly sank to his knees in the stubbly grass and threw up. By the time two other guards got to him he was white and shaking. "In there," he managed. "In there…the carpentry shop…oh my Christ…"

The two guards—Philly and Whitestep—looked at each other, then charged inside after calling it in over their boxes. At that time of day—3:30 P.M.—most of the convicts had been rounded up and brought back to their cells, save trustees and those on special duty. Tony Bob had been out gathering the stragglers and the workers from PI. Last place he looked was the carpentry shop.

And that's exactly where Whitestep and Philly were looking now.

What they saw was so graphic, savage, and over-the-top Hollywood gorefest, that at first it almost seemed like it couldn't be real. But it *was* real and as the stink of blood and meat wafted up their noses and got down into their guts, their legs went shaky and they had to turn away.

Bodies.

The carpentry shop had been turned into a body dump, a death camp litter pile of bloated torsos and gaping rotten egg eyes and stiff, clutching limbs. A communal profusion of the charnel, all of it seeming to ooze and melt, decompressing into a flabby stew of split skins and pink muscle mass and spilled yellow-purple organ.

Words like *disgusting* and *horrible* and *revolting* barely scratched the surface of this beast.

Whitestep said later it looked like the bodies had been caught in a sheet metal press and had the sauce squeezed out of them, but Philly thought that was inaccurate. Because what he saw reminded him of one of those nature documentaries on the tube where they bring up deep-sea fish and they explode from massive decompression. That's how the corpses looked to him: blown up into purple-mottled flesh bags, eyes popping from skin vaults, fluids spread over the floor like a fresh coat of wax, blood sprayed up the walls and over the lathes and table saws. A single shoe had gotten blown clear up into the rafters where it hung, blood dripping from the toe. And down below, contorted faces had opened agonized mouths and vomited entrails in a gushing stew of blood like squashed frogs.

When Warden Sheens arrived and got his stomach under control, he listened to what Whitestep and Philly said even though it was unthinkable and hinted at boundless nightmares. They recognized some of those faces and they belonged to the missing convicts.

Taken away, Sheens found himself thinking as the bodies made cracking and rupturing sounds as they continued to decompose and *dissolve. These men were taken out of here, crushed, imploded, exploded, blown up with gas and suffocated…then dumped back here and how do you like that?*

Honestly, Sheens did not like it very much.

"They're melting," Whitestep said and Sheens decided then and there that there was probably something wrong with him because no man could look at this and not be sickened to his core, but Whitestep was almost clinical in his appraisal.

"How could that be?" said the warden, wincing as a large yellow eye slid from a socket and popped like a soap bubble, spewing gore over his polished wingtip.

"Look, Warden, you can see it happening."

And he could: like flash frozen jelly allowed to thaw. That's how the bodies looked. Like melting ice sculptures. They were dissolving into a fleshy, oozing sea of tissues and fluids and bubbling plasma. In an hour, there would be nothing but one hell of an ugly stain. The coroner would need a mop and a bucket.

"I want a cap on this shit," Sheens said. "This isn't fucking natural and if those shitheads out there get a taste of this we'll have a four-alarm fucking riot on our hands. Not a word. You got me?" He looked at Whitestep who nodded. "Not a fucking peep." He looked at Philly who was as green as the eggs and ham in a particular children's story. "Yeah…uh…yeah."

Then Sheens, who had somehow managed to keep his composure in check and his stomach where it belonged, marched outside, haughtiness in tow…and went to his knees and threw up his lunch.

13

Out in the yard, Coogan smoked, watching, waiting, listening to Luis and Chi Chi talking about things that he did not want to hear about.

"Shit they're talking is bullshit," Chi Chi said. "Ain't nobody fooling no one. I heard about them bodies."

"You don't like the warden's story?" Luis said.

"Hell."

Coogan heard all about it all, of course, and he'd even heard the crazy bullshit story the warden had spun on his loom: a group of cons had gotten crushed by a load of timbers. Even the hacks were making sick jokes about that. As to what had really happened, no one was saying. But there were plenty of rumors.

"Gotta friend over at the Corpse Farm, home," Luis said. "You want the truth, here it is. He overheard the warden talking with the doc. FBI did autopsies on the bodies. Get this, they didn't just puke out their intestines…their lungs were ruptured from methane poisoning, blood full of enriched nitrogen."

"Hell's that mean?" Chi Chi asked. "Where'd they breathe in methane?"

"Not on this planet, home."

"Dead all the same," Coogan said.

"Dead? Shit, man, there's dead and there's *dead*. Autopsy said death by massive decompression. Those bodies were crystallized. Now people say I'm crazy, but it's gonna take a real peculiar set of circumstances to do something like that."

"Whitestep told me they was melting," Chi Chi said. "But you didn't get that from me."

"They were…dissolving. By the time the feds got here, most of the remains had *liquefied*. But there's something even worse, something even weirder."

Coogan and Chi Chi were both looking at him.

Luis looked around, ready to espouse state secrets. "They didn't have any brains."

"What? What do you mean?" Chi Chi said.

Luis licked his lips which were pale as his face by that point. "I mean what I said. The brains were missing from the bodies and there was not a single cut on the skulls. Now, tell me this: how do you extract a brain without so much as scratching the head?"

Coogan sat there, shaking, something invading him, digging deep like rootlets seeking hot red wetness.

14

At Auburn Correctional, the idea to murder Franky McGrath had come when

Coogan walked into the prep room at the prison mortuary where he worked and had found McGrath squatting naked over a corpse he was cutting apart on the floor. The corpse, it turned out, was not some cold cuts from one of the drawers—which would have been bad enough—but the body of slight Hispanic boy of nineteen named Armando Ramirez who had been doing ten years for robbery, repeat offender. When Ramirez disappeared, everyone had assumed he had gone over the wall.

Not so.

Franky McGrath, they later learned, had beaten him and while he lay in the prison infirmary, strangled him and somehow got his body out to the mortuary.

Where Coogan found him.

At the sight of that hulking, feral horror squatting over the body, Coogan just froze there, not sure what he was supposed to do. Jimmy Pegs, Sean Bolland, and another street-eater named Vinnie Scuzzio were on their way over and he hoped to God they'd hurry.

He was speechless.

McGrath looked up at him, huge like a shaved gorilla, naked and heavily tattooed, his red hair hellfire, his eyes glistening grubworms, his hands filled with gore-streaked knives. He grinned with teeth like bloodstained white diamonds in a grave rictus. *"Get that fucking look offa yer face, Coog,"* he said with a scraping, dirty voice. *"This is my thing and it don't concern you or any of the others. This is my thing, this is how I do it and how I stay alive."*

Coogan had been around plenty by that point. He'd seen all the atrocities prison life had to offer. He was truly frightened of no man. But this…it filled his mouth with a taste of rusty metal and sickly sweetness. He could smell the corpse, the blood—like pooling fat and well-marbled meat—and he could only stare at McGrath, eyes locked in orbits like insects in amber.

McGrath kept smiling, teeth jutting from pale pink gums. *"Watch what I do, because you just might learn something. The boys you're running with, it's only a matter of time before you gotta trunk a body, joint a corpse, and I can show you how it's done. Limbs are hard to get free from their sockets, Coog, so don't dick around none, just take a saw and cut 'em. Limbs gotta go. Then the head. No dental records, no fingerprints. Take the pieces and scatter 'em to the four winds, far enough apart that they'll never put Humpty Dumpty back together again."*

Coogan finally asked him why he'd did it in the first place, why he'd killed the kid and then did *this* to him. *"You don't know shit, Coog, none of you do,"* McGrath told him. *"Something happened to me once. Long time ago. Something you could never understand. But since then I been different, you know? On the streets, I killed people to order. And, yeah, I enjoyed it. But it's more than that. Lot of primitive warriors believed that if you killed somebody, you absorbed their strength, their soul, their spirit. See these tattoos on my back? On my chest? Not just tats, Coog, but blueprints, instructions that describe a ritual of sorts. If I kill people in a certain way, if I bring 'em to the point of absolute fear, what's in 'em gets stronger and when I take it, I get stronger. You understand? What's tattooed on my body shows me the ritual and how to perform it, little things like sucking the terror out of them and jointing their corpse in a particular way to gain the favor of them outside…the others…"*

Absolute insanity…yet Coogan had believed it. He could feel the pull of those others waiting on the threshold to take their sacrifice. And the tattoos—arcane words and symbols, skulls and crescent moons and bones and bodies being pulled apart, countless screaming faces, abstract representations of demons with the heads of toads or wraiths with wreaths of tentacles where their hair should have been…all of it intermixed, crowded, clustered on his body so that it took your breath away to follow the maze of inking and see where one thing started and another ended, all of it melting into a hallucinogenic haze of images and words and glyphs.

Coogan later told Jimmy Pegs about it.

Jimmy Pegs, a.k.a Jimmy Pagano, was a made guy in New York's Lucchese family. Not much went on at Auburn that Jimmy Pegs and some of the other old Italians didn't have a hand in. Let the gangs mix it up in the yard all they wanted, guys like Jimmy Pegs practically owned the place. Word came down that McGrath would get whacked as a favor to a certain high-ranking member of the Mexican Mafia; Ramirez had been his cousin. Blood demanded blood. When Jimmy Pegs brought Sean Bolland and Coogan in on it, it was past the discussion phase.

"Friday night, most of the cons in K-block are going to be watching a movie," he said. "I'm going to arrange for Franky to have a little entertainment with a fish I told him about. Only, when he gets into the rec room, won't be no fuck boy waiting for him, it'll be us."

By that point, Coogan had piped a few guys, shanked one man, and beat quite a few others, but he'd never killed anyone. He was a thief. He was not a killer. But he joined up and mainly because you didn't say no to Jimmy Pegs because he was the sort of guy who could make your life really easy or real hard. That was part of it. But the real reason was simply that McGrath was an animal, an absolute animal. And after what he'd seen him doing and those awful things he'd said, that fucker had to go down.

When McGrath walked into the rec room and saw Jimmy Pegs and Coogan standing there with plastic ponchos on and lead pipes in their hands, he knew. Like an animal led out into the slaughter yard and smelling the death-stench of bowels, brains, and blood, he *knew.*

His face grinned like a sacrificial nascent moon.

He charged forward and got his hands on Coogan before he could even think of swinging the pipe. *"You motherfucker! I coulda shown you things! I coulda taken you places—"*

When McGrath's huge, apish hands took hold of him, something happened to Coogan that he could never explain: it was like being electrocuted. An electric surge ran through him like he had just gripped exposed wires in his fists. His body went taut, blazing heat consuming him, and in his head… like a dozen suns exploding with flashing prismatic colors and then collapsing into their own mass, into something like a sucking, whirlpooling gravity sink that yanked him kicking and screaming out of his own head, tossing him light-years through some perverted multi-dimensional hyperspace and into a fractured black cosmos where the stars were oblong corpse-white faces staring down from an abyssal whispering blackness and he saw a great sphere rushing at him. It wore irradiated mist like a mask and slowly, the mask was pulled away to reveal—

But by then Sean Bolland had swung his pipe and it connected with McGrath's head with a meaty impact, his skull cracking open, blood, gray slime, and something like white pus leaking out as he was driven to his knees.

Coogan came out of it and he was on his ass, dishrag-limp, numb, flesh crawling.

Then he was up and they were all swinging their pipes with savage, idiotic glee. McGrath's head was shattered, a soup of blood and brain matter oozing over the floor like congealing pudding. His teeth were scattered like dice, jagged ends of bones jutting at crazy angles from livid, swelling purple flesh. The pipes kept coming down until McGrath was a great distended mewling skin sack of macerated organs and fragmented bones crawling through the slime trail of its own puddling fluids. He looked up once, directly at Coogan, with a remaining good eye that swam in a stew of bile and intercranial fluid, his head a smashed puzzle of skullbone, his face a pulpous raw matter.

And for one mad, unreal moment as that orb of hate drilled into him, Coogan thought he saw something rising up out of McGrath's body—something like a thousand green rubber worms that blossomed into a fungal lunatic forest of grinning emerald-eyed clown faces that themselves divided into the gleaming sugar-bone whiteness of dead children that opened their huge smoldering fissile eyes to reveal a sucking, limitless vortexual blackness that had come to turn the world into a graveyard of well-picked bones.

Then this, too, was gone.

McGrath died with a shrill simian cry of dozens of gibbons being flayed alive and a resounding wail of bleeding ghosts that echoed through the confines of the rec room with a charged, energetic chanting that became a blood mist that dripped from the ceiling and walls.

"It's done," Jimmy Pegs said, standing there in his blood-streaked plastic poncho, his face the color of bleached flour.

"Did you see—" Coogan began.

"I didn't see fucking shit and neither did you," Jimmy Pegs said. "What is done is done and we talk no more about it."

The plastic ponchos and pipes went into a laundry bag and that was that.

At least, that's what Coogan had thought at the time.

15

Two days after they'd shoveled the remains off the floor of the carpentry shop, Buster Cray came up to Coogan. He had a mixed bag of headhunters and ghetto-crawlers with him: black, white, Latino, even an Asian dude with a knife scar slashed across his face ear to ear like a questing pink worm. Badass. Corpse-maker. Looked like he could chew pig iron and piss tacks.

"You Coogan? Johnny Coogan?" Buster said. "Hear you tried to break out of the Hot House, but weren't exactly successful."

"You heard right."

"Got a friend over there name of Raul Mingle," he said. "Call him El Ming around the block. He says you owe him five large and I'm here to collect."

Shit. That's what this was. It was true enough, Coogan owed El Ming the green but he was hoping his escape attempt and transfer to Grissenberg had canceled that out. Not so. The prison grapevine strikes again.

"You tell Ming when I get it, he'll get it."

Buster was fat and soft, a fleshy pink Arkansas hog in blackface. He mopped his sweaty bald head constantly with a towel, degreasing it, a well-chewed cigar butt blossoming from his crooked mouth. He was strictly the non-violent sort, Coogan knew right off. He paid others to hurt people. They called him "Chocolate Pudding" behind his back, but never to his face because death was kept at a low boil in those eyes.

"Ming don't care about your problems, bitch. Neither do I. He wants his money."

"Well, I still don't have it."

"Things might get rough."

"Things always do."

Coogan was already tensed, ready to bust.

He stood at an even six feet, stacked hard with muscle from religiously doing 2000 push-ups a day, working the weights, and hitting the bag. He was known to be easy going for the most part, someone you could talk to, a guy who would help you if you were indeed worth helping. But he was also known for his absolutely fearsome temper. He demanded respect at every joint he pulled time in. It was the only way you survived. In a max joint you were either a predator or you were prey. And if this fat boy thought he could be intimidated, then he was right: things *were* going to get rough.

"There are other ways, of course," Buster told him, coveting absolute indifference. "You could join up with us. We represent a new sort of organization, you see, one based on brotherly love and blind to skin color and racial affiliation and all such bullshit. You want to come on board, you're welcome. We get stuff the rest don't, got hacks on the rake. And that five grand? Forget about it."

Coogan lit a cigarette. "And what might I have to do to wipe out that debt?"

"You know Eddie Sloat?"

Here it comes.

"Heard of him."

Buster nodded, his eyes filled with a vacant sort of fear. "We gonna have some business with him. You know what I'm saying?"

Coogan did and he didn't care for the idea.

Because if he murdered somebody—even a parasite like Sloat—that was life, fucking life in the cage.

Buster mopped his shiny dome. Coogan studied the lines on the man's face, crow's feet splaying out from the corners of his eyes and sutured wrinkles spreading out like hairline cracks in delicate pottery. A line for everything he had done and everything he wished he would never do again. "Things have been funny since that cracker got here," he said.

"Funny how?"

Buster looked to his posse and they all bowed their heads, closed their eyes, as if in reverence to this criminal godhead that walked amongst them.

"What a question, what a question," Buster said, shaking his head. "Motherfucker, you will see it and know it and recognize it as such. That's all I'm gonna say."

It seemed to Coogan that big bad cellblock playa and snake in the switchgrass Buster Cray was trembling on the edge of admitting something, of lancing the poison behind his eyes, maybe squeezing the black blood from his soul. It was close, real close. He needed someone to hear it, someone whose ears were hooked to a working brain—not these hollow-eyed walking mops he had for a posse.

So Coogan took a chance, seized the moment and palmed the meat, as they say. "You're talking in riddles, my friend," he said. "But I understand that. I got one for you. How could a guy who got killed at Auburn four years ago be walking around the yard today?"

The posse studied each other nervously. They were primal, simple things who had just evolved from the black jungle of animal ignorance to discover the fear of the dead.

Buster licked his lips. "Nightmares and reality get soft here, get runny, start to mix together." He pulled off his cigar. "You ever have visions, Coog?"

"Never."

Buster laughed with a harsh metallic sound. "You will, man. Trust me on this, you been here long enough, you will." He looked over at his thugs. "Sooner or later, Sloat is going to get out of the hole. We'll forget about that five large if you do what's right."

Coogan blew smoke in his face. "You want him done, why don't you have one of these fuckheads do him?"

"Because I want you to."

"Ain't gonna happen."

Buster just moved his eyes. "Skin," he said. "Do it."

The Asian dude rushed out with murder in his eyes, but Coogan was ready for him. Skin lashed out with a chopping kick and Coogan sidestepped it, caught his leg, twisted it, and kneed him in the balls. While he was going down, Coogan drilled him in the jaw with a short devastating punch. Down in the grass, Skin vomited out three teeth in a spray of pink foam. Another dude rushed in and Coogan jumped him, twisting his head on his neck and jabbing his thumb into his eye. He went down screaming, crying tears of blood.

Before the others could make a move, Coogan locked an arm around Buster's throat. "Call it off or I'll break your fat fucking neck," he told him.

"Ease up, ease up," Buster said. "Please now…ease up…"

"You want Sloat, get him yourself," Coogan said, pushing him away into his own ranks. "I don't want to get involved."

Buster just stared at him. "Son, if you're here, you're already involved."

16

After Coogan went on his merry way and the boys scattered, Buster stood there alone, surveying the yard, remembering things and feeling things, his stomach turning over and wanting to come spraying out of his mouth. He wished he could tell Coogan, take him aside and make him understand about Sloat, about the big bad wolf coming to Griss City and how sharp his teeth were. But Coogan, as reasonable and stand-up as he was, could never wrap his brain around any of it, could never understand what inhabited Sloat's skin and what its plans were.

But Buster knew because he saw it in his dreams every night.

Buster put his face in his hands, squeezing it, losing himself, forgetting, drowning in rank pools of denial and coveting a numbness that was blank and dreamlike.

He watched the cons out in the yard. Cons throwing balls back and forth. Cons leaning against walls and scheming. Cons huddled in groups, smoking, puffing out their chests, arguing. Cons watching other cons. Cons watching the hacks with their sticks and hacks up in the gun towers. Cons gambling. Cons keeping an eye on the new fish in the yard, sizing them up. Cons leading their fuck boys around, daring anyone to touch them. A game. All a meaningless fucking game in this place that the cons played twenty-four-seven, wind-up toys that never ran out of batteries and clocks that never stopped ticking. All of them puffing out their chests and fluffing their tail feathers, scanning the yard with flat dead eyes and caustic attitudes thinking they had cornered the market on evil and not knowing, never guessing they were amateurs. Because they did not know of secrets kept and secrets tended like dark gardens. Of men who were not men at all but things that laid their eggs in low, steaming places and the terrible things they had done.

Tick, tick, tick.

The clock kept running and Buster knew deep within himself that it was ten minutes to midnight.

The end was coming soon.

17

Daytime in Grissenberg was a constant cacophony of noise blending into a seamless dull roar: men yelling from cell to cell, steel doors clanging, guards shouting, cons hollering at the TVs in the rec rooms, boomboxes blaring, men screaming, religious freaks praying out loud at the very tops of their voices, headcases babbling incoherently at tormentors no one else could see. On and on and on.

But at night, it was the low murmur of a caged animal breathing in its sleep, dreaming ensanguined dreams of blood and meat and death. Water dripped and men moaned in their sleep. Rats clawed at the walls, pipes groaned, ducts ticked as they cooled. Cons whispered and sobbed and begged Jesus and Mary for deliverance. The air was hot and moist with the stink of unwashed skin, sweat, urine, and garbage. Hacks made their hourly rounds up and down the walkways and you could smell their cologne and chewing gum, the smoke of their cigarettes.

By midnight, other than an occasional distant scream echoing into nothingness, there was only the silence of the beast breathing, filling itself with night, recharging itself for another day, hungry for the violence and isolation and intolerance that kept its belly full and its teeth sharp.

18

"Oh, God, here we go," Philly said. Not only was he pulling the night shift but he had to listen to fucking Sloat.

He was chatting away in his cell with his invisible friends again.

Philly set his girlie magazine aside and went over to the cell, preparing to rap the door with his stick, tell Sloat to pipe down.

But he didn't.

He listened.

In a weird, buzzing voice that sounded like the steady hum of bees, a voice was saying: *"We sent them through the White Space, trip-trip-trip they went, falling through the hollow void, tumbling, tumbling, little lost boys, open your eyes, this is Yuggoth, the ninth world…where the terrible darkness rolls… the cyclopean pits of elder fungi…look how warm-blooded life squirms in the cold, the cessation of atmospheric pressure, how your entrails steam on the barren plain, crawling worms…"*

After that, Philly sat in his chair shivering like a kid who was waiting for some goblin-eyed horror to come creeping from the closet on eight spidery limbs. His sweat came in cool-warm rivers, plastering his dark hair to his skull. In his brain there was a perpetual scratching white noise that only barely covered the sounds coming from the cell: slithering and scraping noises, inexplicable metallic screechings and a low whistling drone that he swore made the earth rumble and throb beneath him. There were sounds like things walking about on a multitude of spiny legs, a constant hissing and whispering that seemed to come from a dozen separate mouths. Sloat carried on low, hushed conversations and it all made Philly's skin absolutely crawl.

Good God, what was going on in there?

19

When Coogan closed his eyes that night, the dream came for him immediately.

He saw a field of green energy envelop him, flashes of cobalt and indigo directed at his eyes, laser-bright, blinding him, then letting him see, really see, as he was yanked along by some thermonuclear tidal pull, riding its white-hot wave with incredible velocity towards a yawning zone of blackness that was darker than anything he could imagine. The threshold was reached: a radiant firestorm burning from the inside out like a melting sun…and then he was through.

He had breached.

Yes, that was the word: *breached.*

The threshold was slit open and he fell screaming into a lake of cold bubbling plasma that was impossibly close to Grissenberg and unbelievably distant.

He did not know where he was.

His mind told him it was a world between worlds…a dank gutter in some interdimensional anti-world.

Everything was changed around, turned inside out, flesh made smoke and smoke made flesh, atoms scattered and reassembled. Coogan's mind was a thorny growth of black roses, sprouting, flowering, bursting from his skull which no longer existed in this abstract place.

Before him was a fathomless darkness and right away he saw the city: it looked like crowding, clustered toadstools and greasy, tall mushrooms washed by a gray, bubbling river of creeping fungi. As he got closer, he saw not toadstools but buildings that were tall and narrow like coffins set upon their ends, all spilling blackness and despair and incredible age.

In the dream, he did not walk, but flew, drifting over the city. He saw that the structures were not made of brick and stone, but things like pipes and reeds, femurs and ulnas welded together by mats of what looked to be cobweb, fine filaments of which connected the buildings, consuming them and were woven through them.

The city was a corpse.

In the dream, he knew this. As he drifted about, he saw things like bloated slugs inching about. They were a ghastly, phosphorescent white, crawling in and out of the edifices. They were maggots, weird alien maggots feeding on the rot of the city.

Lamprey mouths sought his warm, pulsing throat and everywhere, decay and slime as the city went spongy with putrescence and the shadows were heady with charnel perfume and that boiling river of fungi shrieked with a hundred scraping voices.

Coogan slid into one of the buildings like a shadow. In an immense convex chamber, he saw shapes moving. Not human. But sentient. Horrible, but not necessarily threatening.

They looked like some kind of grotesque alien insect or crustacean that stood upright on thorny pronged claws. They were a dull orange to fleshy pink in color and made of segmented bands of white-striated tissue with several sets of curving plate-like wings at their backs. Set at the end of a fleshly, wrinkled stalk, their heads were egg-shaped and convoluted, a mass of spiny antennae rising from them. They had no eyes, no mouth that he could see, just bony chambers.

They were absolutely grotesque.

And the closer he looked, the less they resembled insects or crustaceans for it seemed that they were not composed of flesh as such but minute braided filaments and fibers like threads of fungi, interwoven, overlapping, communal. Like a great colonial fungus.

Coogan knew they were seeing him.

Their antennae were changing color, flashing on and off like the chromatophores of deep sea squids. They were communicating. Discussing him and he knew it.

The Mi-Go: the Fungi from Yuggoth, the Outer Ones.

This was how they were called on Earth and they wanted him to know that.

These were the things that had followed Luis from the outer spheres: The Mi-Go.

They began to move in his direction.

He could see McGrath before him on a slab of black stone like a rhesus monkey awaiting the cutting and piercing and changing. Yes, Franky McGrath, but mutilated and broken just as he'd looked after he was beaten to death. He was here now, in this place.

Coogan saw him not through eyes as such, but some other sense that was vivid, yet oddly dreamlike…McGrath looked distorted, obscene, a fourth-dimensional alien interpretation. Purely subjective: a pale white blubbery thing, churning with liquids and fats and filled with gases. A repellent and perfectly monstrous thing.

Though Coogan—or his host—was repulsed, there were necessary things to be done and the delicate triple-pronged crab pincers were doing them with incredible dexterity: rods of light slitting open his cranium, the membrane bisected, the pulsing glob of convoluted tissue that still lived, the severing of millions of nerves.

Then the brain, divorced from its skull, living…still living.

Placed in a canister. One of the canisters he had dreamed about.

Taken from McGrath.

To be put somewhere else.

Coogan drew away from it all. With a hollow and distant scream, he moved away from the things that were dissecting McGrath. He fled through the anti-world, gaining momentum, terror breaking loose inside him, and then velocity, space and time crumbling around him, unraveling and fragmenting.

And somewhere, from distant black gulfs, a buzzing voice: *"You have breached, Coogan. Prepare to breach again…"*

20

Buster Cray could not sleep.

He had been named by Eddie Sloat. It was his turn.

All day long he'd felt it coming for him, creeping in closer, and now he feared it was standing just behind him.

Holding his mother's crucifix to his chest, he said, *"Please Mary, please Jesus, now and at the hour of my death…"*

Enveloped in a sour, yellow stink of fear, he was trembling, beads of sweat the size of chickpeas popping on his brow. As he shook his head slowly from side to side, his eyes did not blink. His face was drawn so tight it looked like the skull beneath was trying to get out.

Behind him, there was a hissing noise.

Something was happening, something was taking shape around him. It was like the atmosphere of his cell was being gutted.

Buster just stood there, eyes wet and wide. *They're coming. Just like in my dreams, they're coming through the light.*

In the corner, right at the very spot where the walls met and the angles died, a seam of blackness appeared. It sheared open like a crack, widening, and a pale blue light came shining through, spreading out and making the entire cell glow with luminous pulsations of matter.

Not just light, but a lambent phosphorescence that was palpable. He could feel the energized particles that made it up crawling over his skin like a million spidery legs.

And he was trapped. Trapped in a steel cage.

He turned this way and that, eyes huge and glassy and staring, ropes of drool flying from his mouth. And then he screamed. A sharp, cutting, absolutely agonized sound that echoed through the cellblock like an air-raid siren. He threw himself against the bars of his cell and beat his face against them until his black skin opened with blossoms of blood the color of dewy red, red roses.

"GET ME OUT! GET ME OUT OF HERE!" he cried between clenched teeth as tears rolled and spittle flew and his fists shook on the bars. *"GET ME THE FUCK OUT OF HERE—"*

And then he saw the figures in the light—crooked, hunched-over shapes like grotesque hobgoblins. There were five or six of them hopping out of the misty blue field in his direction. They made a high-pitched whistling noise like mating katydids in a summer field. As Buster's mind ran like warm sap, he saw something like gargoyle wings spreading out and wavering alien limbs reaching out towards him.

But that was all he saw before he was taken.

21

Down in solitary the voices were speaking from Sloat's cell again and, God help him, but Philly could not seem to stop from listening.

"...they all are knowing now...sensing it...feeling it...seeing it in their visions...near, very near...all those mindless little worms, oh yes, they cannot shut out the majesty of that which comes...it owns them, every one of them!" Sloat began to breathe very fast. There was a stealthy insectile scuttling as something moved across the floor followed by a flapping sound as of sheets on a line...or spreading wings. "The time is ripe and we shall make it so...I have heard voices calling from the green gulfs where the black spheres roll..."

Then that buzzing voice which Philly didn't think a human being could imitate. It was wavering, rising and falling, like a radio signal coming from a great distance:

"...*Iä Iä Cthulhu Fhtagn...as in past days so again...the tall apes no longer hold sway...exterminated by the wrath of...and He, oh sacred and favored lord, shall rise from the sunken city...and as the Black Goat rules the forest so shall the Million Malignant Minds be sated...even now they approach...the Eye of Wormwood... Iä...as in elder lost times...the ancient star-spawn will wake in their tombs beneath the frozen cold wastes...fill the skies...it will be the time of the swarming as of old...give praise to that which squats in darkness...let what waits at the center of primal chaos hear our many voices...*"

Philly was scared white because as much as he told himself that Eddie Sloat was a bugcase and what he was hearing was merely the raving of a diseased mind, he did not believe it. Because something inside him had its back up and was bristling with terror. Philly knew that out there somewhere in the night-black cosmos there was something waiting in chaotic splendor and it was coming for the human race.

22

Lying awake, Coogan heard it quite distinctly: *Click, click, click.*

It came again and it was closer. His flesh began to creep. The spit dried up in his mouth. He wanted to call out to Luis, but he did not dare announce his presence to what was coming up the corridor out there. Noise seemed to be canceled out in the prison, an immense dead silence had fallen. There was only the sound of some tormented con praying in the night and that clicking.

It was coming.

The only lights on were the security lights and they cast a dim, eerie glow over the faces of the cells. *Click, click, click.* Coogan could smell something like dry moldering straw. He knew it was the same stink Luis had smelled in his house when the Mi-Go visited him. Squeezing his eyes shut, beyond simple fear, he waited it out.

The smell got stronger.

An inexplicable chill breezed through the bars.

He opened his eyes but a crack and saw a grotesque, distorted shadow pass over him as something *hopped* past his cell. And then it was gone and the smell faded to memory. But somehow, he knew it was not over, for this was what Luis had called *the taint:* the ability to see those from outside, to recognize them when others could not.

He could hear the sound of footsteps now.

Just the hack making his rounds. Nothing more. Coogan listened as those soft-soled shoes got closer, then paused before his cell. In the dimness he could see the guard…but he could also see someone else standing just behind him…filmy, shadowy, hunched-over like a troll in a storybook. That figure seemed to gain solidity, become more substantial…filling out, fleshing out, like it was being pumped full of helium. Some nightmare cartoon boogeyman filling with stolen, gaseous life…face bulbous and distorted like that of a flyblown corpse, black crystalline eyes sucked down into oblong holes, lips red and bloated like worms mating in a soup of bile.

And the evil, mocking grin.

It was Franky McGrath.

As Coogan laid there, paralyzed with fear, the hack was gone. McGrath came right up to the bars and his face was crawling like moist, oozing pulp. He clutched the bars with boneless fingers. They coiled like greasy white flatworms.

As Coogan cried out with glacial terror, McGrath became a soft, warm plastic thing that melted to a sliding jelly, dozens of sinewy slate-gray ropes bursting from the flaccid central mass of luminous yellow eyes and squirming entrails. They wound around the bars, making them groan as they were gripped with impossible strength. McGrath was squeezing his way through, several tentacles with pulsing bubblegum-pink suckers on their undersides slipped between the bars, twitching and jumping like power cables, sweeping the floor for something to grab, something to latch on—

Coogan could hear men crying out.

A hack shouting.

Luis was praying.

Footsteps coming.

"It's coming, Coog, it's coming for all of you," McGrath's eerie sibilant voice said. *"You want me to open the door? Show you how to manipulate fourth-dimensional space? Show you what's on the other side? I did it for Jimmy Pegs not three months ago. Poor stupid Italian, he went just like the others: a little trip into the well of darkness. Sun never rises on Yuggoth, Coog. Poor Jimmy Pegs writhing on that soundless alien plain, methane rupturing his lungs, water boiling out of his eyes until they blew out of their sockets like runny eggs…but by then the lack of atmospheric pressure…ha! He blew up like a fucking balloon. It only took two minutes, tops. But they were a fucking long, ugly two minutes, Coog.*

"And Sean Bolland? I didn't fuck around at all. I sent that prick right into the Oort Cloud so he could meet the Million Malignant Minds. They took him apart at the subatomic level, scattered his matter like rice, but not before he looked upon them and had every last warm drop of terror leeched from him, his brain pulped and juiced and squeezed dry as a peach pit…

"Prepare yourself, Coog…it's coming now…the time of the breaching…"

The tentacles retreated and McGrath dissolved into a running flux of black jelly that retreated into the shadows.

"What the fuck is going on here?" a hack said, scanning the cells with his flashlight. "Which one of you pissing shitheads screamed?"

But no one was saying.

23

As the prison slept, Luis Cardone had a dream that he was not sure was a dream at all. Again, he was seeing the great Oort Cloud at the very edge of the solar system: a misty sphere that spread in all directions and on to infinity, it seemed.

Subjectively, he saw it as a black hole that had swallowed the blazing, irradiated mass of a neutron star but hadn't been able to entirely digest it, only hold it burning in its throat like flickering witch-light.

Objectively, he knew the Cloud was a slowly rotating chaotic maelstrom of planetary fragments, ice, interstellar gases, and radioactive dust storms, a cold-hot furnace of comets flaring occasionally with jets of superhot plasma and radiant bursts of ionizing matter. All of it being slowly compressed in a web of conflicting, pulsating magnetic fields that were squeezing it like a subatomic fist. The nearer he got to it, caught in the corkscrewing pull of its gravitational field, the more it threw out blue-white geysers of agitated atoms and hot gas like tentacles trying to snare him. He looked into the Cloud, seeing deeper into its anatomy than ever before, right into the cometary nucleus itself, the shifting luminosity peeling away to reveal a core beyond that was spiraling and unbelievably black, an ultracold freezer of absolute zero that was not dead, but alive with something obscene, unnamable, and unbelievably malignant.

Something that was watching him, a cosmic eye of absolute malevolence. And hate.

Then he was pulled away from it, it seemed, funneled into a cycling vortex of white matter with blinding velocity that he knew was near the speed of light if not beyond it. Then he was free, falling, falling like a stone through space, spinning until he thought his guts would spray out of his mouth…and then he opened his eyes.

Coogan was pressing him down into the bunk with one hand and Luis thrashed, his head whipping from side to side. He thought for one crazy, surreal nightmare moment that it wasn't his cellmate but an immense crystallized spider lowering down upon him.

"Take it easy," Coogan told him. "Jesus Christ, you're screaming in your sleep."

Luis relaxed, breathing rapidly in a lake of sweat. He could not stop shaking.

There was a sudden flare of light as Coogan lit a cigarette, his face crawling with shadows. "Hell was it about?"

Luis caught his breath, held it, licked his lips. "The Oort Cloud," he said. "It's here…I think it's here…"

24

Up in the gun tower as the skin on his lower belly moved with a slow shivering crawl, Captain Genzel stared up at the blackness hanging above FCI Grissenberg. It was an immense abyssal darkness beyond anything he had ever seen before. The sort of ebon, pathless darkness that he imagined must exist beyond the rim of the known universe.

It was a clear night, but there were no stars in the sky.

In fact, there was no sky. The blackness *was* the sky.

Mason, an old hand at the prison, came up to him. "What do you make of it, Cap?"

"I…I don't know. Never seen anything like it before. Some kind of weird storm front?"

Mason shrugged. "Radio says clear and calm for the next three days. That ain't no storm."

"Then what the hell is it?"

"I don't know, Cap," he said, his voice nearly a whisper. "But it's been growing in the sky for weeks. And you know what? I was in town last night and you can't see it from there. The only place you can see it is *here.*"

Getzel kept staring up at it, something inside him drying up.

25

About the time Coogan managed to close his eyes and approach something like sleep, there was a huge hollow booming that shook the entire prison and made it feel like something had grabbed it and moved it ten feet.

Coogan was thrown from his bunk as was Luis and hundreds of other cons.

Up and down the cell blocks men were crying out and things shattered as they hit the floors. There was a weird, sharp stink like ozone and another that smelled like fused-out wiring.

And then silence.

A heavy, brooding, deathly silence that lasted for maybe ten seconds and the only sound was an unearthly low howling that sounded something like a distant foghorn echoing through subterranean pipes. It rose and fell in cycles, but never faded away entirely.

Every light in the prison went out.

The backup generators did not kick in.

And every man lying dazed on the floor or pulling himself to his feet, head spinning with dizziness, all had the same sensation: that the very air, the atmosphere of the prison, had been turned inside out as if time and space and the laws of physics had been dislocated and rendered meaningless.

Then men started screaming.

They beat things against the bars of their cells.

There was shouting and anguished cries.

And on C-Block, a single voice rose up above it all with a shrieking hysteria: *"Help me! Jesus Christ, somebody help me! Get me out of here!"* the voice cried. *"There's something in here! It got Joey K! It's coming out of the fucking walls—"*

It was at this climactic moment that every cell door in the prison slid open, releasing convicts into the darkness and what waited in it.

26

Solitary.

Trapped in the darkness, Philly saw a pulsating blue phosphorescence lick around the edges of the steel door to Sloat's cell. It spilled beneath it, spreading in a glowing pool like moonlight.

Then the door blew open and something threw a shadow against the wall like branches moving in the wind. He turned and there was nothing. Crawling away from the blue light on his hands and knees, he heard a sound like a dry rustling just behind him…a clicking noise like chitinous digits rubbing together. He waited there, shivering, heart pounding. He started crawling again, seized by a frantic fear that would not release him.

The noises did not stop.

They were actively seeking him out.

And he knew with a childlike terror that whatever was behind him *wanted* him to see. It was daring him to look upon it.

There was a sudden strong stink like blood and meat and something worse…like dry, rotting hay. A cold shadow fell over him and he buried his face in his hands and began to sob as he had as a little boy when the branch of an ancient oak would scratch at his window in the night.

He looked, knowing he had to.

What he saw in the blue light was not as big as a man, maybe five feet tall, a hunched-over crustacean plated in orange-pink segments that were separated by raised ridges. It had two sets of jointed limbs that ended in something like crab pincers…except they were triple pronged like two fingers and an opposable thumb.

It motioned to him with them.

Philly screamed.

The creature was unmoved. It stood there, on another set of limbs that were thicker, balancing itself on the tips of the pincers. It had wings, several sets of them, that folded up with a leathery, squeaking kind of sound. It had a tail, too, that seemed to be just an extension of the body. It tapered to a point with sharp spines coming out of the bony ridges.

A wavering, high buzzing voice said: *"You have been saved, little one. Come unto me…"*

Philly just sat there, shaking his head from side to side.

He did not realize he had pissed his pants.

Or that his bowels had let go.

Or that he was mumbling and drooling.

He was only aware of the horror standing before him.

It had names, many of them, and they appeared in Philly's head: *Outer One, the Fungi from Yuggoth, the Mi-Go*. None of this made sense to him, but his reeling brain was glad to have something to call it for the human mind requires compartmentalization of all things.

The Mi-Go.

It had a head that was shaped like a bony octagon covered in thin, shiny flesh. It had no eyes, no mouth…just deep oblong chambers set into its face. There was nothing but darkness in them like the hollows of a skull. There were antennae coming from the head, except they were jointed like the legs of a spider. They were flashing different colors and tapping together.

That was the clicking he had heard.

Though it had no eyes, he knew the Mi-Go was looking at him. He had the feeling it was gloating. He knew very little by that point, but he knew it was gloating.

In a tormented, boyish voice, Philly said, "Oh please…oh please…no… don't touch me…don't you touch me…"

"No pain, little one," the buzzing voice said. *"Only deliverance…"*

They were all around him by that point, six or seven of the Fungi from Yuggoth. He was down on his knees before them sobbing with a warm madness in his head. And when they reached out and touched him, his mind ran like sap.

27

Warden Sheens had been working late when the prison shook. He, too, went on his ass and by the time the dizziness retreated from his head, everything was dark.

The phone was dead.

His laptop was dead.

His cellphone was dead.

"What the hell is going on?" he cried out. "Where are the fucking lights?"

And that's when he knew he was not alone in the room. A pale and flickering blue light seemed to spill from the walls and Eddie Sloat was standing there, striding towards him like death.

He was a somnambulant shade with a body of rustling, hungry shadows. He reached towards the warden with fingers like white candlesticks and out of his mouth came two looping black tentacles that were perfectly smooth, perfectly oily, and perfectly deadly.

By the time Sheens thought of screaming, the tentacles were already sliding down his throat and screaming was no longer possible.

28

Chaos, utter chaos.

As the guards pulled themselves up from the floors, many slit open and bleeding from flying glass, the prisoners—now free—went on a rampage, yelling and shouting and screaming. They beat down hacks, cut them, piped them, dismembering them in a manic blood-ritual. They took the prison in minutes, flooding out into the yard and into the administration building as shooters in the gun towers tried to cut them down using sniper rifles equipped with night-vision devices. But there were simply too many.

Within twenty minutes, all the hacks but a few were dead.

The prison was shattered, every corridor packed with bodies and blood, flames engulfing the PI and chapel buildings.

And when there were no more hacks, the prisoners went after each other in slavering packs using shanks and pipes and shards of glass, table legs and purloined guns.

The Mi-Go waited on the high walls like grotesque gargoyles, visible finally, horribly amused by the herds below which ran and raided like swarming white ants on a hillside, killing their own in a great cleansing, a purification, a purge of raw, savage primate aggression. Stretching their ribbed wings and signaling each other with the chromatic language of their jointed antennae, it was exactly as they had foreseen it.

Prophecy fulfilled.

And it was about that time that the black gulf in the sky sheared open with a spinning vortex of gravitational, magnetic, and pulsating kinetic energy.

Nemesis had arrived.

29

The prison was trembling, vibrating with something like seismic waves that Coogan could feel right through the soles of his feet. As the cons raged and the night became a wild shadow-show of bodies rushing down the corridors and catwalks, voices yelling and screaming, he held onto the bars of his cell with Luis at his side. Buildings were burning outside and a flickering orange half-light bathed the cellbock.

"It's here, Coog!" Luis said above the din. "We got to find Sloat! We have to kill that motherfucker! That's the only way this might stop!"

Coogan watched as groups of cons poured down the corridor, crazed, hungry for blood and retribution, gangs going at each other with homemade knives and pipes. More than one man screamed out there as he was thrown over the railing or crushed beneath the mob.

Madness, absolute madness.

Now and again, Coogan thought he saw shapes moving with the crowds…vague, shadowy, indistinct…ghosts that were hopping like locusts.

The whole goddamn prison had breached now.

He did not know where they were, but it certainly was not on Earth. Not anymore. He doubted that very many of them out there knew that yet, but they were feeling it, that everything they had ever known had been sucked into some black transgalactic corridor.

Luis slid something into his palm: a four-inch steel blade with a handle covered in black electrical tape.

"We got to find him!" he said.

Coogan nodded. "If we got to cut our way through every one of them! Let's go!"

They parted, threading out into the mulling violence of the crowds searching for the maker of shadows.

30

Chi Chi was caught up in the madness like everyone else, carried along by the stream of enraged cons, made part of the psychotic, wrathful beast they had become, hitting and being hit, knocked down, trampled, beaten, then clawing to his feet again so he could kill and kill again. Reason was gone and he did not remember what it was, he only knew that he had to survive and that his enemies were to the left and right and all around, drooling subhuman things that wanted to kill him.

He wiped blood from his eyes, searching for a weapon and in the back of his mind a shrilling sing-song voice was saying, *Gather now, gather now, you must gather now.*

He had to go out into the yard; the compulsion was irresistible.

But the rioting mutations around him would not let him. He ducked away from clutching feelers and jointed limbs and slime-covered hands that dripped like hot wax. He crawled on his belly through pooling blood and over ravaged corpses.

He saw cons moving in apish clusters, swinging their arms, most barely walking erect. He could hear them grunting, smell the monkey-piss stink of regression on them.

One of their numbers came in his direction and Chi Chi pulled a baseball bat from the cold fingers of a dead prisoner. The ape cantered towards him, wanting badly to run on all fours. When it got close, snarling with territorial imperative and showing its teeth, Chi Chi hit it in the face with the bat. And when it still moved, Chi Chi jumped up and down on the beast, breaking bones and then, swinging the bat over his head, drove it into his victim until the end was stained with blood and clotted with tissue and hair.

The other apes scattered.

From every direction there were cries and screams from dying and mutilated men, other sounds like braying and howling and strangled bestial noises that could not be from men at all.

And that voice of absolute domination: *Gather now, gather now, you must gather now—*

Three convicts moved up the metal stairs to his left. They crawled on all fours. Their faces were the faces of rats. They dragged serpentine tails behind them.

Chi Chi ducked away from them.

Then he was running again, stumbling down corridors that bled into one another, blurring, unable to hold their shape. Cells were dissolving, iron bars flowing like hot tallow, walls bubbling. The ceiling ran like a river of blood. The mobs of prisoners were reshaping and re-imagining themselves with each step they took. Some became worms that crawled through the concrete walls.

The world moved, shifted, angles intersecting and splitting open. Like melting film, great holes began to burn through the walls revealing an endless blackness beyond. From these dimensional sink holes, *things* were watching with eyes of purple crystal, calling out in voices of shattered glass.

Other things were *swimming* through the holes.

Chi Chi saw pulpy clouds of yellow tissue that were pursued by schools of polychromatic bubbles swimming around each other and *through* each other as if they were made of mist. They were followed closely by great luminous concentric rings of crystal teeth…like living shark jaws.

They moved right through solid walls and floors like they were made of smoke.

Chi Chi felt his mind begin to fold in upon itself.

He saw cons who had the enormous multi-lensed compound eyes of flies. Others that scuttled about on too many legs or suckered themselves to the walls. Everywhere: hopping, jumping, slithering and squealing as gangs met gangs and blood wars broke out.

He was knocked down, kicked mercilessly by a group whose heads had been replaced by squirming protoplasmic pseudopodia that were writhing, in constant motion. Another crowd of convicts that had degenerated into bloated toads gave chase to them.

Chi Chi got to his feet, clubbing down two men who were nursing growths of transparent tentacles at their bellies and was knocked aside by a grotesque dragging thing with flat yellow eyes and gill slits at its neck.

Then a toad-thing.

It hopped in his direction. It reached out for his face with fingers that were puffy, fleshy pads. A black shiny tongue licked blubbery lips. Chi Chi screamed and swung the bat, smashing the thing's left orbit, the eye squeezing out in a tangle of tissue like a pip from an orange. The creature went down making a horrible pained croaking and Chi Chi went mad with it, swinging the bat and breaking limbs, puncturing organs beneath the heaving pebbly skin. With a final shout of rage, he split the thing's head open and that was not enough. He sank blood-sticky fingers into the cleft at its skull and pulled until the head came open and he could get at the glistening frog-spawn it had for a brain.

Splashed with gore, he hopped away from the toad on all fours.

All around him were repulsive subhuman things. He was the only man left and he must stay alive. He must because…because—

Gather now, gather now

You must gather now

But he knew he wouldn't make it for a mixed gang of creepers and crawlers hemmed him in. They moved stealthily forward with knives and clubs and slats of wood sharpened to spears.

"There he is," one of them said. "Do you see him? That's the monster…"

But they were wrong: *they* were the monsters, not him.

As they closed in, their faces were distorted and grotesque as if crushed by intense pressure or melting into threading strands of red-and-white pulp.

When the first spear sank into him and a slashing knife blinded him, Chi Chi cried out in a screeching, defeated voice, but it was not out of pain but out of the remorse that he would not make it to the yard to gather and look upon what was waiting out there.

As he died, he cried out, *"Ph'nglui mglw'nafh Cthulhu R'lyeh wgah'nagl fhtagn…"*

And reached out towards the sky with yellow-suckered fingers.

31

Luis wiped blood from his face, stepping away from the con at his feet that was bleeding out. He watched as the mess hall was enveloped in a fluidic warm green sea that felt like gelatin as it flowed past him, shivering, shuddering with torpid currents. He saw creatures, great and small, that were something like insects, living black and red exoskeletons that swam and flew and often dissolved into agitated streams of bulbous worms that frantically tried to escape gigantic drifting clusters of pink, pulsing eyes that themselves were fleeing vast pulsating bladders with thousands of wavering arms that were composed of a corpse-white jelly.

He did not dare move; afraid they would see him.

They circled around him, passed through him.

He looked down and the floor seemed to be gone.

There were things like craggy, branching tree limbs growing up from a titanic black abyss far below. They bore no buds or leaves, just an immense latticed forest of twigs that wiggled like fingers, reaching out for him.

Screaming, he fell back into the corridor.

32

Coogan was knocked aside by the hysterical crowds. He was hot and feverish, slicked not with sweat but what seemed like a fine layer of mucid slime like afterbirth. His hand felt alien as he brushed his face with it.

Dear God.

There was a fine membranous webbing between the fingers.

He was physically changing, mutating, becoming less human like the others. A monster. He was becoming a monster. The breeching was changing them all.

Sloat. Get that sonofabitch.

Yes.

He moved with a loping gait up the corridor.

An old woman walked through the wall before him. Her face was like threadbare wicker, eaten through with innumerable holes which spilled an inky blackness. She held a plump brown rat in her arms with a human face that grinned malevolently. With her stood three or four tall creatures whose bodies were like tapering barrels. They had great membranous wings and wriggling starfish heads, the arms of which terminated in brilliant red eyes.

Coogan could feel them trying to invade his mind, wanting to draw him into the angles which were fragmenting the prison.

He pulled himself along the wall, a brown fluid sweating from his pores that stank like rotting fish. He came to a barred window and looked out into the world.

Beyond the wall, everything was gone. There was just that greenish mist moving in plumes and eddies.

Rising from it he saw a honeycombed city of red-mottled towers and pipes that looked much like the narrow, elongated chimneys of hydrothermal smoker vents. There were things living in the city, things that swam, propelling themselves about with fanning wings. The red-eyed things that had been with the old woman.

Above, Nemesis was opening in the sky.

His hand. It was swollen, the fingers broad and flattened, that fine webbing between them. The entire thing looked to be made of some white blubbery gelatinous material like pork chop fat. He could plainly see the elaborate system of blue and green veins just beneath the skin that threaded through the hand and forked into the fingers like climbing ivy. It was taking his whole arm.

Then he saw Sloat. He was leading a group of cons down the stairs and they were following him like squealing rats.

Coogan caught up with him just as he made to step out into the yard.

Sloat turned. Too late.

Coogan came at him with a demented instinctual rage. When Sloat turned, Coogan slapped his misshapen fleshy white hand over his mouth and slammed the shank into his chest, burying it right to the hilt. Sloat made a whimpering sound in his throat and Coogan ran his gears—pulling the blade up and over, then down and over like shifting gears in a car.

Sloat fell backwards, arms pinwheeling, a shrill ear-splitting bray breaking from his lips in a mist of red. He tried to cry out, but his throat was filled with blood and all that came out was a stream of scarlet vomit that splashed down his chin as blood fountained from his gashed-open chest and belly.

Coogan stared down at him, his mutant arm throbbing, swollen nodules on his belly tingling.

Sloat looked up at him, his face spattered with blood. For one moment he looked almost grateful…then it was gone, his face pulling into a sardonic mocking grin, the eyes blazing with deranged amusement.

And that's when it happened.

At the very point Sloat should have pitched over and died, what had been living in him, feeding off him like an engorged leech, decided to show itself. Sloat arched backward, his entire body shuddering rapidly with agonal convulsions, a black sap bubbling from his eyes and leaving inky trails like mascara tears down his slack, clown-white face. Milky bile boiled from his mouth and flaring red nodules rose on his cheeks, forehead, and chin…each erupting with a wire-thin transparent tendril like a coiling hookworm. And so many that his face was soon gone beneath the crawling infestation.

Coogan fell back with a cry, gripping the bloody shank.

Sloat's abdomen sheared open like a birth canal with a spray of clear jelly and some writhing, disjointed thing like an undulant amoebic slug pushed up out of the anatomical waste. It was greasy and jellied, yellow eyes like clustered eggs irising open, a dozen oily crimson whip-like appendages like the snaring tentacles of a lion's mane jellyfish emerging and slithering around for something to grasp.

Coogan batted a few away, slashed another open with the shank and it spilled a yellow-green blood to the floor. Another tore out a handful of his hair and yet another, almost lovingly, brushed over his bare arm and it was smooth, silky to the touch.

Then from somewhere outside there came a strident, eerie whistling that was soon answered by what seemed a hundred other such whistles that rose up into a shrill, deafening chorus that reached a single blaring, cutting, ear-splitting note that brought every man in the prison to their knees. It went through their ears like white-hot needles.

Coogan, all the blood drained from his face, pressed his hands to the sides of his head so his skull wouldn't blow apart from sheer internal pressure.

From somewhere, a hot wind of pestilence began to blow with cyclonic intensity.

Nemesis was taking its offering.

33

Luis Cardone barely paid attention to the rioting prisoners or the smell of smoke or the bodies tumbled and heaped about the prison.

Something else was calling to him.

A song of sirens. It was a summoning and it was irresistible. He stumbled along the corridor getting knocked this way and that by a mad flight of prisoners whose eyes were huge and glassy and utterly insane. He could hear something like the manic squealing of a thousand scalded infants and knew it was the men in the yard dying…dying of fright.

He stepped out into the night and looked up into the sky.

The Million Malignant Minds.

Nemesis.

A living primal darkness, an elemental magnetic ghost, a disembodied multidimensional wraith composed of a million malevolent eyes, an irradiated organic dimensional wormhole powered by a seething hot reactor core of decayed alien intelligences hungry for sustenance: human gray matter riven with terror, with fear, with devastating simian superstitious dread.

Luis saw it, gravid with horror, and it reached out to him and found him pleasing and he screamed away his mind until his brain exploded into a soup of blood from a single rupturing, fear-induced embolism that went off in his skull like a cluster bomb.

34

As the prison was overwhelmed, Coogan was enveloped by searching tentacles, dragged screaming into the rising fetal mass of the Sloat-thing. It showed him the face of Franky McGrath and the faces of a hundred others, but he was not afraid. He *attacked,* the shank still in his hand and still razor-sharp. He plunged it into the quivering embryonic biology of the creature as acidic green blood sprayed into his face. Powered by rage and revulsion, he cut and slashed and laid the thing open with pure unreasoning animal hatred.

The Sloat-thing was an abomination.

Mist and slime and bleeding bones, a white unborn spider and a fetal worm and something made of stalks and pulsing bladders washed up on a summer beach in a tangle of deep-sea weed. Stinking and rotting and dissolving. A ghost of teleplasm and undulating entrails and quilts of muscle, all fighting for dominance.

It was these things that Coogan killed.

Sloat's face was hot and pooling, trying to sculpt itself to the stolen bone beneath. But his eyes, they were brilliant and alive and deadly, yellow and smoking. *"And the Old Ones will inherit the carcass of the world,"* he said in a voice of mush, his breath like sewage.

And then he fell apart—a living stew of writhing tentacles and palpitating flesh and oozing jelly and green venom—and Coogan collapsed into him, breathing his last breaths as the ruptured organs within him quivered and the creature's toxic poison turned his blood to cold coagulating sauce. He lay in its remains, the squamous skin of his back prickling, the white gelatinous flesh of his hand pulsating ceaselessly, his belly opening with a watery drainage of black ichor to reveal three budding unformed limbs.

—Coogan closed his eyes—

—he felt a blackness thunder through his head—

—he was sucked from his skull—

35

—but he was not dead—

—agony—

—searing pain—

He felt suction, an intense magnetic pull, a blast of heat and cold as he was pulled up to the thing that hovered above Grissenberg, vacuumed into a funneling gravity of superhot plasma and drowned in pools of liquid methane.

The terror of what he saw stripped his mind to a basal, superstitious level.

He saw images of alien cities rising in witch-cones atop ancient mountains. He saw the black basalt colonies of Mi-Go on hilltops. He saw these cities fragmenting by time, abandoned, collapsing, swallowed by ancient cataclysm only to rise again, inhabited by minds undead and unbodied.

And a voice he had heard in a dream was carried to him by a primal, screeching wind: *"You will be saved."*

The images were gone.

The pulsating black core of the Oort Cloud itself was dragging him in as it sheared open and he saw a million red-litten crystal eyes staring at him, turning his mind to cold mud, those countless deranged monolithic minds spearing into his own like icy blades, laying him raw, his memories and instincts and simple animal drives divorced and dissected as something in him screamed at the violation.

Then he was rejected, spit into the cosm.

Velocity.

Time.

Space.

He was in a foggy-dark dream, a haze, locked in some twitching peristalsis of abject terror, somehow disassociated…a drifting nothingness, a schism that was swallowing itself.

Then sight.

Something like sight.

He stared into faces that were not faces but multi-chambered husks like alien skulls. The Mi-Go. Yes, he knew they were the Mi-Go and he was in one of their buildings on Nithon. Dozens of them were gathered around him, circling him like meatflies about a carcass. He felt their pincers crawling over him like maggots, digging into him, tunneling, slicing and bisecting and changing. He saw his entrails snake free of his belly in a bubbling stasis of blood, he saw them handling his organs and fondling his gut, passing these things from one to the other like children playing a game.

He screamed and it echoed away into dark gulfs.

The Mi-Go were in his head, penetrating his skull and severing his sensory network: careful, meticulous, expert. His brain was an egg, a glossy-gray ova, a sticky, slimy, yolky mass that came free, disembodied, falling into the dark mouth of a pit, plunging into infinite black amniotic waters that were the blood of the cosmos.

A cylinder.

There he waited with hundreds of others all safely secreted in their individual canisters, waiting to be born again, to commune with some distant other. And Coogan could see his other, his host that he would soon commune with: a wriggling, faceless sack crawling through the guttering shadows of a sterile world.

He had been saved from Nemesis, saved to be made whole and made one with a creeping alien pestilence. And it was this knowledge, more than anything else, that caused the entity known as Johnny Coogan to cease to exist.

SPIDER WASP

Moss pulled into town at 4:15, his anxiety spiking as he stepped from the car, a tall knife blade of a man with a face scraped hard by life. His flinty eyes sat in craggy draws, taking in the town, the festivities, the throngs of people that wriggled in the streets like spawning salmon. Place was called Possum Crawl, of all things, a lick of spit set in a bowl-like hollow high above Two-Finger Creek in the very shadow of Castle Mountain. Lots of pastures and trees, hicks towing hay wagons outside town.

This was where The Preacher had gone to ground and Moss was going to find him, drag him kicking and screaming out into the light.

Sighing, he stepped out on the board sidewalk, checking his watch and lighting a cigarette. He carried only a heavy silver case. What was inside it, would be for later. Just like the .38 Colt Special in his gray topcoat.

"Festival," Moss muttered under his breath as he stepped down into the street and merged with the mulling crowds of the town. "Festival."

That's what they called Halloween up here in the yellow and gold hills of Appalachia. Maybe it was about tricks and treats other places, but here in this dead-end mountain town, it was serious business. Festival was not only a harvest celebration, but a time of seeding and renewal, a time of death and resurrection.

The streets were a whirlwind of people, a scattering of autumn leaves blowing down avenues and filling lanes, thronging bodies creating conflicting currents, human riptides of chaos. No one sat still. It was almost as if no one dared to.

Moss could feel all those bodies and minds interlocking out there with grim purpose, a rising electrical field of negativity. One thing owned them, one thing drove them like cattle in a stockyard, and tonight they would meet it.

He walked down the main thoroughfare, beneath spreading striped awnings. Blank white faces with sinister dark eyes watched him, studied him, burned holes through him. It made something inside him writhe with hate and he wanted to open the briefcase, show them what was inside it.

"No," he said under his breath. "Not yet, not just yet."

Not until they were gathered and not until he saw the face of The Preacher.

He avoided the herds as best as possible, taking in Festival. Vines of dangling electrical cords drooped down like snares to capture the unwary. Orange-and-black cardboard decorations leered in every window. Corn shocks and wheat sheaves smelled dry, crisp, and yellow like pages in ancient books. And the pumpkins. Oh yes, like a million decapitated heads, orange and waxy and grinning with dark pagan secrets.

As he passed huts that sold baked potatoes and popcorn and orange-glazed cupcakes, he was amazed at the harmless façade that was pasted over the celebration. What lie beneath it was old and ugly, a pagan ritual of the darkest variety like slitting the throat of a fatted calf or burning people in wicker cages. But in Possum Crawl, it was not openly acknowledged. It was covered in candy floss and spun sugar and pink frosting.

This is what drew you in, Ginny. The carnival atmosphere. The merriment. The glee. The Halloween fun. Your naivety wouldn't let you see the devil hiding in the shadows.

Moss blinked it all away. There was no time for remembrance and sentiment now; he had a job to do and he would do it.

The evil face of Festival showed itself as parade lines of celebrants intermixed and became a common whole that crept forward like some immense caterpillar. They carried gigantic effigies aloft on sticks, grotesque papier-mâché representations of monstrous, impossible insects—things with dozens of spidery legs and black flaring wing cases, streamlined segmented bodies and stalk-like necks upon which sat triangular phallic heads with bulbous eyes. Antennae bounced as they marched, spurred limbs dangled, vermiform mouthparts seemed to squirm. Subjective personifications of an immense cosmic obscenity that the human mind literally could not comprehend.

And here, in this incestuous, godless backwater of ignorance where folk magic, root lore, and ancient malefic gods of harvest were intermixed like bones and meat and marrow in the same bubbling cauldron greasy with human fat, the image was celebrated. Something that should have been crushed beneath a boot was venerated to the highest by deranged, twisted little minds.

But that was going to come to an end. Moss would see to it.

He walked on, a sense of dread coiling in his belly. Not only for what was to come, but what he carried in the case.

As he watched it all, he felt words filling his mouth. Ginny had been fine and pure, a snow angel, eyes clear blue as a summer sky. He worshipped her. She was the altar he kneeled at. She had been perfection and grace and he lived in her soul. Then she had come to Possum Crawl with that little girl's fascination of pageantry and spectacle and this place had ruined her. It had handled her with dirty hands, sucked the light from her soul and replaced it with black filth. Contaminated, she no longer walked, she crawled through gutters and wriggled in sewers.

She loved Halloween. The child in her could never get enough of it. That was how she heard about Possum Crawl's annual celebration, its arcane practices and mystical rituals. That's why she came to this awful place and why the best part of her never left.

But the child, Moss thought. *She should have thought of the child.*

As the shadows lengthened and a chill made itself felt in the air, he watched little girls in white gowns casting apple blossoms about. They wore garlands of flowers in their hair. Symbols of fertility. And everything was about fertility in Possum Crawl—fertility of the earth and fertility of the women who walked it and the men who seeded both. The crowds marched and whirled and cavorted, singing and crying out in pure joy or pure terror. It looked like pandemonium to the naked eye, but there was a pattern at work here, he knew, a rhythm, a ceremonial obsequience to something unnamable and unimaginable that was as much a part of them as the good dark soil was part of the harvest fields.

Moss was shaking.

His brain was strewn with shifting cobweb shadows, his eyesight blurring. For a moment, a slim and demented moment in which his heart pounded wetly and his lungs sucked air like dry leathery bags, Possum Crawl became something reflected in a funhouse mirror: a warped phantasmagoria of distorted faces and elongated, larval forms. The sky went the color of fresh pink mincemeat, the sun globular and oozing like a leaking egg yolk.

Barely able to stay on his feet, he turned away from the crowds that swarmed like midges, placing his hot, reddened face against the cool surface of a plate glass window. His lungs begged for air, sour-smelling sweat running from his pores in glistening beads. After a moment or two, the world stopped moving and he could breathe again. The plate glass window belonged to a café and the diners within—old ladies and old men—were hunched over, mole-like forms scraping their plates clean with sharp little fingers, watching him not suspiciously, but with great amusement in their unblinking, glassy eyes. They looked joyful at the sight of him.

"Ginny," he said, the very sound of the word making him weak in his chest.

He saw her reflection in the glass—she was striding out of the crowds, a swan cut from the whitest linen, her face ivory and her hair the color of afternoon sunshine. Her sapphire eyes sparkled. Then he turned, hopeful even though he knew it was impossible, and saw only the dark, mulling forms of Festival, dark and abhorrent faces greasy with nameless secrets and mocking smiles. He could smell sweat and grubby hands, dark moist earth and steaming dung.

There was no Ginny, only a shriveled beldame with seamed steerhide skin, head draped in a colorless shawl. Her withered face was fly-specked and brown like a Halloween mask carved from leather. She grinned with a puckered mouth, sunlight winking off a single angled tooth like a tombstone thrust from dank earth. "It was only a matter of time," she tittered. "Only a matter of time."

"Go away, you old hag," Moss heard his voice say.

His guts were laced with loose strings that tightened into knots and he nearly fell right over.

"Oh, but you're in a bad way," a voice said but it was not the scarecrow rasp of the old lady but a voice that was young and strong.

He blinked the tears from his eyes and saw a girl, maybe thirteen, standing there watching him with clear, bright eyes. Her hair was brown and her nose was pert, a sprinkling of freckles over her cheeks. She smiled with even white teeth.

"I will help you," she said.

"Go away," Moss told her. He didn't need any damn kids hanging around him and especially not some girl dressed in Halloween garb like the others: a jester in a green-and-yellow striped costume with a fool's cap of tinkling bells.

"I'm Squinny Ceecaw," she said and he nearly laughed at the cartoonish sound of it.

"Go away, kid," he told her again. "Go peddle it somewhere else, Skinny Seesaw."

"*Squinny* Cee*caw*."

Her eyes flickered darkly. She looked wounded, as if he had called her the vilest of names.

Suddenly, he felt uneasy. It was as if he was being watched, studied, perhaps even manipulated like a puppet. A formless, unknown terror that seemed ancient and instinctual settled into his belly and filled his marrow with ice crystals. Again, his eyesight blurred, pixelated, and his head gonged like a bell, his body twisting in a rictus of pain as if his stomach and vital organs had become coiling, serpentine things winding around each other. Then the pain was gone, but loathsome images still paraded through his brain—a psychophysical delirium in which the horned mother parted infective black mists to spread membranous wings over the cadaver cities of men, peering down from the blazing fission of primal space with crystalline, multifaceted eyes.

Then he came out of it and Squinny Ceecaw had him by the hand, towing him away he did not know where. He told her to go away, to get lost, but his voice did not carry. It seemed to sound only in his head. He gripped the silver case as if his fingers were welded to it. He felt weak and stunned.

"It's too early for Festival yet," she informed him.

She brought him through an alleyway and into an open courtyard. Then he was on his hands and knees, gulping air and swallowing a dipper of water she handed him from a well. It was cold and clean and revitalizing. But seconds after he swallowed it, he realized his terrible mistake—he had drunk the water, the *blood,* of this terrible place.

"You've come for Festival?" the girl asked him.

"Sure, kid. That's why I'm here."

He realized he had set the silver case aside. She reached for it, perhaps to hand it to him, and he cried out, "Don't touch that!"

She jumped back as if slapped. He shook his head, wanting to explain, to tell her there were reasons she should not touch it. But in the end, he did not speak. Perhaps, he could not speak.

"Do you live here?" he asked, mopping sweat from his face, pulling the case close to him so that it touched his knee.

"Yes."

"Do you know The Preacher?"

She looked at him for a long time. Her mouth did not smile and her pert nose did not crinkle up with sweetness. He sensed something old about her, something in the shadows behind her eyes, a forbidden knowledge. She studied him suspiciously as if he was playing an awful trick on her.

"Do you know The Preacher?" he asked again.

"Yes, yes, I do."

"Where can I find him?"

"Maybe tonight."

"I figured," he said, wishing he hadn't, because that was giving away more than he dared.

"You have come to Festival to meet The Preacher. Many do," she informed him. "Many, many come but they are not like you. You are special, I think. You are one of the few and not the many."

Tell her, he thought then. *Tell her all about it so she'll know. Tell her about Ginny, about how fair and pure she was until she got stained dark by this awful place, her mind bent and soul polluted until there was nothing left. Tell her how she came for Festival and how she could never leave. How she left you with the baby. Tell her how you came after Ginny that night and dragged her back to the city. How she squirmed like a snake in the backseat until you had to tie her hands behind her back with your belt and gag her with your handkerchief so she'd quit screaming obscenities about the Great Mother who seeded the world, reaping and sowing. And how first chance she had gotten, she slit her wrists, dying in your arms and spewing madness about the festival, Ghor-Gothra, and a ritual known as The Resurrection of the Morbid Insect.*

But he didn't tell her about any of that. Instead, he just said, "Tell me about Halloween."

The girl sat in the grass not far from him, a brooding look coming over her features as she began to speak. "It is not Halloween here. It is Festival, which is much older. It is a celebration of harvest, of leaf and soil and seed," she said as if by rote. "The Mother gives us these things as she gives us birth and life and death to take away our suffering. Once a year we gather for Festival. We celebrate and give back some of what we have been given. It is our way."

Although the degenerate truth of what she said was not lost on him, he refused to listen or accept any of it. He had heard it before and did not want to hear it again. "You should go home now, go to your parents."

She shook her head. "I can't. They disappeared last year playing Festival."

"Get the hell away from me, kid."

Then he elbowed past her, making his way up the alley and to the main thoroughfare, whatever it was called in a pig run like Possum Crawl. He moved through the crowds like a snake, winding and sliding, until he found a bar. Inside, it was dim and crowded, a mist of blue smoke in the air. He could smell beer, hamburgers and onions that sizzled on a grill. The tables were full, the stools taken. Men were shoulder to shoulder up there. But as he approached, two of them vacated their places.

Moss sat down and a beer was placed before him. He didn't even have to wait for service. It came in a frosted mug. It was good, ice-cold. He drained half of it in the first pull, noticing as he had outside that there were no women. Outside, there were old ladies, yes, and little girls, but no teenagers, no young women. And in here, not a one.

Funny.

As he sat there in the murky dimness, thinking about the silver case at his foot, he had the worst feeling that he was being watched again. That everyone in that smoky room had their eyes on him.

Sweat ran from his pores again until his face was wet with it. He caught sight of his reflection in the mirror behind the bar and didn't even recognize himself. He looked dirty and uncomfortable, rumpled like a castoff sheet, his face pale and blotchy, pouchy circles under his eyes that were the color of raw meat. There were sores on his face that he was certain had not been there the day before. His guts turned over. Again, he felt waves of nausea splashing around in his belly and he felt the need to vomit as if something inside him needed to purge itself.

Moaning, he grabbed the case and stumbled back out of the bar. The sun had set. Shadows bunched and flowed around him like pools of crude oil. Faces seemed to crowd him, pushing in, eyes bulging and hands reaching, fingers brushing him. The crowds surged and eddied, hundreds of pumpkins carried on shoulders like conjoined heads. Scratchy Halloween music played somewhere. High above the town, the mountains were dark and ancient and somehow malefic. Their conical spires seemed to brush the stars themselves.

He found a bench and fell into it, gasping for breath. His apprehension increased, the neurotic, skin-crawling feeling that there were things going on all around him that he could not comprehend.

Possum Crawl, goddamn Possum Crawl.

It was like an onion, layer upon layer of secrets and esoteric activities that you could never know nor understand even if you did. The unease flowered into terror as the darkness and silence seemed to crowd him, the sense that he was in an alien place amplified and he heard voices muttering in tongues that were guttural and non-human.

In the glow of streetlights, he saw rooflines that were jagged and surreal. Castle Mountain above seemed to shudder. Fear sweated out of him as his brain whirled and his stomach rolled over and over again. He shivered in the night as a delirium overwhelmed him, squeezing the guts out of him until he became confused, not sure where he was or even *who* he was. The night oozed around him, thick and almost gelid.

He stumbled away, cutting through the crowds, getting turned around and around, hearing a high, deranged wailing and then realizing it was coming from his own mouth.

Moss broke free of himself, propelled in conflicting directions, taken by the crowd and carried along by them until he fell free into a vacant lot strewn with the refuse of Festival: paper cups, streamers tangled in the bushes, dirty napkins and broken bottles and cast aside ends of hot dog buns. He lay there, face in the grass, until he calmed and a voice in his head said, *I will not submit.*

He sat up, lit a cigarette, thinking about Ginny and the night he had taken her from this madhouse of a town. As fevers sweated from him and his gums ached, he was not even certain it had happened. He was no longer certain of anything. There was only this awful place. The night. The cigarette between his lips. He touched the silver shell of the case and his fingertips tingled as if his hand was asleep.

The Preacher.

He had to find The Preacher and do what was right. Do the thing he had come to do which was becoming steadily convoluted and obscure in his brain. He began to fear that his memories, his mind, his very thoughts, were being stolen from him.

Shaking with panic, his identity fragmenting in his head like ash on the wind, a stark image of Gothra floated in his brain, rising, filling the spaces he understood and those he did not—a great monstrous insect, a primeval horror that was part spider-wasp and part mantis and wholly something unknown his feeble brain could not describe even to itself. In his mind, he heard what he thought was the insect's voice, a buzzing/croaking chordal screech. *I am here. You are here. Together we shall bring evil and madness into this world and make it our own.*

No, no, no, that droning, wavering squeal…it could not be a voice. He was coming apart. His mind was failing. He heard maniacal laughter, the sound of sanity purging itself: his own.

Running back out in the street, he was absorbed by the bustling male crowds that carried horrible effigies of Gothra high above them. Faces were twisted masks. The stars blinked on and off like bulbs in the sky. He could smell rotting hay and blood, manure and black earth. Voices jabbered and screamed and shrilled around him. Now the festival was reaching manic, hysterical heights as what he had been feeling for hours took hold of them, too, and carried them forward like a dark river seeking the sea.

"It is time," a voice said at his ear. "Time to meet The Preacher."

It was Squinny Ceecaw, yet it was not her at all. The voice was too mature, all velvet and spun silk, the sort of whispering smoothness one would acquaint with experience and sensuality. Certainly, this wasn't the kid, not Squinny. But it looked like Squinny and as her hand clasped his own, he was certain that it was. Her nearness wedged a seam of pure terror into him. He wanted to throw her off and run. But he didn't; he marched, he melded into the procession that carried pumpkins and flickering candles. Festival was about to reach its terrible climax. The very thing he had anticipated and feared, was about to be realized.

Now no one was singing or crying out. They marched in orderly rows. Many carried pumpkins, but many carried other things—briskets of raw beef, pork loins, shanks of lambs, other primal cuts; dead animals such as rabbits and possum and coyote. Two boys led a massive hog on a rope. Some carried bags of what smelled like rotting vegetable matter.

All of this was so strange and alien, yet so uncomfortably familiar.

Moss knew many things at that moment and knew nothing at all. He walked with Squinny, his mind cluttered, his thoughts muddled. The town was a trap. He knew that much. It had been a trap meant to ensnare him from the moment he arrived and he had stepped willingly into it this afternoon. Possum Crawl owned him now. Festival owned him. Squinny owned him. The people that walked with him owned him. He belonged to them and he belonged to this night and the malevolent rituals that were about to take place. But mostly, oh yes, mostly he belonged to Gothra and the rising storm of anti-human evil he/she/it represented. Now he would become meat and now his mind would be laid bare.

They marched out to a secret grotto beyond the limits of Possum Crawl and up a trail into the high country until the face of the mountain was right before them. And even this opened for them. They passed through a gigantic cave mouth and into the mountain itself.

Moss began to tremble, because he knew, he knew: the mountain was hollow. Hadn't it been this that he was trying to remember when he'd first drove into town? *The mountain is hollow, the mountain is hollow.* Yes, it was really just a sheath of rock and within, oh God yes, within…a high, craggy pyramidal structure of pale blue stone. It rose hundreds of feet above him, illuminated by its own pale, eerie lambency. Its surface was not smooth, but corrugated and carven with esoteric and blasphemous symbols, bas-reliefs of ancient words in some indecipherable language. The pyramid itself was old, old, seemingly fossilized by the passage of eons.

Now the procession moved inside and Moss heard what he knew he would hear—the wet, slobbering sounds, the rustlings, the busy sounds of multiple legs, the chitterings and squealings, and, yes, rising above it all, that immense omnipotent buzzing, the unearthly droning of the great insect itself.

The pyramid was just as hollow as the mountain, its sloping walls honeycombed with chambers, many of which were sealed with mud caps. The women of Possum Crawl had gathered here. They accepted the gifts the men brought. No longer were they women as such, but hairless, pallid things that cared for the white, squirming grubs of the immense gelatinous insect, the all-in-one, the progenitor that all in Possum Crawl worshipped for she brought life, nurtured it, and filled the earth with crawling things and the skies with her primordial swarm.

Vermicular shapes squirmed at his feet, crawling about on their hands and knees, moving with a disturbing boneless sort of locomotion like human inchworms. He saw contorted faces and leering mouths, glistening eyes like frog spawn stared up at him. Flaccid, fungous hands touched him, embraced him.

And now Moss could see her, the Great Mother of Insects, the steaming cosmic furnace of creation, and his sanity ran like hot wax. She was surrounded by a veritable mountain of yeasty gray eggs that glistened wetly from her multiple ovipositors. She was a titanic, bloated white monstrosity, an elemental abomination that sutured time-space with her passing and whose origins were in some deranged cosm where the stars burned black. Her membranous wings spread like kites filling with wind, her thousand legs scraping together, her bulging compound eyes looking down at the offerings laid before her.

Her nest.

Yes, the Earth was her nest.

By then, Moss was on his knees, his mind a warm mush in his head. He remembered her. He had seen her before. Now he understood. He shivered there in her shadow. *Ginny, Ginny, Ginny.* Oh God, he had not stolen Ginny away from them after she was indoctrinated into the fertility cult of Possum Crawl. No, no, she had escaped them and they called out to him, stealing his mind, and he had brought Ginny *back* to them. Yes, in the back of the car, tied and gagged, he had returned their acolyte to the hollow mountain.

But she was not what the Great Insect wanted.

No, Moss was spared, his memories subverted, his will possessed, so that he might bring that which the Mother Insect demanded, the expiation she hungered for.

And now his shaking hands were opening the silver case, fumbling at the locks, working the catches, and then it was in his hands: the reeking mass of meat in the shape of a shriveled infant. The fruit of his marital congress with Ginny. The offering the Great Insect anticipated from the beginning.

It was accepted and found pleasing by her servitors.

Then Moss waited there, his mind gone, his eyes glazed with terror, his stomach pulsing with revulsion. Squinny stepped before him and said, "Your place has always been here. Your destiny is to be meat because all meat has its purpose and all flesh is to be consumed."

He had finally found The Preacher.

He did not fight when the yellow-eyed image of the girl came for him, the avatar of the Primal Mother, when her barbed tongue took his eyes so that he could not look upon the holy rite of birth, the spawning and renewal. He did not even cry out when she jabbed her stinger up between his legs and into his body cavity. He squirmed, he writhed, but no more. Then gray waves of topor washed through him and there was only acceptance.

He was tucked, not unlovingly, into one of the cell-shaped chambers and sealed in there as food. A flaccid, dreaming, unfeeling mass, he did not even flinch when the eggs began to hatch and the wriggling young of the Great Insect began to feed upon him.

WHITE RABBIT

When I woke up that terrible day, I saw the awful thing there on the bureau: a stuffed white rabbit. It was about two feet tall, its fur white and pristine. It was a perfectly innocuous thing essentially, yet it filled me with a weird, disjointed sense of terror. Its obsidian eyes were glassy as the surfaces of mirrors, seeming to look right at me with the most awful sense of menace.

That was silly, of course, but with its eyes glaring at me, it didn't seem as silly as it should have.

"Mason?" I called out. "Mason?"

The silence told me that he had already left for work. Was this his doing? Was this some kind of joke? If it was, I failed to see the humor in it. Or the point. Rabbits were not my thing. I neither liked them nor disliked them. They held no frame of reference, good or bad.

I swung my legs out of bed and stood up. The hardwood floor felt cold under my feet. I stood there, feeling woozy and out-of-sorts. I wondered if I was coming down with something. I had that same fuzzy sense of disorientation generally associated with viral flu.

Then whatever it was, passed.

Tensing, I stepped over toward the bureau. There was my jewelry box, the Horchow catalog I'd been thumbing through last night, my Galaxy S-7…and that damned rabbit.

"I'm pretty sure we never owned a rabbit," I said out loud, trying to be funny, to reassure myself, and only succeeding in amplifying my burgeoning sense of unreality.

There was something else, too.

The bureau was moved. It was not even with the wall. One side was out about two inches farther than the other. It was nothing really, but I was obsessively anal about details. I preferred things uniform and ordered. Had Mason done it? I really didn't think so. He knew how such trifling details annoyed me.

I pushed the bureau back in place. The rabbit teetered, but did not fall. What bothered me the most was the rut in the carpeting. The bureau must have been in that position for some time to press a rut into the pile like that.

Impossible.

I would have noticed such a thing.

Small, insignificant details like that made me uneasy. Don't ask me to explain; I have been like that since childhood. As a girl, my report cards were filed by grade in manila envelopes and my Good Attendance awards were filed alphabetically by teacher. I wouldn't have been able to sleep last night if the bureau had not been perfectly aligned with the wall. Good God, I even organized the food on my plate fastidiously.

Breathing in and out to calm my rising anxiety, I approached the rabbit. It was just a stuffed bunny. Completely harmless, of course, yet those hollow, reflective eyes were staring holes through me. I reached out a trembling hand to touch it, as much to confirm its physical reality as to break the spell of fear it held over me.

Its fur was not soft. In fact, it felt like the bristles of a hog. Tactilely, it was unpleasant, and what made it even worse was that it was warm like the body of a living thing.

I pulled my hand away with a cry.

Enough. It was just the sun coming through the window beaming on it. That's all it was. That's all it could be. These were the things I told myself as I labored over my vegan breakfast of oatmeal and blueberries.

I showered and dressed, got ready for the day in an Emporio Armani skirt suit and heels, refusing to even cast an eye at the rabbit (even though I was certain I could feel it scrutinizing me). I looked good—empowered, chiq, and sexy. And that was exactly the look I was cultivating. If I landed the PacSun account, I was certain to make full partner at Broders.

"I have important things to do today," I told that moth-eaten hare. "And I don't have time for you."

It was moments later, as I checked Evernote on my phone that, again, I was struck by that odd sense of disorientation as if I was moving in one direction and reality (as I understood it) was moving in quite another. I felt dizzy and lost. I closed the app and reopened it. Nothing had changed:

8:15   Prep with Margaret
9:30   PacSun presentation—Nail it!!!
12:30 Lunch at Gregorio's

**Don't forget your dry cleaning!

***Watch for him he is coming

The weight of that last note planted me on the bed. I sat there for some time thinking, fearing, that there were things I should remember, but could not. *Watch for him he is coming.* I had not written that. I knew I had not written that. I had no idea what it could even be referencing. Yet…there was something playing around the edges of my memory, an apprehensive sort of déjà vu that left me feeling jittery and troubled.

Something in my world had changed.

I was certain of it. I just couldn't put a finger on what it was.

Life becomes incoherent now, a voice in the back of my mind whispered and I swear I nearly screamed because for a moment there, I thought it was the voice of the rabbit.

The day moved on and the very unreal texture of the morning was ground beneath the wheels of progress. The PacSun presentation was a hit as was lunch with my boss. I was feeling pretty high and refusing to think about the rabbit or my mad morning.

Mason was already there when I got home. He had that cocky little half-grin on his face that I found so unbearably sexy and so endearing.

"You landed it, didn't you?"

I smiled. "Yes, I did. How did you know? It was supposed to be a surprise."

He came over and scooped me in his arms. "Because, my little Ella, I know you. When you put your mind to something, nothing stops you. That's what I love about you: you're strictly win-win. And look at you in that skirt…God." He kissed me, letting it linger deliciously. "As much as I like you in it, I want to get you out of it in the worst way."

We laughed and I told him all about PacSun and how I had wowed them from start to finish. There was not a single moment of the presentation that I did not feel in control, did not feel that I had them. Not a single clumsy moment or breath of dead air.

"What did Margaret say?"

"Well, she paid for lunch. That should tell you something."

"Good girl."

"How was your day?"

He scowled. "Ah, the life of a PA. I spent the morning with two colicky twins. I had a four-year-old vomit on me. And…oh yes…I accidentally spilled Dr. Bella's chai tea and she called me an insufferable clutz…string of very un-pediatrician like expletives omitted."

The very idea made me narrow my eyes. "She's such a bitch."

"Exactly, dear. That's why I'm looking forward to quitting my job and being a kept man by my rich, successful girlfriend—faithful house-hubby, galley slave, and patron fuck-toy, that's me."

"I'll keep you busy," I told him, pulling him closer and sliding my tongue into his mouth.

"I look forward to it. But for now, I really need to shower. I think there's still vomit down my collar."

"Ew! Please do."

"Oh…and I think I'm taking you out to dinner. You deserve it and God knows I need it." He turned away, then turned back. "Oh, and I love you, Ella-kins."

Ella-kins. Yes, I know it's corny and perfectly ridiculous…yet, when he said it, I nearly melted like butter in a hot pan. I could have dripped to the floor and made an unsightly mess. But that was the affect he had upon me. Even though I was ten years older than him, I knew he belonged to me and no one else. I heard the shower running and felt overwhelmed by love.

This was turning into the most spectacular day of my life…and to think it started with that stupid rabbit. It was laughable now. I'd ask Mason about it when he got out of the shower and the explanation would be perfectly prosaic. Probably a silly gift from one of his little patients. He'd probably left it in the car yesterday and fetched it up this morning before he went in, thinking I'd get a laugh out of it. It was funny how time could change your perspective.

Still smiling about it all, I went into the bedroom and the rabbit was not on the bureau. I saw myself in the mirror, standing there, the smile etched onto my face…only now there was nothing happy about it. It looked positively sardonic.

I told myself either Mason had moved it or I had hallucinated the entire business. But I accepted neither explanation. I went through the motions of looking around for it in closets, under the bed, in the spare room, but it wasn't there as I knew it wouldn't be there. And the reason for that, I began to think, was that this was a private, intimate sort of haunting. It was not to be shared.

I was overwhelmed with a sense of impending doom. It made me feel dizzy and dislocated. It was as if I could sense something taking shape around me, but could not identify it. I went over to where the rabbit had been, placing a hand there for no other reason than I thought I should. It felt warm, warm as the rabbit had felt under my fingers.

Ridiculous.

If this kept up, I'd be on the road to a full-blown psychosis.

I was tired, overworked, coming down from the raw-edged tension of preparing for the PacSun presentation. That's all it was. That's what I kept telling myself.

Sometimes, strict attention to trivial details can clear your mind and soothe what ails you, so I took off my earrings and put them in the jewelry box. I took off my skirt and laid it on the bed. Then I opened the drawer I kept my socks and underwear in. This was when real panic set in. I was always very meticulous about what went in which drawer and how it was organized within those confines. My underwear was always neatly folded on the right side, the socks on the left. Now they had been transposed. Frantic, I opened another drawer and another and another. I found lounge pants in the drawer reserved for tees and sweatshirts. Pajamas where my jeans usually were and—

Everything was in utter disarray.

I didn't for a moment suspect Mason. He would never do such a thing and he was completely incapable of folding clothes with my usual precision. It was quite beyond him.

I began to wonder earnestly then if I was truly losing my mind. Was I doing things contrary to myself and not remembering them? This would have been bad enough for anyone, but for me, dear God, it was a catastrophe. I liked to keep my mind as correlated and catalogued as the rest of my life.

I forced myself into the kitchen and cracked a bottle of Strongbow hard cider. I downed nearly half of it. I was shaking so badly I had to hold the bottle in both hands. I needed to relax and sort this out. Something was afoot, but I had to approach it logically, rationally.

The alcohol helped. Believe me, it did. Still pulling off my cider, I made my way down the hallway. Mason was out of the shower. As usual, he dispensed with vanity, leaving the bathroom door wide open. It was at this point that I would usually admire his form, but what I saw filled me with a vague sense of terror.

He was standing in front of the full-length mirror, eyes glazed, mouth grinning like that of a stuffed fish. As I watched, he stepped back, then, arms held stiffly to either side as if he was being crucified, he began to dance with a swaying, dipping motion, moving backwards in an exacting repetitive circle. The movements were precise, almost mathematically so. It might have been comical if it wasn't for his bulging, unblinking fish eyes and that toothy, mirthless grin on his face.

I wanted to call out to him, but I didn't dare. I merely stood there, trembling fiercely, my eyes welling with tears because either I had gone mad or the world had.

Life becomes incoherent now.

Yes, that seemed to encapsulate the freakish incongruities of my life.

I stumbled off into the bedroom and sat on the bed. My mind was whirling with conflicting thoughts. I felt the same as I had that morning, only worse. Reality seemed to be flaking away and I was afraid what might be revealed beyond its confines. I looked around the room with a frightening, hallucinogenic clarity that made me clench my teeth. Everything seemed… *disordered.* I could not precisely say what it was, but things were different. Askew? Off-center? I couldn't be sure, but it was as if the entire room was warped subtly, distorted in a way only my very precise, manically-ordered mind would recognize.

I recalled seeing Steven Wright a few years before with Mason and Wright had said, *I got up the other day and everything in my apartment had been replaced with an exact replica.* That was the joke, that was the rub—if they were replicas, how could you tell?

But that was the scary thing: I could tell. I could sense the transition. It was there and yet it was not. It was as if some dire mechanism was at work around me, making and re-making all that I knew. There was a crack on the ceiling shaped like a bolt of lightning. A murky darkness seemed to be oozing from it. I knew it had never been there before; it would have offended my sense of order.

Mason stuck his head in the room, dripping wet and naked. He seemed fine. "What're you doing?" he asked.

"How long has that crack been in the ceiling?"

"Since we moved in."

It was at that moment that I realized that he was part of it, too, that he had been drawn into it without even realizing it. There was a wine barrel clock on the wall that his sister had given us. It always hung next to the window. Now it was on the other side of the room near the closet.

My voice would barely come. "When did you move the clock?"

He looked from the clock to me. "I…what do you mean? It's always hung there."

"No, it hasn't, Mason. You know it hasn't," I said. "Just think for a minute."

"You feeling all right?" he asked. "You look a little funny."

Things become fuzzy at this point. He kept talking but I wasn't listening. No, I was staring at a large, dark shadow in the corner. There was nothing there to cast it, yet it seemed to be growing darker and gaining volume until it looked like a great spreading stain.

But it couldn't have been a stain because it began to move with an undulating motion. This was where I checked out. I went out cold.

The sense that everything was in some horrendous process of change and reality itself had been subverted did not lessen, it increased. For two days, I laid in bed sweating out fevers. I was never certain when I was awake or when I was asleep, what was real and what was a febrile dream. The only constant was Mason tending to me or talking on the phone in the hallway, his language sounding like some incomprehensible gibberish.

Of course, there *was* another constant—the shadow in the corner. It stood much larger than a man now, brushing the eight-foot ceiling. It had taken on an unpleasant, fearful solidity. If I watched it for any length of time, it appeared to move. I imagined more than once—or maybe I didn't imagine at all—that it made a grunting, squealing sound like a wild boar, yet low and distant, as if from some faraway place. But getting closer. Oh yes, closer all the time.

On the morning of the second day when Mason went back to work, the rabbit returned. It sat on the bureau as before, but it had changed. Its pelt was no longer glossy white, but a dingy gray like moldering rags. Its eyes were larger or maybe it was just the sockets themselves. It had a drawn, withered appearance like a pet that had been slowly starved to death. I noticed with alarm that a few flies lit off of it.

It was getting so I could not trust what I saw. I was not sure of anything. My head was still spinning and my thoughts confused. Yet, I was certain the rabbit was just as real as the shadow in the corner. In fact, I could smell it: a low stench of putrescence.

While Mason was at work, I made myself get out of bed. Whether it was my illness or what was going on around me or my subjective impression of the same, I felt more disoriented than before. The world was aberrant. I began to feel unreal, as if I had never really existed in the first place. I was losing touch. I was becoming neurotic.

I sat in the kitchen, bathing in a stream of yellow sunlight, fascinated by the motes of dust dancing in it, imagining that the world, the known universe, was but one mote surrounded by countless others.

My phone was on the table. In the twisted depths of my mind, a voice that I did not recognize kept saying, *watch for him he is coming, watch for him he is coming, watch for him he is coming,* until I thought my head might split open. I opened Evernote. It no longer said the above. That was reassuring. Then I opened the Gallery and looked through my photos. Do I dare mention what I saw? There were shots of Mason and I in Bermuda, hiking in the Adirondacks, attending his sister's wedding, all the usual stuff.

The only problem was they were *different* from the ones we had taken.

I mention three specifically. The first was Mason and I standing knee-deep in the crystal blue waters of Horseshoe Bay Beach with weathered, mountainous black rocks just behind us. That much I remembered. But the titanic, seaweed-encrusted effigy rising from the surf, its arms spread as if in benediction over our heads…no, no, that had not been there. It was obscured by mats of yellow kelp, so what it was meant to represent was unknown. The second photo of interest was taken in the wild country above Gleasman Falls in the Adirondacks. Again, I remembered the shot…but not the amorphous, crooked form emerging from the forest that Mason was pointing at. The third photo I bring to your attention was a wedding shot. Mason and I, decked out in summery finery, standing near a fountain. Behind us, was a lurking figure that looked very much like the shadow I kept seeing in the corner.

As in my day-to-day life, physical reality was being altered. There were other photos that equally chilled me, but it was those taken last Christmas that scared me the worst. In each successive image, my face blurred until in the final shots it was completely gone.

Barely able to keep my knees from shaking, I went to the window and looked out over the rooftops. For one dreadful moment, I thought it was an alien cityscape of black towers and egg-like spheres, but it was only my racing imagination.

At least, that's what I told myself.

I was well enough to return to work the next day. I welcomed it. Anything to get out of that oppressive apartment and its otherworldly associations—as well as the very real possibility that I was nearing some kind of breakdown.

As I crept through traffic to Broders, I caught sight of a billboard on Fifth raised high above the bustling streets. It made me smile. It was for one of my campaigns, a perfume called Sinn that we sold unapologetically with sex. It featured a green-eyed, scarlet-haired beauty looking back over her bare vanity-tattooed shoulder, holding a bottle of Sinn. She was practically smoldering, her lips full, juicy, and red as ripe strawberries. *It's not what's on the surface, it's what's underneath,* read the ad copy. That was basically the pitch I gave the suits from Christian Dior and they ate it up.

It made me feel good, positive. I was a force in this world, not some neurotic bitch steadily fading from it. I was now. I was real. You have no idea how badly I needed to feel that way. When I parked in the garage across the street and the resident religious freak on the corner handed me one of his fliers, I even smiled at his mottled, seamed face as I stuffed it into my coat pocket.

Then work. Oh, it was a madhouse, simply chaotic. I was involved in not two, but three campaigns as project manager because Bob Silverman was in the hospital following a particularly bad bicycle accident that left him in traction. It was meeting after meeting, arguing with Creative and Development, barking orders at interns and Accounts…endless. As stressful as it all was, it made me feel safe. I felt insulated from the madness that was beginning to be too commonplace. It even occurred to me, that given time, I might even forget about it all. Then, just after lunch—I skipped food for two vodka martinis—the pandemonium of Broders seemed to switch gears. Everything became calm and pacific. Everyone was suddenly, miraculously, on the same page and it seemed like the agency might survive another day to fight again.

I should have known something was amiss. People all across the office began to cluster in little groups, whispering and gesturing. They had a tendency to scatter or go silent when I approached, which was strange because I had good relationships with just about everyone. But now I was being marginalized, isolated from the social flow. I did not like it. In fact, it began to make my skin crawl as if I was an enemy agent in their midst and they knew it. I began to get very paranoid. People stared at me and old friends ignored me. It was as if everyone was part of something I was excluded from and knew something that I was not allowed to know.

My anxiety increased throughout the afternoon and then eclipsed shortly after five. I went to see the copywriters about a pitch for L'Oréal they were revising. I saw four faces I had never seen before.

"Where's Benji?" I asked.

The four of them looked at each other and then looked back at me.

"Who's Benji?" one of them asked.

"He's your boss if you work in this department," I said.

"We work for Kathleen. Never heard of Benji."

Under ordinary circumstances, I might have demanded an explanation, but I could feel it just as I had at home: things were unraveling. Reality was frayed. What I had known for years was disintegrating. Feeling a mad sort of terror building in me, I went over to Creative. I wanted to talk to Joyce, Broder's art director. Joyce was not there. Neither was Rich or Tom or Carolyn. No one had ever heard of Joyce or the others. I stormed over to Margaret's office. She ran Broders. She was not there either. In fact, there was a supply closet where her office had once stood.

I went back to my own office.

My name was still on the door, thank God. I didn't know what to do. My paranoia was telling me there was a conspiracy at work, that my life had been synthetic, that I had maybe been brainwashed into believing that any of it had been true in the first place. I went down on my knees, shaking and sick to my stomach. Sour-smelling sweat boiled from me in rivers. I was hallucinating. That was it. That's all it could be.

I was clinging to the flimsiest rationale even though I knew it was a lie, a great seething manufactured lie.

With shaking hands, I tried to call Mason, but his number was no longer in my directory. I knew from the moment I saw him performing the dance that he had been appropriated like the others. Soon, I would be alone in an alien, perverse world as reality was turned inside out.

I walked from one end of the office to the other, touching the walls and desk and bookcase, the awards and plaques I had received over the years if for no other reason than to confirm that they did in fact exist.

But in my head, a hysterical voice shrieked, *synthetic, it's all synthetic. Ella Barnes never really existed. You are a nonentity, a shadow, a ghost that is about to be erased by the intersection of something immense, something cosmic and nameless—*

I must have gone out cold.

When I woke much later, I was on the floor. Nearly everyone would have left save the interns and newbies who would be sucking up the extra work of their bosses, trying to make an impression.

I checked my phone, even though I knew it was pointless.

Mason ordinarily would have called by then. He would have been worried as to why I was not home. But he hadn't called. He hadn't even texted. And that was because I no longer existed. Yes, I knew many things now and guessed at others that were literally beyond comprehension.

I grabbed my coat and right away, as I dug for my keys in the pocket, I found the flier the religious freak had given me. It had been balled up, but now I straightened it out, reading the words printed upon it. It did not say HAVE YOU BEEN SAVED? as they always had in the past. No, now it read HAVE YOU BEEN OFFERED?

I walked out into the shadowy offices of Broders…except, they were not shadowy at all.

People were queued up, those I knew and those I did not. They ignored me. I did not exist for them. They were all staring with fixed, manic attention at some huge shaggy form that waited at the far end down where Margaret's office had been.

It was the shape from the corner of my bedroom, I realized with a hot flare of panic in my chest. I tried to focus on its appearance, to finally get a real look at it, but the harder I tried, the more it blurred and became nebulous. It was dark and shaggy with spike-like horns jutting from the top of its head. That's all I knew. That's all I was *allowed* to know.

I backed away, bumping into people who rudely shoved me aside because I was blocking their vision of what waited there. One by one, they kneeled before the beast, making obeisance to the horror. What they did then and what was offered to them, I did not want to know.

I ran for the elevators, then decided on the stairs down to the lobby. All the way, I could hear the porcine squealing of something that stalked me, exhaling hot and sour breath against the back of my neck.

The apartment. The white rabbit, that hideous avatar of what my life had become, was on the bureau, waiting for me. Whereas before it looked withered, now it was decaying—its fur a graying pelt, threadbare and fusty, yellowed rungs of bone protruding through gaping holes. Flies crawled over it. Yet, its huge soulless black eyes looked out at me with wrath and intensity.

"Don't think I don't know what you've planned," I told it.

The apartment was equally as filthy. Dust was layered over everything, dozens of flies speckling the windows. There were jagged cracks in the ceiling and walls, that squirming darkness trying to push through. My clothes were moth-eaten rags in the closet and drawers. In the kitchen, fruit in a bowl was rotted to a blue excrescence of mold.

Out of my mind not just because of the filth and stench, but because my world, my private space, had been reduced to ruin and rot and rabid disorder, I screamed and launched myself at the rabbit. I seized its carcass in my hands and tore it into pieces, discovering that it was stuffed with graying meat and organs and hundreds of plump writhing maggots.

223

After that, I ran. There was little else I could do being that my car was not where I left it. I wandered from street to street, moving down crowded avenues in a daze, looking up but once and there I saw the billboard for Sinn. But the alluring woman was no longer there, instead there was a crude image of the beast and beneath, HE'S COMING GIVE PRAISE.

The tall buildings that rose around me were monolithic and crooked, threatening to fall and crush me. I saw men with the blank, watery eyes of toads. And women, dear God, what seemed hundreds of women and all of them noticeably pregnant.

Finally, my building.

When I reached our floor, I was nearly paralyzed with apprehension. Fear infested me. In my dementia, I imagined some gap-toothed court jester with mad, rolling eyes living inside my skull like a worm in a hollow seed. This was what was left when reality as such fractured like a bone and the marrow of common sense leaked out.

I was not certain the key I clutched in my pale fingers would even fit in the lock. The idea terrified me. The penultimate absurdity. But the key fit and the lock disengaged. I turned the knob and stepped inside. Immediately, I was certain I was in the wrong apartment: the feel, the smell, the very psychic texture was all wrong. I was in an enemy camp and I knew it. Had that abomination from the office been waiting for me, I could have been no more horrified at what I saw.

The furnishings were all different and I sensed the decorative touches of another woman. But that was purely cosmetic. What really disturbed me were the framed photos on the wall. I recognized them. I recognized every one of them. I had been in them once, but now I had been replaced by a leggy, emerald-eyed redhead whose left shoulder and right arm were adorned with vanity tattoos. It was the model from the Sinn campaign. I swear it. Mason was still in them, of course, and was it my imagination or did he look just a bit happier with her by his side than he had with me? Not only had sanity abandoned me and reality failed me, but love had now betrayed me.

Mason, Mason, Mason.

Was this the sort of girl he'd wanted all along? Some bronze-skinned, sapphire-eyed, taut-thighed, bullet-titted whore who would go down on him in traffic or finger herself on the leather seats of his Escalade in a crowded parking lot?

Photo after photo of her wrapped around him, displaying her goodies, grinning with her enticing bee-stung lips and flashing eyes like hot jade…she made him happier in ways I never could.

There was a recent picture of her artfully displayed against a setting sun on a beach, her hands clutching a noticeable baby bump at her midsection.

I began to understand. The white rabbit, the white rabbit. Rabbits had long been a symbol of fertility to the ancients. Mason had wanted children, but my tipped uterus had left me barren. And now, it seemed, he had plowed a richer field.

The final insult was above the fireplace where a tasteful print of Monet's "Lady with a Parasol" had hung. It had been replaced by a bronzed plaque, some revolting pagan travesty, multi-eyed, surrounded by a corona of spidery appendages that seemed to grow from it.

I recognized it because Mason's concubine had a similar tattoo on her forearm surrounded by spiraling letters.

Terror rose inside me on leathery wings because I knew it was a symbolic representation, a holy relic of the shaggy thing that had subverted my life and distorted the very physics of my world.

My stomach turned at the idea of visiting the bedroom where Mason and his perky little fertility goddess joined nightly, probably dancing rhythmically backwards (as he had in the bathroom that day) like Medieval witches tripping on belladonna and henbane, slitting the throats of sacrificial white rabbits and bathing in their blood to ensure fertility, before consummating the act, well-greased like rutting hogs.

I lingered in the kitchen a bit, disturbed at the variety of unnamable spices on my shelves and the quantity of well-marbled red meat in the refrigerator. I also found a quantity of ancient-looking, horn-handled knives in the cutlery drawer.

I had to leave and I knew it. Good sense demanded it. That's when I realized I was not alone. I whirled around, expecting to come face-to-face with Mason's domesticated Circe, the fire-haired Madonna of the fields swollen with child.

But it was Mason himself.

"What...what are you doing here?" he asked, his rugged face and dark, sensual eyes filling my knees with water.

"Wait, just wait," I said, knowing I was a stranger to him now. "Please listen to me. I'm not a thief. Just give me a minute to explain."

But did I dare expose the architecture of my madness? Did I dare tear my wriggling insanity out by its dark roots and let him examine it by the light of day? Yes. I poured everything into it, body and soul, to stir something in him, some shred of remembrance.

"...before this awful thing happened, we were happy. So very happy. Don't you remember? *Can't* you remember?" I implored him and for one solitary, hopeful moment, I saw something shift in his eyes. It was all coming back to him. "Mason...please try to remember. Skiing in Aspen, that weekend with the Rosenbergs in Big Sur, the time we hiked Caminito del Rey...can't you remember? The chateau in Savoie Mont Blanc? The grape harvests?"

Whatever light had been lit behind his eyes, it was now extinguished. He was lost to me and I knew it. I felt my heart clench like a weak fist.

"Listen, lady. I don't know what your problem is or why you had to break into my place," he said, holding the flats of his hands out to stay me. "But you have to go, okay? If you leave now and don't come back, I swear I'll keep the police out of this."

I could feel hot tears spilling down my cheeks. I could barely swallow. "Oh, Mason, please. It's me...it's Ella."

"I don't know you. I've never seen you before. You need to go. I'm a married man. We're expecting and I don't need this kind of trouble in my life."

Everything inside me began to boil. "Why did you have to mention *her?* How the hell could you bring that whore into my house and impregnate her in my bed?"

He made excuses as he always made excuses whenever I caught him being unfaithful. He tried everything, but I wouldn't listen. I saw the beast behind him, squealing and grunting the way *she* must have when he rode her, fertilizing her lush garden.

By then, one of the horn-handled knives was in my hand and I plunged it into his throat. The blood was much redder than I could have imagined. It was hot and meaty-smelling. At first, I was repulsed by it, then oddly intrigued, and finally, excited. I remember kneeling down in a hot pool of it as Mason contorted in his death throes, catching the liquid jet of blood in my hands. How like the rabbit he looked in his agony.

I have no memory of anointing myself with Mason's blood, drawing esoteric symbols over my breasts, belly, thighs, and face.

"I have made an offering in your name," I said to the beast as it watched. "By your hand, make me fertile and rich with life so that these loins I spread for you might bear fruit."

What he gave unto me, I took into my mouth and did so willingly, gladly.

That's when she came in—the whore, the Madonna, the seed-eater, the high cunt of the fields, her belly rounded and full in its eighth month. You know what I did to her and more specifically, to the demon seed she carried. I was still dancing widdershins in the old way (as the beast instructed) over their ritually-harvested remains when the police arrived. They could not understand the significance of what I had done or how I had been called as courtesan into His house.

You, of course, know the rest. I will not speak of it again, not until the stars are right. Soon now, the shaggy savior will come down from the mountain high to claim his offerings beneath the glow of the oblong moon. And I will offer unto him the seed that grows fat and juicy in my belly.

OLD HOPFROG

*(Note: the following is a detailed transcription of what has been called the Lakeside Tapes. For court use only. All video, audio, and documentation will be considered sealed until further notice.)

Guy: The Severn Valley. Brichester. Mercy Hill. Camden. Hardly places to inspire fear. Yet, tonight we may see a ghost. In fact, I fear we may see something far worse. Something primordial and unspeakable that has crawled from the black depths of hell. We're here at Lakeside Terrace, a notoriously haunted bit of hamlet set between the encroaching shadows of the forest and the dark, bottomless lake before us. It's Halloween and it will be an All Hallows like no other.

(Camera pans over a dark and misty lake. The water is uniformly murky and flat, stagnant-looking. Tall, lush stands of grass grow at the water's edge, appearing gray as the lights sweep over them. Reeds and tangled ferns rise from the perimeter. The camera pans from the lake to a row of black-walled houses, each three-stories in height, slouching, crumbling structures that seem to lean out at the viewer. As the camera spots illuminate them, grotesque shadows seem to bob and sway.)

Guy: Tonight, our teams of paranormal investigators led by Annabelle Mathews and Kealan Brightly respectively will spend the night in two of these rather desolate, forbidding houses. They will be locked in for the duration. Here, at the mobile unit, we shall be in direct communication with them.

What they see, you will see. What comes for them, will come for you. For this is *Haunted: Dead or Alive.*

(Guy steps away from the houses and to the mobile unit van parked on the slippery cobbles where the cast is waiting.)

Guy: Well, how do you feel?

(Camera shows a tall, blonde woman. She casts a wary look at the houses behind her. This is Annabelle Mathews. With her is Piers Lyon, her cameraman.)

Annabelle: Honestly, I'm a bit frightened. I've been in some bad spots… but this one…I don't know. It sets my flesh to crawling. Don't you think, Piers?

(Piers steps into the frame. An SLS camera unit is balanced on one shoulder.)

Piers: Weird sort of place, ain't it? You can almost feel something building as if we're expected.

(The camera pans to Team #2. We see Kealan Brightly and cameraman Simon McGee.)

Kealan: I have to agree. I definitely feel a sense of foreboding. I'm not sure what we've gotten ourselves into this time. I only pray we can get ourselves out.

(Simon smiles slyly at the camera which is operated by Bert Taylor, one of the mobile unit team.)

Guy: How does it feel that you won't really be alone? That millions will be watching and millions more streaming live?

Annabelle: It gives me comfort.

Kealan: This might just turn into a global spook show.

Guy: Let's get set up then. It looks like we're in for a long, dark night…

(Video cuts to Brichester, previously recorded material apparently. An old woman sits in a public park. She is feeding the geese.)

Guy: You've lived here your whole life?

Old Woman: Sure, save a stitch in Goatswood after the war when I was a wee girl. But we didn't stay there long. Them in Goatswood ain't exactly right, now are they? (She laughs.) God, must be the age getting into my brain! Saying such dreadful things. Can you cut that out?

Guy: Of course. Can you tell me a bit about the lake?

Old Woman: (Appearing uneasy) Well, I know what I know and I won't have you laughing at me and saying I'm daft and long in the tooth.

Guy: That won't happen. Trust me, we take our subject matter very seriously here at *Haunted: Dead or Alive.*

Old Woman: (shrugs) Well, I've only been to the lake once, you understand. That's when I was fifteen or so. And that once was enough. No, no, I didn't see no phantoms flitting about nor none of that. Just a very bad place. You could feel it in here. (She taps her temple with one finger.) It was very…oh, what's the word? *Oppressive?* My mother always said it was a place to best leave alone. On around sunset, you hear the frogs croaking—loud and strange, like nothing you ever heard before! Goes on all night long. *Cor!*

Guy: What strikes me as odd is there doesn't seem to be any recognized name for the lake.

Old Woman: (Shrugging again) Oh, I've heard it called Dark Lake and Black Lake. People 'round here, you say something's happened up at the lake, well, they know what you're talking about. Lots of wild stories, see? I remember that bit about Mr. Cotsly.

Guy: Mr. Cotsly?

Old Woman: Was when I was a girl. Mr. Cotsly had the next farm over, sheep, barley, rye. He wasn't quite right in the head. He used to fish up to the lake. Used to like to go out there at night, him and a young ward of his. I remember him clearly telling my father that at night when the full moon was shining down from above…very bright, you see…that there were figures carved into the rocks under the water. In the moonlight, them figures would move. And if you watched 'em too long, well, you'd want to move with them, so said he. Course, Mr. Cotsly was crazy and we all knew it. He brewed his own whiskey and it had gotten to his brain. But there's one other thing…I remember my father saying to my mother…the fish…

Guy: Yes?

Old Woman: Well, it was the fish, like I say. Mr. Cotsly would catch 'em up there and eat them. No one 'round here would go anywhere near that lake after dark and precious few would go during the day. Certainly no one would eat anything that came out of that devil's lake—my mother's words—but he did and regular like. My father said he saw one of Mr. Cotsly's catch, awful-looking thing, I guess, a real horror, big like a carp but with sort of feelers where its fins should have been. It had been out of the water two or three hours and it should have been dead, but it wasn't dead enough. *Eyes*, he said, *huge eyes*. Not like fish eyes but the eyes of a person that looked right at you as if they knew something you didn't. *Gawd.* Had regular nightmares as a girl, I did. Fish eyes in my dreams...

(Video cuts to Guy standing before the lake. Must, again, be previously recorded because the sun is just going down. A chorus of frogs can be heard croaking and chortling very loudly.)

Guy: According to local legend, the lake was created by a meteorite that fell from the sky many centuries ago. Just how many is unknown. I spoke with Brichester University geophysicist Dr. Robert Coombes on the subject and he told me he is very aware of the tale. He said it's entirely possible, but without a detailed examination of the lake bed, something which requires major funding, there's really no way to know for sure. What we *do* know is this. Severn Valley folklore tells us that there was a city on the meteorite, the remains of what would appear to be an ancient extraterrestrial civilization. Whatever lived in that city died out during the meteor's journey here... except for a single creature, an evil cosmic entity the locals—those who will speak of it at all—call *Gla'aki*. What this thing is, no one will say. Perhaps they do not *dare* say. One thing is for sure: they believe it is still down there, still very much alive, a living malignance that will one day rise to enslave mankind...

(The camera pans to the walls of the houses. With the floodlights illuminating them, some sort of symbols appear carved into them. Something like a stem with fanning branches. They appear to have been vandalized, defaced, as were the words beneath them which are now illegible.)

Guy: These...symbols are to be found on the outer walls of all these houses, placed there many, many decades ago, it would seem. But what were they? The sign of some esoteric cult? Hex signs? Tonight, we might just find out...

(Video cuts now to real time. Guy is in the back of the mobile unit with Bert Taylor and Susan Pealan. Image must be from a static camera.)

Susan: Okay, we're linked.

Guy: Annabelle, are you there?

Annabelle: Here, Guy. Though truth be told I wish I were somewhere else, anywhere else.

(She is seen standing before a fireplace that looks ancient, cracked and broken. In IR, Piers pans from her to reveal the room: walls water-stained and peeling, uneven floors, boards warped, some completely missing.)

Annabelle: Well, obviously this place is a real death-trap and we have to watch our every step. I don't know if it's just me, but this house is really getting to me. It feels like my stomach's in my throat. Can you get a shot of this, Piers? I've got goosebumps and I don't think it's from the cold.

(Piers zooms to her arm. The image is not distinct enough to see goosebumps. Though it is important to note that she seems genuinely uneasy. Though she may be simply acting.)

Guy: Have you seen or heard anything?

Annabelle: No, not exactly…but the meter on my EMF was jumping wildly about five minutes ago. I have the worst feeling of impending doom… as if…as if this might be the last night of my life. We're now going to investigate the cellar. Wish us luck.

(Video cuts back to the inside of the mobile unit.)

Susan: She's laying it on pretty thick.

Bert: That's her job. She's setting the stage. That girl knows her onions, don't she?

Guy: Exactly. That's why people tune into this rubbish.

Susan: I like the bit about the city on the meteor. Now that's imagination.

Guy: Local color, love, just local color.

Susan (counting down on her fingers): We're live in five, four, three, two, one…

Guy: Glad you could join us. As we speak, our paranormal teams have begun their investigation, penetrating the dark secrets of these lonely, ancient houses.

(Bert is outside the van now, panning the houses carefully. Lit by floods, they appear more than a little menacing; which was probably the intention. Guy steps into the image, silver-haired and regal. An immense, crooked shadow of him is thrown against one of the facades.)

Guy: What grim mysteries can these lonely lodgings tell us? What unspeakable crimes have their walls witnessed? What blasphemous rites were held in the pooling darkness of their cellars? Tonight, God help us, we might just find out. We go now to Team Two. Kealan, are you with us?

(Kealan is seen stalking down a narrow corridor. The ceiling is bowed. A dark doorway off to his left is askew. He is holding a thermal scanner out before him. His cameraman, Simon, sounds as if he's breathing hard.)

Kealan: We're still on the ground floor, Guy. Things were very quiet for some time but now…now as we reach the back of the house…God, noises like you wouldn't believe. Listen…can you hear that?

(Kealan is frozen before the doorway. He keeps licking his lips as if he can't wet them. He casts wary glances from the camera to the doorway. He is either acting or he is visibly upset. He holds the thermal scanner in one hand, a digital recorder in the other. Now what he has been hearing is quite loud in the stillness: a sort of scratching or scraping noise followed by something much like the crunching of bones.

Kealan: We've got something in there. Something…busy.

(He has traded the thermal scanner for a motion detector.)

Kealan: Something's moving…I think it's more than one something. (He turns to the camera) Ready, mate?

Simon: As I can be.

(Kealan, counting off, throws the door open and jumps inside. The image jiggles and sways, capturing distorted images of what appear to be old, very old, furniture. A table. A sofa trailing stuffing. A chair pushed into one corner. And several dozen unknown moving objects that appear shiny, metallic.

Kealan: Oh Jesus, what is that?

Simon: Rats, bleeding fucking rats!

(The image jumps again as Simon apparently backpedals out of the room. Slowly, breathing in and out distinctly, he follows Kealan back in. Whatever was in there has scattered now, it seems, fleeing through an immense hole chewed in the wall.)

Kealan: I don't think they were rats. Rats don't move like that. Those things sort of…hopped.

Simon: What else could they be?

Kealan (preferring, apparently, not to speculate)*:* What was it they were eating?

Simon (zooming in on the remains on the floor): Something dead by the smell.

(Zoomed image shows what appear to be the rent carcasses of large fish. Bones and scales are scattered everywhere.)

Kealan: Fish…never seen fish like that. Those scales have to be three inches across.

(They vacate the room. It is obvious that Kealan is disturbed by the fish carcasses and what was eating them.)

Simon: That was enough to stand my nerves on edge.

(A low guttural mumbling is heard. It is incoherent, garbled. Simon, as if panicking, swings the camera about, searching out its source.)

Kealan (looking angry): What is that you said?

Simon: Not me, mate. Not me at all.

(Simon continues to pan about with the camera. There is nothing to be seen but the empty corridor. He shines a pocket flashlight about. Motes of dust dance in its beam.)

Kealan: Funny, but I think you said it. I saw your lips moving.

Guy: No, I don't think it was him.

Simon: It wasn't.

Kealan (visibly perturbed): I saw your lips moving.

Simon: He's off his bleeding nut.

Guy: All right, you two. We're on commercial here. What the hell are you playing at? This is a live feed.

Kealan: He's saying shit. He's baiting me.

Simon: Piss off, I am not. Don't you see? That voice? It's…it's what we've come for.

Kealan: Ghosts? My arse.

Guy: That's it. Enough of this bloody fucking shit! You're not going to cock this one up like you did at Glamis! If you two can't fucking work together, I'll find two that can!

(Video cuts to the back of the mobile unit. Susan is at the console. Burt is waiting with his camera. Guy looks agitated. He is smoking a cigarette and studying the video screens.)

Guy: Swear to God, those two sods aren't going to make a mockery of this. I'll have their heads. This won't be another Glamis with them picking at each other.

Susan: Ratings were up on that one, Guy. People like the drama of ghost hunters that can't get along. It gives it a human edge.

Bert: Sure, mate. They fight and piss about, but in the end they come together and Scooby-Doo.

Guy: I want opinions, I'll fucking ask for them.

Susan: And we're live in five, four, three, two...

Guy: Things are most definitely heating up at Lakeside Terrace. Team Two has just had a terrifying encounter with rats. And Team One has been picking up measurable temperature drops as they move down to the cellar. God only knows what will happen in the next few minutes, let alone the next few hours. Before we check in with Annabelle, let's view some pre-investigation footage we shot on the morning of this increasingly fateful day.

(Video cuts to an old man sitting on his porch throwing a stick to his dog. He looks to be quite advanced in years, cheerful and happy, a gentle soul.)

Guy: That's a fine dog you have there, Mr. Candliss.

Mr. Candliss: Fine, is he? Ruddy thief is what he is. Ought to be locked up for the safety of the public.

(The dog, a rat terrier, stick in mouth, wags the nub of its tail happily as if it knows it's all too true.)

Mr. Candliss: Lookit him. Mr. Bleeding Innocent. Thief, he is. Robber, highwayman. Steals chickens, toys from the tots crost the way. Even thieved Mrs. Cupp's purse right off her stoop. And her heart pills in it yet.

Guy: Mr. Candliss, I'd like to discuss some of the things we were talking about earlier.

Mr. Candliss: Things about that lake, you mean.

Guy: Yes.

Mr. Candliss: Well, I suppose I know a few bits and bobs. You'll find certain ones 'round here what's afraid to say what they know, but not me.

Me granddam—a right evil cow, bless her soul—used to tell yarns about the lake, but mostly to torment us nips. I recall her saying—on a rare day when she wasn't taking the strap to me—that in olden times, there was a religious cult of sorts that worshipped by the lake. They used to toss people into the deeps, let 'em drown. A sort of offering to what lived below. True enough, I suppose, for those fisher-folk that dared drop their nets in the lake often brought up bones, human-type bones. There'd be funny marks upon them, it was said.

Guy: Did she ever give the cult a name?

Mr. Candliss: Not that I recall. But I was just a nip then, some seventy-odd years back. There was a story, I recollect, about the cult having books. Terrible books. Hell books, some said. Fellah that led the cult—Lee, was it?—wrote them books from dreams sent to him by what was at the bottom of the lake.

Guy: And what was that?

Mr. Candliss: Sort of a foul thing, a monster.

Guy: Did you ever see it?

Mr. Candliss: None that saw it come back to tell.

Guy: Anything else you can tell us?

Mr. Candliss: They held what was called sabbats out there, the cult did. Lots of chanting and singing and blasphemies called into the sky. Lot of the old folk say that even now, on dark, foggy nights, you can hear them voices echoing over the water (he shrugs). Was…was stories about them fish in the lake. How the cult ate 'em and eating 'em, could eat nothing else.

Guy: Why is that?

Mr. Candliss: They said how them fish weren't right, how they sort of changed you after a time. Made you something not rightly human.

Guy: Anything else?

Mr. Candliss: Well…let me think. What was it? Something about that Lee fellow. How someone had seen him down by the lake around sunset when the frogs start their godawful clamoring. He weren't alone. Something with him. Something sort of bloated that hopped. Me granddam said it was his familiar, witch's familiar. She wouldn't say what it was exactly…just that it was unclean…and its name were…*Hopfrog.*

(Video cuts to Annabelle moving through the cellar of the house. Piers pans from her to the cobwebbed rafters overhead. His voice is heard softly counting them one after the other. He pans back to Annabelle. She is scanning with her EMF detector. She appears to be uneasy, tense, as she moves deeper into the cellar. The walls are dirty and cracked. They seem to be oddly stained by some sort of seepage. She freezes.)

Annabelle: Right there! And there! Oh God! Something's happening here. The EMF…hell, right off the scale! (She holds up the EMF. The meter drops immediately.) Did you see that? The field down here is unstable, it's fluctuating.

Guy: We caught that. Be very careful now.

Annabelle: Oh! (She lets out a short, sharp cry.) Saw something…Piers… Piers, did you get it? Right over there. (She points to an archway leading into darkness.) I saw it…*it was right there!*

Piers: I didn't get it.

Guy: What did it look like?

Annabelle (breathing fast): Ah…I don't know…a shape…a figure…it was sort of crawling.

(Piers pans back and forth, getting nothing. They proceed further. Annabelle steps through the archway, moving carefully, and cries out as something bumps into her, a black and swinging shape. She falls backward and stumbles into Piers. The image jiggles.)

Piers: What the hell?

(He has it in view. A figure in a dirty shroud-like shift. Headless and limbless, it is tied off to the beam overhead with a rope. It swings back and forth, back and forth.)

Annabelle (choking back sobs): That's what…I thought it was…oh Christ. For a minute there…

Guy: Tell us, Annabelle. Tell us.

Annabelle: I thought…I thought it was the figure I saw crawling. I was sure of it…because that's how it looked: like a dirty, crawling sack.

Piers (moving in closer): Who the hell hung this down here? And fucking why?

(Very close to it now, he prods it with his finger. The bottom end is tied off with a rope. With trembling fingers, he pulls the knots free. Like an opened bag, a great quantity of something spills out as if it were a piñata of sorts.)

Annabelle: Oh…oh…oh God! Oh Jesus…

Piers: The stink…the stink…

(He zooms in on what fell from the sack dummy: what appears to be a great heap of offal, fish offal, bones and entrails, carcasses and slime and scales.)

Annabelle (practically hyperventilating now): Who did this? *Who the hell did this?* It isn't funny! It's not bloody well funny! (Her voice is cracking as though she may break down in tears at any moment.) Was it you, Guy? Did you do this? Did you fucking well put them up to this?

Guy: Annabelle, please, take it easy. I had nothing to do with it. I swear. Neither did the crew. I don't know what this is about.

Piers (very quietly): Bloody gob'll do anything for ratings.

Guy: We're picking up something…some background noise. Can you hear it? Sounds…sounds like voices.

Piers: Yes…voices. I hear them…

(A garbled string of voices can be heard. But without digital enhancement, they are indecipherable. Annabelle stands there, head cocked.)

Annabelle: I don't hear a thing.

Piers: No…it's there all right…*listen…listen to the words…*

(The garbled voices again. They sound as if they are chanting.)

Annabelle: There's nothing.

Piers: Don't tell me you can't hear it! Christ, it's louder…it's louder! What is it…what are those words…*can't you…can't you hear them?* Bee…bee…bee…at…izzz. That's what they're saying. Bee…at…izzz.

Guy: We're picking up something. Piers, are you sure that's what you're hearing?

Piers: Bee…bee…at…izzz…bee…at…izzz…

Annabelle: Stop it! Do you hear me? Stop it!

Piers (speaking much louder now): BEE…AT…IZZZ…BEE…AT…IZZZ

Guy: Byatis…they must be saying Byatis. It's an entity closely associated with Gla'aki, the inhabitant of the lake.

(Piers continues to mimic what he is hearing. The image is slowly lowering as if he's losing his grip on the camera.)

Annabelle: I SAID STOP IT! I'VE HAD ENOUGH OF THIS SHIT! YOU'RE ALL IN IT! YOU'RE IN IT TOGETHER! I'M DONE! I'M LEAVING!

(The camera image raises back up. Annabelle is clearly sobbing. She looks as if she is at her wit's end.)

Piers (exasperated): Oh, you silly twat! Are you telling me you can't hear it? It's so loud I can barely hear my voice! Listen! *Listen!* It's…oh Christ in heaven…*what is that?*

(The background noise is most clear at this point. It's similar to the sounds of the rats crunching the carcasses, but much louder. It sounds oddly like dogs gnawing on gristly bones.)

Piers: It's gone…gone now…could've sworn it was coming from inside the walls.

(Video cuts to the back of the mobile unit. The static camera shows Bert and Susan at the console. Guy stares blankly at the video. It looks as if Annabelle is shouting at the camera.)

Susan: Oh hell, Guy. You nearly had me. My skin was crawling. When that dummy swung out of the darkness, I almost pissed myself. My God, what a nice touch! And Annabelle…she's going with it!

Bert: Amazing, absolutely amazing.

Guy: We didn't rig anything. Whatever's down there, we didn't put it there.

(Susan stares at him incredulously. One gets the feeling that she believes him even though she doesn't want to.)

Susan (her voice just above a whisper): We're live in five…four…three…

(We see Guy. He appears more than a little distraught.)

Guy: Things are happening at Lakeside Terrace that we can't account for. We believe that our paranormal investigators are caught right in the middle of a full-fledged haunting of epic proportions. Ladies and gentlemen, I warn you that what you may see from here on in might be not only terrifying but disturbing. You have been warned…

(Video shifts to Team #2. Kealan is squatting in a corner, a digital voice recorder held above his head. His eyes sweep back and forth frantically. There is a rumbling background noise.)

Kealan: Guy? Guy? Are you there?

Guy: Yes, we're with you, Kealan.

Simon: Thank God.

Kealan: Are you getting this? Can you hear it?

(A high-pitched sort of throbbing is clearly heard. It has an odd electronic intonation to it. It seems to be getting louder.)

Kealan: We're on the second floor. It seems to be coming from above us…maybe the third floor…or the attic…I don't know.

(Simon zooms in on the water-stained ceiling. Something skitters across the frame.)

Kealan: (holding an EMF detector now): It's spiking! And not just the noise either…we can feel it. It's like the whole house is breathing, rumbling.

Simon: It's quieting again. Keeps doing that.

(The throbbing is barely audible by this point.)

Kealan: We're going to try and track it to its source.

Guy: Be careful.

(Kealan is seen moving down a corridor to a set of stairs. They look like they're tipping to the side, as if they're ready to detach from the wall. He mounts them carefully. The stair rail is loose, the steps creaking loudly.)

Simon (following him): Lucky if we don't break our necks.

(The throbbing begins again. Its tone sounds almost insistent, fevered—like a pumping heart.)

Kealan: Hear it? I think we're getting closer. EMF is jumping.

(They reach the top of the stairs. There's a corridor before them. The IR image of it is disorienting; it appears as if the corridor is crooked, walls and floor not meeting squarely, off-kilter.)

Simon: Claustrophobic.

Kealan: EMF is higher! Christ, needle's nearly pegged!

(Kealan, overcome with excitement, runs down the corridor. Simon follows, the camera image bumping about.)

Kealan: Guy…Guy, are you seeing this? Are you bloody well seeing this?

Guy: What…what is that exactly?

Kealan: Attic door…yes, I'm sure of it. Look…look at those marks.

(Simon zooms in on the face of the door. The marks appear to be symbols or signs etched deeply. Some of them look very much like astrological symbols and others mathematical in nature. They are overlapping and cut into one another.)

Kealan: I'm not sure what the hell this is.

Guy: Some of them look rather like pentacles.

Simon (making a gasping sound): Seen them before…I've seen them before. Somewhere.

Guy: Where?

Simon: I think…can't be…

Guy: What?

Simon: A dream. Had a dream a few nights ago. I saw a city, something like a city…a city in the weeds like it was underwater. Black towers and weird angles. Those symbols were scratched on its walls. I saw them. *I saw them.* It was like…it was like they *wanted* me to see them. Because it meant something. It was the key. The key that opens the door to the below place where *he* waits in the chamber of blue light. The awful light. The light that teaches, the light that punishes…

Kealan: What is this shit?

Guy: Simon, listen to me. According to local legend that's been handed down generation after generation, there's a city beneath the lake. The city that was on the meteorite. Gla'aki lives down there. It lives beneath the city.

Simon (his voice taking on a high, frightened tone): Do not say the name, do not call him from the weeds.

Kealan: Snap the hell out of it.

Guy: Easy, Kealan.

Simon: There are those that know, those that dream. Those that stand at the brink, called through time and blood to make an offering as was done in the ancient days of Hopfrog—

Kealan: Shut the fuck up. I'm warning you.

Simon: I…what the hell's going on?

Guy: Simon…do you think you can continue?

Simon: Yes…yes, I'm fine.

Kealan (sounding very impatient): We've got work to do. We'll hash out the particulars—and your state of mind—later. (He has taken an IR camcorder from his pack now.) Whatever might be behind that door, Guy, I want it documented. *Fully* documented. Apparently, I can't count on Mr. Fumblety-Fuck over here. I'm patching into you…*now*.

Guy: We've got the feed.

Kealan: Here goes…

(Image is switched to Kealan's camera. He reaches out and turns the knob. The door swings noiselessly out. The camcorder's infrared LEDs pick out a narrow set of steps that appear to be well-worn and splintered. There is something glistening on them, not water but a sort of jelly.)

Guy: What is that?

Kealan: I don't…know. Some kind of slime.

Simon: Ectoplasm.

Kealan (ignoring him, prodding the stuff with a pencil): Thick like Vaseline, but stringy. Smells rank. Reminds me of snail slime.

Simon: Something must have crawled up there.

Kealan: Shut your hole, you silly twit.

(Kealan moves up the stairs. He is breathing hard and fast, though probably not from exertion. He reaches the top of the stairs and pans with his camera. Something moves along the wall in a blur with a sort of hopping motion. It appears pale, amorphous.)

Kealan: Shit! Did you see that?

(There is old furniture, cast-offs—a chest of drawers, a frame bed, and a rocking chair. It is rocking though no one sits in it.)

Kealan: You getting this?

Guy: Yes.

Kealan: It was flesh and blood enough to bump into that chair.

(Kealan is holding out his EMF detector. The needle is jumping up and down. He pans the camera towards the bed and something moves, something very fast. It seems to skitter on many legs. The image jiggles as Kealan cries out, bringing the camera around.)

Kealan: It was there! Something…I don't know what. It looked like a woman almost…but creeping like that…

Simon (making a squealing sort of sound in his throat): It touched me! *It fucking well touched me!*

Guy: What was it, Simon?

Simon (brushing his hand against his pants): It was slimy…it was warty… like crawling bumps…

Kealan: This is unbelievable. I've never experienced anything like this before. A physical entity…with substance, volume, and weight.

(He pans around the room with the camera.)

Kealan: It's gone, gone.

Simon (voice only): The toad compels…the toad compels…

Guy: What did you say?

Simon: NOT THERE! NOT IN THAT PLACE! NOT WITH THEM! NOT UNDER THE—

Kealan: Get a hold of yourself!

Simon: My hand, my hand…

(He holds it up briefly and where the entity touched him, it looks oddly scaly.)

Guy: We should look at that.

Simon: No! No one can look! No one can see! Not there where I begin to writhe!

(He runs off and can be heard stumbling down the stairs.)

Kealan: Simon! Simon! Get back here, you bloody idiot!

(Video cuts to the static camera in the mobile unit. We can see Susan and Bert. They are trying to link up with Kealan. Guy hovers over them.)

Guy: Well?

Susan (Shaking her head): Nothing…no feed…I'm not getting a signal.

Bert: Goddammit, Guy, if this is all bullshit, tell us now.

Guy: This is the real thing.

(Susan and Burt look nervously at each other. They both appear genuinely scared.)

Susan (her voice hitching in her chest): Should we…should I cut the feed?

Guy: Why for God's sake?

Burt: Listen…this is…this has gone far enough…

Susan: Do I cut it?

Guy: Not on your life. This is exactly what we came for.

(Susan and Burt look increasingly agitated.)

Guy: In five, four, three, two, one…

(Video shifts to Team #1. Their position in the house is unknown. Annabelle appears to be angry, shouting and gesticulating.)

Guy: Annabelle? Can you hear me?

Annabelle: Don't know…nothing's making sense, mixed up, I'm so mixed up. I—

(She's cut off by a series of coarse, inarticulate sounds, and what might be shrill bleating and croaking noises. It is very loud, echoing and echoing.)

Piers (whispering after it has died away): Now it is revealed, now the shining path is known! Now we dwell in the House of the Toad and are made ready to journey below!

Annabelle: He's losing his mind. I think this is enough.

Guy: Press on, you have to press on.

(She appears to be shaking uncontrollably, her teeth chattering. If it's not just good acting, she might have been very close to a nervous breakdown at this point. The strain is telling. Swearing under her breath, she moves down the corridor to the stairs. Slowly, she begins to climb them.)

Piers: Hurry! We have to get up there! We have to get up there now, you dumb cow! Don't you see? Don't you get it? *This is for us! This is intended for us and no one else! We must get up there! We must see it! WE MUST! WE MUST ALL BEGIN THE WRITHING!*

Annabelle (She stands halfway up the steps. Her eyes are wide. She is still trembling. She is shaking her head from side to side.): You're really fucking crazy! Guy! *Guy!* Get me out of here!

Piers (slowly climbing the stairs towards her, the camera image unpleasantly steady): It's beyond all that, duck. Way beyond that. Don't you see? Don't you see anything? Can't you feel it in your head? (He mumbles nonsensical things under his breath with a raspy sort of growl). I warned you! I told you he was in our minds, crawling just beneath our thoughts! *He*, the sower of dreams and the reaper of minds! *Him! That one! The one who waits beyond the door! Say it! Call him as they called him on Shaggai! It's on your tongue! The 49ᵗʰ Unveiling!* (By this point, Piers has pinned Annabelle against the stair railing, pressing the camera into her face. She is clearly whimpering.) *But you were warned, were you not? Up there, in the darkness, in the attic! They looked upon the sated one, the warted blasphemy squatting beneath the eaves, the bloated carnal toad—*

Guy: Piers! Get a hold of yourself!

Piers (ignoring Guy): Listen…listen now, oh fine fatted calf! Can… you…*hear it? Can you? Well, CAN YOU? It's begun, the cycle has begun! Now we must deliver ourselves unto the living God!*

Annabelle: GET ME OUT OF HERE! GET ME OUT OF HERE! DO YOU HEAR ME? I CAN SEE IT! I SEE THE SCALED HAND! *OH PLEASE DEAR GOD GET ME OUT OF HERE BEFORE BEFORE—*

(At this point, Annabelle screams hysterically. There is a roaring, rumbling noise and something which sounds, again, like the throbbing of a heart. Audio crackles, the video image distorts, breaking up and blurring. It sounds as if a great storm wind is blowing through the house. It is interesting to note that the images themselves, what there are of them, are inexplicable. There is a strobing view of what appears to be dozens of indistinct hopping or crawling bodies, a great many eyes, nebulous shapes that seem to leap in and out of the frame, and something like an immense glassy eye and possibly crawling worms. Annabelle's image is made grotesque as it bends and bloats. A weird sort of pixilation seems to engulf her face. This sequence lasts for approximately forty seconds.)

(The camera image is shaking badly now. It is held at an angle, it seems, from the bottom of the steps. Piers must have fallen. Annabelle, above, at the edge of the light, flickers like a candle flame. She seems to be giggling.)

Annabelle (hissing): Heretic…there's no need to walk if one can crawl.

(The cacophonous bleating and croaking noises begin again. At the sound of them, Piers climbs the stairs as if he's being called or summoned. He passes Annabelle who clings to the railing, her head cocked to one side. Her eyes are very large and unblinking, her cheeks sunken, her mouth moving as if speaking but no words are coming out. There is something very wrong with her image. It appears crooked.)

Piers (sobbing): It begins…dear God, it begins…

(Image is now from the static camera in the back of the mobile unit. Bert and Susan are still at the console. Guy is smoking, staring at the screens.)

Bert: C'mon, Guy! Pull the fucking plug already! They might be dead in there!

Susan (very agitated): Please, Guy! *Please!*

Guy: Yes, yes, I suppose we'll have to...

(One of the screens lights up. There is an image of a set of stairs reaching down into the darkness. The sound of heavy breathing and fumbling footfalls.)

Guy: Kealan! Kealan! Can you hear me?

Kealan: Oh, thank God...I didn't know if you were getting my signal. Simon...I think Simon ran down here, into the cellar...going to look...got to find him...

Susan: No, Kealan! Get out of there! Get out of there!

Guy: Shut up! (Static camera shows him pushing Bert aside) Are we live? Are we live?

Susan: A few more seconds.

Kealan: You need to stop the broadcast!

Guy: Why?

Kealan: Because we've created this haunting, we've energized it! All this gear, all this power...we've activated the memory of this place. Don't you see? What's on the bottom of the lake and what haunts these houses...they were potential energy stored here, waiting to become kinetic and now we've given them the means! We're broadcasting to millions of homes! We're streaming live over the internet! Millions of minds to be tapped into and exploited...a network of raw psychic force...

Guy (under his breath, barely audible): I don't know what you're doing, Kealan, but bloody well keep it up...

Susan: In five, four, three...

(The image is from Kealan's camcorder now. He is down the steps and into the cellar. It is large and gloomy. The lens breaks a few cobwebs, pans over a floor that is thick with dust. We can see a single set of footprints in it. They appear recent.)

Kealan: Simon! Simon, can you hear me?

(Kealan follows the footprints to the rear of the cellar. They pass beneath an archway and to another, much wider set of steps. These move down farther than the light can reach. The mold on them is broken by descending footprints.)

Kealan: He must have gone down here.

Guy: Be careful…

(Kealan moves carefully down the steps. The image shows us a narrow, winding passage of irregular bricks that are crumbling with age. They are filthy and mildewed. Gray water seeps from them. The bottom is reached. The passage opens into a sort of amphitheater. Camera pans over the arched ceiling, the cracked stone floor which is littered with broken bricks and detritus. Kealan moves forward, splashing through puddles. The lights show water, dark, oily-looking water, and what might be fine, scattered bones like those of fish. The LEDs reveal only the outer edge of the pool.)

Kealan: I think…I think this must connect with the lake.

(A splashing is heard. It reverberates with subterranean echoes.)

Kealan: Someone's out there…I can hear them. My lights won't reach…

(He enters the water now. The lights are filled with a foggy, gaseous haze. There are whitish objects bobbing about him. Ahead, a figure emerges from the murk as Kealan goes out farther. The figure is standing perfectly still just ahead, up to its waist in the black, stagnant pool which seems to have no end.)

Kealan: It's Simon! I've found him!

(He gets closer and still the figure has not turned. It appears to be hunched over, but in the haze, it is uniformly indistinct.)

Kealan (hesitation in his voice now): Simon…are you all right? It's me… it's…

(Simon disappears in the darkness and haze. Kealan follows and the water becomes shallower until there is none at all. Kealan pans the LEDs about and it looks like he's in a grotto of sorts.)

Kealan (gasping): He must have gone this way. I think…I think I'm under one of the other houses. I must be.

Guy: Be very careful now.

(Kealan is heard making a sort of whimpering sound in his throat.

Image trembles, probably from his shaking hands. The floor appears to be of shattered flagstones, sunken in places, standing water and silt pooling. There are dark shapes that are too grainy to be made out. Audio is picking up odd squeaking and squealing sounds and that same gnawing/slobbering sound as of a dog with a bone. Kealan is becoming increasingly agitated as forms seem to jump around him, croaking and bleating. Winged shapes seem to swoop from above. Kealan cries out again and again. One gets the feeling he is seeing things the video is not.)

Guy: Kealan…Kealan…can you hear me?

(At this point, the uplink is experiencing a great deal of interference. Audio crackles. Video rolls, pixilates, and is lost in static at irregular intervals.)

Kealan (breaking up): …feel it, it's rolling right *through me!* I can…I can… (audio becomes indecipherable). Jesus, Jesus, Jesus, oh help me! It's in my head! My head! It… (indecipherable)…blow apart! Calling me forward! I can't…can't resist!

Guy: Get out of there, Kealan! Do you hear me? Get the hell out of there!

Kealan (sobbing): I can hear it! *Feel* it! Can't you? Can't you? The Seal of Byatis! The (inaudible) that calls and summons! The throbbing! The throbbing! Like a gigantic heart! CAN'T YOU HEAR THE THROBBING?

Guy: Kealan, get out!

(Kealan does not reply. If he does, it is lost in the throbbing he speaks of that reverberates constantly and with great volume. He stumbles forward through the mud and water as the floor dips into what appears to be a great hollow. The camera pans over heaps of rotting fish carcasses and bones. The video goes in and out, blurring, out-of-focus, breaking up. Forms are seen, indistinct and multitudinous. They are hopping and crawling and squirming about. Kealan, it seems, nearly drops the camera several times.)

Kealan (screaming): OH DEAR CHRIST! NOT THAT! NOT THAT! ANNABELLE! *ANNABELLE!*

(The audio is garbled as he rants. The forms seem to be hitting him from every direction. The video goes out and comes back in, revealing a grotesque, obscured image of Annabelle hunched over amongst the heaped fish remains. Creatures move about her that appear to be human yet almost froglike. Her hair is greased and stringy with fish oil, slime drips from her mouth, her face is shiny with fish scales. Her image elongates, widens, distorts and blurs. She appears to be naked, some writhing plump form pressed to one breast like an infant. It grips her with webbed fingers.)

Annabelle: This is my blood and my flesh…drink of it and eat of it for the time of the rending, the filling, and the spawning grows near as the final (becomes inaudible as her image rolls and pixelates. What can be seen of it shows her stuffing fish entrails and bones into her mouth.) To praise…beneath the hungry moon with the Great Toad and swim beneath to the city where He waits…to breed upon its shores and fill…its graveyard depths…and…

(Kealan screams as something half-seen rises in the hollow in a gushing tide of what appears to be fish roe or frog spawn. The image is unsteady, breaking up. Kealan is fighting amongst the many forms that try to drag him down with them. The rising thing is only partially revealed by the LEDs: immense, noxious, and horribly flaccid, squealing and croaking. A great golden eye is seen….then a blubbery mouth ringed by squirming feelers… flesh that is bumpy, scaled, and wart-covered. It continues to rise, blotting out everything. Video and audio are lost.)

(Video shifts to static camera, rear of mobile unit.)

Guy: Don't know what's happening here…but…*Christ*…everything's going to hell…we need help…*we need help right now…*

(Bert is crouched in the corner, arms wrapped around himself. He is not speaking. Susan is rocking back and forth, sweat beading her face.)

Susan: Not to see until seen, not to know until known, these are my holy sacraments…drink of me and eat of me…the Black Eucharist is offered…

(Video switches to Guy's camcorder as he bursts from the van, moving towards the houses.)

Guy: Kealan, I'm coming! I'm coming!

(But as he nears the houses, they begin to tremble and quake as if they are trying to pull themselves up from their foundations. What seems to be a hurricane-force blow creates a storm of dust and particles and fragments of the houses themselves. Guy is thrown back and down, apparently knocked senseless. According to the digital chronometer, Guy is out for thirty minutes. When he comes to, he grabs the camcorder and stumbles about amongst the wreckage.

Guy (coughing and gagging): KEALAN! ANNABELLE! SIMON!

(The door to the house before him has been blown free. He stumbles inside, panning the camera about. A shape is seen hanging by a rope, swinging back and forth.)

Guy: Oh no, oh God help me…

(The image is the grisly remains of Kealan, his head cocked to the side on a broken neck. His legs and arms are missing. His face is discolored purple and black, horribly swollen as is his body which looks like a great bulging sack. There are fish scales all over him. His lips and mouth appear stitched shut like those of a shrunken head. As Guy cries out, he splits open and disgorges a flood of slime, fish bones and spines, ripped carcasses, and a tremendous outpouring of glistening frog eggs.)

(Guy, whimpering and muttering, turns back towards the mobile unit which has been rolled into the lake, half-sunken.)

Guy: BERT! SUSAN!

(The video goes in and out at this point, but an immense choir of hollow croaking as of frogs is heard. It is a cacophony of chirping and squeaking, bleating and squealing. Guy seems to be crying out but his voice is lost in the noise. Camera still in hand, he records shaking images of what appear to be hundreds of toadlike things hopping and creeping and crawling over one another to reach the dark lake in some unbelievable migration. Seen briefly amongst them are the naked bodies of Annabelle and Simon, possibly Piers. It becomes muddled and grainy, indistinct. The final image is of a slime-covered shoreline, reeds pressed flat as the multitude—human, semi-human, and horribly non-human—splash and leap in the water. Among the grasses, Susan is splayed out, eyes lit and glowing via the IR. Something like a huge white toad-shaped fungus moves on top of her, her fingers gripping its warty back.)

Guy: Oh God…oh Christ…

(The camera is dropped and the image is of the starry sky above which seems exceptionally bright and crowded with pulsating stars.)

Guy (heard in the distance as he scuttles into the water): No…no need to walk when one can crawl…

*(End of transcription)

SCRATCHING FROM THE
OUTER DARKNESS

1

After two weeks of relative silence in which the pot of the world began to boil over, Simone Petrioux heard the scratching again. This time it came from within the walls. Sometimes it came from behind her or the sky overhead. And sometimes from inside people.

2

"You have a marked hyper aural sensitivity," Dr. Wells explained to her. "A form of hyperacusis. It's not unusual for those without sight. When one sense fails, others are heightened."

"But it's beyond that," Simone told him with a singular note of desperation. "I hear…strange things. Things I should not hear."

"What sort of things?"

She swallowed. "Sounds…things echoing from another place. *Busy* sounds."

He told her that auditory hallucinations were known as paracusia. Sometimes they were signs of a very serious medical condition. He did not use the word schizophrenia, but she was certain he was thinking it.

"Just because you hear things others do not, does not necessarily mean there's anything there," he explained.

"And it doesn't mean anything *isn't* either," she told him. "Rocky hears it, too. How do you explain that?"

But he couldn't, of course. Dr. Wells was a good man, she thought, but this was beyond him. Ever since she was a child, she'd heard things others could not. It ran in the family. It was something of a Petrioux family curse—like the blindness—the ability to detect sounds in a frequency beyond that of ordinary human hearing. Simone had been blind since birth. Vision was an abstract concept to her. She could no more describe her acute hearing to Dr. Wells than he could describe sight to her. Stalemate.

Of course, it really didn't matter.

Things had gone far beyond that point now.

3

Feeling very alone and very vulnerable, she listened for it to start again because she knew it would. There had been a two week reprieve, of course, but now the scratching was heard again and it was more frenzied and determined than ever. *Like someone's trying to get through,* she thought. *Trying to dig their way through a stone wall. Scritch, scritch, scrape, scrape.* That was the sound she kept hearing. It was worse at night. It was always worse at night.

Listen.

Yes, there it was again.

Scritch, scritch.

Rocky started to howl. Oh yes, he could hear it and he knew it was bad. Whatever was behind it, it was bad. "Come here, boy," she said, but he would not. She found him over by the wall, fixated on the sounds coming from the corner. She petted him, tried to hug him, but he would have none of it. Beneath his fur, he was a rigid mass of bunched cables. "It's okay, my big boy, it'll be okay," she said, but he knew better and so did she.

The scratching sounded like an animal digging, claws scraping against a door, the sound of tunneling, determined tunneling. She cried out involuntarily. She couldn't bear it any more. Her greatest fear was that whatever was doing it, might get through.

Get through from where?

But she didn't know. She just didn't know.

Night—another abstract concept to the sightless—was a time she had always enjoyed the most. The noise of the city diminished and she could really hear the world. The gurgling of pipes in the ceiling. The gentle breeze playing at the eaves. Bats squeaking as they chased bugs around streetlights. Mr. Astano rocking in his chair on the third floor. The young couple—Jenna and Josh Ryan—at the end of the corridor making love, trying to be quiet because their bed was so terribly creaky (through the furnace duct she always heard them giggling in their intimacy).

But that had changed now, hadn't it?

Yes, everything had changed. These past few weeks, the night breeze was contaminated by a sweet evil stench like nothing she had ever smelled before. Mr. Astano no longer rocked in his chair; now he sobbed through the dark watches of night. For three nights running she had heard whippoorwills shrilling in the park, growing louder and louder in a diabolic chorus. Rocky howled and whined, sniffing around the baseboards constantly. And the Ryans…they no longer made love or giggled, now they whispered in low, secretive voices, reading gibberish to one another out of books. Last night, Simone had clearly heard Josh Ryan's voice echoing through the furnace duct, *"There are names one must not pronounce and those that should never be called."*

The scratching was persistently loud tonight and no one could ever convince her it was hallucinatory. It came from outside, not within. Her nerves frayed, a frost laying over her skin that made her shiver uncontrollably, Simone turned on the TV. She turned it on *loud*.

The voices on CNN were initially comforting but soon enough disturbing. There had been a mass suicide in Central Park. By starlight, two thousand gatherers had (according to witnesses) simultaneously slit their left wrists, using the gushing blood to paint an odd symbol on their foreheads: something like a stem with five branches. The police were saying they were members of a fringe religious sect known as the Church of Starry Wisdom. In Scotland, there had been arrests of a group—the Chorazos Cult—in Caithness who had gathered on the bleak moorland at a prehistoric megalithic site known as the Hill of Broken Stones. Apparently, they had ritually sacrificed several children, offering them to a pagan god known as "The Lord of Many Skins." In Africa, there were numerous atrocities committed, the most appalling of which seemed to be that hundreds of people had congregated at a place known as the Mountain of the Black Wind in Kenya and cut their own tongues out so that they would not, in their religious ecstasy, speak the forbidden name of their holy avatar. There were rumors that the offered tongues were then boiled and eaten in some execrable rite known as the Festival of the Flies which dated from antiquity.

Madness, she thought. *Madness on every front.*

Christians called it Armageddon and began feverishly quoting from the Book of Revelation as, all across North America and Europe, they flung themselves off the tallest buildings they could find, smashing to pulp far below, so that the Lord could wash his feet in the blood of the faithful as he walked the streets of men during the Second Coming.

It was falling apart.

It was all falling apart now.

There was mass insanity, religious frenzy, mob violence, murder, and genocide coming from every corner of the world.

Simone finally shut the TV off. The world was unraveling, but there seemed to be no root cause. At least none a sane mind would even consider.

4

The whippoorwills resumed their eerie rhythmic piping in the park, growing louder and louder, their cries coming faster and more strident as if they were possessed of some rising mania. Rocky began to whine in a pathetic puppy-like tone. At the windows, Simone heard what sounded like hundreds of insects buzzing. It all seemed to be building towards something and she was more afraid than she had ever been in her life.

Now there were screams out in the street, hysterical and rising, becoming something like dozens of cackling voices reaching an almost hypersonic crescendo of sheer dementia. They resonated through her, riding her bones and making her nerve endings ring out. There was a power to them, some nameless, menacing cabalism that filled her head with alien thoughts and impulses. Now the walls…oh dear God, the walls were vibrating, keeping time with the voices and the whippoorwills.

Not out in the streets, but from within the walls.

Yes, echoing voices from some terribly distant place and as she listened, she could not be certain they were of human origin…guttural croakings, discordant shrieking, hissings and vile trumpeting, a reverberating lunatic chanting, hollow noises as of storm winds rushing through subterranean channels.

Dear God, what did it mean?

What did any of it mean?

Feeling dizzy and weak, her stomach bubbling with a cold nauseous jelly, Simone fell to the floor, cupping her hands over her ears as the blood rushed and roared in her head. The sounds were getting louder and louder, the floorboards shuddering, the room seeming to quiver and quake like pudding. There were smacking and slurping sounds, the cries of humans and animals, of things that were neither…all of it lorded over now by a cacophonous buzzing that made her bones rattle and her teeth chatter. It sounded like some monstrous insect descending from the sky on droning membranous wings.

Then it stopped.

All of it ended simultaneously and there was only a great, unearthly silence broken by her own gasping and Rocky's whimpering. Other than that, nothing at all.

A voice in Simone's head said, *it was close that time. Very, very close. They almost got through. The barrier between here and there is wearing very thin.* But she had no idea what any of it meant. Between here and where?

"Stop it, stop it," she told herself. "You're losing your mind."

She pulled herself up from the floor, barely able to maintain her balance. The silence was immense. It was a great soundless black vacuum.

She made it to the sofa and collapsed on it, wiping a dew of sweat from her face. With a trembling hand, she turned the TV on because she needed to hear voices, music, anything to break that wall of morbid silence.

On CNN, there were voices, yes, but they spoke of the most awful things, things that only amplified her psychosis—because it must have been a psychosis. She couldn't be hearing these things, like the veneer of reality was ripping open.

It was reported that several million people had made a pilgrimage to Calcutta to await the appearance of a dark-skinned prophet at the Temple of the Long Shadow whom they referred to simply as "The Messenger." Border skirmishes had broken out in Asia and the Middle East. There was pestilence in Indochina, bloodshed on the Gaza Strip, immense swarms of locusts blackening the skies over Ethiopia, and the Iranians had fully admitted that they were in possession of several dozen hydrogen bombs, each of which were equivalent to fifty million tons of TNT. With them, they would soon "ascend to heaven in the black arms of destiny" via a synchronized nuclear detonation which would bring about what they referred to as the symbolic "Eye of Azathoth."

In Eastern Europe, a terror organization calling itself either the Black Brotherhood or the Al-Shaggog Brigade had been burning Christian churches, Jewish synagogues, and Muslim mosques, calling them "places of utter blasphemy which must be eradicated so that the way be purified before the king could descend from the Dark Star and the Great Father rise from his sunken tomb..."

"Kooks, Rocky," Simone said. "This world is full of kooks."

The idea made her smile thinly. Was it at all possible that the human race was losing its collective mind at the same time? That instead of sporadic outbreaks of insanity there was a global lunacy at work here? She told herself it was highly unlikely—but she didn't believe it.

5

The next afternoon, the UPS man came to her door, knocking gently, announcing that he carried a parcel that had to be signed for. It was perfectly innocuous. He was delivering her new laptop with screenreader software. Yet, as she made to open the door, a sense of fright and loathing swept through her as if what was out there was something hideous beyond imagining. But she did open the door and right away she was gripped by a manic paranoia and a mounting claustrophobia.

"Package for you," the man said, his voice cheerful enough. But it was a façade, an awful façade. There was something sinister lurking just beneath his skin and she knew if she reached out to touch his face, it would be pebbly like the flesh of a toad. Right away, she heard that dire scratching coming from inside him like rats pawing and chewing. In her mind, she sensed a spiraling limitless abyss waiting to open like a black funnel. A voice—his own—whispered in her skull, *has she...has she...has she linked? Have the angles shown her the gray void? Has she seen the black man with the horn?* The voice kept echoing in her head until she felt a cool, sour sweat run down her face.

"Are you okay, ma'am?" asked the UPS man.

"Yes," she breathed, taking the parcel from him with strained, shaking fingers. "Yes, fine."

"Okay, if you're sure."

But deep within her, perhaps at some subconscious level of atavistic fright, she could sense a vortexual darkness opening up inside him. *Show her, show her, it has been promised in the* Ghorl Nigral *as such...let her gaze into the moon-lens and gape upon the Black Goat of the forest with a thousand squirming young...let her...let her...find communion with the writhing dark on the other side...*

"Listen, are you sure you're all right?"

"Yes...please, I'm fine."

But she was not fine. She was blind and alone and a ravening outer darkness was spilling from this man in diseased rivers. She felt scalding winds and dust blowing in her face, a fetid odor enveloping her that was no single stench but dozens breathing hot air in her face with a fungous, nearly palpable odor.

He reached out to steady her, clutching her wrist with a flabby, leprous claw.

She screamed.

She could not help herself.

She slammed the door in his face, ignoring the whining and growling of Rocky. Physical waves of disgust and utter repulsion nearly paralyzed her, but she managed to reach the toilet as the vomit came out of her in a frothing expulsion. And crouching there on the bathroom floor, shuddering, drooling, her mouth wide in a silent scream, she could still hear that voice whispering from unknown gulfs: *Even now at the threshold, the veneer of the Great White Space weakens as the time of the pushing and the birthing draws near—*

6

Enough, by God, it was enough.

She went into the kitchen and made sure Rocky had enough food and water. He had touched neither all day. He was hiding under the kitchen table, trembling. When she reached out to comfort him, he snapped at her. *Even my dog, even my dog.* Feeling depressed and defenseless and without a friend in the world, Simone climbed into bed and tried to sleep. After a desperate round of tossing and turning, she did just that.

Her dreams began right away.

Twisted, unreal phantasms of limitless spaces closing in on her. Immense and shaggy forms brushing against her. Monstrous pulpous, undimensioned things moving past her. Crawling up winding staircases that led into nothingness and being hunted through shattered thoroughfares of wriggling weeds and monolithic towers that felt like smooth, hot glass under her fingertips. And a world, an anti-world, of shifting surface angles where everything was soft and slimy to the touch like the spongy, mucid tissue of a corpse. And through it all, she heard a voice, a booming and commanding voice asking her to make communion with the beautiful, cunning darkness that awaits us all in the end.

A sinister, malign sort of melody was ever-playing in the background, at first soft and silky then building to a harsh feverish pitch, an immense ear-splitting dissonant noise of bat-like squeaking, bone grinding against bone, thunderous booming, saw blades biting into steel plate, chainsaws whirring and jagged-toothed files scraping over the strings of violins and cellos…all of it combining, creating a deranged jarring cacophony of disharmonic noise, filling her head, melting her nerves like hot wires, cracking open her skull like an eggshell until she woke screaming in the deathly silence of her bedroom—

7

Soaked with sweat, shaking like a wet dog, she forced herself to calm down. She was awake and she *knew* she was awake, but the terror and anxiety bunched in her chest did not lessen; it constricted tighter. Her brain was sending a steady current of electricity to her nerves and the result was that her entire body was jittery and trembling. She had the most awful sense that she was not alone in the room, that another stood by her. She could hear a low, rasping respiration, a vulgar sort of sound like that of a beast might make.

"Rocky?" she said in a weak, barely existent voice. *"Rocky?"*

Her voice reverberated around her oddly. Her words bounced off the walls and came back at her like ripples she could feel on her skin.

She could still hear the breathing.

Terrified, she swung her legs out of bed and stood, instantly recoiling because the floor felt gelatinous, a cool mud that was crawling with squirming things that began to slink up her legs. *Dreaming, dreaming, you're still dreaming.* But she couldn't convince herself of that. She reached out for the bed, but it was no longer there.

Panting, she stumbled towards the door and felt an immense momentary relief when it was still there. Something had happened. A pipe had burst or something and she was wading through shit, yet there was no odor save a dank, subterranean smell. She was in the short hallway that led into the living room. She pushed on through the slopping ooze. She reached out and could find no walls. The hallway seemed to have no end and no beginning.

"ROCKY!" she screamed in desperation.

Again, her words bounced around, becoming waves crashing ashore on an alien beach. The air was warm, trembling like jelly.

She kept moving, reaching out in every direction but there was nothing, absolutely nothing to touch. That awful breathing kept pace with her but its owner made no sound as it glided along with her. Her head was throbbing, her temples pumping. A headache was gathering steam, its pain funneling out from the back of her brain to some excruciating white-hot spot in her forehead. There was an explosion of brilliance in her mind that left her reeling, it blazed like white phosphorus, igniting her thoughts into a firestorm of luminosity.

What?

What?

What is this?

Being blind since birth, she did not know sight. She could not conceptualize it. Even her dreams were of sounds, smells, and tactile sensations. Now she was seeing for the first time in her life—a multitude of colors and images and forms like thousands of bright fireflies filling the night sky. And then she saw—if only for the briefest of moments—what stood breathing behind her: a very tall man in a tattered cloak that crept with leggy vermin. He was staring down at her. His face was black, not African, but something like smooth shiny onyx. A living carved mask. Two brilliant yellow eyes, huge and glossy like egg yolks, watched her. And then sight was gone. Whatever had opened in her head, had closed up and she nearly passed out.

The dark man gripped her with fingers like crawling roots and she let out a scream, one that seemed to echo from a distant room. Her hands, unbidden, reached out to him as they had done so many times in her life, finding a face that was greasy and soft like a gently pulsating mushroom. She cringed, but her fingers continued exploring despite the abhorrence that made her viscera hang in warm, pale loops. Beneath her fingertips, nodules rose and from each something worming slinked free. They crawled over the backs of her hands. One of them licked at a cut on her pinkie. Another suckled her thumb. Whatever they were, they came out of him in hot geysers, vermiform fleshy nightmares that gushed over her hands and brought a stench of death—old death and new death—that made her want to weep in her revulsion. Her fingers, seemingly magnetized to the face, continued exploring until they found something like a phallic optic stem growing from his forehead. It held a great, swollen, juicy eye that her index finger slid into like an over-ripened plum soft with rot.

And a voice that sounded as if it was spoken through mush, said, *"You shall make communion with the beautiful, cunning darkness that waits for all…"*

8

When Simone was next aware, she was sitting on the couch. She had no memory of getting there. She had been in bed, having nightmares, now she was on the couch. Her sense of smell, heightened beyond normal ken, gave her a sampling of the oily, fetid odors that seeped from her pores in toxic rivulets.

The TV was on.

A public access channel. She never listened to public access, but here it was. A man's voice was droning endlessly in great dry detail about the cult of the Magna Mater, Cybele-worshipping Romans, and the depravity of Phrygian priests. Little of it made much sense, from the dark secrets of alchemy to thaumaturgical arts and forbidden necromantic rites, from Etruscan fertility cults worshipping the Great Mother of Insects to nameless miscegenations that did not walk but crawled within the slime of the honeycombed passages beneath Salem.

"Was it not foretold?" the voice asked. "Did not Cotton Mather warn of it? Did not his sermons of those cursed of God, born of the tainted blood of those from outside, serve as an omen of worse things to come? Yes, but we did not listen! Was it not known to the mad Arab and his disciples? The time of the shearing and the opening is it hand, is it not? In *Al-Azif*—thus named for the sounds of night insects, some say, but in truth a cipher that prophesied the coming of Ghor-Gothra, the Great Mother Insect—did he not tell us that Yog-Sothoth was the key just as the mad faceless god was The Messenger? *Yes!* Just as he hinted at the blasphemies of the Mother Insect who was the blade that would open the seams of this world to let the Old Ones through!" He ranted on about something known as the *Pnakotic Manuscripts*, the Angles of Tagh-Clatur, and the Eltdown Shards. Becoming positively hysterical as he discussed *De Vermis Mysteriis* and the dread *Liber Ibonis*. "It was all there! All there!"

Simone wanted to turn the channel because these public access stations were always infested with half-baked religious fanatics, but she did not. There was something here, something important.

The voice told her that in 1913 there appeared a novel by Reginald

Pyenick called *The Ravening of Outer Slith,* which quickly disappeared from bookshelves because of its horrendous nature detailing a fertility cult worshipping a pagan insect deity. It was basically a retelling of the ancient German saga, *Das Summen,* which was hinted at in the grand, grim witch-book, *Unaussprechlichen Kulten,* and written about in detail by the deranged Austrian nobleman Jozef Graf Regula in his banned tome, *Cultis Vermis.* The very volume which detailed the history of the Ghor-Gothra cult and the coming age of the Old Ones. Regula, the voice said, was convicted of witchcraft and sorcery for writing it and was drawn-and-quartered in 1723. No matter, despite the suppressed knowledge of the cult, fragments of knowledge persisted in Verdin's *Unspeakable Survivals* and in the poem "Gathering of the Witch Swarm" which was to be found in *Azathoth and Other Horrors* by Edward Derby.

"It was there—prophesy of the ages! The Resurrection of the Morbid Insect! Now *She* comes from the Black Mist to usurp our world and let the others in and we, yes, *we,* shall tremble in the shadow of the true progenitors of the dark cosmos that shivers in their wake. The 13th Equation is on the lips of the many and soon comes the Communion of Locusts, the buzzing, the buzzing, *the buzzing…*"

Simone shut the TV off before she lost what was left of her mind.

9

She was hallucinating, she was paranoid, she was delirious. And listening to the ravings of mad- men was not going to help her.

Do something! You must do something! The time draws closer! It is now!

Frustrated, scared, quivering in her own skin, she called good friends—Reese and Carolyn—but they didn't answer. She called friends she hadn't seen in months—Frank and Darien and Seth and Marion—nothing. No one was answering their phones. Why was no one answering? *Because they're gathering now in secret places, on hilltops and misty glens and lonesome fields to wait the coming of—*

That was insane.

Wiping sweat from her face, Simone called her mother. Mom was at the Brighton Coombs Medical Care Facility, a nursing home. Half the time, she did not even recognize her daughter's voice and when she did, she laid on a heavy guilt trip. *You shouldn't be living in the city alone. Terrible things can happen in those places. Your father would roll over in his grave if he knew.* The line was answered and thirty seconds later, her mom was on the phone.

"Mom…how are you?" Simone said, trying to keep from choking up.

"Oh, Simone, my darling. I'm fine. How are you? You sound stressed. Are you eating enough? Do you have a boyfriend yet?"

Jesus.

"I'm okay. Just lonely."

"Ah, loneliness is a way of life as the years pile up."

But Simone didn't want to get into that. "I'd like to come see you."

"Oh! That would be just fine. I wish you were here now. We're all sitting in the sun room, waiting for the big event."

Simone felt a cold chill envelope her. "What event?"

Her mother laughed. "Oh, my silly little Simone! The event, darling, *the* event. The stars will soon align and *they* will come through. The seas will boil and the sky will crack open. Cthulhu shall rise from the corpse city of R'lyeh and Tsathoggua shall descend on the moon-ladder from the caverns of N'Kai when the planets roll in the heavens and the stars wink out one by one. Those of true faith will be numbered and heretics shall be named…you are not an unbeliever, are you, dear?"

Sobbing, Simone slammed the phone down. When something furry brushed against her hand, she nearly screamed. But it was only Rocky. It had to be Rocky…then it moved beneath her hand with the undulating motion of an immense worm and she did scream. She launched herself off the couch as that thing moved around her, making slobbering noises.

She was hallucinating again.

She had to be.

Through the furnace ducts she could hear Josh Ryan saying, *"She crawls because she cannot walk, she hears but she cannot see. The sign…she does not bear the sign."*

Simone pulled herself up the wall, standing on shaking legs. She heard the scratching again—but this time, it was in her own head like claws and nails scraped along the inside of her skull.

Scritch, scratch, SCRIIIIIIITCH, SCRAAAAAATCH.

The apartment was filled with a hot slaughterhouse stench of viscera, cold meat, and buckets of drainage. She could hear the buzzing of flies, what seemed hundreds if not thousands of them. And the scratching. It was very, very loud now, like giant buzzsaws in the walls.

The barrier was coming apart.

Shifting, tearing, fragmenting, and realigning itself. She pressed a hand against the wall and felt a huge jagged crack open up beneath her fingertips. She touched something that pulsed within it—something busy and squirming like grave-worms wriggling in a peristaltic nest. The buzzing was so loud now she could no longer think. Insects filled the room. They crawled over her arms and up the back of her neck. They tangled in her hair and lighted off her face, sucking the salt from her lips.

She stumbled from the living room and into the hallway as that great furry worm searched for her. Things touched her. They might have been hands, but they were puffy and soft with decay. Worming feelers came from the walls and embraced her, squirming over her face to touch her and know her as she had done so many times with so many others. A mammoth rugose trunk brushed her arm and her fingers slid through a heaving mass of spiky fur. She pulled away, trying to find the wall and succeeding only in finding a wet pelt hanging there that she knew instinctively belonged to Rocky.

Her screams could barely be heard over the constant sawing, scratching noise and something like a great tolling bell.

Sobbing, she fell to the floor and her knees sank into the floorboards as if they were made of warm, malleable putty. This was not her apartment; this was the known universe gutted and turned inside out, merging with another anti-world.

She heard the roaring of monstrous locomotive mouths blowing burning clouds of irradiated steam. They shrilled like air raid sirens as the barrier weakened and the bleeding wound of this world split its seams and the nuclear blizzard of the void rushed in to fill its spaces. Her fingers touched snaking loops of crystalline flesh and things like hundreds of desiccated moths. Mummified corpse flies rained down over her head. *The elder sign, child, you must make the elder sign, reveal the Sign of Kish.* Yes, yes, she knew it but did not know it as the air reverberated around her with a scraping, dusty cackling.

Though she could not see, she was granted a vision of the world to come. It filled her brain in waves of charnel imagery that made her scream, made blood run from her nose and her eyes roll back white in her head.

Yes, the world was a tomb blown by the hissing radioactive secretions of the Old Ones who walked where man once walked, the skeletons of heretics crunching beneath their stride. The blood of innocents filled the gutters and putrefied bodies swollen to green carrion decayed to pools of slime. The world was a slag heap, a smoldering pyre of bones, and no stars shone above, only an immense multi-dimensional blackness that would have burned the eyes of men from their sockets if they were to dare look upon it.

Then the vision was gone.

But she could still see.

The crack in the wall was an immense fissure in the world, splitting open reality as she knew it…and through the gaping chasm, through some freakish curvature of time and space, she saw strobing, polychromatic images of a misty, distorted realm and some chitinous, truly monstrous form striding in her direction with countless spurred legs. Something that was at first the size of a house, then a three-story building, and finally a titanic shape that blotted out the world, *her* world.

She heard the nightmarish whirring and buzzing of its colossal membranous wings. It looked like a grotesque mantis with a jagged, incandescent exoskeleton. It was filling the fissure. Not only filling it, but widening it, its droning mouthparts and needlelike mandibles unstitching the seams of creation.

AL-AZIF, AL-AZIF, AL-AZIF, she could hear voices crying.

Hysterical and completely demented, she tried to escape, but one of the insect's vibrating skeletal limbs reached out for her and she was stuck to it like flypaper. Then it had her, flying off through trans-galactic gulfs, through shrieking vortexual holes in the time/space continuum.

She was dropped.

She fell headlong through a dimensional whirlpooling funnel of matter where slinking geometric shapes hopped and squirmed and then—

Her sight was stripped of meat, her soul a sinewy thing desperate for survival in some godless chaos. She crawled, slinked, crept through the bubbling brown mud and pitted marrow of some new, phantasmal unreality. Hungry insectile mouths suckled her, licking sweet drops of red milk, glutting themselves on what she had left.

All around her, unseen, but felt, were crawling things and sinuous forms, mewling with hunger. She crept forward, razored webs snapping, cobweb clusters of meaty eggs dripping their sap upon her. She was trapped in the soft machinery of something alive, some cyclopean abomination, a gigantic creeping biological mass born in the night-black pits of some malefic anti-universe. She was crawling over its rotten, fish-smelling jellied flesh, sliding through its oily pelt, a speck of animate dust on a loathsome unimaginable life form that dwarfed her world and filled the sky with coiling black tendrils that she could not see but could feel crowding her mind and poisoning the blood of the cosmos.

She was not alone.

Just one of many colonial parasites that crawled through the mire of the beast's life-jelly, swam in its brine and foul secretions and oozing sap, her atoms flying apart in a storm of anti-matter and energized particles.

And then—

And then, it ended.

A rehearsal, perhaps, for what was yet to come. She lay on the living room floor, drooling and gibbering, giggling in her delirium. She wished only for night to come when prophecy would be realized and the stars would be right. There was a knob on her forehead, the bud of an optic stem that would let her see the time of the separating and the time of the joining, the rending and the sowing, the communion of this world and the next, as the Old Ones inherited the Earth and the Great Mother Insect left her ethereal mansion of cosmic depravity in the Black Mist with a swarm of luminous insects and took to the skies on membranous wings.

As spasms knifed her brain in white-hot shards, the stem pulsated and pushed free, opening like a hothouse orchid so it could show her what was coming: that holiest of nights when the world of men became a graveyard and the cities, tombs.

THE BRAIN LEECHES

THE DEVIL'S EYE,
QUEEN ALEXANDRA RANGE,
TRANSANTARCTIC MOUNTAINS

1

The first time Ault saw Mount Kirkpatrick he fell in love.

The entire range took his breath away and filled him with an excitement that was part wonder, part joy, and pure terror. To see those towering heights in the waning light of an Antarctic day was to know all those things simultaneously. The high peaks were ice-free, sculpted in yellow sandstone and red shale with stark black sills and bands of dolerite. They were high and craggy and hunched-over, broken like the backs of hags. Ancient volcanic action had scarred and eaten into them like acid, producing a mountain range that was stunning, yet menacing and clustered by shadows even in the bright glare of a waning February day.

When the sun was still making a regular appearance, Ault and the rest of the team had been flown in via a C-130 loaded with Skidoos, sledges, climbing gear, rations, and a heavy payload of scientific equipment. With winter coming on it was far too cold to live in tents, even though it had been done and many times by people like Robert Scott and the early expeditioners. But that was history. The team would be living in self-contained Hypertats. These were brought by chopper to a sloping ice-plain amongst the rocky cliffs, fallen rubble, and ribbed glaciers of the Devil's

Eye: a bowl-shaped hollow squeezed in between jagged bluffs that had been named thus, for reasons poorly understood, by the British Antarctic Expedition of 1907-09.

The team sledged with the Skidoos for almost three days to reach the Eye, facing blowing snow, subzero temperatures, and a fierce wind that gusted regularly at thirty knots. The smooth, newly fallen drift was easy to glide across, but the serrated blue ice of the glaciers would make the snowmobiles and sledges jump and pitch, the howling winds trying to drag both off into the encroaching crevasse fields. Freak gusts came out of nowhere as they navigated snowy ledges and uplands and they had to hang on for dear life, all of them wishing and hoping for the sheltered bays of the Devil's Eye which seemed impossibly distant.

Well…all of them except for Dr. Crand, who was leading the expedition and had mapped out the area the summer before. Crand was impossibly cool and cerebral. When the winds screeched and the snow blew and the mountains loomed overhead like weathered gravestones, threatening to drop massive ice falls on them, Ault and Marsh and Ellis saw their death in every knob of volcanic rock and every jagged fissure.

And Crand would simply say, "If we had to choose the place of our deaths, then this would suitable…don't you think?"

Damn.

The guy was just as cold and dead as the desolate wastes around him. But driven. Oh yes, Crand was certainly driven.

When he'd discovered the series of caves cut down deep into the southern wall of the Eye the summer before, he showed absolutely no mercy in getting the funding and throwing together a team to investigate. The NSF backed him immediately, even though a winter geological expedition was not only hazardous, but expensive. No one on the team knew what strings Crand pulled to get them up into the Transantarctics with winter coming on, but he'd pulled them—offering the NSF the possibility of discovering something they simply could not resist.

Marsh was there for glaciology and Ault for paleobiology; Ellis was a paleoclimatologist, and Hirvonen was the team geologist. She was an exceptionally gifted post-grad student and Crand's personal assistant. She was very attractive, bright, and gifted. She only had one problem: she thought Crand was God and incapable of making a mistake.

But as the weeks wore by, Ault and the others began to wonder.

Was the expedition merely scientific in nature or was there was something else going on behind the scenes? Because as intelligent, intuitive, and much-awarded as Crand was, he seemed to be up to something. While the team studied rocks and fossils in the depths of the caves, Crand was interested in something else.

Only nobody really knew exactly what.

2

THE MAGNETIC CAVES

Ellis was the one who found it.

Down in the caves, some 500 feet below the crevice through which you entered the system and descended down a myriad system of ladders, he found an immense fossil bed which literally defied interpretation. He'd been the first into an immense sphere-shaped chamber, planning on doing some stratigraphic sectioning and measuring to determine past climactic models. And there, in a great central pit that dropped beneath the cave floor some ten feet and measured three times that in diameter, was the fossil bed. An immense collection of petrified relics rising from the fossiliferous Aztec siltstone that was itself roughly 375 million years old.

That in itself was fascinating—he was already mentally calculating how much time it would take to sort them out—but what was dumped, apparently, atop them was what made him feel uneasy to his core.

He stood there, staring in awe at what he had found in the glow of the battery lights. "How the hell did they get way down here?" he asked, his breath puffing out in white clouds.

And the thing was, Ault just did not know.

He stood there in his insulated caving suit and miner's helmet, feeling the weight of the mountain overhead and the great age of the rocks all around him. The air was dusty and dry, gritty to breathe, but not exceptionally cold.

Not like above. Down here it hovered at about a constant ten to twenty degrees Fahrenheit, which was practically tropical in comparison to above, out in the Devil's Eye, where temperatures were something like thirty below with a wind chill that pushed it down to forty at night…which was nearly all the time now with winter showing its teeth.

But what in the hell was he looking at?

He expected revelation in the depths of the caves, but nothing like this, nothing that he could not even remotely quantify. It was all Devonian rock down here, red and green and gray-banded strata. Up in a narrow passage above, he had been finding the bones, teeth, and scales of primitive fishes. Lobed fishes and placoderms, a dozen new types of acanthodians. All of which fit within the confines of the known fossil record.

But this…

Bodies. Human bodies. At least a dozen of them in a great central heap. Judging by how they were dressed in the tattered remains of antique arctic Burberry suits, reindeer-skin pants, and sealskin parkas, they were from the old days of exploration, the age of Scott, Mawson, and Shackleton.

"Christ," Ault said.

"How did they get here?"

"Probably the same way we did. They were exploring this same system, then something must have happened."

Ellis lit a cigarette with trembling fingers. He was dusty and dirty, looking much like a hard rock miner on his coffee break. There was no joy of discovery on his face as you might expect, but something akin to slow-crawling terror.

"Ault, they look almost like they were placed here."

"That's ridiculous."

"Is it?"

"Yes. Who knows? They could have been washed down here in a spring melt. There's any number of reasons." Still, the tangle of bodies scared him and he wasn't really sure why. "Did you go down there yet?" Ault asked him, trying to get a grip on what he was feeling, which was mostly confusion and awe, but concern, too.

Ellis barked a laugh. "Screw that. I'm not going down there. I have no interest in mummies. I know this sounds perfectly ridiculous, but when I first saw them, I almost came out of my skin. You can't get much more unscientific than that, now can you? But…I don't know…I just don't like the looks of this. The way it makes me feel inside. And, Christ, if you're my friend, don't laugh at me."

Ault was not laughing.

Staring down into the pit, humor was as preposterous as circus bears riding tricycles. The idea was absurd.

He began lowering himself over the edge of the pit.

"What the hell are you doing?" Ellis wanted to know.

"I'm going down there for a better look. This is amazing."

Ellis sat there with his cigarette hanging from his lower lip. "Are you out of your mind?"

"Ellis, they've been dead a long time."

"Yeah, but…" He shook his head and pulled off his cigarette, massaging his temples. "I don't know what the hell I'm thinking. I've been getting headaches ever since we got down to this level. And it's not gas. My detector reads zero."

Ault didn't comment on that.

He knew that Marsh had been getting them, too. Ever since they reached the lower chambers of the third level. And maybe that meant absolutely nothing, but he was starting to wonder. He'd been having funny dreams himself the past couple nights that he woke from in a cold sweat. They were terrible, haunted nightmares but he could never remember exactly what they were about. Something concerning dark, abstract cities and things moving in and out of them.

He jumped down there and Ellis lowered him a flashlight. In the pit, he scanned the bodies up close and personal.

Ault's specialty was vertebrate biogeography, which was essentially concerned with the dispersal of animal populations and particularly those caused by the moving landmasses of prehistory. It sounded terribly dry, but it was his passion and had been ever since he was a kid and had discovered a grouping of fossil shells in the vacant lot where he and the neighborhood gang played baseball. The evolution and migration of species between the

Southern Hemisphere and Antarctica was something still poorly understood. There were too many unresolved questions plaguing modern paleontology. The exact mechanics of dispersal of terrestrial vertebrates such as dinosaurs and marsupial mammals from North America to the Antarctic Peninsula was something that occupied Ault's every waking moment.

Maybe Hirvonen had her cosmogenic argon production and surface exposure dating as evidenced by the evolutionary ecology of gastropods and bivalves of the Eocene. And maybe Marsh was up to his neck in the crustal motions of the ice sheet as tracked by GPS and Ellis had his climatology studies of the Late Quaternary. That was fine and important work, but it couldn't hold a candle in Ault's eyes to Cretaceous dispersal. It was his passion.

And to work in a deep cave system at the onset of the polar winter, man, you had to have passion.

But where was his passion now? This close to the bodies, he felt uneasy like they might wake up at any moment. But mummies didn't wake up any more than rocks or ironing boards did. The transition from organic to inorganic was immutable. Yet, he felt a childlike fear as he stood there next to them.

"Wait a minute," he said.

"What? *What?*" Ellis asked, a note of rising dread beneath his words.

Ault was examining the bodies in detail now with his flashlight. Their faces had dried to brown leather, split open by age, skulls pushing out in yellow knobs. Their eyes were gone, mouths contorted as if they had died screaming. And as disconcerting as that was, he knew that the elements probably had something to do with it, the dry climate stretching their faces, pulling them into fright masks. But none of that explained what else he found.

"Ault…" Ellis' voice echoed. "C'mon, man, get the hell out of there."

"I'm fine. Take it easy."

Which was a great prescription, but one that the doctor himself could not take. Because Ault was shaking now. The close proximity to the remains was getting to him, filling his mind full of dark, creeping forms and faceless, undulant nightmares.

This is insane, he thought. *Absolutely insane. It is and yet it can't be.*

There were eleven bodies and each had the top of his skull removed like a cap with a perfect linear incision and nothing, of course, could explain that but the intervention of a third party. In his light, he could see that the skull cavities were empty. There should have been some trace of their brains, a withered lump of tissue, something, anything...but there was not.

Their skulls were opened so the brains could be removed.

Enough. Seized by an inexplicable fear, he scrambled up and out, Ellis grabbing his arm and hoisting him free. Then he laid there at the lip of the chamber, panting and sweating, but enormously glad not to be in such close proximity to what was below.

"What the hell is it?" Ellis asked him again and again.

So Ault told him.

3

Crand had discovered the cave system the summer before.

Caves were a rarity in Antarctica and mainly because most of the landmass was trapped beneath ice. What he found were a series of naturally-hollowed limestone caves, a vast subterranean labyrinth of chambers and passages that had been dissolved from the bedrock of the Devil's Eye through the erosion of a prehistoric stream or river. Thus far, some three separate levels had been located and Crand was certain there were more lying below.

Not only were the caves impressive, but they were possessed of some strange magnetism that made compass needles act erratically. Hence, Crand named his find the Magnetic Caves.

The system was entered through a crevice that was barely wide enough to accommodate a man. This had been enlarged using small charges so that it was easily navigable by the team and equipment. Once inside, a narrow and high-ceilinged passage sloped downward for about 50 feet, canting at about 45 degrees and terminating in a large subterranean room that was easily 30 feet wide and nearly a hundred feet long, half as much in height. A truly immense and breathtaking chamber whose walls were sculpted with ornate flows and set with an amazing variety of sparkling crystal formations of white gypsum and calcite.

It was here that Ault and Crand discovered their first fossil beds of any significance in a seam of Cretaceous deposits. An immense proliferation of cephalopods, ammonites and belemnites, massive shell assemblages as well as the fossilized remains of seed ferns, angiosperms and gymnosperms, club mosses and unknown fungi. The most interesting things were bone fragments of hadrosaurid dinosaurs and a near-complete skull of Hesperornis, a large flightless bird that stood six to seven feet tall, and what might have been the skull crests of predatory theropods similar to Cryolophosaurus.

And then things got a little more difficult, for the various levels of the cave system could only be reached by a series of vertical fissures. The first dropped down some forty feet and the second, nearly seventy. The passages below were mostly quite large. Some of the rooms themselves were the size of amphitheaters and featured impressive formations of marble and aragonite, the walls rippled with smooth cascades and candlewax flows, crystal boxwork and flowstone deposits. The ceilings and floors were set with stalactites and stalagmites, the complex spirals of helictites.

And it was here, on the third level, the lowest thus far, that Ault found his Devonian deposits. But that wasn't all he found.

Crand had picked his team carefully for underground work in the world's harshest environment. Not only because of their scientific acumen, but because everyone on the team was an experienced caver.

As he told them the night before they flew towards the Devil's Eye, "This cave system will be like no other in the world. You will witness things you will never forget and see things you will scarcely believe."

And on this latter matter, he was absolutely correct.

4

Ellis could not understand it later, but despite his apprehension of the mummies in the pit, something gripped him with both hands, something he simply could not fight against, and made him go down there.

"Just mummies," Ault told him, seemingly glad to see him coming to his senses. "That's all. We've made an interesting historical discovery by sheer chance."

Ellis barely heard him.

At least, with his ears. But some larger, unknown sense of perception heard him just fine. And what he was really saying was, *this is so fucked up, my friend. These mummified bodies. Skull caps removed. Not broken or fractured in any way, but surgically removed. I'm trying hard to maintain my scientific indifference but, God help me, this scares the shit out of me.*

His voice echoed endlessly in Ellis' head as he prattled on nervously, saying everything but what he really felt. Ellis did not bother commenting on any of it; he was transfixed by the mummies. There was a magnetism to them that he simply could not deny. They simultaneously terrified him and fascinated him. The implications of their missing brains was disturbing to say the least, but it was only part of it.

As insane as it seemed, he could almost hear them crying out to him, contacting him on some mental shortwave, wanting to tell him their story whether he wanted to hear it or not.

Their attraction was so solid, so overwhelming, so…*necessary,* that he reached out his hands and touched two of the bodies.

And the circuit was complete.

Ault said something but it was lost on him. All he could hear were the ghosts of these poor men screaming out to him from the past. Maybe it wasn't even their ghosts, maybe it was some weird psychic telemetry, some echo or reflection that originated from the undead essences of the things that had done this to them—the creatures who had opened their skulls and stolen their brains. And maybe it was both of those things amplified by the terrible mountain itself which he saw in his dreams as a great, night-haunted spook house of jutting spires and ancient peaks. A place where the dead slept uneasily and malign forces were gathering.

Ellis cocked his head, impervious to Ault.

Images cascaded through his brain and at such a velocity and with such complexity, that he could make no sense of them. *Buzzing, buzzing, buzzing.* That's what he heard. It was like putting his ear up against a hornet's nest, listening to that terrible life humming inside, preparing to wake and unleash its menace.

Yes, it was the voice of the mountain and the network of arteries beneath it, reverberating, rippling. The dismal and frightening sound of the past given life, thrumming like some huge generator that he was plugged into. *Ghosts,* a voice said in the back of his mind. *You're hearing ghosts.* But to him it was just the mountain itself, a huge rotting box of memories and monsters and reaching shadows whose lock had rusted away so that there was nothing to contain the awful secrets within. They clawed themselves free and filled the corridors of his brain, sending jolts of burning white pain up and down his spine and into the darkest recesses of his mind.

As his eyes stared blankly at the tumble of mummies before him, he thought, *Faces. Oh God, the screaming faces. I can see the screaming faces...I can feel their agony as their minds were devoured—*

Then, whatever it was, ended and he could feel Ault's hands on him, shaking him, his voice calling out the same thing again and again, "...all right? Ellis, are you all right?"

"Yes," he managed. "I'm okay. Maybe we should get out of here."

"Man, you blanked there for a minute."

"I felt weird...light-headed or something."

Which was a complete lie and both men knew it, but as they climbed free of the pit, they spoke no more of it. Ault, because he was afraid to broach the subject and Ellis, because he knew things he just did not dare put into words.

5

Five years before, Kharkov Station—which was southeast of the Devil's Eye and just inland from the Dominion Range—had been the sight of a tragedy. Some twenty people had been wintering-over there and only two made it out alive. And those two—a boiler engineer and the camp physician—came out saying some pretty frightening things, rumor had it. Much of it concerning extraterrestrials and lost cities and parasites that ate human minds. The NSF refused to acknowledge any of it. Their explanation was not quite so fantastic: the crew had died from a propane leak. Regrettable and terrible, yes, but a very concrete explanation.

Some people believed that and some didn't.

The Kharkov Tragedy, as it was known, had become the hub of a mass conspiracy movement…most of it centered on the web, of course. A few books had been written and a few more documentaries made. Word had it there was even a movie in the works. But the bottom line was that it was really hard to know what the truth was. Those two people who came out refused to discuss any of it after their original statements on the affair were met with derision and the NSF maintained its line in the sand: no creepy-crawlies, no Martians down on the ice. Not even Casper the Ghost or Glenda the Good Witch. Nothing. Just an unfortunate accident. Most people claimed to believe what the NSF said. At least in public.

As the years passed, people moved on to more relevant tragedies. At least until the disaster at Mount Hobb, in which the entire crew of twenty-five disappeared in a freak storm. Workers from nearby Icefall Research Station were the first to reach Hobb after the storm had abated and what they discovered were empty buildings and abandoned equipment that they dug from the snowdrifts, but not a single body. An investigatory team scoured the area for two weeks and turned up nothing.

And the stories kept making the rounds, getting worse (if that was possible) with the re-telling. The bottom line was, there was not a single member of Dr. Crand's geo team that were not aware of them. Maybe they didn't speak of any of it, but it was there, deep inside them, grinning at them from the shadows and daring them to doubt its very existence.

6

THE DEVIL'S EYE
TOPSIDE

The Hypertats were really something.

Two of them were set facing the crevice that led to the caves themselves. They were essentially high-tech Quonset-shaped huts with their own generators, water supplies, and plumbing facilities. Inside they looked like something from *Star Trek* with their banks of instrumentation, computer workstations, modular living areas and fold-out bunks. When you were inside, in the warmth and safety of the Hypertats, you could almost forget you were down in Antarctica and maybe fantasize that you were deep in space or living in some futuristic Martian colony. The Hypertats had kitchenettes and bathrooms, HF and sideband field radios and INMARSAT satellite hookups for voice and internet. They shook a bit when the wind blew, but they were securely bolted to the ice and had backup systems to keep you warm, fed, and alive to the point of redundancy.

Although they could be a bit cramped, they beat the hell out of ice tents any day of the week. Ault shared one with Ellis. Marsh was in the other with Hirvonen and Crand. The latter, apparently, to prove to everyone that nothing was going on between the good doctor and his randy post-grad student.

Ellis was still keyed-up, pacing back and forth and looking like he needed a good belt of bourbon. "He's up to something, Ault, and I don't want to be part of it. Crand has a fucking agenda here and we both know it."

Ault chewed his cheese and crackers. "That's pretty obvious."

"I'm not going back down there."

"You have to, Ellis. You know you do. It's why you're here."

"Is it? I'm getting the feeling this is about something else, but I just don't know what."

Well, at least it's not just me, Ault thought.

Ellis finally sat down. "There's something strange about those caves. I get those weird headaches down there."

After they had shown the others the mummies—and, of course, had a lively debate about them, courtesy of Crand, showing off for Hirvonen, no doubt—Crand had led them deeper into the cave system. They'd found some interesting fossil-bearing strata, but Crand kept going until he found something else: a vertical fissure that they sounded out at roughly 125 feet straight down. Tomorrow, he wanted to go down there. He wanted Ellis and Ault with him.

"I just don't like it," Ellis said.

"I don't either. He *is* up to something, but the only way we're going to find out what is by going along with him." Ault finished his snack, brushed his hands together. "Those bodies, Ellis. I'm telling you right now that Crand wasn't surprised by it as if he knew we were going to see something like that."

Ellis did not like talking about the mummies. And particularly what had happened after he touched them. It was a subject he would not comment upon.

"Did you see him when we found the fissure?"

Ault nodded.

Crand had nearly gotten excited. The corners of his lips actually trembled for a moment or two (which made Ault wonder if that's how he looked when he had a lovely little orgasm with his pretty grad student). Regardless, he *was* excited. About as excited as a guy like him got. There was something down there. Something that had stirred him up.

And what might that be?

"I'm not going down there, Ault," Ellis maintained. "All of this is wrong. My headache got worse when I got near that fissure. And that's no bullshit. I got a funny feeling from it like...I don't know..."

"Like what?"

Ellis looked at him. "Like I was looking down into a grave. There's something down there he wants to see, Ault. Whatever the hell it is, I can almost *feel* it down there. Feel it waiting for us."

Ault didn't say anything after that.

He just listened to the wind outside blowing through the valley, the darkness of the Antarctic night pressing down on the Hypertat like it wanted to squash it flat. He didn't say anything, but inside he felt sick with a sense of expectation and discovery of the worst possible sort.

Because, ultimately, he knew Ellis was right.

There was something down there and he wondered if they'd ever be the same again after they saw it.

7

THE MAGNETIC CAVES

They had been down in the fissure for nearly a week now.

It was 125 feet beneath the third level of the Magnetics, which itself was some 500 feet below the crevice itself through which you entered the system or exited to the Hypertats. The first four days down there were really about exploration, because the lower system through the fissure was even more complex and meandering than the upper three levels. Ellis, of course, did not want to make the descent at all because of his suspicions of Crand and the man's ultimate agenda. But Ault talked him into it. Because if they didn't play along, then how would they discover what that agenda was?

"I know he's up to something same as you," he told Ellis. "But if we refuse to go down, he's going to get very suspicious. Jesus, Ellis, we're not only scientists we're *cavers*. That's why he picked us."

Ault wasn't sure how much sense that made, but Ellis bought it.

Essentially, it was the truth. They were cavers. And the Magnetics were some of the most impressive subterranean caves in the world. No true caver would have turned away from them.

So, they went down.

At the bottom of the fissure, they found a rippled and uneven flooring of ice, lime, and frozen sand. The passage angled downward at roughly 40°, but was wide and easily navigable and soon opened into an impressive cavern which turned out to be sort of a foyer into the intricate cave system beyond. The cavern was easily 70 feet in height, twice that in width, and clearly showed the actions of ancient waters: pitted walls of lime scarred with delicate spiderwebbing drainage channels and the whorls of prehistoric whirlpools. It led into a series of large chambers, the ceilings sparkling with multicolored stalactites and beautiful translucent crystalline draperies of purple, red, orange, and green.

Even by flashlight, lantern, and helmet spots, it was all very breathtaking. Ault thought that the Magnetic Caves, both upper levels and lower, might become one of the world's most popular tourist attractions if they weren't set in such a godforsaken country.

The mineral deposits, of course, fascinated Hirvonen because she was a geologist. When Crand had selected her for the expedition to Antarctica, she had been engaged in doctoral research into carbonate sedimentology.

As they explored, Crand led the way with Hirvonen ever at his side. Even in her helmet and bulky, insulated caving suit, she was attractive. Her blue eyes glittered as brightly as any crystals in the caves. But those were only for Crand. Not that this dissuaded Marsh; every time she turned, he was watching her, randy as ever.

All in all, they made an amusing group of cavers.

Crand had his eye on some distant point, some unknown goal he would not share with the others. A visionary in his own crowded little mind. And while his eyes were there, Hirvonen's were on him when they weren't on the crystallized minerals and stratified rocks. Crand led from the front and Hirvonen groveled in his shadow. All the while, Marsh was right behind her, trying to contain his hormones. And behind him were Ault and Ellis, both intrigued by the natural wonders around them, but also wishing that they'd stayed home.

Or, at least, Ellis did.

But for Ault, as a paleobiologist, it was a dream come true. What he had thus far discovered would take him years to describe and when he did, his name would no doubt go down with the greats of paleontology. And that was above, in the upper three levels. But down here, he was seeing even older rocks and had already found nice fossil-bearing outcroppings teaming with the remains of primitive fishes, invertebrates, and vascular plants. There was no time now to adequately even begin cataloging what he had seen, but when the time came, it was going to be rich. The Magnetic Caves were going to be legendary for their Paleozoic remains.

Day after day, they kept going deeper into the network. Crand would not let them slow down for a moment. He was fixated with something and nobody knew what it was. And regardless of how fascinating any particular geologic formation was, he had no interest in taking the time to thoroughly investigate it. He was after something, but it was not rocks.

And that's how it was, day after day after day.

Ault was as unsure of the man as the others, but he was beginning to see a glint in Crand's eye that hinted at manic obsession. He was after something and it was much bigger than the scientific riches of the Magnetics. So big that it was blotting out everything else. Somewhere ahead there was a light at the end of the tunnel, but only Crand knew what shape it would take or how bright it might indeed be when they found it.

8

Ellis was a scientist, a paleoclimatologist, and a veteran caver. He knew his business. He'd seen incredible things under the earth, fossils of everything from Mesozoic dinosaurs to giant carnivorous pigs from the Eocene and predatory birds of the Tertiary that stood ten feet in height with beaks that could have split oak stumps in two. None of it had ever bothered him. Not in the slightest. He was made of staunch stuff and had even once been trapped in a cave-in in a mine shaft outside Rapid City, South Dakota for fourteen hours, alone in perpetual darkness. When he got out, he told people he'd kept it together by keeping his mind busy. A life long Beatles fan, he went through every album song by song reciting the lyrics and then singing them out loud. Even now, when he was nervous, he either hummed or silently sang tunes by the Fab Four.

But the mummies had him spooked. There was no way around it.

When he first saw them, he looked like a little kid who'd just wandered out of a carnival haunted house ready to piss himself or maybe somebody that was terrified of heights and was about to skydive for the first time.

And since then, since he'd touched them, they were on his mind nearly constantly, hiding in the shadows, peeking out at him with death-mask faces that knew awful things, terrible secrets from antiquity.

Whenever they were down in the caves and took a break, he smoked one cigarette after the other which annoyed the hell out of Hirvonen, Crand's attractive blonde assistant, who was a physical fitness instructor and girl's swimming coach in her spare time that ate only organic food and despised things like cigarettes and alcohol and caffeine. Marsh got a kick out of that because he was always real popular with the ladies with his dark good looks, but to Hirvonen he might as well have been a syphilitic leper. He'd been coming onto her since day one, she of the Scandinavian beauty, and she couldn't have been less interested.

Not that she didn't have hormones.

For they were on perpetual, breathy display as she followed Crand around like a lovesick teenager. Crand barely paid attention to her. Hirvonen was twenty-three and Crand had nearly forty years on her, but you would never have known it. She was completely infatuated with him.

Ault watched this all going on around him, thinking, worrying, wondering what Crand's ultimate agenda might be, certain that they were in incredible danger, but a danger that he simply could not put a name to.

He only knew one thing for sure: the deeper they went into the system, the closer they were getting to it.

9

Now they were much further than ever before into the Magnetics and to a man and woman they could feel something building in the air. Maybe something good, something incredible…and possibly something of a darker variety.

Hour after hour, they moved through passages and up inclines, over boulders and squeezing sideways between shelves of rock, lights splashing about and footsteps echoing.

Ellis was clinging so close to Ault it was like having a conjoined twin. Every time he stopped, Ellis would bump into him.

"Please knock that off," Ault told him and told him again.

Ellis would apologize and then start humming. And that was even worse. Ault would tell him to stop that and Ellis would say, "Sorry." For a time, he'd stop humming his Beatles' songs. "Strawberry Fields Forever" would end and then five minutes later as they moved up a rise of gravel he'd be back at it with "Hey Jude" or "Here, There, and Everywhere." It was annoying, but he didn't seem to realize he was doing it. Nerves, just nerves.

Not that Ault wasn't feeling it, too.

There was something about the caves he'd been feeling from the first moment they entered the crevice high above. At times it was a feeling of expectation or exhilaration; at others, an unpleasant suspense, a worming sort of dread as if he was waiting for someone or *something* to jump out at them. It was emotionally draining and the deeper they went, the worse it got. The headaches they'd all suffered came and went. Sometimes they were persistent and throbbing like the sort you got after a hard night of drinking. Other times, they were barely noticeable or so painful that Ault had to grind his teeth and squeeze his eyes shut until they passed. And there was no reason for them. The gas detectors clipped to their suits were showing nothing.

So they kept going.

And Ellis kept humming.

Ault had spent a lot of time underground and it got to where you didn't think much about it, but now and again as their lights splashed over bowed walls and wax flows, he began to feel claustrophobic. Maybe it was the dry air and the cold, that mountain of rock above, but it was there and he could not dispel it.

The caverns went on and on. They were set with huge boulders you had to squeeze between and massive limestone columns that towered above, the sloping ceilings set with variegated bacon-rind banding and immense stalactites. Now and again there were barren fissures and ragged shafts that plunged hundreds of feet below that had to be jumped over. There were rocky inclines to climb and narrow clefts between caverns to be negotiated and great pools of ice to be skated over.

Above, were rounded chimneys reaching to great, unknown heights and dozens of side passages leading off into oblivion, great shelves of rock that could have fallen at any moment and crushed them. But for all the danger, there was impressive beauty beneath the frozen white land. Stalagmitic towers that rose up hundreds of feet. Walls of threading frostwork crystals many inches deep. Wonderfully complex and corkscrewing aragonite helictites. Enormous dogtooth spar crystals, some of which were the size of shovel blades, bright pink and yellow. Oval basin speleothems that looked like giant crystalline bird baths composed of millions of fragile crystals in hundreds of sparkling colors. Amazing, utterly amazing.

This was how time was spent in that new system: in wonder and awe, but with a mounting sense of paranoia and maybe even something like horror at the root of it all.

Because it was there and it could not be denied.

And then they found yet another cavern. It was as large as the others like some colossal amphitheater with a ceiling a hundred feet above and set with an impressive display of marbled walls, gypsum flows, elaborate soda straw stalactites, and ancient dripstones. There were coralloid formations of mineral nodules on the floors and impressive crystalwork in every direction. But at the far end, in a petrified mud flat, there was something else.

When Crand found it, he stopped. "Ault, get up here," he said.

Ault, with Ellis in tow, went up there over the loose scree and pebbles until he stood with Hirvonen and Crand, Marsh hanging back with that carnal smile on his face like he was having some particularly naughty fantasies about Hirvonen. And he probably was. Standing there in their boots and caving suits and hardhats, slicked with clay and dusted with dry earth, it was hard to imagine them in a classroom or lab.

All lights were on the smooth fossilized mud flow before them.

"How would you classify these rocks down here?" Crand said.

"Silurian," Ault said, "clearly older than those above."

"Are you certain?"

"As I can be."

He had been examining the rocks whenever they took a break. Using a hand lens, he had already found the remains of acanthodians and ostracoderms, jaws and scales and fins. And there had been some particularly interesting fossils of land invertebrates, springtails and scorpions, as well as a particularly large spiderlike trigonotarbid. These were very rare finds indeed. But even the cursory examination he'd given them had made him sure this was Silurian strata, the biostratigraphy was most telling.

He sighed. "I think Hirvonen can support me on that."

"Yes," she said. "Definitely Silurian."

She was on her hands and knees examining a limestone deposit. She scraped some white powder from it and dropped hydrochloric acid onto it. It bubbled and fizzed. "Calcite," she said under her breath.

"You're certain then?" Crand said. "Both of you?"

"Yes," Ault said.

Hirvonen packed up her test equipment carefully, looking from Crand to Ault. "Yes, there's no doubt."

"I'm in agreement with you," he proclaimed proudly.

Ault rolled his eyes.

Crand was up to something. That much was obvious. Probably setting up some grandstanding for Hirvonen's benefit to show how wise and wonderful he was. He knew damn well that the strata at this level was Silurian. The green and red banding was indicative. During the Silurian, about 420 million years ago, the land had only recently been colonized by life. Sparse forests of treelike lycophytes and thorny-stemmed proteridophytes would have covered Antarctica, particularly near waterways. There would have been prodigious mosses below and tall green lycopods towering above. On the forest floor there would be mites and scorpions, millipedes and primitive spiders. All of them predatory.

"Now, tell me how you would classify these imprints," he said.

He walked ahead about ten feet and set his lantern down. In the fossilized mud were a series of perfectly preserved casts of what at first seemed to be the leaves of some type of tree, though in the Silurian that was ridiculous. True leaf-bearing trees would not exist for some time. During the Silurian there were no trees as such, just tree-like plants.

Ault had his flashlight beam on them now.

The casts were triangular in shape, maybe seven or eight inches in length, tapering from six inches wide at the fore to an obtuse point at the rear. They were striated with five vein-like markings that gave the impression that what made them had some sort of ridges. Though the idea of leaves was ridiculous, the very pattern in which they were set also ruled that out. For the groupings were systematic, not accidental as in the patterns of falling leaves. Ault counted sixteen such castings and the fragmentary remains of a dozen more.

"It looks almost like a trail," Marsh said. "The stride of an animal."

And it did. Very much. But what sort of animal? Ault's area of expertise was not only vertebrate biogeography, he had also made a very systematic study of trace fossils—footprints, feeding trails, animal burrows etc.—and had even written several papers on the subject. But whatever had left these simply eluded him.

"I suppose they could have been left by some unknown arthropod, possibly a crustacean…I suppose."

"Yes…but by a single creature or a grouping?" Crand wanted to know.

"I can't say…not with any certainty."

Although biology was not Marsh's thing, he had spent a lot of time hunting and tracking game of all sorts. And maybe this particular game had been dust for some 400,000,000 years, but what he saw suggested certain things. "One animal," he said and everyone looked at him. "Look at the stride, the placement of those feet or pads or whatever you want to call them. The stride is repetitious and consistent." He got down there with Ault. Taking a chisel from his pack he began pressing it into the tracks, mimicking what the creature's stride would have been. "See? We have a consistent pattern here of three pads fore and two aft. Again and again and again. When this creature walked, it placed three limbs forward and followed it with two behind, possibly for balance. You can see that stride repeated and repeated."

"But the length of the stride," Hirvonen pointed out. "This creature would have been immense. No arthropod could have been this large."

Ault measured the theoretical stride. It was something like four feet with occasional gaps of five. Fantastic. There was no land animal in the Silurian with such a gait. And the idea of the discovery of a totally new species did not mesh simply because terrestrial evolution of land forms simply could not encompass this. The highest form of life during the Silurian were the fishes. There were huge placoderms, but none of them came up onto land. And they certainly did not walk. As far as arthropods went, the sea scorpion or Eurypterid, sometimes reached lengths of nine feet, but they were strictly marine.

"Well," Ault finally said, "I suppose it's possible that these tracks might belong to some new and terribly exotic lungfish, even though the lungfish did not appear until the Devonian. But it's entirely possible."

"Yes," Hirvonen said. "That makes sense. New species are described all the time."

Ault nodded, but didn't believe it for a minute.

These casts were from no fish; he was certain of that. He could not place them within the known confines of the animal kingdom during the Silurian. Had this been late Devonian or Carboniferous or even Permian strata, it would have made more sense. There were some very large amphibians then… but not in the Silurian. Unless everything they knew about that period was terribly wrong. He figured some of it probably was, but not in relation to basic terrestrial life forms.

Crand arched his eyebrow. "I don't believe these were left by a fish. I believe they were left by an unknown organism. A radically unknown organism. Of course, debate is fruitless at this juncture."

"Wanna take a stab at what it might have been?" Ault put to him.

He shook his head. "Not yet. I believe what we find ahead may bear out my somewhat sketchy and elusive hypothesis, however."

Ault didn't push it. He was in no mood to argue with Crand. Maybe Crand knew something and maybe he didn't, regardless the man was careful. He would take no theoretical stabs at the creature itself that might come back on him and make him appear foolish. If he was pushed, he would simply resort to his usual verbal and argumentative acrobatics.

Besides, Ault was tired. They all were. They'd been down in these caves too long and it had gotten to the point that even the glacial darkness above would have been an improvement. Yes, he was tired. Fatigued. His body aching, a permanent chill having reached into his bones that nothing but a warm bed and a lot of hot soup up in the Hypertat could cure. But that wouldn't be happening anytime soon.

Ellis could not stop staring at the prints with his helmet light. His facial expressions jumped from one emotion to the next—fear, shock, surprise, anxiety. He pressed up close to Ault like a frightened puppy, then he let out a sharp, agitated sort of laugh that got everyone looking at him, wondering if he was on the edge of a nervous breakdown.

"Yes, yes, yes," he said, suppressing a giggling beneath his words. "Whatever could have made such prints? What possible advanced lifeform walked upright in the Silurian?"

"Are you okay?" Ault asked him.

"Of course, I'm okay. Just ask Dr. Crand. He'll tell you just how okay we all are."

Crand eyed him hatefully. "Of course, we're okay."

They pushed on.

10

Ellis followed along, humming "The Long and Winding Road" under his breath, his eyes filled with a wild, terrible knowledge. *Oh, Crand, you fucked up egotistical little sociopath! Like you don't know what left those fossilized prints! Like you don't know where it is you're leading us, you sonofabitch!*

He could hear that curious, awful buzzing in the back of his head as he had when he placed his hands on the mummies in the pit. The deeper they went into the system, the louder it became until it seemed to echo in the confines of his brain like a scream in an amphitheater. He could hear something buried in it, a distant agonized sound and he knew it was the final cries of the expeditioners from the pit. Something history had forgotten, but the mountain remembered quite well. It was the sound of their final, ultimate violation at the hands of the things that had haunted Kharkov.

Oh, yes, yes, yes, they'll get us, too, because that's what Crand wants. He's offered us up to those alien horrors because he doesn't give a rat's ass about human lives. All he cares about is expanding his knowledge and we're the guinea pigs that can give him that.

Ellis tried to shut out the voices, but they wanted to be heard and as he heard them, he heard something else, too, something far worse than the horrible deaths of those poor men—the sibilant murmurings of the aliens themselves, trying to crowd out his own thoughts and replace them with something inherently inhuman. Yes, they were filling his mind with eggs that would soon hatch and obliterate his humanity.

"I am the Eggman," he said under his breath. "I am the Eggman. But who is Mr. Kite?"

11

Cavern after cavern, the shadows crawled around them, their lights like knife blades laying back the stygian flesh of the underworld. The air was dry and chill, but warmer than above. There was a constant mean temperature of nearly ten degrees in the first level, so it was getting warmer the farther down they went. That was intriguing. There were great wonders to be had in those caverns and grottos, but Crand had no interest in stopping for study. He kept marching them along, a look of absolute desperation in his eyes.

So, on they went, their boots echoing like thunder, the stillness and desolation of the lower Magnetics making it feel like they had been buried alive in some primal catacomb.

Ault was feeling that headache coming and going.

And that strange, ever-building sense of exhilaration and suspense that was making the flesh at his spine actually crawl. He couldn't understand what it was, but he could feel it. In his belly, in his head, along his spine and over the backs of his arms…a tingling, creeping sensation that he equated with a discharge of energy. As if some great kinetic machine nearby was sending out a charge of static electricity. He felt very nervous, very wired as if he was pumped full of amphetamines.

And it wasn't just him, because he was seeing it in the faces of the others. They were tense and agitated. Ellis looked like a college kid who'd been up three days straight cramming for exams. His eyes were bright, his face tight, a tic in the corner of his lips.

Standing on a rocky ledge that wound away above a great chasm that the light beams could not plumb, Crand suddenly stopped. He was holding his compass. "Look," he said. "Look at this."

They all gathered around. The compass needle was erratic. It vibrated madly from side to side, then spun so fast that they could not even see it. Being near the Geomagnetic Pole, compasses often acted strangely…but not like this.

"Some sort of intense magnetism," Marsh said. "Much stronger than above."

"The rocks?" Ellis said, his voice squeaky and hopeful.

"I don't think so," Hirvonen said. "No ore in the world has that kind of draw."

They had seen some of this before, of course. That's why Crand had named the system the Magnetic Caves. But this was much more pronounced.

Marsh kept watching it. "I've seen this before," he said.

All eyes were on him now.

He shrugged. "Compasses spin like that in the presence of an electromagnet. A big electromagnet or electromagnetic field."

"Down here?" Ault said.

Crand put the compass away and Ault saw his face for a few moments in the lantern light. Yes, his eyes were wide and wet like the others, his face corded and tense…but there was something else there. An expectation the others did not have.

"We must be getting close to something, Dr. Crand," Ellis said, then pressed a gloved hand to his mouth as if to stop himself from saying anymore.

They moved on.

Now the caverns were not just large, they were immense. Whereas the ceilings might be a hundred feet up before, now they were twice that, roofed by thousands of stalactites. Great valleys and chasms opened up in the cavern floors. Glittering crystal growths grabbed the lights and held them. All in all, it gave them a feeling of insignificance, like ants crawling over the floor of a train tunnel.

Thirty minutes after the compass incident, they were struck by alternating currents of freezing air and then plumes of heat that actually made sweat break out on their faces. They passed through a cavern whose floor was a frozen lake that went on for nearly a mile. The ice was black, smooth, and impossibly old.

"Not far now," Crand said when they'd reached the end and entered another passage. "Not far at all."

"Not far at all to what?" Ault said. "Don't you think it's time to clue the rest of us in on it?"

Ellis leaned in close to Ault and said, "There are secrets that no man can know and few can imagine." Then he giggled, blowing out rolling white clouds of condensation.

"You need to relax," Ault told him.

Crand was oblivious to all of it, walking ever forward, playing his light around. Had Ault not been so damned tired he would have grabbed him and beaten him to the ground. The others just trudged along in stony silence. And then they entered another gigantic cavern and on the far side they were met with a wall of black stone that was incredibly smooth and perfect. Like basalt or black onyx, utterly without so much as a blemish. It was shiny and they could see ghostly reflections of themselves in its mirrored surface. It rose up hundreds of feet and went in either direction farther than their lights could reach.

"It…it looks artificial," Hirvonen said.

And Ault thought: *This is what your father figure cum prophet has been leading us to all the while: this wall. This perfect wall of artificial design. No lava flow in the world could mimic this. It's too perfectly smooth. And Crand knew it was here all along. He didn't give a flying fuck about fossil remains or cave systems or mineral deposits. He was after something much bigger…*

"Like quartz," she said. "But definitely artificial."

"Artificial?" Marsh said. He had been growing quietly antagonistic for some time and now it was surfacing. "Are you out of your mind? *Artificial?* Down here for chrissake?"

And Ellis said, "The whole Kharkov thing…remember? Gates, the paleobiologist, said there was an ancient city under the ice…"

Marsh turned on him. "Yeah, and I've heard that comic book bullshit ad nauseum. Last thing I need now is more of it. Aliens. Dead cities. My white fucking ass."

"Pull your head out of the sand. Things have happened down here," Ellis pointed out. "And they're still happening."

Marsh's mouth got tight, but he said nothing.

Pulling out a rock hammer, Hirvonen tried to chip the wall. The hammer wouldn't leave so much as a scratch. She tried her files and chippers. No good. Marsh took her hammer and swung it, kept swinging it until sweat ran down his grimy face in clean trails. He could not even mar it. But the echoing sound of him striking it boomed and echoed weirdly.

"Feel it," she said, her bare hand pressed against it. "It's…it's warm."

Ault did. Yes, it was warm. And not only warm, but thrumming subtly like the beat of an infant's heart. *Thump-thump, thump-thump.* He pulled his hand away, a blade of pain cutting through his head.

"That's it," Marsh said, turning on Crand. "I've had enough of this shit. You're going to tell us and tell us right now what this is all about."

You couldn't have removed that smug, knowing look from Crand's face with a belt sander. It was permanently etched. "I think we'll all know soon enough."

Marsh made a choking sound in his throat and grabbed Crand. Grabbed him and swung him up against the wall, that odd booming sound echoing out again. "Listen to me, you fucking pretentious asshole! I've had my fill! Tell us what this is about or I swear to God and the fucking saints that I'm going to beat your face in!"

Ellis and Ault pulled him away and he fought them off, pacing in circles and swearing.

Crand was not bothered by any of it.

He walked away, swinging his lantern, and shining his light around. Nobody followed, not at first. Hirvonen looked at his retreating light, then looked back at Ault and the others. Her eyes were wide like those of a frightened rabbit. Ault held out his hand and she came and took it.

"I'm...I'm scared," she admitted.

"Yes. We all are."

Together, they went after Crand and found him about two hundred feet down the wall. He was grinning and shaking with excitement. "There!" he said. "Do you see? Do all of you finally see?"

Oh, they saw all right.

There was a perfectly circular tunnel cut through the black stone. It was huge. Its rounded ceiling had to be at least fifty feet up. Inside, it was shiny and black like the wall itself, its surface glassy. It reached farther than their lights. It was so perfectly symmetrical that it looked as if some immense drill bit had channeled it out.

"Who do you suppose cut this?" Crand said.

"Who or *what*," Ellis said under his breath.

They all put their lights on it. Hirvonen put hers up high near the top where the tunnel was cut into the black stone. Up there was what looked like a plaque or a bas relief, a very intricate and abstract representation of a spiral galaxy, arms radiating outwards, a weird vortex whose epicenter looked like a great eye.

Ellis felt himself grow cold just looking at it. Some unknown, ancient terror had seized him with icy hands, squeezing the guts right out of him.

Marsh made a choked, sobbing sound in his throat. It was more than the sound of anguish, but as if the breath had been sucked from his lungs. "That symbol...oh, Jesus Christ, that symbol..."

It hit them all in a very personal, intimate sort of way. Ellis had to lean against the wall so he didn't go out cold. His entire body was shaking and quaking. He made a series of inarticulate noises like a frightened animal. Hirvonen's lips were pulled in a tight, gray line. Her eyes were huge and glistening.

The only one untouched by it seemed to be Crand. He studied the symbol with great fascination, sweeping his light over it and nodding his head. "The gateway," he said. "At last, the gateway."

Ault was pretty sure that none of them wanted to know what it was a gateway to, but they followed behind Crand into the passage. Bunched together and shaking, feeling things just ahead that made their flesh crawl, they followed, seemingly having no choice.

But by then, there really was no going back.

12

They hiked about two hundred feet into the weird tunnel, not speaking, not doing anything but following the beams of their lights like donkeys following a carrot on a stick. The analogy worked, Ault figured, because in this place with the very real fear of who and *what* had built it, they were pretty much mindless beasts of burden led forward into something which would probably be a limitless horror.

Though the headaches seemed to have faded for the most part, he kept getting a bright surge of pain in his head like a white-hot spike was pounded through his skull. Every time it occurred, it filled his mind with static and grating noise. He could not understand or account for it. It was as if his brain had been turned into a radio receiver, one that could not lock onto any specific channel.

He kept looking at the others, what he could see of them in the enclosing darkness, but as to whether they were getting it, too, it was hard to say.

At first, he tried to ignore it, but it was impossible. And it wasn't just the pain, but all that damn noise gathering between his ears and rising to a shrill squealing. Then he tried to work with it, to tune it if such a thing were even possible. He concentrated and fixed his thoughts into something like a straight line, trying to gather it all in that linear arrangement. And when he nearly had it, he sent out a thought, *who's out there? What do you want?*

But there was nothing.

He was both relived and disturbed.

Marsh finally stopped and refused to go any further. "This is ridiculous," he said. "We need to go back."

"Absolutely not," Crand said.

Ault looked at Hirvonen and he could see the fear in her eyes. She was carefully concealing it, but it was there. Ellis looked about twenty years older than he had when they first arrived. They all needed a break. It was not only physically exhausting, but mentally draining.

"No, he's right, Dr. Crand," Ault finally said. "We're low on everything. Our water's getting down, we're short on food. And if we keep at it like this for another day or two, we won't have any batteries left for the lights. And I'd say the chances of our making it out of here in the dark are slim to none."

Crand didn't like it. Everyone agreed with Marsh. It amounted to open rebellion to him. And by that point, even Hirvonen had slipped the collar he put on her. He tried to reason with her, ignoring the others, but she wouldn't have it. She was far past humping the leg of her master for attention.

"Well, I'm not going. We're close. Dear God, we're so very close now. Think of the science. Where is your curiosity? Your sense of discovery?" he said, trying to appeal to the scientists in them. "You're on the outer edge of the most significant find in human history. Doesn't that mean anything to you?"

"Means I'd rather be alive and ignorant, than dead and informed," Ellis said, encapsulating what they were all thinking and feeling.

Marsh was getting angry. This time Ault was certain he was going to hit Crand, but he didn't. He just sighed and shook his head. "Hate to point it out to you, Crand, but what we've already found down here will ensure our names in the history of geology and paleontology. We've found enough to keep us going for decades. I can think of four papers I want to write on what we've seen already."

"But we're close!"

"Close to what?" Hirvonen asked. "Please, can't you spell it out for us?"

But Crand just shook his head, incensed at all of them. Maybe he was afraid to put a name to it for fear that it would vanish like a treasure in a fairy tale. But by that point, they all knew what he was after and the mummies of the explorers they had found and the indescribable set of fossilized prints were part of it. But just the very extremity.

"We need to go back," Ault said. "It's the sensible thing to do. We need to re-provision. That's a fact. And we need to get on the radio and let McMurdo know we're still alive. For all we know, they might have already organized a rescue team."

"Then go, I'll stay," Crand said.

"Down here? All alone?" Ellis found the very idea akin to madness of the most severe variety.

"Yes."

Elis looked over at Ault and it was easy to read his mind: *This guy is fucking bananas. He's certifiable.*

Nobody argued with him. There was no point. They all knew how obsessive he was by then. A rock had more flexibility. So they left him down there. Nobody was comfortable with the idea. It was as if they were abandoning another human being to a terrible fate. Yet, they had to consider survival. The greatest discovery of all time was fine and dandy, but if you weren't alive to tell of it, what possible difference did it make?

Ault tried again and again to change Crand's mind, as did Hirvonen, but he was firm: he was staying down there and that's all there was to it. Marsh didn't seem to care one way or the other and Ellis just wanted to get out of there.

Finally, they left him alone in the darkness.

13

It was a long journey up to the Hypertats and when they got there, they radioed McMurdo, got a ration of shit for not calling in daily, then showered and ate and rested. When they went back down, they planned on being in good shape. It was then that Ellis, who'd been going slowly mad ever since he'd stumbled upon the mummies, announced he would not be going back down. Ault did not blame him.

"Somebody should stay up here," he said. "Somebody should be monitoring that radio. We agreed to do that when we came here. The NSF made us sign a set of rules and we—"

Marsh went red, then purple as a rutabaga. "Coward. You're nothing but a coward. You're afraid to go back down there."

Ellis was not offended. "Afraid? Oh yes, I am afraid and if you had any sense in that litter box you use for a brain, you'd be scared, too. Scared of what's down there. Scared of Crand. Scared of what that maniac is leading us to. That's not cowardice, friend, it's common sense."

"He's right," Hirvonen said. "Somebody should stay up here."

"Yes," Ault said.

"Things are going to happen down there," Ellis told them. "Terrible things. It's all part of Crand's plan. Can't you see that? Can't you feel it in your head?"

"You're crazy," Marsh said.

"Of course I am. But it doesn't make me wrong."

Marsh started laughing, but there was no humor in it. It had a grim, morbid tone to it, sardonic, mocking. The laughter of someone about to launch into a real good horror story. "Okay, Ellis. You stay. Up here. All alone. Out there, nothing but the wind and the blackness and the cold. You enjoy it. But you remember what the old explorers used to say about how the wind would become voices that call you out into the darkness and you remember what happened at Kharkov Station and Mount Hobb and all those other places. What's down here likes to get people like you alone so it can call you off into the storm and eat your mind."

Ellis looked pale and Ault could pretty much figure what was going through his mind and the myriad ways his imagination was going to torture him in the coming days.

Before they left, he told him, "Three days. Give us three days. We're not back, you call McMurdo and tell them you need help. Don't hesitate. Our lives might depend on it."

"Will do."

14

They journeyed back down and when they reached that black wall over twenty-four hours later, Crand was gone. They knew where he'd went and went after him. Some 500 feet into the tunnel, they still could not find him. So they went another 500. Still no Crand.

"I'm not going any farther," Marsh announced. "If that wingnut wants to get lost, the hell with him."

"Just a little farther," Ault said.

They moved forward for another hour and found nothing. They called Crand's name at regular intervals, listening to it echo and echo down the tunnel. Finally, they turned back. The tunnel might have gone on another mile or ten for all they knew. Hirvonen led the way back. She was just ahead of them and when she let out a cry.

"What?" Ault said, jogging up to her.

But then he saw, too.

They were trapped.

Somehow, some way, the tunnel had closed up. It was impossible, entirely impossible, and yet it had happened. The tunnel was large, about fifty feet in diameter give or take, and perfectly smooth. They had carefully studied every inch of it as they penetrated deeper and deeper and there was no sign of any doors or hatches or anything that could possibly explain what had now happened. A wall had appeared where none could be. They were in a colossal tube with no egress, no outlet. The mystery wall was only about twenty feet behind them now and up ahead, another wall. They were bottled up like bugs in a jelly jar and like them, the reasons were equally as incomprehensible.

"This can't be," Marsh said. "It just can't fucking be. This tunnel is straight. There's no way way we could have diverged. Do you hear me? There's just no way."

With that, he crumbled.

It was quite a show. Devilishly handsome, confident, always the big man on campus, he lost it. He started screaming and shouting, pounding and kicking the smooth walls. The sounds of his cries echoed around with a maddening volume. He ran back and forth and finally, fell to his knees and began to sob uncontrollably.

Hirvonen was terrified by then, too.

Who wouldn't have been?

She was Crand's beautifully Nordic post-grad student and faithful lapdog. He had been a god in her eyes…at least until they found the wall and he'd shown his true, aberrant colors. Then she'd jumped off his lap and had clung to Ault like a frightened schoolgirl. Which was fine by Ault, because by then he was little more than a frightened schoolboy himself.

"Marsh," she finally said. "Please try and relax. Panicking will only make this worse."

"Fuck you," he told her.

He was inconsolable after that. He just climbed into his hole and pulled the hole in after him. Ault and Hirvonen spent their time marching off the tunnel, studying every aspect of it. It was their scientific minds that held them together: here is a problem, let's look at it rationally and logically, gather our facts and hold the whole thing up to the scientific method. So they paced off the tunnel, examined it minutely, and came to the very unscientific conclusion that they were most seriously screwed.

15

Endless, endless, endless.

Alone, Crand wandered through the perpetual darkness of the endless passages, a lost little boy on the edge of hysteria, his mind beginning to fold in on itself because he knew there was no escape. He would die here and his bones would lay in this subterranean hell for an eternity. He used his light sparingly, trying to be rational, trying to use common sense and reasoning, but sometimes it got the better of him. He began to shake and moan, chattering endlessly to himself. He was certain he was neither going backward or forward, but caught in some interminable loop. Nothing seemed right, nothing felt right.

And whenever he stopped, trying to think, he could hear voices calling to him, summoning him to something that he knew would destroy his sanity.

He had seen things since the others left and he became trapped. Incredible wonders, scientific marvels, things that would have captivated him intellectually if he hadn't been so goddamned terrified all the time. Fearing that he was alone and fearing, at the same time, that he wasn't.

Now and again, the tunnel echoed with weird squealing noises, electronic static, and a strident piping that made him seize up, his stomach rolling over out of sheer dread.

The darkness was so big and he was so small that he began to feel like a little boy as he was haunted by childhood terrors that he thought were long extinct. He had been afraid for so long now he could not remember what it was like *not* to be afraid. The terror was inside him and outside him, closing in, bending his mind out of shape.

Finally, exhausted and trembling, he fell down and sleep took him.

When he woke, minutes or hours later, he became aware that something was happening to his brain. It was as if something was crawling in his skull, filling his head, feeding off his waning mental energies.

It's them, he thought with a feverish, childlike terror. *They've found you and they're reaching out to you, taking you over, remaking you in their own image.*

His eyes darting around wildly, sweat breaking out on his face, he panned his light around, seeing all the awful and grotesque remnants of their civilization, prehistoric things that were dead but not dead enough. He couldn't seem to think. The pressure in his brain increased. He let out a cry and then bit into his tongue until he drew blood. Urine coursed down his leg. His thoughts were muddled, he couldn't seem to remember who he was—

I am…I am…I am…I am…

But it was lost in the haze and he screamed one last time and then everything went black. For how long, he did not know. His eyes opened and there was a calmness, yet a terrible sense of dislocation. He was here, yes, but he was also somewhere else.

He licked his dry lips and a voice, *his* voice yet not his, said from somewhere impossibly distant: "I am ready. I am willing. I will be chosen because there is nothing else…"

Then his brain began to work again and it was like he was back at the university, lecturing.

Witches, he heard his voice say.

Funny how so late in the day for mankind all the old superstitions and legends and whispered folktales are suddenly taking on greater concrete and prophetic meaning. So long denied and suppressed by reason, intellect, and the anthropocentric ideals of the conscious mind. Delusions, they were called. Yet, they were not delusions, but memories of ancient pre-human rites that had been instilled into humankind as racial memory, locked up in the core of the human brain for eons, passed along as inherited memory, and re-invented in the anthropomorphisms of demons, devils, sorcery, and witchcraft itself. The demons and devils were but anthropomorphic versions of the Old Ones themselves. Spells and pagan rites were but bits and pieces of alien ritual. Psychic abilities were simply natural attributes of the Old Ones that had been bred into us so that we would be like them at the time of the great awakening of the human hive. And things like witchcraft and sorcery, when coupled with psychic ability, were only crude, humanized versions of an incredibly ancient and systematic alien science. Thought projection, telekinesis, telepathy, even prophecy itself...only techniques of this science.

Who can say how many innocents were hanged, dismembered, tortured, and burned out of superstitious terror and blind unreasoning fear during the witch persecutions. Christianity, of course, had a strong hand in this, the great suppressor of pagan belief and pre-human memory. But much of it was probably the human race itself and its inborn fear of the Old Ones and the surviving vestiges of their culture which clung on as witchcraft and black magic. Perhaps we did not recognize these memories and primal fears, but it was there, in our subconscious minds, the drives that sought to eliminate and sterilize any remaining limb of the alien tree. Now and again there were those that were born with certain faculties intact or had them activated by the hive mind itself...witches. Many were no doubt killed by hysterical primitives frightened of not only witches, but the witches residing within themselves. And that was the greatest adversary of all...the devil within that could wake at any time. But some of these few true witches did survive and did establish cults and the rituals survived.

Crand knew much now that he was not only here in the hive, but plugged into its memory. He knew not only the above information, but something even more startling.

So much of who and what we are, he realized, were imitations of the makers and enslavers themselves.

And he was grateful here at the end of self-imposed human dominion, that it was all revealed to be cyclical in nature. As we stood upon the brink of destiny, on the threshold of the future, the past owned us completely and irrevocably. As it always, always had. For we were never anything but a human colony of the gods themselves.

Forever and amen.

Crand opened his eyes again and he was somewhere else, a place he had long wanted to go.

He was in some sort of immense semi-spherical chamber illuminated by a soft blue light. It was like the inside of a channeled whelk, but on a grand scale. The floor and lower walls were rippled and flowing like candle wax, black and shiny as the carapaces of stag beetles, rising up and up, flaring ever outward in a pattern of ridge whorls and revolving lines as the sphere widened and then narrowed again high above in a webby profusion of strands and fibers.

He heard a rustling behind him, soft and secretive. He turned and fell down to his knees with a curious combination of fear, excitement, and madness. An Old One stood there. It was no ancient, dead thing or filmy ghost, but a living representation.

It towered over him, easily eight feet in height. Its wings were entirely unfolded, spread wide in a defensive display. Its brilliant red eyes set atop erect stalks were practically luminous. It reached out to him with clusters of emerald green tentacles that ended in triple-pronged slender red tendrils. It held these out like the claws of a bird of prey.

The threat of the thing was only too apparent in its posturing. Its wings trembled. The fingerlike tendrils were like hooks. The eyes were bright, tiny pinprick black dots that might have been pupils watching warily. It made a low piping sound that made Crand's ears ache.

He wanted to serve it, if only it would share a fraction of its knowledge with him. His voice, when it came, asked, "What is it you want of me?"

It sent images into his mind, a piping voice that was indecipherable. But he knew what it communicated. He translated it with some ancient vestigial sense buried in his subconscious mind. *I've come to take you away to a place you've always wanted to go.*

Along its barrel-like torso, there were some sort of squirming parasites hanging. They were about three inches long, gray unpleasant things like gelatinous slugs. It plucked one free with its tendrils and held it out to him.

He didn't really start screaming until it attached itself to his face.

Then a thundering blackness enveloped him and there was no escape.

16

"How long now?" Marsh said. "How long has it been?"

Ault did not bother looking in his direction because it was pitch black. Nor did he bother turning on his helmet light, because his batteries were getting down. He had one more set for his helmet and flashlight and then—

"Three days," he finally said, surprised by the rusty sound of his voice.

Three days.

Three days.

That seemed incomprehensible: they'd been in this fucking black tunnel for three days? The idea of that made something grip tightly inside him, panic rising in ever-increasing waves. God, how could it be that long? The chronometer did not lie...still, it was too much.

No, you moron, he thought, *it was too much two days ago, now it's just insane. Like Alice going through the looking glass and never, ever being able to find her way out again.*

As things stood, they were nearly out of food, short on water, battery power getting very low...and when that ran out: *darkness.* An absolute, unthinkable darkness. Ault knew what that would be like because they were sitting in it now, conserving batteries. He was very familiar with the literature concerning people trapped in the dark. The general psychological consensus was that about four to five days of absolute darkness was about as much as the human mind could take before it descended into madness.

The tunnel was so smooth, so glossy, so black. The thermometer he wore on his suit told him the temp was an even fifty degrees. Not a nice day at the beach, but certainly warm enough to survive without fear of freezing. But he would have taken a cold cave at that point. Something with uneven rocky walls and rubble. Anything but the unnatural uniformity of the tunnel. It never, ever changed and there was something about this that put him over the edge. Several times, thinking about that uniformity and feeling the perfectly symmetrical walls closing in on him, he had had to push his fist into his mouth to stop from screaming.

And he couldn't do that.

Marsh and Hirvonen were teetering on the edge of a great abyss as it was. One little push and they'd both go completely stark mad.

With you taking the first plunge, he thought.

Maybe that was so. God knew that the once well-stitched seams of his mind were beginning to split. And day by awful day, the situation was getting only that much worse. Hirvonen, on the other hand, had proven that she was made of some very stern stuff, her mind extremely well-disciplined. And Marsh…well, he was living proof that the tougher men were on the outside, the weaker they were on the inside.

Hirvonen and Ault had gone over it from every possible angle and what they arrived at was this: the wall was artificial as was the tunnel. So, with that in mind, the tunnel had closed-up on them by some equally artificial process, possibly an intelligence, that wanted them to stay. Either that or the tunnel itself had been designed to do what it had done. And, of course, there was also that darker third possibility: it was all in their minds.

Group hallucination.

Not a random act on their part, but more along the lines that they thought the tunnel was closed off because someone or something *wanted* them to believe this. And where did that get them? It simply brought them back to the bane of modern Antarctic urban legend—aliens and dead civilizations that maybe weren't so dead after all. Just like those two that had come out of the Kharkov Tragedy had said. Maybe this tunnel was part of one of those cities. It made as much sense as anything. And if that was a maybe, what was a certainty was that Crand, their beloved leader, had had an agenda from day one. He had known something like this would be down here and had led them unflaggingly toward it.

"That was it, you know," Ault said to Hirvonen, their second day of imprisonment. "He knew that alien crap wasn't crap at all and we were here to help him find them or their remains. Whatever. We furthered his ends."

"He always scoffed at that business," she admitted. "He got almost belligerent when I brought it up."

"I'll bet he did."

She sighed. "But what now? What do we do now?"

"If it closed, it can open." Boy, that was great. A little pearl of wisdom he tossed out. It sounded positive and upbeat, nearly masking the shivering horror he felt inside. "We have to wait for that. Unless this thing is operating independently of those who built it. If that's the case..."

"Yes?"

He shrugged. "Then maybe we triggered something."

"What?"

"I don't know."

And now a day later, he still did not know.

Yet, he sensed a certain underlying logic to it that he was having trouble getting at because of simple animal fear. If they triggered something... what was it? A switch of some kind? Had they broken a beam or stepped together in some precise mathematical pattern that they had not been able to reproduce? Or was the technology behind this thing even beyond that? Did it have something to do with thoughts or emotions, discharges of mental energy? Ault liked that approach because he remembered very well the stories that came out of Kharkov. Lots of wild tales were thrown around, but what kept coming up was that the aliens were a race with not only highly-advanced intellects, but unbelievable psychic powers. That manipulating physical processes and bending mental energies to their will was as natural for them as eating and walking and shitting were for the human animal.

Three days, though.

Jesus, they couldn't hold out much longer.

If there was a key to this cage, now was the time to find it.

But still, there was that other possibility that dogged him: that they were being held here by an intelligence that did not want them to leave. He both believed and disbelieved that. Before they'd discovered the wall that day, when they had encountered that magnetism that made their compasses spin madly, they'd all felt something. A building energy that had nothing to do with magnetism. Something that was vibrant and kinetic and electrical. They'd all been amped-up by it. As if every cell in their bodies were hooked, direct current, to a power source. And maybe they had been. And maybe it had been the psychic emanations of the aliens themselves.

He remembered that the further they descended into the Magnetics, the worse the headaches had gotten, the more the nightmares and weird visions had persisted, and, more telling, the more that feeling of utter dread had risen up in him. Ellis had felt it from the first. And Ault supposed he had, too, but had tried to sweep it away with the broom of reason.

But it had been there.

The sense that something was waiting up ahead for them. Something huge and fantastic and, yes, devastating.

These past days in the tunnel, the headaches continued to come and go. When he closed his eyes, the dreams threaded thickly through him, knotting him up with visions of malefic, cyclopean cities and the monstrosities that called them home. Dreams. Images. Race memories, maybe. Thing was, Ault felt like he was plugged into some system of knowledge that was not only atavistic, but hard-wired into his very being.

He did not believe the aliens were dead.

He could almost *feel* them. Sense their eyes on him, their minds. Like some ancient door of perception had been gradually opened. Like Ellis, he wasn't fighting it and, yes, what he was seeing through that doorway was scaring the shit out of him, but it was also…*enlarging* him, activating something inside him that had long laid dormant.

And at times that something was not only a psychological thing, but seemingly organic. And interlinked with it was an irrational fear of those that had built this place. Wonder, yes, and curiosity, certainly, but a primitive terror that was immense.

And as the absolute realization of this settled into him, he could hear a weird, scratching voice in his brain: *Fear? Of course, there's fear. You were designed to fear us. If all else failed, we owned you by fear, by showing you that which terrified you the most. You fear us because you're SUPPOSED to fear us. We are your masters and you are our slaves. Never, ever equals. No more than a crop is equal of the farmer that seeded it. We are the first dream of a god you ever had and we will be the last. You are not and never have been in charge of your own destiny. You are ours to seed, to cultivate, and to harvest. You think your minds are so advanced, but they are nothing but a global battery to be drained dry. Remember that. Know it. Accept it. Embrace it. You are as we designed you—*

"Listen," Hirvonen said, sitting up in the darkness. *"Listen!"*

"What?"

But then he heard it, too. He heard it quite distinctly: footsteps. And they were coming in their direction, slowly, inexorably. By then, everyone was on their feet with flashlights in their hands. They illuminated the tunnel, waiting, waiting.

Slowly, a shape came into view.

17

"Crand!" Marsh said.

He stood there, waiting for them, his pale face streaked with dirt, his caving suit ragged and filthy, his miner's helmet snapped tightly on his head like the lid of a pickle jar.

"It's taken you long enough," he said.

Nobody said anything for a moment. There were no words that could describe what they were feeling, a mixture of surprise and relief, uneasiness and absolute terror.

In Ault's mind, it was summed up thusly: *He's just been waiting out here? Alone in the darkness and he hasn't gone completely insane? That seems a little hard to believe.*

"How did you get through?" Marsh asked him. "There was a wall…"

Crand said, "I could hear your voices from the other end. There was no wall."

"It was there!" Marsh snapped.

"It was," Hirvonen said.

Ault didn't like any of this. The wall was there. There was no doubt of that. It hadn't been there, then it appeared. And now it had vanished. The logic behind that was dizzying.

311

None of this made any sense. Crand should have been out of his mind by now. It would have been easier to take if they found him curled up and sucking his thumb, completely irrational…or even dead. That would have made sense. But this, like the disappearing wall, it just didn't *feel* right, even if that made no sense at all.

Marsh looked absolutely terrified. "And you…you just waited here? Hoping we'd find you?"

"Yes. There wasn't much else to do." Crand smiled, but it never touched his eyes which were watery and bloodshot, sunken back into their sockets as if there was nothing to hold them in place. They never seemed to blink. "I did some exploring and I found….well, come with me. You'll want to see this."

He turned to lead them away, shuffling with a straight, stiff gait. Hirvonen looked at Ault, then they both looked at Marsh. He shook his head slowly, side to side.

They followed Crand, their helmet lights bobbing and flashing. The labyrinth of passages and tunnels were all made of that same glossy black material that you could not even chip with a rock hammer or a drill. Crand led on, that same dogged determination in his eyes. The eyes of a messiah, a self-appointed savior. Ault followed right behind him, knowing there was no choice and Hirvonen was at his side. Marsh grumbled.

Ault was beyond being tired, beyond being worn down.

The physical suffering of these last weeks and particularly that of the past five or six days had taken a toll on his mind. No longer was it the marvelous thinking machine it had been. It cringed in superstitious fear and uncertainty. It called out the names of gods it had never even believed in. And, probably even worse, he could no longer trust it.

The line between reality and fantasy seemed to be eroding.

Is this real? Am I really here? Or is it all just some demented fever dream?

His reasoning powers had gone belly-up with his instincts. He could only stumble along blindly with Crand, led even deeper into the maze that would terminate with something that he could not even begin to comprehend. More than once it had occurred to him that Crand was not even Crand anymore, but something less than human. But he had never been actually human to begin with, now had he?

312

He's like one of those cows that lead the others down the plank to the slaughterhouse, Ault thought. *A decoy. A deceiver. A traitor. He's leading us into the arms of something that will destroy us.*

How could you gauge Crand?

How could you really gauge him?

Even back at the university, he was not like other men. He was ambitious, yes, but it was more than that. He had been like some mindless drone serving a higher power and, in his case, that was knowledge and perhaps something beyond what men would consider knowledge. Even when they'd gotten to Antarctica and up into the Devil's Eye, things like fear and death and suffering had meant nothing to him. There had always been that allegiance to something else. Maybe it was science to the others, but to Crand there had always been that other unspoken objective, that agenda. And he would have walked over their corpses to get to it.

And look at you now, Ault thought, *blindly following him into a place that you know is not only toxic to anything warm and human, but inherently evil.*

All of it now, all the anxieties and fears and bad feelings, were coming together and he would soon see the horrors that inspired them. For so long he had denied the possibility of the aliens themselves, even though he had felt them from day one, haunting the bones of his existence, a noxious influence chewing away at his mind hour by hour. Each step took them closer to the black, beating heart of the beast.

He knew he should have been much more afraid than he was.

At the very least he should have been functionally insane like Marsh. Maybe he was, but he didn't think so. He doubted his mind, yes, he doubted everything, but there was no real fear. And maybe the human mind only had so much fear to offer before the well ran dry and it scraped bottom.

Up ahead, getting stronger and stronger, was the massive, unbelievable group mind of those who had built this place and engineered life from non-life. They were up there, waiting, and Ault knew he would look upon them. And when he did, it would not be as some brain-dead, hysterical savage at the feet of his resurrected god, but as a *man.* He would look upon them and he would not shudder. He would know disgust and loathing, but they would not bring him to his knees with their godhood.

He would stand straight and tall and inflexible.

Mind games. That's all. A matter of perception management. Inside, he would be shaking and full of yellow fluff. And they would know it. God yes, they would smell the fear on him like mad dogs and look through the dusty windows of his mind and see all the shivering white things hiding in the corners that made up a man named Ault.

The maze was an eternity. It was lit by a soft glow. Not all of it, just the passages that Crand led them down. Whether he had something to do with that or it was automatic, Ault could not pretend to know. Crand brought them into something that almost looked like a train tunnel, except it was threaded like a screw and the roof above had to be a hundred feet up. It went on and on and then…

"Now you will see," Crand said to them. "Now you will see the womb itself which has been waiting down here since long before things such as men or mammals evolved. Indeed, long before there was such a thing as life on this world…"

Ault uttered a bitter, taunting laugh and he could not choke it back down. Hirvonen reached out and clutched his hand, held it tightly. He shook his head to tell her he was not having a nervous breakdown.

Too late for such niceties, my dear.

He was readying himself as a perfectly smooth and flat wall ahead of them melted away. This was the place where the aliens were, the inspiration of every demon and dragon and crawling night-terror men had ever known or would ever know.

He looked at Hirvonen and she looked at him and he felt emotions run through him. Human emotions. He felt protective of her. In love with her. And, yes, he wanted her. She was so beautiful even with her dirty caving suit and miner's helmet and grime-streaked face: the honey-blonde hair and high cheekbones, full lips and even white teeth. And those big blue eyes. How could you look at something as exquisite as a perfectly-proportioned, drop-dead beautiful woman and not see the hand of a higher power? How could you ever write it off to simple organic evolution and gene transmission?

That's how it was for Ault.

As his humanity edged closer to extinction, science was replaced by spirituality and poetry. He wanted to take Hirvonen in his arms and make love to her. She was his flaxen-haired warrior maiden and he wanted to pull her up onto his horse and take her as his bride off across the fjords to the marriage bed that awaited them. Hand in hand, mouth to mouth, loin to loin, they would fill this Earth with wheat-haired, blue-eyed children.

Hirvonen smiled at him, her eyes lit with a hunger and purpose as if she understood exactly what he was thinking and dreaming about. His thoughts were her thoughts, his dreams married to her own.

Dear God, I really am losing my mind, he thought.

Crand passed through a circular opening in the wall and warm, decayed smelling air rushed out at them and encapsulated them in a stench of fetid germination.

"No…no….not this place," Marsh said.

Hand in hand, Ault and Hirvonen stepped into the hive.

17

It was like breaking a seal.

They all felt it to varying degrees. It was as if they had encountered some elastic, invisible membrane that pushed back as they tried to push forward. It held them in stasis for several moments and everyone tried to speak, to connect their brains to their vocal cords and cry out the same vexing question: *What is this? It's like glue and we're stuck in it…*

But they could not speak.

They could not move.

They could not think.

They existed in some warped gulf of space-time that was everywhere and nowhere simultaneously. It held them like flypaper and like flies, the bigness and impossibility of it was beyond their simple mammalian brains to comprehend.

And then the membrane no longer tried to hold them back—it pulled them in, it sucked them into its depths. Like stones sinking into the same bottomless black lake, they sank without a trace…

18

For Ault, it was like some black, fluttering veil descended over him, wrapping him in darkness and nonexistence. He was, again, a stone dropped into a pond and the ripples muddied the universe, turning his vision not outwards but inwards, creating enormous, titanic vistas beyond simple human understanding. He felt a white-hot pinprick of pain in his brain that became a whirring, tunneling drill bit of agony that macerated not only his subjective thoughts, but his ability to think in any rational way.

He was and he was not.

He existed and yet he was a ghost.

A fragment.

A reflection.

A dismal protean memory…

19

For Hirvonen, as her mind was emptied like a cup, reassembled in abstract forms like scattered atoms, she heard a voice speaking in her head in a language that was no language she could possibly understand. Part of her remembered hearing it eons before echoing through the grotesque tangle of an alien city, a complex collection of angles and geometry, part machine and part living thing, and all completely arcane and nameless.

And then all that was blotted out by an absolute eruption of pain inside her skull, a tidal wave of agony that flooded her brain with boiling lava.

20

For Marsh, there was defiance.

As he felt something noxious invade his mind and the soft, dreaming pink meat of his brain, he fought. It was how he'd reacted his entire life, using his intellect, when possible, but when that failed him, lashing out with his fists.

The problem was that as his mind surged through unknown gulfs of time and space, achieving impossible velocities, he did not know what he was fighting against. His brain was filled with burning agony, his thought processes no longer interlinked but scattered like a 1,000-piece puzzle dumped on the floor. Waves of emotion rioted through his head. Guilt and grief and anguish and loss and self-contempt. But not the way he had ever felt them before. These emotions were not just emotions, not simple self-defeating things, but things with shape and volume and contrast and color. Physical things that punched into him again and again like fists, each blow making him weaker than the last, making his head reel in waves of redness and black and uniform gray.

He was sent reeling into some dead-end universe inhabited by nameless lifeforms, a cosmic colony of termites, and he sank into a bloated and white mountain of writhing flesh with thousands of oily eggs bursting free, squirming larvae hanging like podia, reaching out, touching him, writhing over his body and infesting his mind. It was like being caught in the living, fleshy tendrils of a man-o'-war jellyfish. For the briefest of moments, all was revealed to him and he saw, he *knew,* he understood what it was all about.

And he screamed.

21

When Ault came out of it, he was on the ground, squirming and mindless… then slowly, he relaxed, breathing rapidly, trying to make sense of what just happened. The membrane. He remembered encountering the membrane and then…he could not be sure. In fact, he could not be sure of anything.

Hirvonen was a few feet away, her helmet lying at her her feet. She was on her knees, grasping her head and moaning. Tears had cut fresh trails through the dust on her face. Marsh was on all fours, gasping and grunting. Finally, he vomited and fell over.

Crand, however, was completely unfazed by any of it.

"Don't try to talk," he told them. "Moving through the barrier is rather… devastating. It…it seems to squeeze the guts out of you for a time. You'll feel better in a few minutes."

He was right.

Ault seemed to come out of it first. And when he did, his mind seeming to coalesce and find its bearings once more, he said, "You knew that would fucking happen to us. Goddammit, why didn't you warn us? Why didn't you give us a choice?"

"There was no choice to give," Crand told him in his dead, monotone voice.

Ault just laid there, his body aching, his head throbbing with waves of discomfort. A strong, overwhelming sense of déjà vu played in his head. He could remember…*nothing*. It was there and then gone, what he had seen and where he had been.

"You prick," Marsh said to Crand and that pretty much encapsulated their feelings for him.

"You'll be better in time," Crand reassured him.

Time.

Time.

Yes, that was part of it, part of what Ault was trying to remember and piece together in some rudimentary way. He pulled up the sleeve of his caving suit, the layers of polar fleece beneath it to check his watch. Peeling back the protective Velcro flap from its face, he studied the readout.

"Three hours," he said. "Goddammit, Crand, where have we been for three hours?"

"Right here. Have no worries, I was watching over you the entire time."

As Ault looked at Hirvonen, reading the fear in her eyes, he knew that was the thing that concerned him the most.

22

Ault was amazed by what he saw opening around him. Not just some secret burrow, but an incredible, fantastic, and geometrically-profuse underworld. Although he could not be certain, certain of anything by that point, it looked as if it went on for miles. An interconnected series of spherical chambers each hundreds and hundreds of feet in diameter.

They were made of that same glossy black material, but veined with delicate fingers of cool gray and mother-of-pearl white. Each of them were tremendous in scope and reminded him of snail shells set on their ends, spiraling whorls radiating ever outward and outward as they climbed high above in ever-narrowing convolutions where they terminated into smooth borings and corkscrewing tunnels like the shells of moon whelks and periwinkles. Some of the chambers were set upon mound-shaped platforms, others dropped down below. Tombstone-shaped archways separated them.

"Incredible," Hirvonen said.

It was. Ault could not help but be awed and overwhelmed by it. The danger and nightmare truth of this place paled next to the majesty and scientific wonder of those who had built it and what their reasons might have been.

Marsh was trembling...with fear, with anger, it was hard to tell.

"This is enough," he said. "We need to get out of this fucking tomb."

But Crand led them deeper into the hive along narrow walkways (or something like walkways) that connected the chambers themselves.

The only good thing, Ault noticed, was that his headache was completely gone. And maybe that was because he was in the hive. Like being in the eye of a hurricane, the calm of a storm, you did not feel the emanations of the storm itself when you were in its belly.

And in his head, a weird and wavering voice said: *The entities who built all this were called Old Ones. Old Ones. For they are indeed old. But they are not alien. Essentially, yes, in that they are of extraterrestrial origin...but in the general usage of the term, no, not alien at all. They migrated here. They were the first inhabitants of this world. Its original colonists. We exist through their good graces.*

Ault looked over at Crand and he was staring at him, smiling.

Ault did not smile back. The sight of Crand disturbed him in ways he could barely fathom. Maybe he always had, but now it was worse. Something had happened to him in this place. He'd been alone here for days, wandering through this labyrinthine graveyard and no man could have come through that with his mind intact. Even without the constant nagging, debilitating race memories of this primal womb, it would have stripped any mind bare as a wire. Maybe he acted perfectly sane, but he wasn't and Ault knew it. He had changed in this place or been *made* to change.

And don't forget, he thought, *about the missing time. Those three hours, those three long hours.*

It was something that disturbed him and flooded him with a crawling anxiety.

They moved forward through the massive complex and then, right before them, set in an oblong cell in the wall was an Old One.

Marsh let out a strangled cry and went white as if the blood had been sucked out of him. It was dead, but that did not lessen its threat: the terror of finally, actually seeing one.

The mummy was dusty and leathery, great holes eaten into its barrel-like body, its wings like old ragged umbrellas. It must have been dead for thousands of years, but in life it must have been a true horror, easily standing seven feet in height. Ault was a scientist. He should have been fascinated by what he was seeing, an actual alien lifeform, but he wasn't—he was unhinged at some primary level. He didn't want to study this thing; he wanted to take up an axe and chop it to bits.

Something happened then…his mind filled with impressions of the Old Ones, the Elder Things of antiquity. They moved in his head like elongated shadows, a parade of them: walking tentacles writhing like the legs of spiders, wings flaring and flapping, blue-gray flesh flashing with colors like the chromatophores of a squid—radiant cobalt blue and sparkling green, pale gray and then violent red. One of them stopped and looked at him with red bulbous eyes. There was no hate. No threat exactly. Just a cold and cunning curiosity that made him feel weak inside like a butterfly waiting for the net of a collector.

The images continued, crowding out his thoughts.

The creatures appeared then disappeared at will. They were here, then there, then hovering high above, then gone completely for a few seconds before appearing somewhere else.

And a voice in his mind, not necessarily his own, said, *It's no stage show, no parlor tricks. It's physics, you idiot. They move at will through the third dimension by jumping in and out of fourth-dimensional space-time as they see fit. They are threading the needle of hyperspace.*

In the phantasmagoria of his dreaming brain, the creatures vanished and reappeared dozens of feet from where they had last been. Even those that were flying above were doing it. They were like fireflies on a summer night, lighting up five feet away and then thirty feet from where they had been.

"They do not move in the spaces we understand," Crand said and that brought Ault instantly out of his psychic mind-trip.

"How did you know what I was seeing?"

Crand stared dumbly at the mummy before them. "Because you're seeing what I saw," he admitted. "I was here for days and their memories were in my mind until they became part of me."

Which made Marsh giggle madly.

And why not? It was all insane and Ault had a mad desire to laugh as well. Laugh at the absurdity of who and what he was—an evolved ape stumbling through the halls of the gods themselves, too stupid to understand anything but a fraction of what it all meant.

Hirvonen, her scientific curiosity getting the better of her, took a rock hammer out of her pack and gently nudged the mummy with it.

"It's dead," Crand said, as if reading her thoughts. "It can't hurt you."

"*Can't* it?" Marsh said.

Crand kept staring at the desiccated husk. "It's very important at this juncture that we do not allow ourselves to be overcome by superstitious fear. We must embrace what we find in this place, not shrink from it."

Ault scowled at him, a surge of pain in his head making him rub his temples.

Crand led them away deeper into the ancient hive and the odd lambent glow faded until they were in absolute blackness guided only by their flashlights and helmet lights.

Grotesque shadows were thrown against the walls which were no longer the glossy black material but stone carved right out of the bedrock itself. The chamber they found themselves in was triangular in shape, the apex at least seventy feet above them. To either side, were dozens of the oblong cells and in each of them were alien carcasses. They were not crumbling things like the other one, but in a high, nearly-perfect state of preservation. Other than some mottling from great age, they looked as if they could have woken up at any time. Their wings were intact, even the dangling eye pods, all of which were closed.

There's eyes in them, too, Ault found himself thinking. *Bright red eyes that can open at any time, eyes that can suck the soul right out of your head like a pimento from an olive. And you can be sure of that.*

Marsh, his eyes full of secrets and nameless traumas, said, "These don't look dead, Dr. Crand. Did you notice that? I said, *did you notice that?"*

Crand nodded, but had no real comment on it and that made Marsh grow angrier. There had always been bad blood between them, but now it was seeping with poison and toxic fumes. Sooner or later Marsh was going to punch his lights out and when that happened, Ault knew that he would not interfere. No, he would stand and watch and perhaps inside, he would cheer.

He tried to imagine what it must have been like down here for Crand alone, finally finding those he had come so far to meet. Fawning at their feet, mumbling his eternal devotion to their inestimable intellects and glorifying in their diabolic plans for the human race. Crazy as a bee in a bottle, he would have called out to them and they would have answered because these fucking carcasses were not dead, they were only dreaming.

Waiting.

And Crand would have dreamed with them, happily so, his mind twisted like a root, his sense of humanity—which had been fleeting at best on a good day—shriveling inside him. He had found his gods and he was their vessel.

"Ault?" Crand said. "I think we should move on."

Ault came out of his dreams, but not to Crand's voice but something else—rustlings and scrapings, muted screeching noises and weird trillings. It was there and then it was gone.

Both Marsh and Hirvonen were scanning the cells with their flashlights, searching for the source, but all the mummies were silent, unmoving.

"If these fucking things are dead, Crand, what was that sound?" Ault put to him.

"I didn't hear anything."

Marsh giggled. "Oh, he heard all right, but he's not saying. It's part of the game he's playing. I wonder who taught him this game?"

Crand did not respond to that. Ault found that particularly telling because the old Crand would have told Marsh what a simpering, superstitious fool he was. In fact, he would have turned it into a ten-minute lecture. Because that's the kind of guy he was. Or had been. Now, he simply let it go.

Hirvonen noticed it, too. In her eyes, there was a slowly dawning horror because she knew something was terribly wrong with her old mentor and it frightened her.

There's something wrong with all of us now, Ault thought without really knowing why.

"This is bullshit," Marsh said, starting to back away. "I've seen enough of this fucking sideshow. I'm going back."

Crand looked at him. "There's nowhere to go, Marsh. This is all there is now."

Marsh looked from Ault to Hirvonen for support, but got none. A nervous, jumping grin played over his face. "He's crazy! You both know he's crazy! Look where we are! Look where he's brought us!"

Hirvonen said, "We have to go on because we can't go back! Our retreat has been carefully closed off in case you haven't noticed…"

Marsh made a sobbing sound in his throat, breathing very fast.

"Lead on," Ault told Crand.

23

Another few hours of it was about all they could take. The vaults and passages were endless, repetitious, geometrically abstract. There seemed to be no plan, no beginning and no end. All of it an experiment in gigantism. A cyclopean maze. It taxed the mind.

But Crand led on and on. He seemed to know where he was going even if the idea of that was absurd. There was no forward or back, it was all just around and around, sideways, inside-out, upside down. And as they walked through immense chambers and along narrow walkways with limitless depths below them, Ault wondered, and not for the first time, if he was trying to get them so mixed-up that they'd never find their way back to that weird membrane that led them into this madhouse in the first place.

Finally, in a huge spherical chamber, Crand said, "We better rest."

No one argued with him. Marsh sat down, leaning against a canting blue-black wall and closing his eyes. He was no longer speaking. His eyes were glazed and from time to time he made whimpering sounds.

"Just where is it we're trying to go?" Hirvonen asked.

"Out," Crand said. "I'm trying to find a way to get out."

He's up to something, of course, Ault thought. *He has been since the beginning and you know it. Whatever you do, don't close your eyes because if you do, things will happen. Who knows how many hours you'll lose this time and what dreadful places you'll visit.*

But as he stretched out next to Hirvonen on his sleeping bag, his eyes closed automatically. He forced them open once or twice and each time he did so, Crand was watching him with his vapid, dead eyes.

What is it?

What is it you're going to do with us?

Then his eyes closed again and the dreams began right away and through it all, even in the depths of the nightmares, he knew Crand was watching him, staring into his head and plotting mischief.

24

Marsh woke with a surge of bright agony in his skull. He let out a strangled cry because it was like a thousand voices were screaming in his head, a terrible wriggling sensation in his brain. His hand clawed around and found his flashlight. He clicked it on and the moment he did, what was in his head vanished.

Ault and Hirvonen were still sleeping.

Maybe they were dead.

Anything could happen in this place.

His light picked out the convex walls, the rippled ceiling high, high above. A sort of buzzing static filled his mind and then was gone. He panned his light around and found Crand. Crand was not sleeping. He was wide awake and staring at him.

"I've found a way," he said.

Marsh cleared his throat. "What…what do you mean?"

"A way out. A way back to the Hypertats."

Something came to life inside Marsh for the first time in what seemed days. *A way out? Is that what he said?* He shook his head from side to side because he didn't believe it. Something inside him *refused* to believe it. Yet, optimism and hope dawned, and he said, "How? A tunnel?"

"Yes. C'mon, I'll show you."

"I better wake the others."

"Let them sleep," Crand said. "If it works, I'll come get them."

Well, that sounded reasonable and Marsh was so eager to get out of that tomb that all he really cared about was his own skin. He stood up and followed Crand off through a maze of passages, knowing that he would never find his way back again and part of him was just fine with that. Because in the Hypertats there were beds and food and water and coffee and safety and everything he needed so badly.

"Look," Crand said. "The Star Funnel."

There was a circular tunnel ahead of them that was luminous with a soft, blue glow. It was slowly turning counter-clockwise.

"What...what is that?"

"A way out. A way out." Crand's lifeless eyes were filled with secrets. "It'll take you away from here. It's the sort of conveyance *they* use to travel great distances."

Trembling, Marsh licked his lips. "I don't know."

"Close your eyes now. That's how it works."

Marsh did.

Right away, there was a veritable explosion of screeching semi-human voices and an eerie trilling in his head. It canceled out his thoughts. He felt a deep, gnawing pain in the depths of his brain, a crawling sensation, a suckering pain as if something was sucking the blood from his gray matter.

His eyes opened, widened into glass balls. *I know and I do not know.* The Star Funnel was reaching out for him or he was reaching out for it. He saw strange symbols and glyphs and arcane mathematical figurations inside it as it revolved. They glowed yellow like digital displays. As he studied them, they seemed to change, reconfiguring themselves, abstract equations becoming radical geometrical shapes and non-linear expressions that taxed the brain.

He looked back at Crand and he seemed to be thirty or forty feet away, growing smaller and more distant with each passing second. Marsh felt feverish and disoriented. He had only stepped a few feet into the tunnel, yet he was deep into it and it was spinning faster and faster and he was being drawn further into it, pulled toward some nameless destination. He cried out, but his voice was weird and echoing, seeming to come from somewhere behind him.

(MARSH MARSH)

It was Crand's voice, cycling around him, seeming to be in his head, yet echoing from the blackness ahead, reverberating off the walls as the tunnel continued to spin and the equations became more complex, intersecting and massing and changing with dizzying speed.

(MARSH YOU'RE LEAVING US IT'S A LONG WAY BUT YOU'LL BE THERE IN SECONDS)

Accelerating now, faster and faster and faster into a spinning womb of matter and neon light and mist and motion and forking lightning and flashing bursts of green-red-yellow fire, melting like a candle, coming apart, fragmenting, particulating, dandelion fluff caught in a tornado. He screamed. God how he screamed for help, for Crand, for Hirvonen and Ault and his mother and father as the velocity increased and his screaming voice continued to reverberate around him and in him. The flesh was torn from his bones, his brain ejected from his skull with a searing atomic kiss of crackling/burning/freezing/mushrooming energy and—

(YOU'll DRIFT FOR CENTURIES IN THE VOID BUT YOU'LL RETURN TO US YES YOU WILL RETURN)

And then the tunnel ended and he fell into an endless black vortexual gulf populated by trains of polychromatic bubbles and squirming cubes and inching tesseracts as he swam through a green soup that felt thick as molasses. He was in hyperspace and the part of his brain that could still think, knew it.

His body elongated and shrank, then stretched like Silly Putty until his agonized face was miles long and his screams were rivers of blood surging around him, sluicing and boiling, populated by clusters of cyclopean eyes that breathed like lungs. Black depthless voids opened like mouths. Maggoty crystalline worms that were flesh, then fog, then arcs of energy, then writhing heaps of decay, fed upon his body and sucked the sweet juice from his mind.

He saw incredible panoramas of geometrically impossible cities like broken shards of luminous glass hanging on the edge of pathless gulfs, and crumbling eons-old cities on dead worlds whose blade-like spires reached into boiling purple skies. Black stars shrieked in chasms of white space and constellations throbbed like beating hearts.

He was an incorporeal, sentient cloud of atoms in some terrible anti-dimension, soaring into a rising nightmare landscape of wriggling fungi.

Then he saw something rising to meet him—a great swirling mass of matter and black mist that became a noxious, flabby seedpod bulging with eggs that snapped open like an umbrella to embrace him. It was a perfectly alien, ridged, and rugose thing that pulsated in time with the distorted stars high above. It exhaled steam and burning slime and flickering colors and then he had intersected with it, become part of it, his atoms mixed with its own, creating some malignant hybrid whose eggs burst like bubbles, each disgorging a pallid worm that mewled with an all-too human mouth to be fed. One of them drilled right through his eye in a white-hot explosion of pain and then it was tunneling into his brain, chewing and slurping and ingesting, devouring all that he was and replacing it with something full and fleshy and alien.

And he understood.

Oh yes, he understood it all.

It was he and he was it.

Then it all played in reverse and he was drawn back, pulled, yanked, ejected into a searing cosmos that whirled around him faster and faster and he could feel everything breaking apart, disintegrating, becoming form without flesh and flesh without form.

Then, after what seemed a billion dizzying lifetimes, he was once again in the tunnels of the Magnetic Caves. He opened not one mouth, but many, and cried out not for help but for *food*...

25

Ault woke to screaming beyond anything he'd ever heard before. A resounding, ear-splitting hysterical cry of absolute terror that shocked him awake like ice-water thrown in his face. He scrambled for his flashlight and clicked it on and saw—no, he knew he could not be seeing this—a familiar form pressed up against the wall, mouth wide in an agonized wailing.

"NO! NO! NO! NO! I CAN'T BE HERE! I CANNOT BE IN THIS PLACE!" the voice cried, tears rolling down its face. *"I'M NOT HERE! I'M SOMEWHERE ELSE! I'M ABOVE, I'M NOT BELOW! OH JEZUUUUZ THIS IS NOT HAPPENING! CAN'T BE HAPPENING!"*

"Ellis!" Hirvonen called. "Ellis!"

But it couldn't be Ellis, Ault knew, because Ellis was up in the Hypertat. He couldn't be down here; he just couldn't be. This was a trick, a mind game the aliens were playing because the only way Ellis could be down here was if he had come all the way through the Magnetics and the tunnels…no, it just wasn't possible.

Then he was with him and so was Hirvonen. They were trying to calm him down and by degrees, he mellowed or simply ran out of steam.

"Why? Why?" he asked. *"Why the hell did you bring me down here again?"*

"We didn't," Hirvonen said.

And Ault was glad that she had because nothing was making sense and he couldn't seem to get his feet under him. He felt like an untethered balloon that might drift away into impossible depths high above. Because he did not trust reality and he sure as hell didn't trust his own thoughts which were asking, *but did you? Did you go back and get him somehow? Are you sure you were even asleep or that you're even awake now?* He shook it from his head because he had to deal with what was on his plate. This was what was served and it required attention.

"I don't know how you got here," Hirvonen told him and when she tried to touch him, he flinched. "We were sleeping. We're lost down here."

Which made Ault look around as everything that had happened rushed into his groggy mind. "Where the hell is Crand? Where's Marsh?"

Ellis kept shaking his head from side to side. "I was up in the Hypertat. I went to sleep. I know I went to sleep." He pulled away from Hirvonen. "I had nightmares. Awful nightmares. *God, that pain in my head! That chewing! That fucking gnawing!* I can't be here. There's just no way I can be here."

"Well, you are," Ault told him. "We'll figure out why later."

"Where are they?" Hirvonen asked.

"I'll bet Crand took him somewhere," he said and although he did not know it to be true, he was certain of it because Crand was not right. Hell, Crand was not even human anymore and he knew that, felt that, sensed that from the moment they'd found him again. Crand was not Crand and Ault knew he was not alone in his thinking. Just looking into Hirvonen's eyes, he knew she was thinking the same thing.

He took a few moments to bring Ellis up to speed, so he could understand what had happened to them and what might be happening now.

"We have to look for them," Hirvonen said.

"I can't be here," Ellis said one last time, as if repetition might break the magical spell that had brought him to this awful place. "You don't understand. I can't be here."

"Stop it," Hirvonen told him.

Grabbing their packs and rolling up their bags, Ault led them off into the depths of the hive.

26

Why was this happening?

What was the point of it all?

Why hadn't those monsters just drained their minds off already? What were they waiting for? Why all the damn mind games? Why did it have to come down to this? The questions ran through Ault's head at what seemed light speed, one after the other after the other. There were no answers. There never could be answers and he knew it.

They moved down the tunnels, one after the other, calling out to Marsh, hoping he would answer and maybe in some small, frightening way, hoping he wouldn't. Despite the size of the passages and the mammoth chambers they led to, it was all very claustrophobic and confining.

Crushing, Ault thought. *This goddamn place is crushing us all and squishing the life and spirit out of us.*

Meanwhile, Ellis never seemed to stop talking about his dilemma. "Gotta be a dream. Yes, that's what it is. I'm in the Hypertat. I'm sleeping. None of this is *really* happening. Can't be happening."

"For God's sake, can you shut up?" Hirvonen told him in a severe, strict voice that said quite plainly that she was sick of his shit.

"Yes, yes, yes," Ellis said. "I won't say a word because I'm not really talking anyway. This is all going on in my head and it's just going to play out and be over with. Just like it did above. Then I'll wake up and have a cup of coffee, go over my notes, and call into McMurdo." He cackled softly, then grimaced. *"My head! My fucking head!"* He was grasping it in both hands. "Can't you feel it? In your brain? Can't you feel something eating you?" He shook it off and sighed, humming "Across the Universe" and that made him laugh hysterically. "Oh, I am the Eggman and I know who Mr. Kite is because—"

"Shhhh!"

She had stopped now and Ault could feel her tensing next to him, pulling tight like a spring. Her eyes were wide and very bright. Her head was cocked slightly to the side. She was listening.

"What is it?" he asked her.

He was sensing something, too, but not necessarily with his ears. The atmosphere of this subterranean hell was constantly pernicious, but suddenly it seemed even worse. There was something in the darkness ahead. What form it would take, he couldn't even guess at. He played his light around the grooved walls of the tunnel, disturbed dust whirling in its beam.

Then…a wet sort of noise. A slithery sound.

"I heard it," Ellis said, very calmly. "Like snakes moving around."

He had honestly convinced himself now that this was just a dream and there was really nothing to fear. Ault did not bother trying to talk him out of it; sometimes ignorance and delusion were the best insulation against the terrors of the unknown. He had found his sedative and it mellowed him. Maybe that was enough.

But Ault was not mellow. He was easily as tense as Hirvonen. She started to move again and he knew she was on the trail of something. She led them deeper into the tunnel and it opened into a spherical chamber. Another passage led off of it and this was where the sounds were coming from.

"Marsh?" Hirvonen called out.

There was a moist sliding sound and a liquid dripping. Then a voice that was shrill and terrible came out of the darkness. *"No...no...no, you can't. Don't come after me...please do not come after me...the hunger...I'm so damn hungry..."*

It was Marsh's voice and it wasn't. The tone was eerie and wavering as if it was sped up or slowed down, echoing in the most disturbing way like he was speaking to them through a network of pipes.

"Marsh," Ault said and his voice was so weak it barely even carried. "We just want to help you. That's all we want to do."

Marsh...if it really was Marsh...did not reply as such, but there was a low bubbling growl that sounded like it was full of mucus.

Ellis, firmly convinced that it was all a dream, stepped forward and put his light into the tunnel. They all saw what it revealed. Hirvonen gasped and Ault took an involuntary step back in disgust. The light illuminated a great wriggling heap of tendrils and blunt fleshy hoses that looked like slimy entrails, all moving and looping in some webby network. When the light struck them, they pulled back further into the tunnel. For one fleeting moment, it looked like dozens of eyes shined out from the darkness.

If this was indeed Marsh, then some unbelievable and dreadful mutation had taken place. They could hear him/it up there, squirming with a sound like guts slopping into a bucket. It was revolting. If there had been anything in Ault's stomach, he would have thrown it up. Despite the unreal, freakish tone to Marsh's voice, one thing was for certain: he had been trying to warn them off. Maybe he had become something less than human in this hellish place, but there was enough humanity left in him to do that.

Ault took hold of Hirvonen's arm and pulled her back, quietly and gradually.

Ellis, milking his delusions, stood his ground. He was out of his mind. He was really out of his mind. "Goddammit, Marsh, quit playing around and just come out of there," he said. "This is all a dream...don't you know that? I'm not really here and you're not really a monster. Makes a body stop and think, don't it?"

Hirvonen made to step forward and Ault pulled her back again. The threat level was now very high, only Ellis was too delusional to realize it.

"Ellis," Ault said in a low voice. "Step back with us. *Now.*"

But he didn't because he couldn't conceptualize the absolute danger he was in. He stood there in the beams of their helmet lights, a smug look on his face as if he was daring Marsh to do something.

"Ellis!" Hirvonen cried. "Get away from there! Get the hell away from there!"

But he didn't and he wouldn't and whatever shred of humanity was buried deep in the thing Marsh had become, could not stop what happened next.

There was a squishing, gelatinous sound and something came out of the tunnel in a gray and seeping wave of grotesque anatomy. Hirvonen screamed and Ault was certain he did, too. Marsh was like a yellow-green oozing protozoa, a mountain of plastic flesh that flooded out of the tunnel, steaming and exuding a river of slime. Dozens of whipping rubbery appendages flayed the air and countless blood-red eyes irised open. The mass split lengthwise as it engulfed Ellis. He was trapped in its swampy mass like a fly in amber.

Ault knew it would drown them as it had Ellis and make them part of it.

They turned to run and one of those snaking appendages lashed out. It had a mouth at its end and it seized Hirvonen's arm, tearing away the material of her caving suit and biting into her flesh. She screamed and thrashed. This along with Marsh yanking on her, got her free. He half-dragged and half-carried her away as she moaned in pain.

"It'll be all right," he told her. "It'll be all right."

27

He had no idea where they were going, only that they needed to distance themselves from the creature. Lights bobbing, they retreated the way they had come, getting lost in one branching passage after another. Finally, when they could no longer hear the thing, they stopped. Hirvonen slipped from Ault's grip and went down on her knees. Her arm was red with blood.

As Ault dug his medical kit from his pack, he thought: *Oh, Jesus, she'll need stitches to close that up. The infection. The trauma. And down here, down here of all places. That fucking thing with its dirty, filthy alien mouth.*

She was barely conscious as he cleaned her wound. The flesh hadn't been torn out exactly, just punctured by the thing's teeth. The punctures were deep, but he got the bleeding under control and wrapped the wound after giving it a dose of antiseptic spray. It was the best he could do under the circumstances.

Hirvonen trembled in his arms. She felt very warm, blazing with fever, and he didn't like that at all. They were lost. Trapped. Even if a rescue team came to the Devil's Eye, they'd never find them down here.

We'll be entombed for an eternity.

Then lights flashed over him and his heart leaped in his chest. It was Crand. He stood there like a wax figure. He didn't even look alive.

"You're safe now," he said.

"Marsh…he was a thing…he killed Ellis," he tried to explain. "He bit Hirvonen."

Crand still had not moved. His helmet light plunged his face into shadow. The only thing alive were his eyes which were huge and glossy like those of a nocturnal animal.

"He went into the Star Funnel."

"What are you talking about?"

"Marsh went into the Funnel. He crossed the threshold like *they* do."

Ault just shook his head.

Crand stepped forward and explained what had happened. "I believe the Star Funnel was used by the Old Ones for long-distance transference. Marsh stepped into it. Who can say where he went or how far? My guess is we couldn't measure it even in parsecs."

"You're not making sense."

"Oh, but I am," Crand said. "Marsh took a trip through fourth-dimensional space as the Old Ones do, but as to where he went and what he encountered, I don't know. He moved through hyperspace, Ault. He teleported. *They* do it all the time, you see. Or, at least, some of them do," Crand explained in that awful monotone. "There's no real danger if you know how, if you do it rightly and properly. He must have gone somewhere…to a space outside anything we can know and his atoms became mixed up with those of another organism that is perfectly alien to us."

Ault just sat there with Hirvonen. She was lying next to him, spasms passing through her now and again as if she was in great pain. "I don't know how you know these things, Crand, and I'm not going to ask. I don't want to know." He licked his dry, flaking lips. "She's in bad shape. We need to get her back to the Hypertat. The medical kit there has things that can help her. If you know a way out of here, tell me. Help me. Help me to help her."

"It's out of my hands."

"Please, Crand. I'm begging you."

But Crand was unmoved. He knew many terrible things now and he seemed pleased at the idea. "They don't want her to leave. They want her here. You see, she's part of this experiment. We're all part of this experiment. She in particular is necessary."

Ault was on his feet, his blood beginning to boil. "Why?"

"A rare opportunity is afforded her—she is being colonized by another entity. Something far beyond anything we can possibly imagine, Ault. A life form that is essentially a god…endless, eternal, she is becoming its avatar, a holy relic."

"Fuck that! Goddammit, Crand…she practically worshipped you. Help her! Don't turn your back on her now when she needs you. Act like a human being…"

Crand smiled thinly. "Really, Ault, let's not translate this into simple-minded simian emotions. She is being given the honor of becoming a vessel for the eternal and undying. It's all part of the experiment."

Ault stood there while it all sank in. An experiment which Crand knew all about. He was not just an innocent bystander, but an active participant. And Ault was willing to bet that Marsh hopping off into the fourth dimension was no accident, but part of the overall plan.

"We all have to go, Ault. It's the entire point of the experiment, you see," Crand told him. "A journey from this reality to another where we can commune with other entities who wish to come here."

Hosts. That's what he means. We're to be hosts for extradimensional life forms.

That's when something boiled over in Ault. It had all been too much and Crand was responsible for it all. He had put them in danger with his fucked-up ambitions and now Hirvonen was going to become God only knew what and he was perfectly okay with that.

Ault let out a wild shrieking cry and charged Crand who didn't even flinch. He punched him in the face two or three times and Crand folded up as blood like blue ink burst from his nose and split lip. He hit the floor of the chamber on his knees and his helmet was knocked off. And Ault, who was planning on kicking his brains out, stopped dead because he couldn't kick something out of Crand that he didn't have.

With the helmet gone, his true nature was revealed—the top of his head had been sawed off and the inside of his skull was perfectly empty. *Just like the expeditioners.* That was horrifying in of itself, but there was something much worse—his brain was not only gone, it had been replaced by a pulsating slug-like creature that filled the intracranial space of his skull. It was beet-red, bloated, slowly throbbing as it lifted itself free, four rubbery and segmented feelers reaching out, an oval chewing mouth opening and closing.

Ault felt his blood drop to his knees, his head spinning, a lunatic moaning coming from his throat. *It ate his brain,* an insane voice in his head informed him. *It's engorged with his gray matter.* Crand wasn't even human—he was a living puppet, a host for that alien brain leech which operated him like a machine.

"We face a dilemma," Crand said, his glazed eyes staring out blankly, the tendrils of the creature playing over his forehead. "It's very important at this juncture that we do not allow ourselves to be overcome by superstitious fear. We must embrace what we find in this place, not shrink from it."

Yes, yes, the very words he'd said when they found the mummy of the Old One. Crand was like a doll: you pulled a string and he spoke.

Ault trembled on the floor of the passage. He tried to move, but his limbs would not obey.

Crand held out his hand. His sunken eyes were glassy like those of a stuffed bird, "Hirvonen, come with me now. You have great distances to travel and wonders to behold."

"No!" Ault shrieked. "Get away from him! Get the hell away from him! *Don't...don't let it touch you!*"

But Hirvonen, eyes glazed, feverish and disoriented, reached out a shaking hand and Crand took it.

Ault tried to rise, but an immense, unknown force put him to his knees, a kaleidoscope of dizzying colors exploding in his head. He could not get up. It was as if some immense weight was bearing down on him, grinding him into the earth. In his mind, he saw himself being crushed like a frog under a heavy boot, his stomach forced from his mouth in a bloody discharge.

But even as he was pinned and squeezed by that enormous pressure, he saw that Crand had become a palpitating, squamous horror that writhed and crawled.

And that was all he saw before the lights went out and he passed out cold.

28

Hirvonen woke sometime later, sluggish, confused, in pain, but mostly disoriented because her body did not feel right and some formless terror at the center of her being told her it never would again. In the back of her mind there was an analogy that was disturbing and irrational—she felt the way a baby bird must when it wakes up in an egg and tries to peck its way free.

A shell. I'm trapped in a shell.

She tried to focus her eyes, to remember, but nothing seemed to work. She blinked and blinked, her dry mouth tasting like blood. Her blonde hair stood up in dirty spikes, her body aching. Her eyes swam in their sockets, bloodshot and bleary. She was seeing things, but not necessarily those around her. She heard a distant insectile sort of buzzing. Part of her trembled at the sound, but another, larger part understood.

Then her memories returned as if they had been suddenly downloaded in her head. She remembered Marsh. She remembered the horror he had become and what he had done to Ellis and, perhaps worse, what he had done to her.

And then…

And then—

Crand. Holding out his hand, wanting her to take it. He promised her things, told her he would take her places she'd never dreamed of and show her sights no mortal mind had ever seen before. And though part of her was repulsed by him—she had a nightmare vision of him as a noxious, furry toad holding out a limp, slimy hand with pulsating suckers on the fingertips— and wanted to reject him and anything he was associated with…there was another part of her that still held some silly teenage crush for him and wanted him to touch her, a man twice her age.

Take my hand, child, and walk with me, he said, his voice echoing in the back of her mind, whispering like satin. *It is what you want and what you must do.*

His flaccid hand enclosed her own. It was warm and flabby like the belly of a maggot. Then there was no fight left in her, not a shred of disobedience, only a fuzzy, dream-like acceptance of her destiny. As they walked, an ethereal green luminescence lit their way and she was only vaguely aware that it came from her host.

He had a secret name that was older than Hyperborea. It had a musical sound to it as he whispered it to her. But she could not pronounce it in her delirium. He spoke softly to her of the Yellow Sign and the caverns of Yuggoth, the Temple of the Toad and the Formless Spawn that squirmed at his feet.

When they reached the ever-revolving Star Funnel, she made the Sign of the Dark Mother that he had taught her.

"Are you ready to cross?" he asked her.

"Yes. I must cross."

"Of course. But first, you must call up what's inside you. Do not fight against it like Marsh…it is part of you. Summon it."

She did as he instructed and there was a searing hot pain inside her skull as the brain leech made itself known, suckling her brain, chewing and slurping and devouring it in soft pink globs, ingesting it. Then her head cracked open and it emerged like a snake from an egg, distended and pulsating, tendrils wiggling in the air.

It knew the way.

Piloting her, the brain leech made her step into the Star Funnel which pulled her in, making her skin glow with a flickering indigo light. Yellow mathematical expressions and geometrical equations and impossible angles danced about her, opening spheres of reality that made something at her core scream. They fired in intricate, converging patterns like neurons and synapses, ejecting her into a black void of shrieking wind.

Her flesh crawled over her bones and her brain quivered in her skull with the convolutions of the leech and then she raced through hyperspace, achieving incredible velocities. Time and space as she understood it melted like wax as she wormholed into a deranged, multi-dimensional hell. Disembodied, her thoughts spanned black voids and linked with an insane geometrical reality of wriggling crystalline lifeforms that worshipped an immense entity in the form of a malevolent spiral galaxy whose very epicenter was a gigantic eye. Yes, yes, the same vortexual horror that had been on the bas-relief.

But this was no representation, but the real thing.

A limitless, cosmic whirlpool that was eating time and space.

Then it all turned inside out, sucking into itself in a shrilling trans-galactic maelstrom. She saw barren fields that teemed with slithering blue-gray fungi. There were distorted circles of impossibly convex stone pillars and loathsome crawling things that bowed before them, thirsting for blood offerings. Then the worming vortex came out of the sky and opened like a leering yellow eye.

She was drawn into it, tangled in the fleshy web of its anatomy—and then expelled like a mewling, grotesque fetus from a womb, skating the perverse curvature of a space she could not know nor comprehend of.

And then she fell out of the funnel, thoughts and imperatives that were perfectly alien and obscene

(i am i am i am SHE who calls to you)

filling her head, eclipsing her mind with their malignant awfulness. She cried out, trying to force them from her parasitized brain, but there was resistance, a powerful and dark resistance that was growing and growing, dividing like a cell and consuming her until she no longer existed as such.

(i am SHE who summons you)

(the ALL-MOTHER i am you)

Everything mixed in Hirvonen's head as she felt that execrable dominion growing, its dark roots taking hold, digging deep into her psyche and into her flesh. She tasted blood. She felt pain. Horror. Being and non-being. Her mind reached from the awful truth of the Devil's Eye and what had happened there to things that made no sense, and yet, in a larger and frightening way, made more sense than anything she'd ever known.

No, no, no, no, please God, no, a voice screeched in her head.

(the all-in-one the OLD MOTHER the mother of toads SHE creeps in the spaces between and beyond and walks in unknown spheres)

Hirvonen felt her body contort, draw up tight, then release again and again. The contractions were painful as if she were giving birth and maybe she was at that. A cool, sour-smelling sweat seeped from her pores, her eyes rolled back white, her mouth was filled with a dark sweetness.

(look)

(look inside you)

She screamed because she was being violated both physically and mentally. She could feel noxious fevers gripping her, cold poison running through her veins, black ice expanding in her chest. And if that was bad, what was happening in her mind was far worse—someone was in her head, an entity that was vast and omnipotent and blatantly evil. It was communing with the leech, eating her brain in juicy globs. She could not only feel it sucking at her gray matter, but hear it slobbering and chewing.

It was paging through her mind like a book, reading her memories, learning everything she was and wanted to be and would never be, all the things she loved and hated and wanted and despised and wished for so it could crush them beneath its pounding hooves.

Please please oh please get out of me and leave me alone, her voice sobbed in her head. *I only want to be me to be Ava Amelia Hirvonen my dad was Roger and my mom is Ingrid and I I I won a prize for my chemistry paper in eleventh grade and I was on the swim team I played soccer and I kissed Ryan McCandliss and I graduated with honors in geology and earth science from Penn State and got my masters in planetary science from Stanford I was/might actually have been in love with Dr. Crand and oh my head my fucking head hurts so damn bad…*

(listen to the words that are spoken)

(listen)

(you will listen)

(to the voice)

(you i we are the Great Mother she who is concubine to Him-Who-Shall-Not-Be-Named the All-Mother who treads through the Great White

Space the undimensioned one from the Black Spheres that feeds upon time and space give praise in our name bring sacrifice complete the circle and call us forth with the Ritual of the Black Goat)

Hirvonen fought with everything she had as that terrible infection from beyond time and space grew inside her skin and owned her.

Please let me go let me go let me go oh help me Jesus God help me help meeeeeee...

(Iä! Iä! Cthulhu fhtagn! Ph'nglui mglw'nafh Cthulhu R'lyeh wgah-nagl fhtagn)

There were screams in her head, filling all the empty spaces that were closing, collapsing, being turned inside out.

(WE are joined WE have become)

Hirvonen felt herself descend into some monstrous whirlpooling pit of blackness where the stars were wrong and the constellations crawled like great cosmic worms and something like whippoorwills shrieked with great earsplitting volume.

When she came out of it, something quite different than Hirvonen looked out through her eyes. Ault was waking up and he looked over at her, asking her questions that made no sense.

All the while, another voice was speaking to her in a language she did not understand, yet seemed to understand all too well. It was coming from the wrapping at her wound. It throbbed as it spoke. She frantically tore the crude dressing away.

She wanted to scream, but she had no voice because what had taken up residence inside her had not granted her one. She tried to turn away from what she saw in disgust, in horror, but it was not allowed—she needed to look, to see, to understand what had seeded her. The bite from the Marsh-thing had mutated into something hideous that made her skin crawl and her heart palpitate. There was black, coarse fur growing around it and the wound itself had become a set of blubbery pink lips puckering away from gnarled, yellow teeth.

It made horrible smacking and sucking sounds and she could feel a sickening, feverish heat rising from it. It stank like an infected sore.

She held out her hand and her wound said, in an ancient, crackling voice, *"Ault, come with me now. You have great distances to travel and wonders to behold. Now you must cross."*

29

Ault was mad and he knew it.

His concept of reality had been inverted, subverted, turned inside out, blown up like a fucking balloon animal and popped with a pin. He charged down one passage after the other, escaping the horror that pretended to be Hirvonen while he listened to her screaming voice echoing from a dozen different tunnel mouths.

"Take my hand, Ault, take my hand..."

He called out to her in that shadowy realm and his voice echoed eerily around, but there was no answer. He cast the beam of his flashlight to and fro and it showed him darting/dematerializing/shadowy images of the Old Ones themselves. They were here and they had him, yet he scrambled about like a mouse in a maze or a rat in a box. Any of them could have swatted him like a fly...but maybe he frightened them somehow the way a wild beast might frighten him if it roamed his house at will. For surely that's what he was to them: a wild, primitive beast. And an emotional one at that. A beast governed by unpredictable moods. Savage. Unstable. Bloodthirsty, perhaps.

But Hirvonen...dear God, she sounded like she was in agony.

No, no, no, you idiot! Think! You must think! that voice said to him. *She's gone! Marsh is gone! Ellis is gone! And Crand has been gone longer than any of them! Hirvonen is dead! Do you hear me? Dead! It was like Crand said—she was colonized by another entity, made into the avatar of the holy relic! And that thing is screaming now to lure you in!*

He was trying to think, trying to understand. He could remember Crand taking Hirvonen away, but now she was back. He remembered the membrane, the loss of three hours and distorted images of where he had been. It made him cry out. There was a churning, tearing, suctioning agony in his head that made blood run from his nostrils.

Remember! You must remember what happened!

But the harder he tried, the more he felt a perfectly alien sense of invasion, a crawling, slithering sensation over the convoluted surfaces of his brain. His

341

knees went weak and he fell to the floor, crawling, inching forward, every slight movement an agony.

He tried to sit up again and again, falling over each time as his mind spun and that crawling feeling in his skull increased, amplifying into white jolts of agony.

He stumbled into a new chamber and a pair of Old Ones were waiting there, their brilliant red eyes appraising him like a pretty new butterfly in a cage. They spread their wings and made rubbery, coiling sounds with their tentacular appendages.

You know, don't you? he thought at them. *You know why I'm being spared.*

If they read his thoughts, they gave no indication. They just fluttered their wings and dove off into the upper regions of the chamber.

They were everywhere now. They hid no longer. They circled him like a noose and their minds began to focus in on him with heat and energy and raw psychic force.

But Ault was not done. Not quite yet.

He would die as a sacrifice for the entire race of men that had been molded, enslaved, and subjugated by these monsters since the dawn of time. To do anything less would be a declaration of inhumanity.

The Old Ones pressed in to contain him and Ault ran at them, everything inside him ready to die, to go out with one last blaze of glory. He dove at the nearest one and actually gripped its slick body tentacles and squeezed them, crushing them in his fists…and then those tentacles were burning like red-hot bands and he felt his hands dissolve as he gripped them, running like wax and he fell to the floor, screaming in agony.

And by then the hive mind had him.

His brain was filled with a spinning, burning void of blackness as they pushed forward, eager to toy with their writhing scrap of protoplasm on a Petri dish.

Oh yes, they most certainly had him.

Ault pressed his hands against his ears because he couldn't take any more of it. His mind was a kettle of bubbling white sauce that was superheating and would run out of his ears at any moment. He inched across the floor, then crawled like a terrified infant, then he was on his feet, running, bumping into horrors and impossibilities, tripping over his own feet but moving ever forward because he had to escape this lunatic asylum. It went on and on and on, a surreal madhouse, a deranged set from a German expressionist film.

And then something stopped him.

It wasn't a wave of force this time, but a field of spinning green particles that engulfed him and forced him to his knees. He could not fight. He could not move. He could not do anything but wait there at the foot of his god which was an Old One that towered high above him, wings flared, red eyes leering at him from lowered stalks. He wanted to cry, to scream, to slit his throat and put a gun in his mouth...anything but this.

Then it was gone.

Time blurred, stretched out.

It went on for hours, for days, Ault crawling, running, hiding, dragging himself through one passage after another. He rested. He dreamed and felt his mind fly from his body to distant spheres. When he woke each time, the pain was worse in his head.

That three hours, a voice taunted him. *What happened to all of you in those three hours?*

He scavenged and scampered like a rat, but eventually, there was nowhere left to run and nowhere to hide. And finally, Hirvonen found him. He screamed at the sight of her—her wound had completely engulfed her, morphing her into a furry, scaly abomination that called him by name and he could hear her voice shrieking in his skull: *"I am...I am...I am She that was dead and now lives again! We...I...We are made one! Born from the cold black fire of the Crystalline Dimension where the engorged stars scream! She...I...the split maidenhead of interspace! She that rules at the throne of the Locust God and He that waits at the center of chaos! Iä! Shub-Niggurath! Iä! Shub-Niggurath! The Black Goat of the Woods with a Thousand Squirming Young!"*

And her diseased, infested skin began to split open, dozens and dozens of gelid whipping appendages rising from her as her contorted, slime-dripping mouth screamed his name and a mountain of jellied softball-sized spheres gushed out. *Eggs.* They buried Ault alive in a sea of bile and pulpous yolks from which brain leeches were born by the thousands, entering him, piercing him, threading him with their squirming larval forms as the one already in his head sucked his mind dry.

Hirvonen squealed like hundreds of rats as they were finally made one, a monstrosity that pushed out an ocean of eggs like massed fish roe, sliding forward on a gushing carpet of them that would enslave the world of men.

Ault was made ready for his journey through the Star Funnel.

The End

PUBLICATION HISTORY

"When the Seas Run Hot and Cold" appeared originally in *Terror Cell,* 2016, Thunderstorm Books

"Cult of the Black Swine" appeared originally in *N,* 2021, Stygian Fox Publishing

"The Eldritch Eye" appeared originally in *DarkFuse #2,* 2014, DarkFuse Books

"The Slithering" appeared originally in *The Slithering and Others,* 2007, Rainfall Books

"The Penumbra of Exquisite Foulness" appeared originally in *The Court of the Yellow King,* 2014, Celaeno Press

"Blowfly Manifesto" appeared originally in *Eldritch Chrome,* 2014, Chaosium Books

"Nemesis Theory" appeared originally in *Cthulhu Unbound #3,* 2013, Permuted Press

"Spider Wasp" appeared originally in *What October Brings,* 2018, Celaeno Press

"White Rabbit" appeared originally in *Creatures of the Night,* 2019, Corpus Press

"Old Hopfrog" appeared originally in *The Children of Gla'aki,* 2017, Dark Regions Press

"Scratching from the Outer Darkness" appeared originally in *Return of the Old Ones,* 2017, Dark Regions Press

"The Brain Leeches" appears here for the first time

ABOUT THE AUTHOR

TIM CURRAN is the author of Skin Medicine, Hive, Dead Sea, Resurrection, The Devil Next Door, Dead Sea Chronicles, Clownflesh, and Bad Girl in the Box. His short stories have been collected in Bone Marrow Stew and Zombie Pulp. His novellas include "The Underdwelling," "The Corpse King," "Puppet Graveyard," and "Worm, and Blackout." His fiction has been translated into German, Japanese, Spanish, and Italian.

ABOUT THE ARTIST

Steeped in the enthralling fantasy and science-fiction illustrations of the 1960s, '70s, and '80s, artist and illustrator **K.L. TURNER** brings a bit of old-school painterly style to today's methods. With more than 30 years of experience in the arts, he expertly brings an expressionistic style into his illustrations to create compelling works which captivate and draw the viewer in. His works are found in media and galleries around the world, and celebrated in pop culture. A versatile creative type, Turner is also accomplished in the mediums of photography, sculpture, and the fine arts. Choosing to live and work on the beautiful front range of the Colorado Rocky Mountains where he was born and raised, he continues to derive inspiration from nature as well as cultural influences both at home and in his travels.

WEIRD HOUSE PRESS

https://www.weirdhousepress.com

Made in the USA
Middletown, DE
21 February 2024

49517537R00213